THE MAD KING AND THE FALSE QUEEN

HOPE ABROM
AMANDA ABROM

Copyright © 2024 by Hope Abrom and Amanda Abrom
Cover design by Seventhstar art.
All rights reserved.
No part of this book may be reproduced in any form or by any electronic or mechanical means, including information storage and retrieval systems, without written permission from the author, except for the use of brief quotations in a book review.

To those who are always counting spoons
To those who will do anything for the ones they love
And to the pet best friends who are sitting beside you as you read

ILUSAURI

Ilusaurian Castle

Elsynoire

Lousevve

Field of Valor

Sailonne

Nouchenne

Mirror's Edge

Moreio

Tydal

Sapphire Pass

Pillars of Fate

Seitlee

Celesta Tower

CELESTAIRE

Mystic South

Spirit Guardian
Guardians that command with air and flight

Guardian Sora Amai

Mind Guardian
Guardians that project dreams or nightmares

King Claude Mirage

Soul Guardians
Guardians that manipulate plants and rock

Queen Sanyal Dhara
Princess Kiran Dhara

Life Guardians
Guardians that mend injuries and bend water

King Bogdan Krol
Prince Aleksy Krol

In lands of myth where magic reigns,
Four realms entwined, the last contained

The first, where guardians rule the air,
Banishing darkness and despair

The second, beneath the starry veil,
In silver light, phantoms prevail

The third, where ancient treasures flow,
Trails of leaves and soil grow

The fourth, the songs of waves and tide,
Harmony in currents where secrets hide

Four locks unseen, to trap a foe,
A final crown will be bestowed

PART ONE

The Coronation

CHAPTER 1
Dagmara

Dagmara felt safer when her gloves were laced with poison.

The sun was setting over the cliffside town of Gorzhelm, casting a pink hue on the pastel-colored buildings. The town was bustling with villagers and foreigners, preparing for Princess Magdalena's coronation the following morning.

Honing in on her target—innocent Greta—Dagmara passed underneath a flag with the royal sigil, brushed past a couple, and knocked into the barmaid.

Greta let out a squeal, stumbling back a few steps and dropping her keys.

"Oh, my apologies!" Dagmara said before Greta could utter a word. Swooping to pick up the keys, Dagmara placed them in Greta's bare hands, giving her a firm grip.

"My fault." Greta's face was flushed as she accepted the keys. "Thank you."

"Long live the guardians," Dagmara added before sweeping into the flow of the crowd once more. She meticulously removed the gloves and slipped them into a nearby wastebasket. Rounding the corner, she eyed Greta, noticing her pace was already sluggish. It wouldn't be long before one of the nice citizens of Gorzhelm ushered her to the doctor. By then, the trace of bilans would already be out of her system, and the doctor would simply advise her to rest.

Continuing with diligence, Dagmara proceeded to the tavern, tightening her cloak to shield herself from the chill.

The main square was flooded with citizens not only from Gorzhelm, but from all of Azurem. The central fountain held a spectacular waterworks display, in an attempt to mimic the water manipulation the Guardians of Azurem possessed. Children jumped near the edge, pretending they could harness the magic of the guardians. Tomorrow, Princess Magda would rise to become a guardian of Azurem, joining her father and brother as a Guardian of Life. Everyone was here to witness the day she received her magic.

Dagmara watched the children for a brief moment as they played with their pets in the square. Some were weak with bloodshot eyes, indicating that they might already be infected with the kingdom's most deadly illness ravaging the countryside. It only affected children, so Dagmara was safe, but no one knew how exactly it spread in the first place.

"Long live the guardians." A woman stepped in Dagmara's path, extending a single poppy flower toward her.

"No, thank you," Dagmara said gently. "Long live the guardians."

She knew better than to accept handouts on the street, especially during the time of the coronation and when an infection was spreading. She checked her money pouch, single dagger, and potions pouch out of sheer habit as she picked up her pace. Her heart rate started to intensify, and her breath was shallow. She had been walking for too long. She hadn't stopped to rest since she left the royal fortress. Urging herself to continue, hating the constant reminder of her imperfect health, Dagmara pushed her body despite her condition and reached the tavern.

The tavern was hot and smelled of sweat and alcohol. All around her people danced to the fiddle's music, illegally gambled, or shared secrets after a long day working in the mines. The Azuremi crest hung in every corner of the room, softening the ambiance with pastel pinks and blues. Above the bar was a wolf carving, appropriate for the name of the tavern.

She noticed her victim almost immediately in the corner from his boisterous gestures. King Bogdan had described him well. Jacek's beard was dripping with alcohol, making his graying hair glossy, and his shirt was half unbuttoned. He struggled to stay upright in his chair, slurring his words as he cheered on the gamblers.

Dagmara spotted an open seat at the bar and almost let out an audible sigh of relief. She wouldn't be able to stand much longer. Slithering through the patrons, shoving aside the drunk miners, she almost made it to the barstool when she slammed into someone's shoulder. He knocked her completely off balance and she stumbled to catch herself on the bar. As she turned around to face him, she noticed he also braced himself against the bar, his arms on either side of her.

Dagmara looked up...and up at him.

His eyes were a rich chocolate, and his black hair fell to the bottom of his ears. He was tall and broad, adorning a black vest with silver stitching and a black diamond crest. It was unfamiliar to her, but it must have signified some noble household. His skin was tanned, and his jawline was chiseled. His gaze was hypnotic. The way he stood demanded attention, almost as if he was a guardian himself.

By the guardians, he was the most attractive man in Azurem.

Her lower back was pressed against the bar, and he was nearly leaning over her with his hands braced on either side of her body. Dagmara could only stare as he parted his lips.

"Pardon me," he said with a soft accent, remaining close to her.

All the warmth vanished from Dagmara's body. He wasn't Azuremi at all. He was Ilusaurian. What was someone from Ilusauri doing on Azuremi soil when the kingdoms cut ties over a decade ago? What was the Mad King of Ilusauri scheming now?

Dagmara's skin prickled. She had never met someone from that monstrous kingdom. She was very young when the kingdoms broke ties, and hadn't understood all the politics surrounding the split.

She didn't have time to think about that. Someone let him across the border, so he had to have permission to be here. Maybe King Bogdan invited representatives from each kingdom to the coronation? Maybe he was here on business? It didn't concern her why the dreamy man was here at all.

"You're excused," Dagmara replied curtly. With a small nod, she shoved his arm out of the way and stole the barstool, trying desperately to ignore the inviting raise of his eyebrows. As soon as she sat, her heart settled, and the dizzying nausea dissipated. Her breathing slowed, and she let out a sigh of relief.

The man's gaze lingered as he passed by, reaching the other end of the bar. He leaned his elbows against the wood, and muscles rippled at every inch of his body. A smirk crossed his face, and he glanced in her direction.

She snapped her head away with a shake, clearing her mind. She was here for one reason only.

"On the house for the prettiest girl in town," the barkeep said, his voice raspy. He was barely as tall as the bar, and his skin was lined with wrinkles. He set down a jug intended for beer, but instead held Kvas. She was here often enough for him to know she didn't drink. At least not at the Wilk Tavern. Whenever she was here, she was on business.

"Thank you, Andrzej." She flashed him a smile and his cheeks reddened.

The fiddler squeaked on a high note, but everyone was too drunk to notice. Dagmara took a sip of the Kvas, having the perfect view of Jacek from her spot at the bar. She eyed him over the rim of her glass, waiting for her moment. Her sheathed dagger pressed into her waist underneath her cloak, and her bodice was laced with throwing stars. However, if she did this correctly, she wouldn't have to use either of those weapons. Instead, she had her potions pouch.

The bar shook as someone slammed their palm against it. Dagmara snapped her head to view the commotion. The barkeeper was standing on his step stool to be at eye level with a patron—yet he was still a few inches shorter than the man across the bar.

"I do not serve Ilusaurians in this tavern! Go back to your mad king!" The barkeep wagged his finger in the man's face. It was the attractive man she had the fortune of bumping into earlier.

The foreigner's voice was sonorous. "Surely you can make an exception."

This could not get out of hand. If anyone else knew there was an Ilusaurian at the tavern, there would undoubtedly be a fight, and she didn't need the town knights to make the crowd disperse. She wouldn't risk losing Jacek. Not yet.

"Andrzej," Dagmara called.

The barkeep bounced at his name. "Yes, milady?" His raspy voice croaked, struggling to yell over the chaotic patrons.

"Give the man what he wants."

"But he is an Ilusaurian!"

Dagmara slipped her hand inside her cloak and withdrew three golden coins. They were thin between her fingers, and she faintly could feel the raised outline of the elk, her kingdom's symbolic animal. She set them on the bar in front of her, sliding them in his direction.

Andrzej's eyes widened. He hopped off the stepstool and rushed over, greedily snatching the coins as though they would disappear if he hadn't grabbed them in time. "For you, milady, anything." Andrzej gave her a smile, showing a full set of yellow teeth.

He wasn't doing it for her, he was doing it for the coin.

"And here I thought Azuremi women despised the Ilusaurian."

The man's voice was deep with a thick Ilusaurian accent, but he retained a hint of humor.

Was everyone from Ilusauri this attractive?

The thought struck her, and she instantly shoved it from her mind.

He started to reach into his pocket.

"I don't want your money," Dagmara said.

His hand froze halfway inside his pocket. "You paid him double."

"I did."

"Where did you get so much coin?"

Dagmara sat taller on the barstool. "It is not polite to ask where a woman gets her money."

"Hmm," the young man mused. He pulled the empty barstool beside her closer to him and sat down. "I'm not surprised. You are stunning, with the curves to capture any man in this room. I'm sure you make a lot every night."

For a moment she was flattered, her cheeks turning bright red. Then her jaw dropped. "I am not a prostitute."

The man raised his hands defensively. "Forgive me, I was mistaken. I'm simply impressed by your generosity."

"I'm impressed by your Azuremi." Whoever this man was, he had training in foreign languages. That could only mean he was wealthy or came from a noble background.

The side of his cheek rose into a smirk. "Oh, a compliment. Are you flirting with me?"

Dagmara snapped her head away, taking a large gulp of Kvas and spotting Jacek in the crowd once more. It calmed her to see him in the same spot he had been moments ago.

"My name is Sabien," the young man introduced himself, a melodic tone to his rich voice. "You are?"

"Dagmara."

Sabien smiled. "Sounds very similar to dagger."

"It is a common Azuremi name."

"Even so, your name is as sharp as your tongue."

"Keep bothering me, and you'll see how sharp my tongue can be."

"I have no doubt you're very skilled with it."

Her face paled, caught off guard once more. She fumbled for words, but he casually went on. "I didn't think I would like Azurem, but it's growing on me," he stated. Then he gestured toward the carving on the wall. "And all the wolf sculptures are immaculate. I always loved those fierce creatures. Don't you agree?"

"I've never given it much thought."

"Maybe you should." Sabien winked. "Now, I don't like to be indebted to someone. How can I repay you for the drink?"

" 'Thank you' would be sufficient. Or do they not have those words in Ilusaurian?"

He let out a short laugh that rumbled in his throat. "Ah, so you *do* despise Ilusauri."

"Along with everyone else here."

Sabien shifted in his chair, leaning his elbow against the bar. "Maybe Azurem should ask to be allies again."

"Why? Ilusauri impulsively invaded Celestaire. Ilusauri could invade us too."

"Impulsive? Do you know why King Claude is at war with Celestaire?"

"Because he's selfish, and he wants control of all kingdoms."

Sabien's jaw clenched. "You don't know anything about him."

"The Mad King? I know he murdered his father when he was thirteen. That's all I need to know to agree with the rest of my people that he is a monster."

The two stared at each other with fire behind their eyes. They waited for the other to break first. Dagmara gripped her drink until her knuckles turned white.

Andrzej interrupted them, setting Sabien's drink down on the bar. "Here you go, Ilusaurian! Another for you, milady?" The crowd seemed to get more rowdy by the minute.

"No," Dagmara said. "You seem to have your hands full."

Andrzej wiped sweat from his brow. "Well, Greta has abandoned me on the busiest night of my life! Where is that girl?" He hobbled away, attempting to calm a crowd of miners that had just gotten off their shift.

Dagmara's gaze shot in Jacek's direction again. His table would be asking for another round shortly.

"You have special business with that old drunk?" Sabien nodded his chin in Jacek's direction.

Dagmara glared at Sabien. She didn't waste her time with an answer. Instead, she prodded him with her own question. "Why are you here in Gorzhelm?"

Sabien picked up his mug and took a slow sip. He set the mug down gingerly, taking his time to lick a stray drop of alcohol from his lips. He finally answered, "I'm here for the coronation."

"They won't let you in," Dagmara said. "They're being much more strict on invitations with the spreading infections. Besides, it is for guardians and Azuremi citizens only."

"Maybe I was sent on Claude's behalf."

"The Mad King of Ilusauri wasn't invited."

"How would you know?"

Dagmara hesitated.

"With your wealth of knowledge about the fortress, your wealth of coin, and…" he paused to let his fingers skim the hem of Dagmara's cloak, "…the expensive fabric of your cloak, I suspect you have a very prestigious place there."

Dagmara yanked the fabric away from him, scooting sideways on the stool.

Sabien grinned. "So, if you work at the royal fortress, what are you doing here the night before the coronation, Dagger?"

"Dagmara," she corrected.

"I like my nickname better. You wouldn't happen to be seeking one final night of freedom before your big day, would you?"

Dagmara's face paled. Did he think she was Princess Magdalena?

A glass shattered behind the bar, and Andrzej let out a slew of curse words.

"Let me help," Dagmara stated, rising from the barstool. Disregarding Sabien's questions, she shoved by two drunk men to round the bar.

"Ah, milady, I couldn't ask that of you," Andrzej said, already sweeping up the glass, the front of his shirt drenched in beer.

"You said your barmaid didn't show, let me at least help until the rush dies down," she said.

Andrzej looked up at her like a lost puppy. "Would you?" he reached out and patted her cheek. "You're a doll."

"You stay here, I'll deliver another round to the tables in the back," Dagmara announced. Everything was going according to plan. She dropped down behind the bar, finding the pitcher she had hidden there a few nights prior. It was a special pitcher, with a secret compartment for the poison. With a shift of the thumb, the poison would be able to flow out alongside the alcohol. Shift it back, and only the alcohol would dispense. After dropping a pinch of smierc from her potions belt into the pitcher's poison compartment, Dagmara rose from behind the bar with the pitcher in hand.

She was keenly aware that the Ilusaurian was still watching her. His gaze made the muscles in her stomach tense.

"Can't take your eyes off me, huh?" she called over her shoulder as she filled the pitcher from the keg.

"Is that a problem, Dagger?" he replied.

She swirled on her heel to face him. "It's Dagmara."

"I heard you the first two times."

"So it's not your hearing, it's your memory that sucks."

He smirked. "I have a perfect memory of the moment I had you trapped against the bar. Unless...you'd like to remind me of that too?"

Forcing herself to ignore the butterflies that churned in her stomach, she made a straight line to Jacek. It would be a problem if

Sabien continued to watch her. She was supposed to remain discreet.

Reaching Jacek's table, she channeled her best acting. "One more round for the table?" She flashed the five men a cute smile. They all shouted something incoherent before slamming their jugs down. Meticulously, she poured the four mugs first, then with a little shift of her thumb, she poured the last jug for Jacek. The poison blended perfectly with the alcohol. They were all too drunk to notice the slight hole beside the spout.

"Long live the guardians!" she exclaimed. As she went back to the bar to get another round of alcohol— without poison—for the next table, she still sensed Sabien's presence. She had to get rid of him. She wouldn't let an Ilusaurian ruin this.

She proceeded to the next table, weaving through the customers, and began to fill their drinks. She saw a woman on her right, lounging against a wealthy noble.

Dagmara grabbed her by the hand and leaned in. "Don't tell anyone, but I heard there's an Ilusaurian at the bar."

The woman's eyes widened as she covered her mouth with a gloved hand. "No!" she exclaimed.

"Don't tell anyone," Dagmara repeated before returning to the bar once more. Her heart began to accelerate, not from nerves, but from her health. Her mission was almost over. She could push through. She wouldn't let her condition define her.

Timing was key. Timing was everything.

But the noise and heat intensified. Darkness started to crowd her peripheral vision, threatening to pull her unconscious.

Then someone took the pitcher from her hands. "Why, you're as pale as snow!" Andrzej's raspy voice scraped against her temples. "Go get some air."

"Thank you," Dagmara let out. She swerved through the remaining patrons and burst out the back door. A nearby crate caught her as she fell to a seated position. The chill from the night air flooded her body, preventing her from overheating any more. The world returned to normal.

She let out a deep sigh.

Then the silence was broken by a wave of shouts coming from the tavern. Catching a few words here and there, everything from the Mad King to the brutal murder of his own parents was shouted at Sabien. As expected, the bargoers turned on one another, and soon a brawl broke out. The front door burst open, and a wave of customers rushed to the streets. It wasn't long before a whistle pierced the air and the stampede of boots pounded the cobblestone as half a dozen knights arrived at the scene to break up the fight.

The backdoor swung wide, nearly missing her feet, and a few more drunk patrons stumbled into the back alley.

Lastly, she heard the retching. Glancing across the sleek alley, she saw Jacek grabbing his stomach, coughing up more than alcohol. He must have escaped the tavern as soon as the smierc hit his system.

Gliding to her feet, Dagmara used the commotion to her advantage. She reached Jacek's side just as he was crumbling to his knees, blood coating the cobblestone.

Dagmara gripped his hand, "By the guardians, I'll get you a doctor!" she told him, lithely slipping his ring from his finger in the process.

Her voice would never be heard over the reinforcements that rushed to break up the bar fight. She pocketed the ring to bring back to her king and fell into the stream of people, making her way toward the bridge back to the Azuremi fortress.

Passing through town, the bridge finally came into sight. It was dimly lit by torches on either end. Puddles of light cloaked the bridge in uneven areas. The clouds covered the moon, casting more shadows around the street. The crowd was far behind her now. No one would have any reason to cross the bridge aside from her. Everyone attending the coronation was staying in town and arriving at the fortress in the morning. Everyone participating in the coronation who was at the fortress was long asleep, including the Guardians of Life. She pulled up her hood, hiding her blonde hair that made her visible in the night.

Just as she started across the bridge, a hand grabbed her wrist. Swirling around, she slammed into someone hard.

She looked up and could barely make out his face in the shadows as she whispered, "Sabien?"

CHAPTER 2
Dagmara

The Ilusaurian stared at her. His chocolate eyes were neither afraid nor accusatory, but rather curious. He cocked his head. "I caught you in the alley with that man, stealing his ring after you poisoned him."

"That is quite an accusation," Dagmara snapped.

"I'm waiting to hear you say, 'It's not what it looks like.'"

But it was, in fact, what it looked like.

She didn't want to kill someone who wasn't on the list. She was an assassin, not a murderer. There was a difference, she often told herself. An assassin was a job title, much like an executioner, whereas a murderer was driven by free will. Dagmara had no free will. She was hired by the king and in return she and her brother lived in luxury at the fortress.

The king's only rule was to have no witnesses. If she broke her agreement, what would happen to her brother?

She would not be caught like her mother had. She had no choice but to kill this handsome foreigner.

At least that's what she convinced herself as she reached for her dagger.

She withdrew her blade with one swift motion, creating an upward arc, remembering the techniques her mother had taught her.

Sabien was faster than she anticipated. He dodged, before clobbering the side of her face with his fist.

She staggered back, clutching her cheek with one hand. Her mouth was agape. He had punched her.

"Don't fight me, Dagger," he said under his breath, "You won't win."

Dagmara could feel the dizziness begin to set in. Her heart rate was increasing, but her adrenaline pushed her to stay alert. "You underestimate me."

She lunged forward to stab him, and he countered out of the way, withdrawing his own dagger. As Dagmara whirled around, she saw the knife coming toward her chest. She barely dodged in time, and the tip of his blade raked across her shoulder. She felt it pierce her skin, slicing across her collarbone.

She would not meet the same fate as her mother, dying as an assassin for the Azuremi King. Dagmara was the only person her brother had left.

But she was never as good as her mother. Not with her condition. That's why she learned how to adapt.

Yanking a vial from her belt, Dagmara threw it at the ground. As soon as it made contact, the glass shattered and released its contents. It combusted into a blinding light and a pillar of smoke rose. It was enough of a distraction to send her dagger into Sabien's stomach.

Through the smoke, she could barely make out his expression. His lips parted as if to say something, shock written across his face. She saw the Ilusaurian crest on his vest and knew no one could discover his body in this kingdom. Azurem couldn't risk going to war with Ilusauri, especially when the Mad King of Ilusauri was so unpredictable.

She yanked the dagger out of his stomach, and a rush of crimson blood oozed from the wound. She hiked up her dress and kicked him with all her might. He went toppling back over the edge of the bridge.

She didn't look over the edge. She knew he wouldn't survive the rapids in the rushing river at the bottom of the ravine.

"I'm sorry," Dagmara said under her breath. She wiped the blood on her dress before sheathing her dagger once more. She had never killed anyone but her targets before. The blood from the wound on her shoulder began to trickle down her arm.

She brushed aside the guilt that coursed through her veins. He was a nobody from Ilusauri...it didn't matter.

She hoped that was true as she fled into the shadows, returning to the fortress. She hardly made it to the front gate before darkness flooded her vision, and she fell unconscious.

CHAPTER 3
Dagmara

Dagmara jolted awake in the infirmary. Her breathing was rapid, and blood pulsed at her temples.

"It's alright," the nurse attempted to calm her. "You're safe."

Dagmara took her time examining the room, ensuring her own safety, before settling on the cot. Now that she was out of danger, she could feel the pain burning from the slice across her collarbone. A headache pounded at her skull, and the light was far too bright.

The nurse had stripped Dagmara's cloak and removed her corset, leaving her upper body in a thin chemise. She had withdrawn her one arm from the sleeve, letting the top of the chemise hang from one shoulder to under her other armpit, so it would be easier to wrap the wound. The white fabric was stained a dark crimson.

Nausea erupted in Dagmara's stomach at the sight of the slash across her shoulder, and she turned away.

The nurse was nearly finished cleaning the cut. "It isn't too deep, milady, but it will leave a scar," the nurse stated.

When the nurse poured cleansing alcohol onto the wound, Dagmara winced and clutched the edge of the cot. Dagmara cursed under her breath, trying to steady her voice. She didn't know the nurse's name, and only uttered, "Thank you."

"There, not too bad," the nurse said, setting down the rag and alcohol next to a bowl of clean water. She picked up a bandage. "Let me wrap it before attending to your eye."

The curtain to the private area flew open, sending a rush of air inside. At the sight of the prince, Dagmara instantly grabbed the top of her chemise, pulling it higher on her chest to cover the gash. She shot upright, moving too quickly, and grimaced as stars danced in her vision.

"Your Highness!" The nurse curtsied low to the ground.

Dagmara's mouth remained shut.

The prince's silver hair was tousled on his head, and his oversized white shirt revealed the top of his chest. His eyes were illuminated, and shadows were cast on his sharp jawline. He was young, barely three years older than Dagmara.

"Rise," Prince Aleksy said to the nurse before giving his attention to Dagmara. "What happened?"

When the prince's eyes were on Dagmara, it was like nothing else existed. His full attention was on her and only her.

"What are you doing here?" Dagmara answered his question with another.

"The knights informed me they took you to the infirmary. They said you were unconscious."

"They informed you?"

"They always inform me of your return."

"They don't inform your father."

"Because he never asked them to. I did."

Dagmara's face paled. That was new information.

"So?" Aleksy prompted.

"It was nothing," Dagmara replied, her words slow and drawn out, her chin lowering slightly.

Aleksy knew her well, and that meant she didn't want to discuss anything in front of the nurse. He read her thoughts and said, "I can take it from here," before crossing to the nurse and taking the bandage from her.

"Your Highness..."

"I assure you, the patient is in good hands with me." The prince gave her a soft smile that would convince someone of anything.

The nurse gave a hesitant nod before making a swift exit.

Aleksy stepped closer to Dagmara, and her face flushed. She had grown up with Aleksy, moving to the castle when her mother was hired as King Bogdan's assassin. She acknowledged that he had grown more attractive as he aged. However, ever since he acquired his gift, he had been pulled more into the inner court, and they hadn't crossed paths as often. When they did get a moment to see each other, there was far more tension.

Aleksy reached for the bowl of water on the side table, and a blue magic sparkled at his fingertips. The misty water swirled around his hand as he raised his fingers to her.

"I don't want you to heal it," Dagmara said. Healing open wounds and minor injuries was simple magic for Guardians of Life, but she needed the scar as a reminder. She wanted to feel the pain for much longer—it was the price she would pay for taking the Ilusaurian's life when she didn't have to.

Aleksy's eyes stopped glowing ice-blue, and the dusting of water evaporated. He inclined his head, about to argue, but he must have thought better of it. "Then let me help you without magic." His fingertips grazed the back of her palm, and he guided her hand down so he could see the laceration across her shoulder.

Aleksy's voice was sensitive. "Tell me what happened."

Dagmara kept her hand at the top of the chemise, making sure it didn't drop too low. She was already acutely aware of how revealing she was.

"You can't tell your father," she said.

"I won't."

"There was a complication."

Aleksy let out a soft laugh. "I gathered that much." He began to wrap the bandage around her shoulder, safely covering the gash. Yet every time she spoke, he made sure to maintain eye contact.

"Someone saw me. I don't know how..." Dagmara muttered. "Then I just thought about how my mother was caught, and I reacted."

"You won't die like your mother did," Aleksy said.

"I'm not afraid of death. I'm afraid of being tortured and leaving my brother to fend for himself."

"Teos is stronger than you think," Aleksy said. "In fact, he has no mercy when it comes to cards."

Dagmara's laugh was soft as she thought about her brother Teos. The prince smiled.

"Maybe...it's because of your condition?"

"What?" Dagmara jerked back.

"I-I'm just wondering...if it's getting worse," Aleksy said.

"Other people have it worse than me."

"Most people aren't assassins. Maybe we need to find you a new...occupation."

"You don't think I can do this?"

"I worry about you," he admitted. "What if you got into a chase? You can't outrun them."

"I have other solutions."

"Potions and smoke bombs won't work forever."

"They aren't just any potions."

"Maybe it's time to tell my dad—"

"No!" Dagmara snapped. "I'm not having this conversation with you again."

The prince hesitated, but then nodded.

Aleksy tied off the end of the bandage. She watched as he reached for the water bowl, letting his hand hover over the liquid. First, his eyes shifted to a light blue hue, so vibrant it only could have been magic. Then a small amount of water rose from the bowl, levitating in the air underneath Aleksy's palm. It began to mold into a cube, transforming into ice. Then the prince grabbed the ice from the air and wrapped it in a thin cloth.

He didn't think twice before he separated Dagmara's knees with his hand, letting himself step even closer to her. Dagmara's breath hitched in her throat as he stepped between her legs before he raised the ice to her face, and his eyes returned to their normal color.

When the ice touched Dagmara's cheek, a rippling pain pulsed through her temple. She winced but bit her lip to fight the pain.

"Sorry," Aleksy said. He was so close, she could smell the mint on his breath.

"It's fine," Dagmara breathed.

"Are they dead?"

She knew he was referring to Sabien. She gave the prince a small nod.

"Who were they?"

"Some Ilusaurian."

Aleksy's brow furrowed. "Here? Why?"

"Supposedly he was here for the coronation."

"We didn't extend an invitation to Ilusauri."

"I know," Dagmara replied.

"Was he a nobleman? Or from King Claude's court?"

"I hope neither."

"As long as he wasn't the king, it will be alright."

"Maybe the world would benefit from the Mad King's death."

Aleksy grinned. "It would, but we're trying to avoid going to war with Ilusauri."

Aleksy dropped the ice cube back in the water bowl and let the rag drop to the cot. He then ran two fingers through the poultice that the nurse had made before touching the ointment to Dagmara's cheek. His caress was soft.

"Thank you, doctor," Dagmara said.

Aleksy's cheeks reddened. He cleared his throat. "You'll definitely have a bruise for the next few days."

"How noticeable is it?"

"It's...uh...it's pretty ugly...I won't lie."

She exhaled sharply.

"But you're still beautiful."

Her face flushed, and all of the sudden it felt like there wasn't much air in the room. She couldn't even manage a 'thank you.'

Aleksy cleared his throat once more. He wiped off his hands on a clean rag before picking up her cloak, holding it up for her to put on. "I'll walk you back to your suite."

They were silent as the prince escorted her back to her chambers. She could feel the tension rising between them with every step, and her heart pounded against her chest. Sure, she had flirted with him for fun on multiple occasions, but she never thought he would reciprocate the feelings. Was she imagining it? It was the middle of the night. Her exhaustion could have been clouding her judgment.

Maybe Aleksy's judgment was also clouded because of the coronation tomorrow. Certainly, he had to be nervous that Magdalena was receiving her gift, knowing he would have to face off against his sister soon in the trials to see what sibling kept the magic.

When Aleksy and Dagmara arrived at her suite, her hand lingered on the doorknob.

"Thank you, for tonight," she said. "I didn't know that you ordered the knights to inform you of my return."

Aleksy shifted his weight, taking time to search for the right words. "I can't really sleep on the nights when you have a mission. Knowing you arrive back safely puts me at ease."

"Oh." It was a terrible, stupid response. However, she couldn't quite think clearly with her nerves erupting inside. His gaze was intense. She bit the inside of her cheek, restraining herself from ruining the moment by saying something she regretted.

To her relief, he continued. "I...worry about you sometimes." He corrected himself. "Often, actually." His face was getting redder. "But maybe that's just me."

"It's not just you," Dagmara blurted out. Her breath was shallow and the air around her began to thin. It was now or never. They had eyes for each other for a long time, but neither had acted on their attraction for one another. That was what was going on, right? Dagmara suddenly feared she was misreading the prince.

He took a step closer.

She shifted forward, nodding, telling him exactly what she wanted with only her eyes.

The prince swooped his arm behind her back, pulling him against her chest. He cupped the back of her head with his palm, pressing his lips to hers.

She felt like her entire body was on fire. The pain in her shoulder and face no longer mattered. She wrapped her arms around his neck, pulling him closer and feeling his body against hers. Her heart rate intensified, and it didn't have anything to do with her health.

Footsteps down the hall made Dagmara pull away from him. "Someone's coming."

His forehead was against hers, and he only wrapped his arm tighter. "I don't care."

Dagmara laughed, and he cut her off as he kissed her once more. Between kisses, she said, "You don't mean that, trust me."

"You make me forget I'm a prince."

The footsteps echoed in the corridor, signifying that they were getting closer.

Dagmara pulled her lips away, despite wanting more. "We can't get caught the night before the coronation. Come inside."

Aleksy watched her carefully. "Are you sure?"

"If you'd rather leave..."

"I'd rather not."

He pressed his mouth to hers once more, deepening the kiss. He reached behind her back, opening the door to her drawing room. Her bedroom was only one door away. He supported her around the waist as he gracefully led her backward into the room. They didn't stop kissing for one moment. He kicked the door shut with his boot before pressing her against the wall. She arched into his embrace as he swept his tongue into her mouth.

The sound of someone clearing their throat loudly snapped Dagmara out of the trance.

She jerked away from Aleksy, gasping for breath. Her eyes immediately found her fifteen-year-old brother seated at the desk, holding cards in both hands.

"Teos!" Dagmara's blood turned to ice.

Aleksy ran his thumb against his lips, turning his back to Teos in embarrassment. His hand was propped against the wall next to Dagmara's head, and he leaned his forehead into his bicep.

Dagmara slithered out from underneath Aleksy. "What are you doing here?"

"This is my suite too," Teos said.

"I mean—what are you doing up?" She gestured toward the door to his bedroom on the opposite end of the room.

Teos let the cards flop onto the pile between his hands. He leaned closer, propping his elbows on the table. "What are you two doing up? I thought you were working tonight." He raised his eyebrows and tried to repress his smile, but two dimples formed on his cheeks.

"It's..." Dagmara's voice ran dry. She didn't want to say it was nothing. She didn't know what it was.

Teos tilted his head, his blonde hair flopping on his head. "You know I can see you, Aleksy?"

Aleksy let out a breath, turning around to face Teos. His cheeks were bright red, and he scratched the back of his neck as he tried to think of an excuse. "I...wasn't thinking you'd be awake."

"Clearly," Teos laughed. "You didn't have time for a card game tonight with me, but you have time to make-out with my sister?"

Dagmara's face paled. "Teos!"

"No, no," Aleksy held out his hand to prevent her from rushing forward. "You're right, I'll make it up to you tomorrow."

"Tomorrow is the coronation," Teos reminded the prince. He picked up a card and began to flip it between his fingers. "By the way, does Magda know about this?"

Dagmara glanced in Aleksy's direction. No, Aleksy's sister and Dagmara's best friend didn't know about this. Dagmara hadn't even known about this until a minute ago. Her heart still pounded loudly against her chest, and she wanted to kiss him once more. Would they return to being cordial with one another tomorrow morning? Aleksy didn't break eye contact, no doubt wondering the same thing.

"I'll take that as a no..." Teos said, extending the last word. "Is this a one-night thing? Or should I find somewhere else to spend my evenings because three doors away is not nearly enough space between my bedroom and yours."

Mortified, Dagmara held her face in her palms. "I'm sorry," she muttered under her breath to Aleksy.

"No, I'm sorry," Aleksy replied. "I should go."

He opened the door and began to exit, but stopped at the threshold. "Teos," he said over his shoulder, "How about I sneak away during the coronation for a card game? It'll be our secret."

Teos nodded, a knowing expression in his eyes. "I'm good with secrets. Don't think I'll go easy on you though." He pointed the card at the prince.

Aleksy smiled. "Of course not." He then met Dagmara's gaze. "I'll...see you at our meeting in the morning."

She nodded.

Then the prince left, closing the door behind him.

"This was not my fault," Teos said.

"I know," Dagmara groaned. She crossed to the chaise and plopped down, her mind running wild. She propped her feet up, letting some of her blood return to her head. Now that she was resting, her body began to settle. She remembered Aleksy's lips against hers and couldn't help but smile. She grabbed the pillow on the couch and held it against her stomach, squeezing it tighter.

"You do remember he is the prince, right?" Teos asked.

She forced the smile off her face. "Yes. Maybe it's best that it stopped."

"How long has this been a thing?"

"Just tonight," she replied.

"Please. You two have been flirting with each other since before you knew what flirting was."

"How would you know?" Dagmara asked.

"Because I'm not an idiot." Teos eyed his sister, shuffling the cards in his grasp. "What happened to your face?"

She had nearly forgotten. "Someone punched me."

"Ouch. I'd hate to see the other guy."

She scoffed. "You won't."

"And Aleksy still thought you were attractive enough to kiss?"

"Oh, shut up!" She threw the pillow in his direction. He braced himself with his forearms, and it pitifully bounced off his shoulder before flopping onto the ground.

He cackled. "Well, I've had enough excitement for one night, I think it's time for bed." He grabbed his single crutch, propping it under his shoulder as he rose to his feet.

"Oh, *now* you go to bed?"

"Goodnight, sis," he called over his shoulder in a melodic tone. Then he headed toward his bedroom, utilizing the crutch for support.

He had been in an accident the month after their mother died, and the bones never healed correctly. His knee and ankle were still not aligned, and he would never be able to walk properly again.

It was part of the reason Dagmara was committed to staying an assassin. If she and Teos hadn't been living at the fortress, Teos would not have received the advanced medical care and could have lost his left leg entirely. Being an assassin and living at the fortress was the better alternative, especially with the raging disease sweeping the countryside.

"Wait, Teos," Dagmara called.

Her brother paused.

"Your jasny concoction—the light explosion—saved my life tonight."

A smile creased his face, revealing two dimples. "Told you it was amazing." Then he proceeded to his room.

Dagmara remained on the couch for a moment longer, even after Teos had shut the door behind him. She didn't have the energy left to make it to her bed, even though it was only a room away. Every ounce of her body burned with exhaustion, and she would pay for it tomorrow. But she had to keep going for Teos. She had killed Sabien for her brother. All this work as an assassin was to give her and Teos a better life.

She simply prayed Sabien wasn't an Ilusaurian nobleman.

Also…what would she tell Magda about the prince?

CHAPTER 4
Magdalena

The morning air was crisp, and harsh wind beat against Magda's face. Magda picked up speed, dashing through the field on her horse.

Odie sprinted beside her. The dog barked playfully as he crashed through the poppy field, drifting further away from Magda's view. But his black and white fur and floppy ears were always easy to spot against the blood-red flowers.

Magda picked up speed, urging her horse to follow Odie's lead. They flew together across the landscape, cutting a path straight through a layer of snow and red flowers that carpeted the ground. On the horizon, the sunrise peaked through the mountains. It was the heart of winter, and the peaks were still white.

Here, despite the soft layer of snow, fully grown poppies marked the path with a sea of scarlet. Some said that the flowers were magical, able to withstand treacherous winters and remain in full bloom. The elders said that these were flowers from the wars long ago, marking the graves of all the men and women who had been slain in wars with their ruby petals. That was before, when the fight over the control of magic belonged to everyone. The ancient stories said that magic lived in all things—the ground, the water, and in people's minds—and that one only needed to know how to tap into the ancient magic all around them.

That was what the coronation today was truly about, and she was quite nervous. Today, Magda would officially become an heir to the Azuremi throne, naming her a true royal, and a Guardian of Life.

She broke free from the poppy field, emerging onto the banks of an ice-cold river. The rough rapids descended all the way from the glaciers in the mountains, traveling next to the castle before twisting through the rocks toward the town and under the bridge that led into Gorzhelm.

Odie darted to the water, lapping it up with his pink tongue, but even he knew better than to play in the deadly rapids.

Magda pulled the reins to a halt and dismounted her horse. Then, she gingerly tied the reins to a nearby tree. She pensively approached the water with outstretched hands, attempting to mimic the same position that her brother and father always demonstrated when displaying their magic to the court. She squeezed her eyes shut, focusing on moving the frigid stream with her fingertips, but when she opened them, nothing happened.

Odie seemed to understand, letting out a sad yelp next to her.

Magda dropped to her knees. "Don't worry," she smiled as she scratched behind the dog's ears. "Aleksy says I'll be able to channel the family magic after the coronation." It wasn't a lie...her older brother had explained the sensation of harnessing the power of water millions of times. She could almost hear his voice in her head right now, explaining the pure strength needed to hold back the rapids, move glaciers, and burst springs from the earth.

Suddenly Odie's ears perked up, and he began running off along the riverbank alongside the rocks. He sensed something Magda couldn't, but by the way his tail began to wag, shaking his entire body, she knew who was nearby.

"Odie!" yelled Magda, "Come back here!"

Magda sprinted after her pet, but it was impossible to keep up with his pace. While Odie scaled the rocks elegantly, maneuvering down the river at ease, Magda struggled to keep up. She bounded across the riverbank, following around the bend just in time to see Odie leaping up into Aleksy's arms, letting out a slew of friendly barks.

"You followed me?" Magda called.

"I thought you might be running away." Aleksy laughed.

Magda let out a huff. "You know I would never skip the coronation."

"Good boy," Aleksy patted Odie, kneeling down and stroking the dog's fur. Then he turned his attention back to Magda. "I figured I would find you here...near the poppy fields where we always practiced."

Magda shrugged her shoulders. Something passed between them, the knowledge that both of them wouldn't be able to keep this gift, and at a certain point, it would stay with only one of the siblings.

"You're thinking of the trials?" Aleksy read her mind.

"It crosses my mind often," said Magda. It was scary to think that someday, she and Aleksy would be forced to go up against each other in a fight, proving who had mastered the water magic better, and who should be the Guardian of Life for their generation. If they had more siblings, they would have to fight each one of them.

"Don't worry. I'll go easy on you," Aleksy joked.

"You will not!" Magda laughed.

"I mean, I do have a three year head start."

It was true. Aleksy was crowned three years ago, and once Magda was crowned, she had one year to master the magic before she would have to challenge him in a trial. If they never challenged one another, they would both lose the gift. It had been years since trials had been held in Azurem—their father, King Bogdan, had challenged his two older brothers, defeating them both. Now, one brother worked as an ambassador, and the other disappeared to the countryside, too ashamed to have lost his magic.

"Are you nervous for the coronation?" Aleksy changed the subject.

"No. I just needed a bit of fresh air," Magda confessed. "It feels like a huge weight is about to be put on my shoulders."

He spoke, "Before I was crowned, I was terrified I wouldn't be able to channel the magic in front of everyone."

Magda stared back at the rushing, white rapids that pummeled across the rocks. Unlike Aleksy, she had never channeled the water magic while growing up. Even though the coronation marked the moment in time where the Krol descendants would receive their full powers in front of the court and be named official guardian's of ancient water magic, Aleksy had shown early signs of his powers. When he was only eight, he could turn a glass of water into ice, or sprinkle a drop of cool mist across Magda's face. But Magda, on the other hand, had never exhibited any indications that she would be as powerful as her brother or father.

"Are you sure you're alright?" asked Aleksy, reading her face. "I mean, it wouldn't be the first time you missed a royal ceremony," he paused, "or tried to run away for that matter..."

Magda hit him across the arm playfully. "We all know that you are the golden child. Try not to rub it in, okay?"

"I am not," Aleksy laughed, his big eyes beaming. "You're just *a little* more adventurous than me."

"Adventurous...," Magda's voice trailed off. "Yes, that's what all the servants say about me behind my back."

They both stood at the edge of the riverbank, staring at each other and trying everything not to laugh as memories flashed between them —until Aleksy broke first.

He blurted out, "Remember when you dressed Odie up as a royal prince and told mom and dad that he was your date to the winter ball?"

"Or when I convinced you to use your powers to create a giant ice sculpture in your room?" she laughed.

"Or when you kissed your tutor's son when you were supposed to be studying!"

"Oh please," said Magda, "I'm sure you've had your fair share of kisses in the fortress." She raised her eyebrows.

Aleksy's face turned bright red, and he began walking back to his horse. He raised his arm in the air as he said, "And on that note, we're going to be late for the coronation, you know. I also have a meeting with dad I can't miss."

Magda nodded. "I'll race you back to the fortress."

Aleksy turned back to his sister, smiling. "You're on."

The two returned to their horses a few paces down the riverbank. Then they dashed along the trail that followed the bends of the river. They raced along the path, each urging their horses faster, as the fortress appeared on the horizon.

Magda and Aleksy's home was perched on a hill that overlooked the crystal-clear river. Ahead, the red roofs matched the surrounding poppy fields on the opposite side of the body of water, and large, cylindrical towers jutted from the shape of the building in an asymmetrical pattern. On the towers, a banner depicting their mother's coat of arms fluttered in the wind, and the pastel-colored flag backlit a white elk shining in the morning sun. Snow reflected off the roof's peaks.

At the main entrance, they spotted a caravan of carriages approaching the main gate. As far as the eyes could see, disappearing around the mountains, was a line-up of elites and celebrities arriving for the coronation ceremony. Magda noted the crowd was much smaller than during Aleksy's coronation, for their father was weary of the illnesses spreading through the kingdom and didn't want to spread any infections through the event.

"We're going to be late," Aleksy shouted loudly over the rumble of the horse's hooves.

"Not if I have anything to say about it!" Magda laughed, and her horse sprinted forward even faster.

They made their way to a side entrance of the castle, mainly where the stables and kitchen were located, and dashed across a bridge that took them across the rapids below, until they emerged in a brick-laid courtyard.

Magda dismounted first. "Beat you."

Aleksy scrunched his face. "It was a tie, but I'll let you have this one today, *guardian*." He emphasized the word, reminding Magda once more of the weight of the coronation. After today, she would be an official heir, second in line to the throne after Aleksy.

Magda began walking away. "And the *guardian* has to get ready!" She turned back to her brother, giving him an over-dramatic curtsy before starting a light jog back to the royal quarters. It was true, she was extremely late and her mother and Urszula would likely be furious with her. "Come, Odie."

She heard Aleksy's voice echo behind her, asking about the horse, but she was already bounding into the fortress.

Magda turned the corner, heading through a set of large double doors. The entrance to the royal wing was via a walkway across a shimmering pool. Water cascaded down from the ceiling, cresting into the pond on either side and creating the illusion that there were two walls made of water, flanking the path.

The royal wing had its own personal staff, chambers for all members of the family, spare bedrooms that were meant for more children—or potentially grandchildren—and a private library. The library was where the Scribestone was located, allowing immediate contact between all royals across the kingdoms.

Magda turned up a staircase ascending to the royal bedchambers, racing Odie to the top. Odie bounded beside her, sometimes lingering behind and sometimes darting in the front, as if he knew where they were heading. She passed nearly a dozen knights, adorned in silver breastplates and donning the pastel pink and blue crest with the elk. They nodded their heads, giving a gracious smile to the princess as she passed. Two of Bogdan's wolves prowled beside them, acting as guard dogs.

Finally, Magda raced through the parlor connecting the family's suites and offices, emerging into her bedroom. Her mother and handmaiden, Urszula, leapt from their seats when Magda and Odie entered.

"Where have you been?" her mother Bernadette scolded immediately. "Come, come quickly." She wasted no time in ushering Magda to a raised pedestal at the far end of the room.

Odie dashed to his large pillow at the foot of the bed, twirling twice before settling down in a comfortable position.

"Look at you...," Bernadette's face wrinkled upon examining Magda in the mirror, "And you smell like a horse."

"Mom!" Magda let out a huff.

"You know you shouldn't be outside with the infections spreading," she sighed. Then Bernadette motioned to a bouquet of red flowers on the desk. The crystal-blue vase contrasted against the blood-scarlet poppies. "These are for you. A tradition in honor of your coronation."

"Thank you. They're beautiful," Magda confessed.

"And this is your dress." Bernadette crossed to an armoire and threw open the wardrobe doors.

Magda couldn't take her eyes off the dress hanging in front of her, designed to appear as waves of the ocean with ice-like crystals resembling the glittering salt that was found in the kingdom's scattered mines. She imagined what it would feel like to slide the dress over her body and step into the role as a Guardian of Life. Did royals in all of the kingdoms feel different after the coronation? Even those that controlled the earth, air, and the minds of others?

"What do you think?" asked her mother.

"It's the most stunning thing I've ever seen."

"I had it made for you." Bernadette's eyes softened as she placed her hands on her daughter's shoulders. The two could have been twins if they were the same age. She said, "This is an important day for us all. I love you, but I will not have you attending the most important day of your life in this state. We have visitors coming from all over the kingdom!"

"I know, and I'm sorry for running off."

Bernadette waved her hands in the air. "No more excuses. You and your brother are always getting into mischief." Then she turned on her heel and darted out of the room, but not before calling over her shoulder, "I want you ready in one hour!"

Magda let out a sigh before examining her appearance once more in the mirror. Her silver hair was wild from the wind. Behind her, her handmaiden Urszula peered over the princess's shoulder.

"I think you look great," Urszula laughed, placing her hand on her hip and sinking into it.

"Thanks. But I feel like my mom is going to kill me."

"I was being sarcastic. Your mom is going to kill *me* if I let you go to the coronation like that." Urszula walked toward the bathroom, disappearing around the corner. "I'll draw your bath," she called back. "Then we'll make sure you look like you could actually become a queen someday."

After Urszula helped Magda wash off as best as she could, she entered her bedroom once more. Upon seeing the princess, Odie's head perked up from his pillow at the foot of the bed, letting out a friendly bark.

Urszula quickly excused herself, "Your new crown should be polished by now. Let me go fetch it."

With that, Urszula crossed to the door and exited.

When Magda was alone, she approached the stunning dress once more. She ran her fingers over the crystals, sliding her hands along the rough rocks. They were unlike anything she had ever seen before, appearing different from the crystal-like salt in the Azuremi mines. As she touched the stones, the rocks moved underneath her fingertips, flattening until they were a smooth liquid, dripping down the dress like molten lava.

Magda jumped back, startled at the sight. She moved away from the window, looking at the dress at a different angle and hoping that a trick of the light had made the crystals appear to move. But it was not the case.

The shape of the crystals had changed exactly where she had touched the dress. Instead of existing in their distinct shapes, they had molded into one, large crystal, blended together as if a piece of stained-glass had been manipulated by a blacksmith's torch.

Magda gasped and reached back out to touch the crystals. Once again, as she moved her hand, the rocks changed underneath her fingertips. She waved her hand again and again, until the waves on the dress were nothing more than an undefined swirl of color.

What was going on?

Magda snapped her head behind her to Odie. "Did you see that?"

Odie's ears perked up, and his head tilted at the sound of Magda's voice.

"It's Soul magic...," Magda's voice trailed off.

Her heart fluttered, and Magda looked frantically around the room for anything else that reminded her of the Guardians of the Soul and their earth magic. Her gaze snapped to the bouquet of poppies that her mother had gifted her.

Quickly, she extended her hand toward the flowers, pulsing a burst of energy through her arm and extending to her fingertips. She remembered everything Aleksy had taught her about channeling magic when they had trained for her coronation ceremony. As she clenched her hand into a fist, the poppies shriveled into black, coiled stems. Dried, flaky petals fell to the table in a heap of ashes.

Magda jumped back, and her hands flung up to cover her shocked expression. When she did so, the poppies reformed in their beautiful, red glory, extending higher than they had before.

Magda's hands shook. She raced to the mirror just in time to see the yellow glow fading from her irises. The evidence of earth magic couldn't be clearer. She had seen it explode from her fingertips in two separate instances.

How was it possible that she was exhibiting signs of earth magic? Earth magic belonged to the Guardians of the Soul in Flaustra, while Azurem held the Guardians of Life. Her father was a descendant of a line of royals who had all been blessed with the gift of water. That meant Magda was supposed to display Life magic at today's coronation ceremony.

If she had earth magic, and not water magic, she could not inherit the Azuremi throne. She would be stripped of her title, and forced out of the fortress. She would be disowned by her entire family.

She jumped to a series of conclusions that all seemed outrageous. What if she wasn't her father's child? Her heart sank to the pit of her stomach as the thought paralyzed the rest of her body. Maybe she could accept the fact that she wasn't a royal to the Azuremi throne, and that her and Aleksy were possibly half siblings, but what would happen to her when everyone realized that she was in line for a different throne? What would happen to her mother if they thought the queen had a daughter with another royal from a foreign kingdom?

She couldn't let that happen.

There was only one person who could help her.

Magda dashed out of her room, and Odie trailed behind. She exited the royal quarters and made her way to the knights' wing, bursting into Dagmara's suite without knocking. Her best friend had to be here getting ready for the coronation.

"Dagmara?" Magda called and looked around. After a few moments, it was clear that neither Dagmara nor Teos were inside.

Magda darted to the sofa, picking up a pillow, before crouching down and shoving it towards Odie's nose. "Can you help me find Dagmara?"

Odie's ears pricked up as he sniffed the object.

"Dagmara," Magda repeated before giving her dog the search command, "Go find."

CHAPTER 5
Dagmara

The throne room always captivated Dagmara with its three-story ceilings and sparkling glass chandeliers, made to look like glittering pieces of pink salt. All around the outside of the room, were two layers of balconies that faced the raised dais, creating a theatrical element to the space. Large banners in pink and blue pastels hung from the rafters and salt-carved statues of the royals were placed in stained glass windows. At the front of the room, the Krol family crest hung over four thrones, and a majestic waterfall streamed down the wall behind them. A large fountain at the center of the room added a soundscape of rushing water to the area.

Now, only two thrones were occupied. One by King Bogdan, the ruler of Azurem, and one by Prince Aleksy. Dagmara forced herself not to make eye contact with Aleksy for fear her face would flush.

It had taken every ounce of her strength to show up at the meeting this morning. Her neck and shoulders throbbed, and her scalp prickled, similar to the pins and needles that danced in her fingertips. She was both cold and sweating, and her brain felt as though it were blanketed in thick fog. However, she didn't have time to rest. She couldn't let the king question her absence and discover her illness. Having an invisible condition was a double-edge sword; she was able to hide it, but no one believed how much it affected her.

Taking a deep breath, she approached the throne. The king and the prince quickly stopped talking about the salt trade and turned their attention to her. After giving the king a low bow, Dagmara extended her palm out toward King Bogdan. Jacek's ring was in the center of her hand.

Bogdan eyed the jewelry. His face was filled with wrinkles, and he had bushy, gray eyebrows which were more expressive than his personality. For his age, he still had a large head of silver hair. His face was clean-shaven, and his light blue cape, lined with white fur, hid his figure.

"He is dead?"

The comment jarred Dagmara. The king knew what her job was. He had never asked for confirmation before. By the way Aleksy shifted forward in his throne, he was taken aback too.

"Of course."

As you requested. She wanted to add. She kept her hand extended toward him uncomfortably, waiting for him to take the ring. Did she not powder her face enough this morning? Could he see her cheek was swollen? Did he know that there had been a complication?

Bogdan let out a deep sigh before rising from the throne. "My gut is telling me our intel was wrong." He approached his first knight who willingly handed the king a scroll of parchment. Bogdan unraveled it and examined the scroll with a furrowed brow.

"Father," Aleksy rose, "Jacek was the target."

"Yes, but what if there's another one? What if he has a team?"

Aleksy took the ring from Dagmara. When his fingertips grazed her palm he lingered a moment longer than usual, sending a shiver down her spine. He glanced at her softly before becoming rigid once more as he approached his father.

"You sound paranoid," the prince said.

"I have a right to be," Bogdan replied, his voice staying calm. "What if King Claude has been wrong all along?"

Dagmara's blood turned to ice. "The Mad King? What does this have to do with him?" To her knowledge, the people she had been assassinating were conspirators against the Azuremi throne. They were from Azurem. Rebels, for lack of a better word. They weren't foreigners or associated with King Claude in Ilusauri. She had never wanted to know specific details in case she ended up in a similar situation as her mother—kidnapped and tortured. Someone could easily use truth serum on her and all the secrets of Azurem would be exposed. But sometimes she wished she knew more about why she was assassinating these people. What put them on the list?

Aleksy started, "Someone said they witnessed Jacek with..." his voice ran dry when he saw his father's eyes widen in warning. She, and perhaps the other knights in the room, weren't allowed to know whatever secret the king and the prince shared.

"What motive would King Claude have to conspire against us?" Dagmara asked. "He outright attacked Celestaire. Why would he enlist our people instead of outright attacking us too?"

"Well, he isn't exactly predictable," Aleksy countered.

"But he is predictable," Dagmara insisted. "He killed his parents to have full control of Ilusauri. Now he's attacking Celestaire. Maybe he wants control of every kingdom. Thank goodness Celestaire's forces are impenetrable."

"We don't know that for certain," Bogdan said. Bogdan let out a low sigh before he rolled up the parchment and shoved it into his first knight's chest. Then his expression fell somber. "Celestaire's head of foreign correspondence wrote to me personally through the Scribestone this morning. Guardian Sora has been in and out of hiding."

Dagmara knew the Scribestone was a magical system designed for the royals of each kingdom to communicate with one another almost instantly. Anyone had the ability to use it, but as it was a tablet stationed in the royal library, it was mainly reserved for the royals. Supposedly there were identical versions in each kingdom.

"You think King Claude is going after Celestaire's guardian?" Dagmara asked.

"I don't know what King Claude's intentions are, that is the problem," Bogdan said. "The illness plaguing children—zowach—has spread through almost all the villages in the north. Without the trade routes open, we can't get medicine from Claude's kingdom. Eight years ago it wasn't a problem, but I'm receiving word that a third of the youth are dead before adulthood. Our population will be wiped out in a few decades at this rate. Claude is withholding medicine, and it's killing us at the same rate as if he was killing us with his army. Maybe this was his plan all along. I'm telling you, he can't be trusted." Then the king of Azurem looked at the crown prince. "For all we know, everything he said to us has been a lie."

Aleksy nodded, but his expression was laced with skepticism.

"All of this is just to say..." Bogdan's words were slow and precise as he deliberately shifted the conversation away from Claude, "...we need to keep our wits about us this evening. No one connected to the men we have previously taken care of can be present, including Jacek's friends. I don't need to remind you, Dagmara, that Magdalena's life is in our hands. She will be in front of hundreds of people tonight. If one person slips by our guard, I entrust you to keep her safe. Don't leave her for a second."

"Your Majesty, Magda—the Princess—is like a sister to me," Dagmara said. "Her safety is always my priority."

"I guess that makes you my second daughter." A tender smile formed on his face.

Dagmara couldn't help but smile back. She had barely known her real father.

"If you ever feel unsafe in your current position..." the king paused to scratch his temple. No...he wasn't scratching his temple. He was gesturing to Dagmara's bruise. Her heart sank, both concerned and pleasantly surprised that he had noticed. He finished his sentence, "I could transfer you to be Magdalena's full-time knight. She will need one now that she is a guardian."

It was as if the floor fell out from underneath Dagmara. Stop being an assassin and become Magda's full-time knight? If she accepted a new role, she could be with her best friend at all times and ensure her safety. But would Teos still have the same access to the royal nurses?

"I'll let you think about it." Bogdan said. "Let's make tonight a trial run, and we can discuss in the morning."

She was so lost in her thoughts that she almost missed the relief on Aleksy's face. He looked at her with a pleading expression, almost as if he was begging her to take the job right there.

"It would be an honor," Dagmara said, having to calm her shaking voice. She dipped her head respectfully before turning to the exit. Then a thought struck her. "Last thing, Your Majesty. Do you know an Ilusaurian noble by the name of Sabien?"

"Sabien...any surname?"

She shrugged.

"No...I can't say I know of any noblemen with that name."

Dagmara tried to suppress her sigh of relief.

"But..."

She froze.

"...Sabien Renaud is the captain of the Ilusaurian royal guard. Only been there for a few years. A real ass if you ask me, and he's far too young to be so entitled. I guess he takes after King Claude. Why?"

Goosebumps ran down her arms. She didn't spare a glance in Aleksy's direction, afraid her expression may reveal too much.

Shoving aside the fear, she leveled her voice and said plainly, "No reason."

The king didn't seem convinced, his head inclining slightly. "If there is something you know that I don't then I implore you to speak."

If the Sabien she had stabbed and sent off the bridge to his death was truly the captain of the Ilusaurian royal guard, King Claude would be after her head. She wouldn't admit to killing Sabien in this room, especially with all these witnesses. She would wait until they found his body—if they even did in the spiraling rapids at the bottom of the ravine. Suddenly she regretted asking the king this question so publicly.

However, Sabien had been in town. People had seen him. She had to tell part of the truth.

Dagmara kept her expression calm. "I saw him at the Wilk Tavern last night. He was arguing with the barkeep."

"He's here?" Bogdan questioned. "On Azuremi soil? Why?"

Sabien had explicitly told Dagmara that he was there for the coronation, but there was no reason to confess she had spoken to him. It wasn't like he would be going to the coronation anyway.

Dagmara shook her head. "I don't know, Your Majesty."

"Hmm," Bogdan mused. He turned to his first knight. "Patrol the town, I don't want him here. Ask if anyone spoke to him. I don't care if he came to provoke us or came for a night at the brothel. I want him gone. But don't think about touching him, I don't need King Claude to have a reason to attack. We're walking on thin ice as it is."

The first knight nodded. "Yes, Your Majesty. We will scour the streets until we find him."

Dagmara swallowed the lump in her throat. She hoped they wouldn't find him. Maybe when he washed up on shore his body would be too mutilated from the rocks that he wouldn't be recognizable.

"Thank you," Bogdan said to Dagmara.

"You're welcome."

She turned to go once more, and couldn't help but meet Aleksy's gaze for a half-second.

His expression was unwavering, his jaw clenched.

The prince knew.

Hastily, she exited the throne room. Her heart was pumping so fast, she could hear the blood rushing to her temples. The wound from Sabien's blade still stung underneath her clothing. She had to get back to her room and lie down.

How could she have killed Ilusauri's Captain of the Royal Guard? Surely she couldn't have gotten herself into this mess. If anyone found out, would King Bogdan cover for her? Or would she be sold out to the Mad King?

She didn't have time to reach a conclusion. Someone grabbed her arm and yanked her into the shadows.

CHAPTER 6
Magdalena

"There you are!" Magda shouted. They were tucked away in a side-hallway, deep in the royal wing of the castle. Odie was beside her, and brushed up against Dagmara, his tail wagging happily. Magda was grateful Odie had led her right to her friend.

"I thought you were getting ready for the coronation," Dagmara replied, reaching down to acknowledge Magda's pet and gently stroking his fur.

Magda didn't know where to begin. How could she tell Dagmara she had exhibited Soul magic? Even the thought was impossible. Beyond that, how could she explain to her friend that she wouldn't be able to display water magic at the upcoming coronation ceremony?

So she said, "I have a huge problem."

"Add it to the list." Dagmara sighed, her face paler than usual. She sat down beside Odie, letting out a deep sigh, and proceeded to scratch behind his ear. Odie tilted his head, his tail wagging.

Knowing her friend was using Odie as an excuse to sit down, Magda took a seat on the cold stone beside her. "Why, what's wrong?" asked Magda.

"First you."

"Fine, but after we deal with my problem we deal with yours," Magda said assertively.

Magda hesitated before speaking the next words. Although she considered Dagmara her best friend in the fortress, it still scared her to reveal that she had magical abilities no one ever anticipated. The ramifications of this decision were beyond what she could logically imagine.

"Promise me you won't tell anyone what I'm about to tell you."

"I promise."

"It would destroy me and my family...including my brother."

Dagmara's brow furrowed. "Tell me."

"I think...," Magda gulped. "I think I have...Soul magic."

"Like...a Soul Guardian? You can control the earth?"

Magda nodded.

Dagmara froze. "That's impossible."

Magda reached into the front of her apron to pull out a set of poppy petals that she had stolen from the bouquet in her room. She opened her palm facing upward to Dagmara. A soft glow emitted from Magda's hand, and slowly, the petals dried out, curling into a set of wilted, dead ashes.

Odie turned away from the girls and sniffed at the dead flowers that scattered the ground.

Dagmara's hand flew to cover her open mouth. "How is that possible?"

Magda stood, unable to remain in one position with the nerves racing through her. "I don't know."

"But...Bogdan is your father. You're supposed to be a Guardian of Life, right?"

"I don't know!" Magda let out a huff, her emotions getting to her. Then she calmed down. "That's what I need to find out," she said, "but right now we have a bigger problem. Hundreds of guests from all over the kingdoms are coming to watch me display my magic...*water* magic."

Dagmara nodded, realizing the gravity of the situation. "If they think you are some sort of imposter, they would imprison you immediately until they figured out what to do with you, and the outcome would be much worse."

"Which is why I need to run away," said Magda.

"No." Dagmara shook her head. "Then everyone will know you have something to hide."

"Then we need to stop the coronation. Cause a scene that will prevent me from actually going through the entirety of the ceremony. We can figure out the rest later."

"Do you realize what you're asking me to do? If people knew I sabotaged the coronation, it would end my job and position here at the court. And Teos…"

"I thought you were good at not getting caught," Magda said, a pleading smile forming on her face.

"Not anymore it seems," she grumbled.

"What?"

"Nevermind."

Magda crouched to be at eye-level with her friend. "Please, Dagmara. You know I would do anything for you."

Dagmara was slowly coming to terms with the situation. "This is bigger than us," she said.

"Why do I have the feeling this has something to do with your problem?" asked Magda.

"We'll get to that later," said Dagmara, using the wall as a support as she climbed to her feet. "Just get ready. Go through the motions. I promise you I'll find a way to stop the ceremony."

CHAPTER 7
Dagmara

Her mind whirling, Dagmara laid flat on the chaise in her suite, staring at the ceiling. She was supposed to be getting ready for the coronation, and now she was devising a plan to sabotage it. And Magda...with Soul magic? It wasn't possible. *How* was it possible? She was biologically the child of a Life Guardian. Right?

And now Azuremi knights were scouring the streets for a dead man. The man she killed.

Sabien Renaud.

She clamped her palms over her face, blocking out the light that exacerbated her headache. She couldn't think about Sabien. One step at a time. For now, the coronation was the priority. The people of Azurem couldn't know Magda had magic belonging to a different guardian line. They would say she had no place being an heir to the Azuremi throne.

She wished she could ask her brother for advice, but he was with the nurse to regain mobility in his injured leg, leaving her alone. Surely Teos could help her come up with a strategy. By the guardians, if only her head didn't feel like it was shrouded in a thick blanket, maybe she could think clearly.

Sabotage the coronation.

Dagmara laughed. Bogdan certainly wouldn't let her become Magda's knight after that.

The door opened abruptly, and Dagmara jolted upright in alarm. Darkness danced in her vision at the sudden move, but as her vision cleared, she saw Aleksy in the threshold.

He was frozen. "Sorry, I should have knocked."

She was both shocked to see him and relieved. Her battling emotions continued to spiral out of control until she suppressed them all. "It's fine, come in." She propped her feet underneath her, sitting upright.

Aleksy closed the door behind him. "*Please* tell me the Ilusaurian you killed wasn't Ilusauri's Captain of the royal guard."

"Shhh!"

"Teos isn't here," Aleksy said before crossing to her in three strides. "Dagmara, answer me."

"There...is a strong chance it was the same man," she admitted.

Aleksy cursed under his breath before running his hand through his silver hair. He plopped down on the chaise beside her. "It's alright. We'll figure this out."

"We?" she questioned. "I'm the one who killed him."

He grabbed her hand. "We're in this together."

She could feel her stomach erupt with emotion as she felt his touch against her skin, but she had to focus.

She pulled her hand back. "I have...stuff to do."

"Stuff?" He let out a single laugh. "Really?"

She shrugged. "I have to get ready for the coronation."

He stared at her intently. "I know you do. I was only coming here to ask about Sabien Renaud, nothing else."

"I know, I'm sorry, but I have more important things to think about than Sabien at the moment."

"What could possibly be more important than the captain's death?"

"Is this captain really that important?" asked Dagmara. "We haven't associated ourselves with Ilusauri in years. I've never heard of him in my life."

"My father knew him. When people find out that King Bogdan's royal assassin has murdered the Mad King's Captain? That's an act of war."

"I can't think about that right now," Dagmara blurted out. "I have other major concerns on my mind."

"Such as?"

"The coronation."

"Unless Magda's been kidnapped I don't think the coronation ceremony is more important than a potential war between two kingdoms."

Kidnapped. Dagmara pondered the idea. Then she shook her head suddenly. She couldn't cause too much of a scandal.

Aleksy's expression wavered with concern. "Where is Magda?"

"She hasn't been kidnapped."

"So what is going on?"

She couldn't respond.

"Dagmara?"

She continued to remain utterly silent. Magda had entrusted her with the biggest secret of her life. What if the prince told his parents? What if others found out and stripped the princess of her title? Or worse...would the whole family be called false royals?

"I need to sabotage the coronation."

His body tensed. "What?" He sounded like a prince again. "Why?"

"I can't tell you."

Aleksy let out a deep sigh, which broke off into a laugh. He stood, distancing himself from her.

"You're going to sabotage the coronation but you can't tell me why? I need something, Dagmara, if you don't want me to have you locked up until the coronation is over."

Her mouth dropped open. "Lock me up?"

"You admitted to wanting to sabotage my sister's coronation!"

"I never said I wanted to."

Aleksy frowned. He massaged the back of his neck, exhaling sharply. "If you can't tell me *why* you plan on sabotaging it, at least tell me *how* you plan to."

Dagmara hadn't gotten that far in her plan. However, as she stared at Aleksy, suddenly it hit her. What if she didn't need to sabotage it at all, but rather make everyone believe Magda had the gift of water? No one would be the wiser, and there wouldn't need to be a scene.

Dagmara sat forward on the chaise, her eyes wide with revelation. "How far away can you be from a water source to use your gift?"

"I...what? Don't change the subject."

"I'm not, please, how far?"

"As far as I can see."

She rose slowly. "So...?"

Aleksy's brow furrowed. "I don't know, a mile or two? Depends on my vantage point. I'm not a sorcerer."

"Debatable."

"What is this about?"

Dagmara grabbed his hand, "Come with me, and I'll tell you."

She tugged him along, tearing out of the room and racing toward the royal wing of the castle.

"Is this part of the sabotage?" he asked.

"Maybe."

"Are you taking me somewhere secluded to kill me?" There was a hint of humor in his voice.

"If I took you somewhere secluded it wouldn't be to kill you," she said, flashing him a smirk.

His face reddened.

Without wasting any more time, Dagmara led Aleksy to Magda's chamber. Luckily, he didn't seem to press her further with questions. She was flattered he trusted her so much.

First, Dagmara knocked, hearing a soft 'come in' before she entered the room. Dagmara opened the doorway, seeing the chambers bustling with commotion. Magda was in the center of the room, standing on a platform, while maids rushed to and from. They were simultaneously doing her makeup while others laced up the bodice of her dress—or at least one of the many layers. Urszula, her personal maiden, seemed to direct everyone, clapping her hands lightly to ensure they kept up the pace. Odie, on the other hand, was napping at the foot of the bed.

Magda made eye contact with Dagmara through one of the floor length mirrors. "Urszula," Magda said, shying away from a brush. "I need a moment alone to speak with Dagmara."

Nobody stopped working. In fact, the commotion continued. "A moment?" Urszula asked, her voice respectful but stern. "You have now run off twice, and we're already behind!"

"It won't take long," Dagmara said, though her statement went unheard.

"We only need a minute." Aleksy's voice was commanding as he stood behind Dagmara in the doorway.

Immediately, the room was silenced. They whirled to face the crown prince, curtsying until they were nearly kneeling. Scattered "Your Highness!" flew throughout the room.

Urszula cleared her throat. "I will give you five, Your Highness." Then she began waving her arms, silently shooing the maids. Urszula was the last to leave, stopping at the threshold and pointing her finger at Magda. "Five minutes. So help me, I will not let you be crowned a guardian without looking perfect. Your mother will have my head." Then she gave a sharp curtsy, flashed a smile and exited, closing the door behind her.

"What is he doing here?" Magda demanded of her friend before sharpening her gaze on her brother.

Aleksy parted his mouth, but was at a loss for words.

"Magda," Dagmara started, "I found our solution."

CHAPTER 8
Magdalena

"You told him?"

"No, of course not. I promised you I wouldn't tell a soul. But I have a plan that involves telling Aleksy."

"Telling me what?" Aleksy shut the door behind him as he crossed to the two girls.

"I...," Magda stammered. This was her brother, someone that she trusted more than anyone else in the world. If there was anyone that would help her, he would.

Magda noted the crimson boutonniere pinned to her brother's chest. He was all ready for the coronation, dressed in regal attire, and his golden crown was pressed to his head. Her head spun as she demonstrated the magic she had exuded already three times today. In a flash, the petals disintegrated into dust as she destroyed the boutonniere. The flakes fell to the floor like airy, blood droplets.

"Your eyes...," Aleksy reached out toward his sister. "They turned yellow."

"Apparently, I have Soul magic," Magda went back to the mirror. She stared deep into her brown eyes, trying to glimpse the lingering yellow tint, but to no avail.

Aleksy's hand was trembling. "You must be related to the Guardians of the Soul."

"How is that possible?" Dagmara asked.

"I don't know...somewhere in our family line, maybe the lineages crossed..." mused Aleksy.

"I know what you're thinking. Maybe dad is not my real dad," Magda said.

Aleksy shook his head, not wanting to believe the possibility. "All those times that we went to the embassies when we were growing up, spending time with Kiran and Claude—"

"Don't talk to me about Claude," said Magda, wanting to press her palms to her ears. Rumors of her childhood friend turning mad, his mind intoxicated by the same magic his parents once controlled had spread terror across the kingdom. She couldn't remember the last time she had seen the King of Ilusauri. The entire story had made her fearful to inherit any magic herself.

Aleksy composed himself before taking a deep breath. "It doesn't matter to me, at all." He reached out, engulfing Magda in a warm hug. "You're still my sister, and nothing will ever change that. Don't you forget it."

Magda held him tightly, forcing her mind to remember the moment to assure herself that everything would be alright. "I need you now more than ever."

"I'm here." He squeezed her once more before letting go. "So what do we do?"

"For now, we go through with the coronation," Dagmara revealed her plan. "Magda will act as if she's performing the water magic in the ceremony, and Aleksy will be the one actually manipulating the water. Can you be discreet?"

Aleksy appeared concerned, but he answered, "Yes."

Magda grabbed her thin, silver crown on the top of the dresser, forcing it onto her head. Then she marched purposefully to the door.

Aleksy grabbed her arm before she could leave.

"I won't let anything happen to you," he said. "Try not to be afraid."

"I'm not," Magda replied.

"Good," Dagmara said, "Because if we can't pull off this act, they'll charge you for treason, Magda. Us and your mom too."

Magda said firmly:

"We're keeping this family together."

The coronation was held in the throne room. Ahead were four thrones framed by a rushing waterfall and the family crest, as if they were a stage for all to see. Around the edges of the room, were two layers of balconies, decorated in pink and blue banners. The entire room was already crowded with guests.

Today, the large fountain in the center of the space was gushing with water, and aisles of chairs were set up all around it.

The four royals stood at the entrance to the throne room, with Bogdan and Bernadette in the front, followed by Aleksy and Magda.

"You look beautiful in that dress, honey," Bogdan turned around.

"Doesn't she?!" Bernadette said excitedly. She whipped to Magda, also seeing the dress on her daughter. Upon noticing the skewed gemstones, she mouthed, "What did you do to the dress?"

"Ready?" Aleksy stole Magda a side-eye before turning back to the front of the room.

Magda was grateful that he had saved her from answering her mother's question. She didn't have time to explain that she had practically melted the gemstones with her fingertips due to her recent discovery that she was related to Guardians of the Soul.

Magda rolled her shoulders back and shifted to the balls of her feet. "Ready."

A horn blasted, announcing the arrival of the royal family. Instantly, all the guests stood to their feet. Bogdan and Bernadette entered first, followed by Aleksy and Magda straight behind. They all were dressed in the periwinkle blue that represented the cool rivers and southern oceans.

"Announcing His and Her Majesty, and His and Her Highness, to the arrival of the coronation of Princess Magdalena!" a voice sounded from the throne.

Magda stole a side eye at Aleksy, and he gave a reassuring nod.

The four stepped in the room, walking elegantly around the large fountain in the middle of the space and toward the thrones. Then, they turned to face everyone that was waiting to greet the royal family and witness the ceremony.

"Welcome to everyone here," said Bogdan, his voice echoing through the courtyard. "We are honored that you have joined us in this momentous and timely coronation. This is a time of celebration, where we appoint another guardian of magic. It is a day where Princess Magdalena will not only display her powers, but she will be entrusted with the knowledge of the royals." Bogdan paused to smile in Magda's direction.

Then Bogdan thrust his hand toward the central fountain, and bursts of water sprayed toward the heavens. The water fanned outward like dozens of shooting stars, and approached each individual guest throughout the room. Magda cupped her palms in front of her, and a water droplet found its way to her hands before swirling upward into a glass made entirely of ice. In an instant, servants were rushing towards the guests, pouring ample glasses of wine into Bogdan's magical ice goblets.

"A toast. To the newest Guardian of Life, Princess Magdalena," smiled Bogdan.

"A toast!" The guests echoed all around the room.

Magda and Aleksy downed their glasses quickly, before they disintegrated into thin air. It wasn't the first time they had tasted the rich wines from the fortress cellars.

The crowd began to adjust their positions in the room, finding their seats for the ceremony that was about to begin. A few of the nobles approached the king and queen to pay their respects before the coronation began.

"Princess," a voice said on Magda's right. "I have to extend my congratulations to you."

Magda turned around to see the Queen of Flaustra standing before her. She was a short woman, with long black hair tied into a braid on the side. She wore a golden, wrapped-dress that fell straight to the floor and a set of decadent earrings and necklace complemented her dark lipstick.

Magdalena's breath caught in her throat at the sight of Queen Sanyal Dhara. Flaustra was one of their main allies, and the royal families always had a good relationship. It was the kingdom of earth magic, host to the Guardians of the Soul, so Magda had no idea if Queen Sanyal would be able to see right through Magdalena's fake ceremony. It would be the end of her time at the court.

"Queen Sanyal," said Magda, her breath shaky. She bowed in order to not meet the Queen's eyes and continued, "Congratulations are hardly in order yet."

Sanyal said, "When you pass the test at the ceremony, it will be nice to have another woman as a guardian. Kiran will enjoy your company at our embassies."

"How is she?" asked Magda, remembering the princess of Flaustra, who was only a year older than herself. When their parents had meetings growing up, some of the heirs would spend time together playing in the hallways of each palace, getting up to no good. Was it possible that Magda was somehow related to this royal family? It didn't make any sense.

"She's taken to her role as a guardian quite well," said Sanyal, "but times have been quite difficult, and I'm sure your father and brother will tell you everything after you are appointed. If you ever need anything from our kingdom, please know that our doors are always open to you."

"Thank you," said Magda.

"Now, I must pay my respects to your parents," said the queen.

Magda nodded and began making her way toward the throne. Before she sat down, Aleksy caught her arm, pulling her close and whispering in her ear.

"I just made up an excuse to mom and dad," he said under his breath. "I'll go find Dagmara and get into position."

Magda nodded.

Aleksy disappeared behind the thrones, heading out a side door of the room. What excuse could have gotten him out of the coronation that easily? Why would their father let him leave on the most important day of her life?

Magda shrugged off her feelings. She didn't have time to perseverate. Instead, she sat down on the throne, letting her disfigured, crystal dress spread out around her feet. Then she looked out at the hundreds of people. They were all watching her.

The audience's attention snapped to the sage in the middle of the room, who began reading from his scroll in front of the glorious fountain.

The ceremony had begun.

This was it. It was time to deceive her parents, the court, and the kingdom.

CHAPTER 9
Dagmara

Dagmara strolled through the courtyard with her brother by her side. The sun helped warm the cool air of Azurem, and the smell of flowers danced in the air. In the small courtyard adjacent to the throne room a few children were playing, pretending to be guardians. The servants played along with them, happy to have a day of rest and join in the festivities happening around the many towns. King Bogdan had declared today a royal holiday, and he had even halted work in the mines.

Dagmara wished she could run and play with the children, but stayed in the shade for the sake of her health. She couldn't exhaust herself too early in the day, especially when she had used all her energy for the week on her mission the previous night. The only reason she was still functioning was because of the adrenaline and nerves.

Teos coughed, barely covering his mouth with the crook of his elbow.

Dagmara snapped her head in his direction. "Are you alright?"

"Fine," Teos said, clearing his throat.

"You're not sick, are you?" Dagmara placed her hands on either side of his face and tilted his head up. His eyes weren't bloodshot, but coughing was the first side of zowach, the illness that was killing youth all through Azurem. Without a medicine supply from Ilusauri, any child or teen that caught zowach was practically given a death sentence.

Knocking her hands away, Teos jerked back. "I said I'm fine. How would I catch zowach in the fortress? I'm one of three teens there."

"I walked by some kids that may have been infected last night."

Teos rolled his eyes. "You think I caught zowach because you've been going into town? Doubtful."

"We don't know how it is transferred."

"How hard did the guy punch you last night? You're being paranoid." Teos laughed before intentionally changing the topic. "Oh, I have something for you." He propped the crutch underneath his armpit before reaching into his vest. Her brother cautiously withdrew what appeared to be a metal ball. "I've been experimenting."

Dagmara stepped directly in front of him, covering the object with her body. She glanced around hastily, but everyone was deep in their own laughter and conversations. "What is that?" she demanded.

"Calm down." Teos chuckled. With a twitch of his head, he brushed a blonde lock of hair out of his eyes. "Instead of the jasny we use for the light explosion, this is a little more powerful. Try it."

"No." Dagmara wrenched the object from his hand and shoved it back in his vest. "Why would you bring it here?"

"Well, I wasn't going to leave it in our room where someone else could stumble upon it."

"You're experimenting?"

"Sis," Teos inclined his head, his jovial tone wavering. "We're a team. My light detonation helped you escape last night, didn't it?"

"Shhh!"

"No one's paying attention, but if you keep acting like that someone will."

Begrudgingly, Dagmara replaced her serious expression with a halfhearted smile and crossed her arms. She leaned against the wall nearby for support, pretending to appear like she was having a good time.

"We're a team," Teos repeated. "You handle the potions, and I handle the explosions. I'm better at it anyway, and I don't know a thing about poisons."

"You shouldn't have to handle anything."

"Don't you think mom would have wanted both of us to be assassins like her?"

"No, frankly, I don't think that's what she wanted. She accepted Bogdan's offer so we could have a better life, not one like hers."

Teos let out a sigh. "Well she's gone now, Dagmara. And if we want to keep our plush spot in the castle with money for days, we have to fill her role."

"*I'm* filling her role."

"You'd be dead if it wasn't for my explosive last night."

Dagmara bit her lip, remembering when she killed the captain of the Ilusaurian army. Her stomach curled.

Teos continued, "I can't survive outside the fortress, but you can't survive without both of our concoctions. Unfortunately, this is what the guardians ordained for us," Teos gestured to his twisted leg, "so until I can walk correctly again, which will never be, and until the doctors find out what is wrong with you, which will never be, we're a team."

A sigh escaped her lips. She only wanted to protect him, but she wished he wasn't right. How different her life could have been if she were born to another mother. How different Teos's life would be if he wasn't involved in the accident at the cliffs. How different her life would be if she was someone else. Sometimes, she wished she was.

She opened her mouth to speak, but her brother cut her off. He said:

"Dreamy prince, northwest, five seconds until arrival." He batted his eyelashes at her mockingly.

Shoving his shoulder, Dagmara said, "Knock it off."

Teos rolled his eyes, ending in a boyish grin.

"Ceremony is about to start," Prince Aleksy said when he reached their side. Even though Teos had given her a heads up, her heart still fluttered at the prince's proximity. "You ready?"

"Yes," Dagmara said.

Aleksy flashed Teos a smile. "We can sneak out for our card game after the ceremony, when it gets boring."

"Sounds like a plan," Teos replied. "I'm going to take my seat inside."

With that, Teos headed off, entering the throne room and making his way to a seat on the first floor.

Once Teos had gone, Aleksy beckoned Dagmara. With a gesture to follow him, Aleksy headed toward the back of the throne room, on the other side of the courtyard. There were two identical circular staircases, wide enough to fit four people across. Aleksy led the way up the stairs, Dagmara following, meticulous about her breathing. Stairs were her worst nightmare. Something seemingly trivial was what spiked her heart rate the most. It was embarrassing, and disappointing. And once again a constant, incessant reminder that she would never be normal.

They reached the upper balcony. There was a side door, nearly concealed by the way it blended in with the wall. Making sure no one was looking in their direction, Aleksy opened it, revealing another set of stairs.

Letting out an exhale, Dagmara readied herself.

"I can do this by myself," Aleksy said, noticing her hesitation.

"No." Steeling herself, Dagmara scaled the next flight of stairs. She wasn't going to let the flights of stairs stop her, not in a moment like this. They were about to fool the entire kingdom, and she wanted a front row seat.

By the guardians, she would be in bed the rest of the week.

They reached the third-tier balcony, this one closed off to the guests. It was almost amongst the rafters, and there was no seating, just a simple 'U' shaped roundabout. A thigh-high wall barricaded the edge of the balcony, and a few pillars supported the weight of the ceiling. A few of the banners and flags were tied off to the ropes along the rim of the third floor, revealing the behind the scenes of the glorious display on the ground. It was lined with stained glass windows, casting in pastel colored hues. They weren't nearly as large as the ornate windows on the second story, but they were still the size of a full-grown man.

At the center of the balcony, Aleksy lowered to a crouch on the ground, his elbows resting on the balcony wall while he peered at the sight below.

The ceremony below had already started, and a sage was reading in a booming voice from a scroll at a central pedestal. Magda was sitting in her throne, completely done-up in her blue dress, and her silver hair fell loosely around the crown. Beside her, sat King Bogdan and Queen Bernadette.

Dagmara crouched down, leaning her back against the wall, facing the opposite way of Aleksy. She didn't need to see the scene yet. She would know when the display began. For now, she was catching her breath. She wanted to loosen the corset around her waist, but decided better against it, remembering it was concealing the dagger that she had used to kill the Ilusaurian captain. There were too many people here, and it made her nervous.

"Do you think it will work?" Aleksy asked.

Unable to answer right away, Dagmara steadied her breathing, her heart pounding against her ribcage. There was a shooting pain at the center of her ribs, and she clutched her chest, waiting for it to cease. "Fooling the entire kingdom?" Dagmara panted. "It has to. We don't have another option."

"And what happens after the ceremony?"

"What do you mean?"

"Do the three of us take this secret to the grave? Shouldn't we tell my dad?" Aleksy fired question after question. "Someone is going to find out eventually. Then Magda won't be the only one to blame. All of us will go down with treason."

Dagmara put her hand on his shoulder. "It'll be alright," she said. "Let's get through this plan first. Then we will come up with another. No use figuring out what comes next if we don't know this will work yet."

Aleksy gave her a soft smile. She thought he was reaching for her hand, but instead, he removed her hand from his shoulder. "It's almost time." He stood to his feet, getting a better vantage point, but still remained in the shadows. No one could see them from up here.

The gesture stuck with her. Was he mad she was roping him into this? Did he blame her? She was only trying to help Magda.

She couldn't think about any of that. She shook her head, readying her breath, when a shadow flickered in her peripheral vision. It could have been a trick of her eyes, or a cloud masking the sun. However, the hair on the back of her neck rose in alarm.

The room felt eerily silent, except for the echoing voice of the sage downstairs, and she could hear her own breathing. There was a creak in the rafters, and her heart lurched in her chest. They weren't alone up here.

She looked at Aleksy. He was focused, his hands at his sides, and his gaze dead set on the center of the room below, waiting for his sister to approach the fountain and display her magic. A blue sparkle began at the center of his irises. She couldn't distract him now.

Quietly, she scrambled to her feet, ducking in a crouch as she rounded the 'U' shaped balcony. She let her palm skim the wall, making sure she was underneath it. The last thing she needed was to cause a noise and have the whole audience—or one person for that matter—look up and see Aleksy orchestrating the magic.

Slipping between two columns and brushing underneath the backside of a few ropes holding the banners, she saw a figure. Whoever it was remained crouched, their head barely peeking out over the wall.

She scanned his appearance, first noting his thin-soled shoes. He came from a warmer climate than theirs. The glistening dagger on his belt notified her that this was not a friend from the court. Then she saw his black doublet, stitched with silver.

Whoever this was, they were Ilusaurian.

CHAPTER 10
Magdalena

Magda's stomach dropped when she heard her name called. The royal sage was standing in the center of the room, beckoning for her to come to the fountain. This was the moment of truth—the moment where the entire room expected her to put her powers on display.

Magda stepped forward, off the platform and toward the central fountain. She was aware of hundreds of gazes, scrutinizing each one of her steps with their beady eyes.

"Princess Magdalena Krol, you will now officially become a guardian upon your own display of water magic. Only you will know how your powers live inside you."

Magda gulped, scanning the two levels of balconies above for any sign of Aleksy in the darkness. She knew he was hiding in order to conceal his magic. She never doubted that he would be there for her, waiting in the shadows, ready to exhibit the water magic in her place.

Magda nodded toward the sage, showing that she was ready.

He spoke, "Upon the rising of the water from this fountain, I hereby declare Her Highness, Princess Magdalena Krol the next Guardian of Life, following in the footsteps of both His Highness,

Prince Aleksy Krol, and His Majesty King Bogdan Krol. She will take on the duties of the guardians, and due to her diligence and duty, never again will the First Prince reign."

Magda's face flushed, and her heart dropped to the pit of her stomach. She extended her hand, letting the spray of water from the fountain tickle her arm, but quickly put it down, for her entire palm was shaking. She let out a deep breath before closing her eyes, making it appear as if she was searching somewhere inside for the answer. Time went by, moment after moment, until Magda was sure she was putting on a convincing act.

She opened her eyes, raising her hand and then thrusting it toward the fountain. Just before Magda slammed her eyes shut again, she caught a glimpse of a glorious shower of water shooting up toward the sky. It was as if she and Aleksy were perfectly in sync.

All she could hear was the fantastic awes of the crowd, and she felt the wind beat against her face and hair, combined with a falling mist that rested in the atmosphere. She wanted to open her eyes and see what Aleksy had majestically inspired in the room, but she kept them sealed tightly.

The exclamations continued, and Magda couldn't help but let a smile creep over her face. They were doing this—really doing this. How had they successfully pulled off this scheme in front of the entire court and the royals?

A sprinkle of water danced across her face, until the liquid in the damp air had faded from a drizzle into a faint mist. It was cool, as if she had stepped outside on a frosty morning, where the poppies were covered in dew after a light shower.

Magda took a deep breath. The magical display must have concluded, since the room was cold and the audience silent. She opened her eyes, hoping no one would see deep into her irises and realize they had never once turned blue.

Magda was about to raise her arms in triumph, when a creaking noise sounded from above. Magda looked up to see a figure falling from the balcony. She stepped back with a gasp, just as a limp body dropped onto the center of the fountain, clattering against the hard metal in a gruesome display of lifeless, twisted limbs.

In an instant, the room was in an uproar. Screams echoed, and the audience members leapt from their seats, pointing to the rafters in between shrieks of confusion and mayhem. They darted into the aisles, or jumped over the pews, heading in a massive stampede toward the door.

Magda's eyes were fixed on the body before her. She backed up, but not before she heard a faint scream behind her:

"Magda!" her father's voice was loud and clear.

He sprung forward, covering her with his massive body, just as a slew of projectiles rained down on them. They both fell to the floor, and Magda struggled to breathe under her father's weight.

The room around her was in pandemonium, and a mix of blood-curdling shouts and a stampede of footsteps flooded her senses.

"Dad!" she yelled. "Dad, get up!" she screamed underneath his hefty body, kicking and yelling so that someone would hear her. But the entire room was in an uproar, and no one had noticed that both the king and princess had fallen.

Magda's vision blurred as she tried to stay in the moment. All around her, the multi-layered shouts blurred into one jumbled sound. This was an attack, and she needed to stay alive.

Magda inhaled, using all her upper body strength to roll her father over and turn him onto his back. Then she stared down at the king.

His eyes were nothing, as if the glossy tears in the corners were windows into a void she couldn't bring herself to describe. A single arrow protruded from the center of his chest.

"Dad!" Magda screamed hysterically, throwing her body over his. Even though he was underneath her, he felt heavy, as if the breath once filling his lungs had been sucked out completely. She almost blacked out, pulled into the madness all around her.

Gushes of wind flew past her head, and she wasn't sure if more arrows were being launched in their direction. She scrambled backward, away from her father, crouching down next to the fountain for cover.

Magda's eyes scanned the balconies, looking for Aleksy or Dagmara, but they were nowhere in sight.

Then she turned back to the throne. Her mother was hysterical, attempting to rush toward Bogdan while she was being dragged away by royal knights to a safe place behind the thrones.

All that Magda could do was stare at her dad, but she couldn't run to him. She wanted desperately for him to be alive, for there to have been some type of mistake. She played the sequence over and over in her head, wondering why he had jumped in front of her and what she could have done differently. But no matter how hard she stared, no matter how hard she tried to imagine him sitting up, he didn't move.

Magda realized she wasn't breathing, and gasped for air. All around her were the sounds of nightmares. She crouched behind the fountain, realizing she had nowhere to run, for she wouldn't escape the arrows coming from above. Anger threatened to consume her completely, but at the last second, her mind sharpened at the sound of something familiar.

BARK!

Magda snapped her head to the right. Odie was in between the pews, as if beckoning her to run to safety.

Before she could stop herself, Magda leapt over her father's body, dashing between the pews and laying on her stomach, right beside Odie. But Odie continued barking, leading in the direction of the side of the room.

Magda crawled on her stomach through the chaos. When they got to the edge of the pews, Magda knelt behind Odie as they dashed to the side of the throne room, behind a set of columns that was holding up the side balcony.

"We're safe now," Magda said, holding her pet. However, she

knew it wasn't true. The closest door was at the front of the throne room, past the fountain and all the way down the long aisle at the front of the building.

There was no escape from their attackers. Magda could only hope that they wouldn't be found.

CHAPTER 11
Dagmara

Dagmara had no intention of letting the man slide off the railing, but when she drove her dagger into the back of his chest, right through his heart, his weight nearly took her off the side with him. Her grip slipped and he toppled stories below landing in a contorted position on the top of the fountain.

With a dagger in hand, she raced back toward Aleksy. The room had already erupted in chaos, and she could barely hear her own thoughts. Aleksy was gripping the rail, screaming something down to his family. He saw Dagmara and instantly shouted, "We have to get down there to protect them."

That's when Dagmara noticed another figure, on the opposite end of the 'U' shaped balcony. He had a bow in his hand and arrows strapped to his back. Two assailants? But this one was making a straight line for the staircase as if he knew his cover had been blown.

"Aleksy!" Dagmara shouted.

Aleksy saw the target across the rafters. With a rise of his hand, he summoned water from the fountain below. A dozen droplets manifested into dagger-like icicles before they hurled toward the intruder.

Throwing up his forearm in attempts to block, the intruder rolled to the ground. The water-daggers lodged into the wall and the railing in a cacophony of shattering ice and splintering wood. The intruder was on his feet as fast as he had dodged, his bow in hand as he withdrew an arrow from the case on his back.

Time froze as Dagmara stared at the assailant. He was dressed all in black, aside from a white mask. The white mask was thick, covering his whole face aside from slits for the eyes, and a black symbol was painted onto the center of the forehead.

Lurching back into reality, Dagmara noticed with stark horror that Aleksy was weaponless to fight in this close of quarters.

The intruder set the arrow and released, Aleksy barely dodging in the confines of the rafters. The arrow made contact with one of the stained glass windows, shattering it to oblivion and coating the ground in pink glass.

There was something else. The intruder's gloves had claws on the back of their knuckles.

Aleksy charged forward as the intruder tried to ready the next arrow. The prince kicked him in the side of the hip before decking him across the face with a punch.

Unfazed, the intruder backhanded Aleksy. Aleksy tried to dodge, but the claws caught the side of his cheeks. With a rake of his foot, the intruder tripped Aleksy, sending him to the ground.

"No!" Dagmara yelled. She didn't know what came over her. Wielding nothing but a dagger, desperately wishing she had the explosive from Teos, she raced forward, aiming for the intruder's chest.

The intruder, with horrifying accuracy, grabbed Dagmara's wrist, bending it backward before the dagger was anywhere near his chest. She screamed in pain, the dagger flying from her grip. She watched in horror as it was tossed out the open window, disappearing from sight.

Looking up at the intruder, she knew with certainty that this was the end. He had an iron grip on her wrist, and could easily knock her out or use the bow to strangle her.

Instead, he released her and shoved the ball of his palm into her throat. She was on her back in an instant, choking for breath from the blow. Her hands flew to her neck as she gasped for air. Then the assailant turned his back on her and reached for another arrow.

As Dagmara begged for air, she knew he had let her live. This wasn't an attack on Azurem. This was a coordinated group of assassins after one thing only.

The guardians.

Luckily her distraction had given Aleksy enough time to summon more water from the fountain below. When the assailant turned to face him, the prince wielded a magnificent ice sword, glittering in the sun that poured in from the open window. With one overwhelming thrust, Aleksy drove the blade of ice through the intruder's chest. The enemy was dead on impact, and as Aleksy withdrew the blade, the enemy fell to the ground with a hard thud.

Aleksy raced to Dagmara's aid as she continued to struggle for air.

"Are you alright?" he asked, his eyes twinkling with piercing blue light. He was dazzling, his pale skin almost glowing with magic. Three claw marks raked down the side of his cheek, and blood poured from the open wounds.

"Your face..." Dagmara's voice rasped.

"I'm fine." Aleksy offered her a smile. He lifted the iceblade slowly, showing her his magic. The iceblade melted in his grip, and she could see the water slither up his arm, his chest, and reach his face. The water brushed over his porcelain skin, healing the wounds immediately. All that was left was drops of blood on his doublet.

He was a true Guardian of Life.

She gave him a breathless smile, relieved.

He rose to his feet and extended a hand down to her. She gripped his hand to let him help her to her feet, when a throwing knife whizzed through the air. The deadly weapon found purchase in the center of Aleksy's chest.

A shock rippled through their connected hands, an electrifying jolt singeing her palm. She screamed, scrambling to her feet and catching Aleksy as he fell backward. She landed hard on her knees, his head cradled in her lap.

"No, no, no, Aleksy!" she shouted, her palm touching his cheek.

But the knife was perfectly thrown, stabbing through his heart. It may as well have been stabbed through hers.

"You're going to be alright, you can heal this," Dagmara said, brushing a silver lock of hair off his forehead.

Aleksy choked, blood sputtering from his lips.

A sob burst from Dagmara's throat. "Please, Aleksy, please don't leave me."

The prince met Dagmara's gaze one more time. "Save...Magda."

His body fell limp.

"No!" The scream erupted from deep within, tearing through her throat. Looking up, she desperately searched for who had thrown the knife.

That's when she saw the figure in the stairwell doorway. He was broad, wearing the same attire as the other two, holding another throwing knife in his hand. The white mask covered his face, but the dread seeping through Dagmara's body made her realize that his eyes were directly on her.

He inclined his head slightly, and a chill ran down her spine, casting her whole body in an imaginary state of ice. Suddenly the room felt colder, and the air harder to breathe. The assassin looked at her, and it was almost as if time was frozen.

Then he turned on his heel and disappeared down the stairwell.

She remembered Aleksy's last words.

Save Magda.

Three assailants. Three targets.

Setting Aleksy on the ground, she rose to her feet, peering over the wall to the ground below. The crowd was massive, and a stampede was still trying to make its way to the exit. She scanned the area around the fountain, her heart plummeting in her chest upon spotting the limp body of the king.

But on the side of the room she saw movement.

Magda.

Dagmara knew she would never beat the assailant downstairs. She would never be able to push against the flow of the stampede to get to the front of the throne room.

Swooping to pick up a shard of glass from the broken window, she raced to the ropes that were holding up the banners. By the founding guardians, help her if this plan didn't work.

Gripping the rope of the largest banner—or what she hoped was, she couldn't entirely tell with the way they were intertwined—she used the shard of glass to saw through its restraints.

"Please, please," she begged under her breath, feeling the glass simultaneously cut into the inside of her palm.

The rope snapped.

She dropped the shard and gripped the rope with both hands. Using the railing as a foothold, she leapt. Swinging from the rope, she flew over the crowd, feeling the rush in her hair as her stomach catapulted inside her. Jumping down from the rope before it swung her to the opposite wall, she landed in a roll, feeling the impact ricochet through her body. Her head spun as she pulled herself to her feet, and her hands burned, but her adrenaline surged a new spark inside her.

Dagmara skidded to the ground, sliding on her hip as she reached the princess's hiding spot. She was surprised to see both Magda and Odie behind the column. Three other guards were cowering, their shields up to protect the princess. At least they had found her.

Magda flinched back, but upon seeing Dagmara, a relief flooded her eyes.

"There's a panel to exit in the back!" Dagmara yelled, quickly shouting instructions to find the secret exit door. "You three," she pointed at the guards, "protect her with your life."

They obeyed immediately, flanking the princess and making their way toward the exit. It wasn't their fault for cowering. They didn't know where the threat was coming from. The exit was the best way to escape, but it was smarter that they had stayed hidden.

Dagmara, on the other hand, knew there was only one assassin left.

Rising from the hiding spot, Dagmara faced the room before her. It was empty now. The crowd had completely exited. There was only one silhouette in the center aisle, backlit by the open doors behind him.

He was holding his throwing knife, and Dagmara knew his aim was deadly, and she was weaponless. Her body was exhausted, her muscles trembling and her hands shaking. The knights had to have been protecting the Azuremi nobles or the Queen, and only a few were left, standing in front of the podium with their shields extended.

The assailant's gaze shifted from Dagmara to the back corner. He saw the group making their escape. He had his gaze set on Magda, not bothering to waste time on Dagmara. He lifted the throwing knife, taking his aim.

"Magda!" Dagmara screamed in warning.

Before the intruder had a chance to throw, something skittered across the ground, rolling out from underneath the pews. It was a small, metallic ball, a few yards ahead of the intruder, blocking his path down the center aisle.

The assailant and Dagmara simultaneously realized what it was.

An explosion lit the throne room. The assassin threw up his hands, blocking his face from the rubble that scattered across the ground. Shards of the surrounding pews broke off, flying in haphazard directions. Dagmara felt the earth rumble underneath her, and she extended her hands for balance.

The smoke cleared, revealing the assassin behind, his figure menacing. He had been too far back from the explosion to be killed, but nevertheless, it had saved the princess. It had bought Magda enough time to make it to the exit.

With one glance toward the back exit, the assassin came to the conclusion that the princess had escaped. Then the assassin met Dagmara's gaze once more, but she stood, unwavering. It was almost as if he gave her a promise that he would be back, before he turned and fled.

"Go after him!" Dagmara commanded the few guards that remained in the throne room. They obeyed immediately, charging after him.

After the throne room seemed to fall silent once more, the air thick from the small blast, Dagmara heard shuffling. She strode forward to the noise at the center of the throne room before dropping down and seeing her brother under the pews.

"I knew I wouldn't make it in the stampede so I hid," Teos's explanation came tumbling out before Dagmara could ask.

But she didn't care. Dropping to her knees, she reached out and grabbed his arms, pulling him out from underneath the pew before embracing him. The destruction of the explosive—his explosive—was still scattered around them.

"What did you do that for?" she let out, gripping him tighter and burying her cheek into his blonde hair.

He hugged her back, leaning all his weight into her. "We're a team."

A heavy weight fell over her, and she felt the tears rushing to her eyes. Squeezing him even stronger, as though she was making sure he was still there, she looked up to the rafters.

"He's dead, Teos," Dagmara gasped, a choked sob escaping her mouth. Her gaze shifted to the king, sprawled on the stage at the front of the throne room. "They're both..." she had to look away from the king, the only father figure she ever had.

Then she looked at the dead body in the fountain—the first intruder that had fallen over the edge. His mask had snapped off his face, rolling farther down the aisle.

She didn't recognize the symbol on the center of the mask. But she knew she wouldn't forget it for the rest of her life.

"We're safe—" Teos broke off into a fit of coughing.

Dagmara jerked back, taking in his face. Her heart plummeted in her chest as she met his bloodshot gaze.

"Teos..." she breathed.

"I-I'm fine," he muttered. "It's the dust and debris."

The next cough was a gurgle, thick with mucus.

Gasping, Dagmara pulled him tight into an embrace. Denial and desperation coursed through her as tears rolled from her face. It wasn't the debris making him cough. It wasn't the dust turning his eyes bloodshot.

He had zowach, the deadly illness that plagued the children of Azurem. Maybe she had brought it back from one of her assassinations. She had no idea how the illness operated. If Teos was lucky, he had a year left before the disease took his life. He wouldn't survive without medication.

The only cure was in Ilusauri, the kingdom with uniforms identical to the assassins. If the Mad King sent these assassins, there was no way he would send Azurem medicine. He probably liked watching Azurem's children die.

Because of that monster, Teos was as good as dead.

CHAPTER 12
Magdalena

Magda threw herself across her bed and cried into the pillow. She had never cried so violently in her life. Greeting guests at her brother and father's funeral was worse than anything she had ever endured, and the grief was slowly turning from sadness to anger.

Magda sat up, throwing the pillow across the room and into a portrait on the wall. It swung, but didn't crash to the ground. She let out a scream, letting the grief consume her as she clenched her hands in anger. All of the sudden, a loud shatter pierced her eardrums. She was aware of the bouquet of poppies on the table that her mom had given her. Thorns had sprung from the vines in all directions, puncturing the glass vase and sending the pieces everywhere.

Odie shot up from his space at the foot of the bed.

Magda screamed again. A burning rage was growing inside of her, and she seized onto violent daydreams of her unleashing wrath on all of the assassins who had killed her family.

If only she had the courage to summon all of the magic from the earth and tear down the houses and families of the killers.

Technically she could do just that. She did have Soul magic which could control the earth.

Magda thought back to the coronation, and Queen Sanyal's invitation to come to Flaustra. She had to find out the story behind her birth, and why she was different from Aleksy. It wouldn't be long before the entire castle would find out that she wielded earth magic and not water. When the royal court found out she wasn't a Guardian of Life, and no other Guardians of Life remained alive, she had no idea what they would do to her. She had to leave Azurem as soon as she could.

Magda got up and marched out of her bedroom and into the parlor. Her mother sat on a chair, her head in her hands.

"Mom, I need you to be honest with me," said Magda.

"What?" Bernadette asked, looking up to reveal red, watery eyes.

There was no more time for lies, so Magda blurted out, "Was dad my real father?"

"How can you say that? At a time like this!"

"Please...," said Magda, "I need to know."

"Oh, sweetheart, of course he was," said Bernadette. "Why would you ever think otherwise?"

Suddenly the question seemed ridiculous, and Magda felt horrible for even asking it. She didn't want to burden her mother with any more grief today. She couldn't let her mother know that she wasn't a Life Guardian, not while the kingdom was still in chaos. Her mother had to believe Magda could continue the Life Guardian lineage and that their entire livelihood in the fortress wasn't in jeopardy. So she said, "Because I'm different from them. I deserve to know what they were going to tell me after the ceremony. Please tell me what the guardians have always known."

Bernadette wiped the tears from her eyes and patted the seat next to her. Magda crossed to her mother and sat down, before the queen explained:

"Those secrets were part of what your father was allowed to tell you once you became a guardian," she explained. "He was looking forward to this day so much, so that he could tell you the full story."

"But what does that mean?" asked Magda.

"I'm not a guardian myself. Your father and brother would have told you everything. I'm so sorry, Magda, but there are forces of magic in our universe that no one fully understands." Bernadette reached out to touch her daughter.

"Then how am I supposed to know how to be a guardian?!" exclaimed Magda. What was worse, she didn't have water magic at all, she had earth magic.

"That is not our main concern," said Bernadette, "My concern is that whoever killed Bogdan and Aleksy might come after you. You're not to leave the fortress until we get to the bottom of this."

"Do you know who the assassins were?"

"No. I'm told they were dressed in Ilusaurian attire, but the mask they wore had the symbol of the First Prince on it."

"The First Prince? The character from the legends I was told as a child?" asked Magda. "Wasn't he the one who tried to kill his siblings outside of the trials to ensure he kept the magic? The stories say he was destroyed."

"Yes, but it's more than a legend, Magda," Bernadette spoke. "I don't know why his symbol has resurfaced now."

"I thought the First Prince was a fairytale, to teach guardians the importance and rules of trials, and that only one sibling may be the guardian of the generation." said Magda. "You're saying the First Prince was real?"

"I'm not a guardian, so I don't have the answers."

"Then I have to talk to the remaining ones. Guardian Sora, Princess Kiran, or Queen Sanyal." Or dare she say it—her childhood friend—King Claude Mirage.

"That won't happen as I've told all the knights that you are not allowed to leave this fortress—or the royal wing for that matter. Not until we get to the bottom of this."

Magda let out a huff. She wasn't going to be able to help anyone being stuck in the fortress. She had to find out why her family was targeted, and she had to understand the secrets that her brother and father held so close.

Magda walked out of the parlor, heading to her father's office. She didn't care that her mother saw where she was headed. If there was anything that her father had been keeping from her, surely he would have written it down in his endless notebooks. She crossed the royal hallway and banged the door open to her parents' room.

Like Magda, they had a parlor area, and a string of consecutive rooms led to a study and finally to their bedroom. Magda marched into the study, going right to her father's large mahogany desk that took up the majority of the space.

She sifted through the papers on the tabletop, before opening the drawers on either side of the desk. Magda tore through scrolls, ledgers, and notebooks, skimming for any mention of ancient magic, the guardians, or their family history, but she couldn't find a single mention of any of those topics. All her father had kept in his records was notes after meeting with nobles, maps, ledgers, and battle plans. Nothing seemed at all significant to Magda.

Afterward, she went to the bookshelves, flipping through every book to see if there was a scribble or note inside. The books were in pristine shape, as if her father had never read them at all, but rather they had been mere displays.

Odie whimpered from the half-open doorway and made his way over to Magda.

"Oh, Odie," said Magda, dropping to her knees and allowing the grief to consume her once more. She hugged the dog tightly, pressing her face up against his soft fur. For a brief moment, Magda felt a sliver of comfort.

Odie perked up and began wagging his tail, whining in excitement before racing back over to the door and letting out a hopeful whimper.

Dagmara was standing in the frame, her eyes red and indicating she had been crying. "Odie, you found the princess." She validated the dog in his search.

"How is Teos?" Magda asked instantly. Last she heard, it was confirmed he had zowach.

The muscles in Dagmara's neck constricted. "He's alright," she lied before changing the topic. "There's news on the investigation into your dad and...," she paused, as if the next words were difficult to say, "...brother's deaths."

"What?" asked Magda, standing up.

"It seems as if early leads point to Ilusauri being responsible. The assassins were wearing Ilusaurian uniforms."

The words cut through Magda like a knife, threatening to break her. She fought back tears as she assessed the situation. If it was true that Ilusauri was behind this, they had to pay. But how could they be sure this was linked to the Mad King of Ilusauri—Claude?

How would she make this decision as a ruler? And how was she going to rule when she knew nothing about being a Guardian? The only option was to speak to another guardian, one who had the same magic as she did, in the land of Flaustra. Which meant sneaking out of the fortress and past her mother.

"I need you to continue the investigation," said Magda, fighting back tears. "But first, come with me to the Scribestone. I need to send a message." There was only one person that she trusted to tell her about the ways of the guardians.

"To who?"

"Queen Sanyal."

A few minutes later, Magda, Dagmara, and Odie entered the royal library. It was a small, circular room that extended up into one of the large towers at the corner of the fortress. All around, bookshelves wrapped along the walls, extending upward to a small window at the top of the tower. In the center, a wide spiral staircase extended along the outside walls, allowing easy reach to access the manuscripts.

In the center of the room, was the Scribestone. It was a large statue of a book that glowed with a hint of iridescent magic. Anyone that wrote a message on the book would be able to send it to one of the three identical statues that lay in the libraries in Flaustra, Celestaire, and Ilusauri.

Magda approached the Scribestone, with Dagmara close behind.

Odie paced across the room, sniffing the ancient scrolls.

"I'm going to send Sanyal a message and ask to meet with her," said Magda. Quickly, she grabbed a quill pen from a shelf and began writing on the magical stone.

Queen Sanyal,

I must speak with you. Please allow me to come to Flaustra to visit with you and your children. Without my father and Aleksy, I have no idea what it means to be a guardian, or how to use my powers, and I need your guidance.

Sincerely,

Magdalena Krol

Magda finished the letter, and in an instant, the message had sunk into the stone, completely disappearing. Soon, it would reappear on the Scribestone in Flaustra. The message would only appear for the person whom it was addressed to, meaning Magda didn't have any reason to fear it would be intercepted.

Suddenly, the Scribestone glowed bright.

Words flashed upon the stone:

One message from Claude Mirage, Ilusauri.

Magda gasped. "Claude?"

"The Mad King?" Dagmara echoed.

Odie let out a whimper and padded across the floor to reach Magda's side. He placed his snout against her knee, and she idly ran her palm against his head.

Magda pressed her other hand to the words, touching her fingerprints to the letter.

Dear Princess,

It has come to my attention that your brother and father were murdered during your coronation ceremony. My heart goes out to you and your kingdom, and I extend my greatest condolences.

I fear that you are unsafe and that these assassins won't stop until they find you too. Let me offer you a place of refuge in Ilusauri, a chance to rebuild a grieving heart and a broken friendship.

Marry me.
With love,
Claude

Magda's eyes widened. It had been ages since she had received any communication from Claude, her childhood friend, and his new reputation only made her uneasy. She never wanted to fully believe in the stories—from withholding food from his population, to forcing people out of their homes with no explanation, to having fits of rage or holding public executions—but she had no evidence to believe otherwise.

If what Dagmara said was true, and the Kingdom of Ilusauri really was behind the death of Aleksy and her father, then they had to pay. Nothing in this letter could change that.

But now, the Mad King was asking for her hand in marriage.

CHAPTER 13
Dagmara

"I don't believe it." Magda let out a sharp breath. "King Claude wants to marry me."

"What?" Dagmara gasped.

Magda stepped aside to make room for Dagmara, and Dagmara quickly scanned the letter.

Disbelief flooded through Dagmara's body.

"He sees Azurem as weak," Magda deduced. "Now he wants full control of it."

Odie let out a yelp, almost in agreement.

"A guardian has never married another guardian before," Dagmara objected. "Merging the life and mind lineages?"

Magda snapped her head up to Dagmara. "The life lineage doesn't exist anymore." Her lip quivered ever so slightly.

Dagmara could feel the onset of tears. She went to Magda's side and nestled her head on her friend's shoulder. "I'm sorry."

"I can't go through with the marriage," Magda said. "Sooner or later, he will discover I am a Soul Guardian. I can't control it. What then? Azurem is history."

Dagmara listened in silence. This was Magda's decision, even though Dagmara may have her own opinions on the situation. Until Magda asked for her opinion, she kept her mouth shut.

"What would Claude have to gain from this alliance anyway?" Magda asked.

Dagmara faced her friend. "More troops so that he can finish taking over all the kingdoms?"

"I'm serious." Magda frowned.

"I'm serious too," Dagmara replied. "I hate him. He's holding onto the cure that could save Teos's life."

"If there was a marriage, we could negotiate medication. Azurem would benefit from reopening the trade routes."

Dagmara hadn't thought about that. Would the Mad King even be interested in negotiating? Was there a way to get the medication from Ilusauri after all?

Magda asked, "We don't have proof Claude was behind the assassinations, do we?"

"No, but he killed his parents. And he invaded Celestaire," Dagmara explained. "I think it's easy to see a pattern."

"What were you doing for my father?" Magda asked. "Why were you assassinating Azuremi nobles if Claude was behind everything my father feared?"

She had a good point. There was something Bogdan and Aleksy kept from Dagmara...something that pieced together that exact information. If only she had known what it was.

"If I accept this marriage, we have access to Claude's castle. We can find proof. Maybe he's working with other people."

"You can't be serious," Dagmara shook her head. "The potential for the trade routes is enticing, but if you accept the marriage, you could be killed the moment you walk across the border."

"Or...he may actually want an alliance." Magda turned away from the Scribestone, and the sparkling letters disappeared. "That didn't quite sound like a mad king to me."

"You remember him from your childhood," Dagmara objected. "People change."

Magda nodded and then froze. Her eyes widened in realization, her mouth slightly agape.

Dagmara shrunk back. "What is it?"

"People change," Magda echoed before biting her lip, lost in thought.

Odie sat upright, recognizing her shift in emotion. He tilted his head in curiosity.

"I can't go. We can't risk him discovering I have Soul magic," Magda said. "But, forming the alliance would benefit both kingdoms, and if we had access to his castle we could find the proof we need to bring him to justice for the murders. So, we send someone disguised as me."

"Who?" Dagmara asked.

Magda gave an awkward shrug of her shoulders before gesturing forward.

"Me?" Dagmara gasped. "That's ridiculous!" She gripped the Scribestone to prevent herself from falling over.

"Just hear me out." Magda was pacing, lost in furious thought. "We already look similar. All we have to do is dye your hair, put on heels, get rid of that bruise on your eye, say I filled out since the last family portrait, and you're practically me!"

"Magda!"

"You're the only one I trust, and I don't have the sleuthing abilities you do," Magda tried shifting her approach.

"You're worried he's going to find out about your magic. What if he finds out I *don't have* magic?"

"It's far easier to say you don't want to show it off," Magda said. "I can't control it. It could come out at any time and both my life and Azurem's are over."

"What about my health?" Dagmara countered. "Guardians are perfect—what if he finds out I'm not?"

Her friend's face softened. "You can say it's your time of the month. A man won't know the difference."

Dagmara knew she had a point, but it wasn't enough. "I'm not a princess, and I'm certainly not fluent in Ilusaurian."

"Neither am I!" Magda shrugged with a sheepish grin. She wasn't a good liar.

Dagmara let out a sigh, walking over to the spiral staircase and plopping herself down on a step. One way or another, they had to find proof if Claude was behind the assassinations. Dagmara had to know why Bogdan sent her on missions. She had to avenge his and Aleksy's deaths.

Her heart hurt remembering the coronation.

Magda crossed to her friend, putting her hand on Dagmara's. "I know you loved my father and brother as family."

Tears began to well in Dagmara's eyes. Aleksy's lifeless body replayed in her mind like a nightmare.

"If you don't want to do it for them, do it for Teos. The alliance will return the medicine supply. Or, you can do it for me?" Magda gave a half-hearted smile. "Going in my place will protect me more than you staying by my side. I fear declining his proposal more than anything."

A shimmer in Magda's eye was the only indication that she was on the verge of tears. She was so strong. There was so much about her that Dagmara admired. If only Dagmara was a guardian too.

For now, she would have to be as strong as she could be, in her own way.

Dagmara wasn't trained in political negotiations, but she was good with words. If there was a slim chance she could get medicine to save Teos's life she would do whatever it took. Worst case scenario, she would find the Mad King's stash of leku and steal it herself.

Dagmara nodded. "I'll do it."

Magda let out a sigh of relief before engulfing her friend in her embrace. "Oh thank you!"

An excited bark rang through the room as Odie jumped up onto Dagmara's lap and nuzzled against them, wanting to join the hug.

The two burst out in a laugh, with a quick moment of respite, wiping away their tears and giving Odie much needed attention.

"What happens if I don't find proof before the wedding?" Dagmara asked.

"You always have to have everything planned out, don't you?"

"But think about it...what if he isn't behind the attacks? Then what? I'm the queen of Ilusauri?"

A soft laugh escaped Magda's lips. "It won't get that far. If it does, we can switch. We'll figure it out."

It wasn't the reassurance Dagmara was hoping for. "One more problem. I may have killed the Captain of the Ilusauri guard."

Jerking back, Magda's face flushed. She stammered, searching for words, but eventually regained her composure. "All the more reason to agree to this alliance to smooth that over before it is exposed."

"What about you?" Dagmara asked. "You'll stay in hiding here?"

"No," Magda replied. "I have to learn why I have this magic. So I'm going to the source of it. I'm going to Flaustra."

CHAPTER 14
Magdalena

Magda's mother couldn't understand why she would even consider a marriage proposal to the Mad King, especially given rumors that he was behind the deaths of the Azuremi royals. So, Magda made a deal with her mother. Magda would go to the Ilusaurian castle for approximately one season of courting time, and then she would decide if she would go through with the marriage or not. It was enough to buy her some time, and for her mother to allow her outside of the fortress for one season.

So, she went back to the Scribestone, writing a different note to Prince Claude, saying:

Claude,
  I accept your proposal, but we must speak soon. I think about you often. I will come to visit you and stay with you until the wedding.
  With all my love,
  Magda

It was a bit manipulative, but she needed Claude to think that she was on his side. She only hoped that Claude didn't remember specific memories of their encounters growing up. For in reality, Dagmara would be going in her place. She and Claude hadn't seen each other in over ten years, and he wouldn't remember exactly what she looked like or acted like now that she was older.

At the Scribestone in the library, Magda was surprised to see another message.

One message from Sanyal Dhara, Flaustra.

Magda pressed the letters once more, opening the message.

Dear Magdalena,
   I can respect that you are looking for answers from a close ally, but right now it is too dangerous to leave the fortress. You must not come to Flaustra. You must stay in Azurem. It is for your own good. I will write to your mother and let her know the same.
   Queen Sanyal

Magda cursed under her breath upon seeing the letter. The plan was already in motion, and she had already sent back a response to King Claude. Also, she had already told her mother the news, and Dagmara was making preparations to change her appearance so they could pull this off. If Queen Sanyal wrote to Queen Bernadette, Magda wouldn't be leaving this fortress for her entire life.

No. She still had to go to Flaustra, whether Queen Sanyal liked it or not. Magda was close to Princess Kiran, Queen Sanyal's daughter, who had been crowned a year ago. Kiran would tell her everything... she just had to give the princess a bit of warning.

Magda picked up the quill once more.

Kiran,
   I'm coming for a visit to Flaustra. Please tell your officers to be expecting me. I can't wait to see you. I fear we have a lot to catch up on.
   Your friend, Magda

After leaving the Scribestone, Magda slipped into her mother's study. Queen Bernadette had a beautiful workspace that mirrored King Bogdan's. Magda knew that inside one of the drawers there was a false bottom, where emergency money was kept for safe-keeping.

Before anyone could stop her, Magda crossed to the desk and opened the central drawer. Then she pulled open the bottom and grabbed three, small bags of golden coins. One bag had golden coins stamped with the elk on one side and water on the other, representing the currency of Azurem. The others were the golden coins of Flaustra, stamped with a tiger. Then, she also grabbed a few rings and gemstones from her own closet. There were so many expensive items she had been gifted, and she would be able to survive for years in other kingdoms. When Magda was sure she had enough, she packed a sturdy backpack with a hidden pocket on the bottom, perfect for storing money for her travels.

Two weeks later, the day came that Magda was set to travel to the Kingdom of Ilusauri. She stepped outside into the courtyard with her mother, handmaiden Urszula, and Dagmara. In front of them was a carriage leading a caravan of servants, gifts, and Magda's chests.

Unlike other days, Dagmara wore an overcoat and a tight wrap around her head. It was necessary if they were going to pull off the switch before they got to Ilusauri.

"Goodbye, sweetheart," said Bernadette, giving Magda a soft hug.

"Goodbye, mother," said Magda.

"Remember, Claude killed his parents, and there's no telling what he'll do to you if he also killed the rest of our family."

"That's precisely why I have to go to him," said Magda. "I'm a guardian. I'll be fine."

"Don't let him control your mind."

"Mom, you know his compulsion doesn't work on other guardians," Magda assured her.

"Claude will have medicine in case you catch any of the diseases on your journey through the countryside. Don't be afraid to ask him for it."

"Mom, I'll be fine."

"Yes, yes," Bernadette said, sniffling. "Do what you need to do. I love you."

"I love you too."

Giving her mom one final hug, she knew keeping her magic a secret from her mother was the right thing to do. Bernadette most certainly wouldn't let Magda leave to find the truth about her powers, and learning that the Life magic died with Aleksy and her father would be too much for her mother.

Magda turned to Urszula and Dagmara. "Ready?"

"Ready," they both nodded in unison.

She nodded to Odie who was prancing in excitement. "You seem ready too," she laughed.

The knights flanking them on either side stepped forward and opened the carriage for the three girls. The head butler reached out his hand, allowing Magda to place a gloved palm inside it before she stepped into the carriage.

Odie hopped in next, helping himself up onto the bench even though he was too big.

"Oh, Odie!" Magda laughed, ruffling his fur.

"I hope Claude isn't allergic to dogs," Urszula laughed.

"Too bad if he is," said Magda.

The door slammed shut, and Magda looked at Dagmara, who wore a concerned expression.

"Don't worry," said Magda, "I hardly remember anything about him from when we met as children. You will be fine."

Urszula watched the exchange between the two with a confused expression.

"Move out!" yelled the driver, and in a flash, the carriage was bumping up and down along the cobblestones, being pulled outside of the courtyard, across the narrow bridge, and down the hill toward the rushing river.

They continued along the pathway, rolling across the dirt paths and into the forests that surrounded the edge of the Azuremi kingdom. About ten minutes into the journey, they were cutting through the poppy fields, still dusted with light snow, heading in the direction of Ilusauri.

Dagmara pulled off the wrap on her head. Her bleach-blonde hair was now sprayed on the ends with a shining silver. She wore dangling, jeweled earrings, representative of a royal. Then Dagmara pulled off her heavy overcoat, revealing a blue, embroidered dress with a sash around her waist, as well as a string of pearls dangling down her neck.

"Dagmara...," Urszula let out an exclamation. Then she turned to Magda, "Did you give her your dress?"

Magda grabbed Urszula's hands. "I'm not coming with you."

"But King Claude expects you to arrive in the next week."

"I know," said Magda.

"I'm Princess Magda from now on," explained Dagmara.

"You!? You'll never pass for Magdalena." Urszula laughed.

"I need you to help her." Magda said to Urszula. "Please, you've been with me at all my royal engagements. It will be easy for Dagmara to act like me if she has you."

"But why?"

"I'm going to Flaustra. There's too many mysteries I have to solve. But I promise you that it will help Azurem, and my family."

Urszula appeared skeptical, "You two are serious?"

"Yes," they said in unison.

Urszula shifted in her chair to bang on the back of the carriage. "Stop! Stop at once!"

Dagmara lunged forward to grab her arm. "Please, this is what Princess Magdalena wants."

Urszula frowned. She fired a glare at the princess. "How long must we hold up the ruse?"

"A few weeks, maximum," Magda said. "I have to speak with Queen Sanyal. Then I'll be in Ilusauri before any wedding happens."

Her maiden let out a deep sigh. "Fine. But hurry back. I don't like the idea that I will be lying to a Mad King. You hear he's wiping people out of their homes? Taking a full village and ordering everyone to leave for no reason! Not only are his people starved, they're now homeless!"

"I've heard, yes," Magda replied. She could sense her best friend getting uneasy. Then she leaned over to hug Urszula. "Thank you." Then she reached over, grabbing the wrap and fur-coat, before putting on the clothing items. She took off her shoes, quickly giving her heels to Dagmara before trading them for Dagmara's boots.

Then Magda leaned over and gave Dagmara a hug. "I'll write to you as soon as I can. Stay strong," she said.

"I will. Be safe," Dagmara replied.

"You too," said Magda. "Continue with the plan until you hear from me, unless he puts your life in danger."

"Alright," said Dagmara, "but you better come to Ilusauri soon."

Magda released her friend and let out a sigh. "Come, Odie." She beckoned her pet before cracking open the carriage door. They were still pulling through the poppy fields, and it wouldn't take long to retrace her steps back to the castle and get her horse.

The carriages glided along at a snail's pace, and Magda easily jumped down to the ground, Odie just behind her. The knights were up ahead, scouting the terrain in the distance. Magda pulled the wrap further around her face before darting off the path and into the forest.

From now on, she was no longer a princess.

PART TWO

The Guardian of the Mind

CHAPTER 15
Magdalena

Magda and Odie traced their way back to the Azuremi fortress, sneaking inside to secure her horse, before trotting out of the stables and down the road. She circled away from the fortress, careful to hide her face from the knights, before cutting south and heading toward the coast. Odie followed every step of the way, darting across the fields, grateful to be free from the palace walls and exude his never-ending energy.

The shores along the southern coast line were rocky and gray, lined with square houses in bright colors. In a few days' time, Magda would find ships, decorated with the pastel flags and the crest of her parents, heading to Flaustra each daybreak. Surely, someone would grant her passage to the south, and she had enough gold to pay her way.

Inside, her heart burned for Aleksy, wishing that he was taking this journey with her. Even the thought that he was dead didn't seem real in her mind. It was almost as if she was going on a trip, and he would be waiting to greet her back at the Azuremi fortress when she returned. Mere memories of her brother made her throat close and glistening tears threaten to form at her eyes, knowing he was no longer breathing. But those thoughts didn't manifest as sadness, rather as anger. Why did it happen to them? What had they done to deserve it? Their deaths weren't fair. Magda's anger was slowly building into a fierce determination to avenge both Aleksy and her father's death.

Magda decided then and there that she would solve the mystery of the origin of her powers as quickly as possible, and she would do whatever it took to find the answers. She didn't have much time, and she needed to get to Dagmara quickly to ensure that the kingdom of Ilusauri didn't discover their hoax.

Magda continued riding, determined to get to a town by nightfall, where she could buy a proper wagon and food for the rest of the journey. When the sun was setting, she stopped in a small village, but not before pinning her bright, silver hair underneath her cloak.

Magda dropped off her horse at the stables and grabbed her knapsack, before ordering that a wagon be hitched up to him upon her return the next day. Then she turned around and headed toward the town square. "Come on, Odie," Magda called, and he raced to catch up with her. He was still energetic, as if the sprint to the town had exhilarated him.

As Magda stepped outside of the stable, she looked up at the charcoal sky to see a wisp of falling snowflakes. Magda shivered and pulled her scarf tighter over her mouth and her hood further over her face. Odie jumped up, lapping the snowflakes with his tongue.

To her right, was a group of dogs who looked well taken-care of, darting around the town square. Despite their presence, Odie stayed by Magda's side as she walked toward the central inn.

Once inside, Magda slipped into a dark booth in the corner of the tavern, hoping to not be recognized, and Odie trotted beside her. There were other customers with dogs, and no one paid Magda any attention when she beckoned Odie under the table.

Luckily, no one in these parts of Azurem had actually met the princess. She hardly even left the area surrounding the fortress. It was clear she was in a small mining town—likely many of the people here spent their days mining salt from the depths of the earth. Most of

Azurem's economy was based on the royal salt mines, which were a significant industrial operation. The mysterious labyrinths beneath the surface of Azurem were known as the underground kingdom. They extended all the way to the fortress, and Magda remembered touring one of the royal mines when she was just eight years old. Nevertheless, the memory stuck with her, for they had walked through chamber upon chamber of decorative salt pieces, including a hand-carved statue of her father.

Magda was promptly served a bowl of soup, slices of meat, and a loaf of bread. The waitress that served Magda coughed into her sleeve. Magda withdrew from the waitress, not wanting to catch any illness herself. She hadn't realized how many people were affected as everyone in the fortress was safe.

She listened in as she fed Odie scraps of meat under the table. For an instant, Magda forgot the fact that she was a princess, but the villager's conversations brought her back to reality.

"What do you think of the king and prince's deaths?" a hoarse voice rang through the room. The man broke off into a fit of coughs, but no one around him seemed to care.

"Shows you that the guardians aren't gods as they say they are. If a few rogue actors can take them down, how strong are their powers really?"

"They just want you to keep your head down. Keep working in the royal mines, making them richer while making us sicker."

"Yeah...what do the guardians *actually* guard?"

"Nothing!"

The room was filled with boisterous laughter and continuous coughing. Magda listened in as the conversation turned to the most deadly illness, zowach, and the fact that nearly no child or teen who got it survived. It seemed to be a bigger grievance than the lack of any form of governance, a dead royal family, or a Mad King that threatened to invade. All that Magda could do was agree with their every word. Her family already knew about the lack of medicine and the illnesses plaguing the kingdom, but was anything being done about it?

Maybe a marriage to Claude wasn't such a bad idea after all.

Magda stayed at the inn that night. The next day, she picked up her horse and a bright new wagon before continuing on the rest of her journey toward the port. While Magda rode her horse, Odie played in the back of the wagon.

She continued riding for hours and hours, not taking her mind off the task at hand. Throughout the day, she only briefly stopped for lunch and a few more breaks for her horse. Every town she came across had some form of the illness. Soon they arrived near the coastline, where the pungent smell of the ocean breathed life into Magda's nostrils. The salty air was a reward at the end of a long quest, and the setting sun alerted her that she needed to make it to the docks soon to find a place to stay for the night. The harbor town was known as Frostmere, named for exactly what its title suggested.

Magda urged her horse along the pathway, circling down through the myriad of villages that dotted the rocky coast. The wagon bumped behind her, and Magda turned a few times to look back at Odie—her most precious cargo. As the sky grew orange, Magda must have traveled through approximately one dozen villages, descending with the landscape after passing through each one. Upon reaching the shoreline, she spotted four ships docked in the harbor. Three of the ships hosted glorious pastel flags, fluttering briskly, as if the embroidered elks were about to gallop off in the wind. The last ship's flags were down.

Magda led her horse and wagon along the road, traversing through numerous villagers either on foot or in carriages. They were heading to trade on the docks, hoping that their money would be worth enough to barter for Flaustran treasures at a discounted price now that they were on Azuremi soil. When she reached the dock, she pulled her horse to a halt and gracefully dropped down into the sand. Instantly, a young boy rushed up to her, grabbing the horse's reins. "How many nights in the stable miss?"

"Keep him indefinitely until I return," Magda replied, dropping a coin in his hand, which likely was worth his entire yearly pay.

The boy's eyes widened, giving her a slight bow before rushing to the wagon. He opened the small door, and Odie jumped down to the ground. Then the boy handed Magda her knapsack and side-bag before leading the horse away.

"Odie," Magda called her dog, and they both continued into the crowd. Magda headed up a set of wooden, creaky stairs, and shoved herself through the rowdy peddlers. A ship ahead was unloading imports—or as the Azuremi called them, treasures. All around, auctioneers screamed out, attempting to attract those with the deepest pockets, but some of the opening bids were still too high for the Azuremi citizens.

Odie circled next to Magda's legs, not once leaving her side or getting distracted by the newfound commotion. She noted quite a few Azuremi had dogs with them, but none were the same breed as Odie.

Magda searched the docks for anyone who was selling passage across the sea. Her mind spun, as she got a glimpse of words being shouted in Azuremi, Ilusaurian, and Celesta.

Then—to her surprise—she heard the beautiful language of Flaustran. Magda turned around to view the last ship on the dock. The pounding wind inflated the white sails, and a loud commotion came from the sailors as they darted from one end of the deck to another, pulling on the golden ropes. The sailors began releasing their flags into the sky, and out unfurled the symbol of a raging tiger, marking the ship as Flaustran.

Magda's eyes lit up. This ship was leaving soon, and if she moved quickly enough, she might be able to gain passage.

She rammed her way through a group of women who were all clamoring around a pile of fabric. As she did so, she pulled her winter scarf higher on her face in order to keep her identity hidden.

Ahead was a female officer, with a handaxe attached to each hip. Her black hair was slicked back into a perfect bun, dressed in turquoise and bright yellow. The colors of Flaustra.

"One passage to Flaustra," Magda announced when she stepped in front of the girl.

"I'm sorry," she replied curtly, her accent thick in Magda's native language. "That's a cargo ship. You can wait for the next tourist transport."

"And when will that be?"

"One week's time."

"I don't have one week to spare." Magda's eyes flicked to the ship as the clamor increased. It was clear they were almost ready to set sail. "Please, I'll pay my way," she begged.

"Even if you had enough money to interest me in that proposal, you're not getting on that ship. It's completely full, and I'm short staffed as it is."

The wheels were turning in Magda's head. Here, using her title as a princess wouldn't help her get by. She would have to convince this woman with her words and wit. What would Aleksy do? He would have charmed them no doubt. And Dagmara? She would have had a plan before approaching this woman. Too late for that.

So she said, "I'll pull my weight, don't worry."

"You look like you've never worked a day in your life."

Magda was taken aback by the girl's brisk responses, and she frantically tried to come up with an argument to get her on the ship. Did she have any skills? Would she be able to cook food for the sailors? Would she be able to help them navigate?

When the woman realized that Magda wasn't going anywhere, she rolled her eyes and said, "Do you have money or not?"

Magda nodded. She dug deep into her pockets to find the last remaining pouch of gold stamped with an elk. There were approximately twenty-five pieces inside. She wouldn't need them where she was going, for she had stolen other currency from her parents' study, so Magda plopped the pouch in the woman's hands.

The woman's expression changed after she peered into the pouch. She switched to her native tongue before asking, "Do you even speak Flaustran?"

The words were spoken so quickly that Magda almost didn't have time to register what the woman had said. Magda dug deep to remember her Flaustran classes with her private tutor all throughout grade school. She switched to the language before replying. "I do."

The woman scrunched her eyebrows and looked down at Magda over the brim of her nose. "You'll have to work on your accent. And this one?" She looked down at Odie.

Odie wagged his tail in response.

"He's coming too," Magda answered.

"Are you sure?" the woman asked, her eyebrows raising in surprise.

"Of course."

"Suit yourself. Let's go."

The woman in the turquoise coat walked down the dock, beckoning Magda and her pet to follow her. As she turned to board the ship, a golden cufflink flashed in the setting sun, drawing Magda's attention. It was a symbol Magda had only seen in her lessons—a peacock feather—the mark of the Fowler's Guild.

This ship belonged to one of Flaustra's infamous guilds that informally controlled all of Flaustra's economy, as well as all trade in and out of Flaustra. The kingdom was famous for its luxuries and markets above all else, and some of these treasures nobles would kill for.

The Fowler's Guild was known for traveling to the Mystic South, a no man's land filled with precious gems and metals, as well as large beasts that they hunted for their thick fur. Because of Flaustra's location as the closest kingdom to the mysterious south, Flaustra was a marketplace of priceless artifacts, and traders would bargain at all hours of the day for the best deals. This had boosted the guilds to the status of unofficial royals that controlled the entire Flaustran economy. They were well-funded, well-organized, and impressive fighters. They even had so much influence that the royals often had to include them in official decision-making.

The woman broke Magda's thoughts:

"I'm Ishani. Captain of the Starway."

Magda hesitated. Obviously, it wouldn't be appropriate to reply with her real name. It would possibly reveal the fact that she was a guardian, or a royal. But she hadn't had too much time to consider a new identity. Quickly, she replied:

"Dagmara."

"Nice to meet you. It's a long way to Flaustra. You better make yourself comfortable, and I hope you don't get seasick."

They all stepped onto the plank leading up to the ship, and boarded the magnificent vessel. When they jumped down onto the wooden deck, Ishani began shouting orders to the sailors that were preparing to set off. She was speaking Flaustran too rapidly for Magda to understand. When she was done screaming at those nearest to them, she switched back to Azuremi and said, "This is Dagmara. You better treat her well...or else." Ishani's hands shifted to her waist, and Magda's attention was drawn to the two hand-held axes hanging from either side of her belt.

The sailors around Magda all nodded their heads in obedience, but they were more drawn to Odie, giving suspicious glares and whispering in Flaustran under their breaths. Had they never seen a dog before?

"Get back to work!" Ishani yelled, ordering them back to their tasks.

Magda thanked Ishani before crossing the deck and leaning out over the side of the ship below to watch the dark blue water crash onto the rocky shore. Odie trotted beside her, his paws clicking against the wood. The gray beach below blended into the cliffside beyond, and the villages were like speckled rocks nestled on the snowy hills, marking the pathway back to the castle.

"We made it, Odie," Magda sighed, leaning further over the railing.

It had been years since Magda had traveled to Flaustra as a little girl. She guessed that the capital city of Flaustra had also greatly changed. She knew the city was heavily guarded, with checkpoints and guild leaders acting in dual roles controlling the economy and the royal officers. Eyes were everywhere, and she had to be careful not to be spotted and her identity revealed. Surely, the well-traveled people of Flaustra had seen a portrait of her before.

A loud horn blasted through the air, causing everyone on the docks and throughout Frostmere to watch the incredible ship push off into the open sea. Magda stumbled to catch her footing as the ship departed, gliding off into the glittering waters, heading for the horizon.

In a matter of time, Magda would be in Flaustra and discover the truth about her magic.

CHAPTER 16
Dagmara

The trip to Ilusauri was arduous and long. In total, it took a few weeks, departing from the eastern port city Bergclow. Dagmara thought she would get seasick on the boat that took her to the Mad King's kingdom. Each day was filled with more Ilusaurian words, but every time Urszula quizzed her, she felt like she retained no information. How was she supposed to impersonate Magda if she couldn't speak Ilusaurian fluently? All the guardians learned every language.

The sun was sweltering, and Dagmara spent most time in her cabin on the boat lying down, her legs propped up. She missed the cool air of Azurem. She missed Bogdan and Aleksy. The onslaught of grief surprised her, and she buried it deep next to the grief for her mother.

Her mother...caught and tortured to death while preserving secrets for the king of Azurem. What if Dagmara was caught for impersonating Magdalena? She would take Magda's secrets to the grave, that was her only option.

She would not meet the same fate as her mother. Teos needed her.

If she could find a way to convince the Mad King to send a shipment of medicine to Azurem, then everything would be worth it. She had to save Teos. There was no other option. Even if she had to steal the medicine from Ilusauri herself.

Besides, she was impersonating Magda. She had to channel Magda's courage and spontaneity.

If only Dagmara could be as naive to the world's dangers as her friend.

After disembarking the ship in the small port town of Elsynoire, which was a stark first impression of Ilusauri, Dagmara was even more unstable on her feet than before. Stiffness radiated through her limbs, and pain laced through her shoulders. She was used to her body aching for no reason, but it was worse today. She could never anticipate when she would have a good or poor day.

The port was eerily dead, with no other ships entering or exiting. A light drizzle fell from above, and the air was foggy. She kept her hood up, concealing her face from the Azuremi knights that accompanied them. They couldn't know she and Magda had swapped. She also couldn't let the rain wash out the temporary silver-tinted spray in her hair.

Ahead, a group was waiting for them, flanked by an Ilusaurian carriage. Had the Mad King come to greet her? A shiver ran up Dagmara's spine.

"Let me speak with them," one of the Azuremi knights said, taking the lead to address the Ilusaurian guards.

Dagmara stood still beside Urszula. Her throwing stars were already sewn into a hidden pouch on her corset, and she knew she had her poisons and potions stored underneath her makeup case as a disguise.

Then a female Ilusaurian guard stepped forward, clearing the distance between her group and Dagmara's entourage. She was beautiful, appearing in her late twenties, and she remained professional with her arms behind her back. She was tall and muscular, with piercing eyes and dark skin, and her brown hair was cropped short. Weapons lined her armor from her corset to her boots.

"Princess," she said with a thick accent, giving a small bow. "I'm Martine D'Aramie. I've been entrusted to accompany you to the Ilusaurian Castle. I can be your translator, advisor, or guide. Anything you need at the castle, I will be by your side."

Someone to watch my every move. Dagmara fought to keep her thoughts silent. For all she knew, Martine was here to kill her, and that would be the end of her time in Ilusauri. She wouldn't have even made it across the border. If Martine wanted her dead, she would be. It was better to earn her trust and learn anything she could about the king in advance.

"Join me in my carriage for the rest of the ride?" Dagmara asked.

Martine nodded. "As you wish, princess."

One of the Ilusaurian guards opened the carriage, and Dagmara climbed in alongside Urszula and Martine. It was a tight space, and she could feel her knees against both of theirs. Before long, they were moving once more.

"Urszula and I were just talking about what the castle will be like," Dagmara said, taking the moment as an introduction. "I'm sure you know all about it."

"Yes, I have been there for many years," Martine replied.

It wasn't much. Dagmara would have to pry information out of her.

"And the king? What is he like?"

Martine's solid expression faltered slightly, but it was impossible to tell whether it was just from a bump in the road. "He is our guardian," she responded without any inflection in her voice.

Dagmara was about to press for more when the window caught her gaze. They were passing by what looked to be a field, but it was brittle and gray. Only portions of the vegetation were visible and still seemed to have a coating of dust on them. It was almost as if a fire had torn through the town, but left everything standing. It made no sense.

Another field came into view, and the grass was yellow and

brown. Gaunt cows were scattered across the landscape, but there were no other animals in sight.

Then the carriage passed by a row of homes. Children played with the mud in the street, and those old enough to take on heavy labor struggled to repair holes in their houses.

That's when a series of shouts broke out. The overlap of the screams made it indecipherable. Dagmara couldn't translate quickly enough.

Then a rock smacked against the glass window. A gasp escaped Dagmara's lips as she scooted back in surprise.

Martine slid the curtain shut, covering Dagmara's view of the outside. "I think it is best to leave this closed until we get to the castle." Her voice was surprisingly calm.

All Dagmara could do was nod.

After a long, silent ride, the carriage pulled underneath a metal gate with the royal crest of Ilusauri: a black diamond stamped with a silver, iron-clad bear.

The carriage jolted to a halt.

"We're here," said Martine.

Dagmara nodded. She adjusted her clothing and flipped her braid to the front of her shoulders. Then she rolled her shoulders back and held her chin in the air, attempting to embrace as much of Magda's persona as possible.

When she stepped out of the carriage, Dagmara stood in front of a towering castle, both elegant and menacing due to its sheer size. Its outer walls were built of light-colored stones, and vines snaked along them, displaying silver and purple flowers. The rectangular, three-story building was marked with symmetrical wings on each side of the main entrance; its square windows were perfectly spaced out. Directly above the front door was a balcony overlooking a front garden and a fountain.

Dagmara turned behind her to admire the garden. Between the castle and the gated entrance, were beds of pastel roses, in colors that

Dagmara had never seen before. They were in perfect bloom, despite the overcast and brisk weather. The fountain in the center appeared magical, as if the water sparkled like diamonds in the sun, although there was no sun peeking through the clouds today. To Dagmara's right, she noted that the castle stood on the outskirts of a purple field of lilacs, stretching as far as the eye could see.

If this was how the Mad King lived, no wonder his subjects hated him. They were dying in ash-ridden villages and their crops had turned to blight.

"This way," said Martine. She led Dagmara through a checkpoint of four guards and through the front gates. The Ilusaurian castle was drastically different from what she was used to. Instead of the calming pastel colors that decorated her home, black and silver spanned the entirety of the room, making it appear smaller. There were reflective panels along the wall that weren't quite mirrors, but blurred where the room started and ended.

Then, a woman nearly fifty years old began to descend the staircase, flanked by four guards. Her black hair was swept up into a tight bun and fastened with a metallic headband. Long pieces of whimsical, silver fabric draped from her wrists and connected to the back of her shoulders, giving the illusion that she was floating down the staircase.

Dagmara knew Claude had killed his parents eight years ago, so this couldn't be his mother. She racked her brain with all the knowledge she had studied for this exact moment.

"Your Highness," the woman said, giving a subtle nod of her head, then she started to speak in Ilusauri, her words too fast for Dagmara to piece together.

Dagmara stared blankly, her mind reeling. This was why she had studied on the entire trip. She thought she was ready. She knew Ilusauri well enough to hold a conversation, so why was her mind drawing a blank now?

The woman's lips thinned. "I thought they taught princesses to speak foreign languages," she said, now speaking Dagmara's native language. "I guess the education in Azurem is lacking. Lucky for you, His Majesty speaks seven languages."

Embarrassment raced through Dagmara, but she didn't have a chance to respond.

The woman repeated her introduction in Azuremi, "I'm Madame Annette Beaumont, advisor to both the King and Captain of the royal guard."

Was she referring to Sabien? They still didn't know that he was dead? Or had he already been replaced?

Annette continued, "I have worked here for over thirty years and anything you should need will be run by me."

"Magdelena Krol," Dagmara said, giving a soft curtsy and growing uneasy. If Annette truly worked at the castle for thirty years, she had to have worked with Claude's parents whom he murdered.

"I know," Annette replied with no humor in her voice. She then acknowledged Urszula. "Her baggage?"

"It is in the carriage out front, milady."

"Wonderful." She made a gesture, and the four guards surrounding her began to exit, no doubt heading toward the carriage. Annette continued, "His Majesty has summoned you upon arrival. I will escort you to see him now. Alone, I might add." Annette fired a razor sharp glare at Urszula.

"Yes, Madame," Dagmara said before adding a smile, "I have been looking forward to meeting him."

Annette eyed Dagmara from head to toe before finally saying, "Hmm."

Then she whirled on her heel and stalked away, expecting Dagmara to follow. Quickly, Dagmara flashed a goodbye glance to Urszula before scampering forward to follow Annette.

As they made their way through the castle, Dagmara was fascinated by her surroundings. Mirrors were plastered on every wall, creating reflections everywhere, and the illusion that each space was bigger than the last. Everything was gilded with silver, but its bright metallic shine was almost unnatural.

Being in the Ilusaurian castle reminded Dagmara of her missions as an assassin for King Bogdan. There had been many times where she had to infiltrate a new place, or go to a location she was completely unfamiliar with, but she had always done so in secret or by blending in. Never in her life had she been in such a public position—so vulnerable and so easily scrutinized for any mistake she could make. It made this mission all the more precarious.

Each room they passed through, Dagmara counted at least three more guards. This place was heavily protected, and each new doorway was blocked by an armed man or woman. It would not be easy to snoop around without being noticed.

"You're quite different than I recall," Annette stated.

"Recall?"

"We still have your family portrait from years ago. Before Azurem cut ties with Ilusauri, as you know."

Dagmara stiffened. "Well, that was a decade ago. I have matured since then."

Annette side-eyed Dagmara's figure before returning her attention to the path in front of them. "Yes, clearly. I didn't expect you to be so...filled out."

Dagmara's heart dropped in her chest. "Artists can do anything. Maybe you should get a portrait commissioned sometime. I'm sure the artist could even make you look beautiful."

Annette whirled to face Dagmara and grabbed her wrist, forcing her to stop in her tracks. "You would be wise to watch your tongue around the king. He is short tempered."

Dagmara already feared meeting the king. Now, having his royal advisor give a sharp warning only made Dagmara even more fearful.

Taking Dagmara's silence as resignation, Annette continued, this time at a brisker pace.

The entrance to the royal wing was far different than Azurem's.

Instead of an elaborate cascade of waterfalls, the walkway was made entirely of mirrors. The walls, floor, and even ceiling were reflective, making the dozen chandeliers and guards feel infinite. Unease crept through Dagmara's entire body. She could barely walk straight or find the next door amid the chaos.

Then they stopped at a black door, lined in silver. Annette raised her hand and pounded against the frame. "Princess Magdalena has arrived," she announced, nearly shouting.

There was a moment of silence that stretched on forever. Finally, Dagmara heard one word, crisp and terrifying:

"Enter."

Annette gave Dagmara a smile, though it wasn't kind. "Good luck, Your Highness."

Dagmara swallowed the lump in her throat. Letting out a deep breath, she reminded herself why she was here. She was saving Magda. She was getting medicine for her brother. She would find proof that Claude killed Bogdan and Aleksy, and that would be the end of this ruse. She didn't fear Claude because he was a murderer—she feared he would discover her true identity.

And what if he didn't kill her if he found out? He would know she wasn't a guardian, and he could use his mind powers on her, torturing her.

Shuddering, Dagmara shoved everything from her mind as she entered the room to meet the King of Ilusauri.

CHAPTER 17
Magdalena

Magda's eyes barely opened, heavy with debilitating grief. Her body jolted forward, and her stomach surged with a falling sensation. She stood in a dark space—alone. All around her was a void of darkness, with no apparent escape.

"You run from me," a voice echoed from every direction.

Magda held her breath, startled at the sound, searching every inch of the dark realm for the source of the voice, but not a soul could be seen. "Who's there?" she called out. Was it her brother, trying to reach her from the great beyond?

A stark silence followed, as if there was no breathable air to carry the voice in the empty space.

"Who's there?" she shouted louder, spinning in all directions.

But the desolate blackness didn't respond.

Magda jolted awake. She snapped upright in the bed, realizing she was on the bobbing Starway. Her face and neck were clammy with sweat. She shook the nightmare out of her thoughts. She had expected that the recent terrorizing events would follow her even outside of the fortress, but the dream had felt too real.

Suddenly, Odie's tongue streaked over her face.

"Odie, stop!" Magda laughed, pushing away his soft fur.

Suddenly a horn sounded, announcing their arrival. Odie's ears perked up and Magda beamed in excitement. They darted out of their cabin and up onto the deck. Magda was the first to race to the stern, with Odie bounding beside her, getting a glimpse of the grand, urban sprawl beyond.

Up ahead was the capital city of Flaustra, Eloquas. It was a tightly interwoven and dense city, home to the largest number of people in all the kingdoms. On the outskirts were rolling hills of lush farmland, and great structures for irrigation brought glacial water down to the crop fields. Great plants and vines twirled down from the jungles, snaking through the city. The city itself sat on the banks of a river, and was dusty and crowded, for it hosted too many people within its gates.

BARK! Odie pointed his snout in the air in the direction of the city, before turning to look up at Magda.

"Yes, that's where we're going," Magda answered.

Soon the ship docked next to twelve others. Magda recognized the flags of Celestaire and Azurem on the opposite ships. Even though all of the kingdoms had cut off ties with Ilusauri, it was a well-known fact that there was a black-market for Ilusauri goods in Flaustra. Only certain guilds were willing to trade with the Mad King behind Queen Sanyal's back. Making deals with the guilds had proved difficult for Magda's kingdom, and it was never a reliable source.

Magda slung her knapsack on her back and bag over her shoulder before crowding next to the sailors. Then they all began making their way down the plank and onto the docks. Odie trailed her closely as they disembarked. Before them, an immigration officer stood at the end of the plank. He patted down each one of the sailors, looking for stolen or compensated goods. It wasn't clear if he was acting on behalf of the royal family or one of the guilds.

When Magda's turn arrived, she was also patted down. They searched her belt for any weapons. Luckily, she had already spent all of her elk-stamped gold, although it wasn't worth anything in Flaustra. Here, the currency was a brighter, yellow gold stamped with a tiger, which she had taken from the fortress and hidden at the bottom of her knapsack. Bartering was also accepted, hence why she had stolen so many jewels from her mother's study.

"Welcome to Eloquas. Registration card." The guard held out his hand to Magda.

Registration card? That was something Magda had never heard of before. She didn't have such a thing in Azurem. In fact, she had no way to prove her identity.

Odie whined beside her.

She searched for the proper words in Flaustran. "It's..." but they didn't come quick enough. Her accent gave her away.

"So you're Azuremi? And alone?" The immigration officer looked her up and down. "I've never seen an Azuremi girl aboard the Starway. What business do you have in Flaustra?"

"I'm here to purchase some fabrics," Magda lied.

The immigration officer didn't seem pleased by her answer. "The guilds control what comes in and out of this kingdom. So, as for you, I think you should get back on the next trip to Azurem."

"But..." Magda tried to protest, but once again she couldn't find the words.

"Officer!" a loud voice sounded from behind Magda. "She's with me." The voice said assertively.

Magda turned to see Ishani, the Captain of the Starway, strutting down the plank in her clicking heels. Today she was wearing flowing green pants, and a jeweled shirt that showed her entire stomach. Her hair was slicked back into a bun, and a jeweled headband hung down onto the center of her forehead. A sash hung across her body, revealing the pin of the Fowler's Guild. Both axes were on full display.

The officer raised his eyebrows. "She's with you?"

Ishani placed her hands around Magda's shoulders and leaned close to her. "Don't try too hard and maybe I'll invite you to join us next time," she said with a twinkle in her eye.

The officer seemed intrigued. "You said I wasn't your type."

Ishani sighed. "It's amazing what a few months at sea will do to you. So, are we good here?"

"What about the dog?" he motioned to Odie, who cocked his head curiously.

"Also with me," Ishani answered.

He nodded and stepped to the side, allowing them to proceed.

Ishani interlinked hands with Magda and then brushed past the man, intentionally knocking him in the shoulder as she passed. Odie followed their lead, dashing behind them. Soon, they were hustling through the crowded docks, in between immigration officers dressed in turquoise and yellow.

"What did you do?" Magda snapped, finally able to find her words in the foreign language. It was rudimentary vocabulary, to say the least.

"Stay with me. There's one more checkpoint before getting inside the city."

Magda gritted her teeth as she whispered in Ishani's ear. "Why are you helping me?"

"You're not just any Azuremi girl," Ishani laughed, before switching back to Azuremi. "Your hair, the lack of dark circles underneath your eyes, and those crystal-studded earrings say it all."

They approached the next checkpoint, and this one was more secure than the last. There were exactly four lines of people waiting their turn to get into the city. They each were checked by a group of three guards, while another one stood by and observed the entire production. The people that had animals were undergoing even more scrutiny.

When Ishani and Magda approached the guards, Ishani simply flashed a smile to the man in charge of the group. He too, wore a peacock pin attached to his upper-right shoulder, just like Ishani.

With a silent nod that passed between them all, Ishani and Magda walked through the gates and entered the city of Flaustra without showing any identification papers. Odie stayed close to Magda's legs, his fur brushing up against her knees as they exited the dock.

The streets of Eloquas were jam-packed, almost unwalkable, and all around were merchants pushing carts and wagons, threatening to trample everyone in the roads. To their right and left were tiny store fronts with makeshift, bright-colored signs displaying the prices of the newly bought goods that were being brought in on the ships. Magda spotted a store—full of Azuremi salt cubes—that were going for twenty times their normal prices. Vines and plants snaked around the sandy-colored, dense buildings.

When they reached the end of the street, Magda turned to Ishani, "Thank you, but I can take it from here. I didn't ask for your help."

"But you needed it," Ishani said. "Have a good trip. And if you need to find me to get back home, I live on the Starway. I'm happy to take your money again once you realize that you want to leave Flaustra and head back to Azurem. Don't be afraid to come find me. I'll tell my men to expect you." Ishani began walking away before adding over her shoulder, "Dagmara."

Magda watched Ishani leave until she was certain she had completely gone. At least she had passed the checkpoints and had safely arrived in Flaustra. It was mid-afternoon, and she wanted to get to the palace as soon as possible to talk to Queen Sanyal.

Magda continued on her way. She headed straight, directly down the overcrowded street, pushing her way through the peddlers that shoved their merchandise in front of her face.

"A dog?" someone on her left whispered. That was vocabulary Magda had mastered in Flaustran.

Magda picked up her pace down the road, and suddenly she and Odie were inside a store covered with a purple tapestry as a roof. Then, upon taking a few more paces, she was outside on the road again. The street continued as so, with storefronts and merchants spilling out in every direction, with no indication of where the street ended or began. She passed stores with items from Celestaire and Azurem, and others that seemed like they would be storefronts for blackmarket goods—those could only be entered for a hefty sum.

Smells of heavy spices and hot porridges, along with Flaustra's signature tea, filled her senses. Behind the commotion of voices was the sound of a soft but beautiful instrument, singing high over the cacophony of noise. To the left, a young street musician played a dashing tune on a violin. He had drawn a significant crowd, who were in awe over his music, quick fingerwork, and lush bow-strokes. In-between lyrical phrases, the small audience dropped trinkets into a tin can at his feet as a token of appreciation for his efforts.

Odie noticed Magda's interest in the musician. Shooting ahead, Odie charged forward toward the musician, wagging his tail as he went.

"Odie, come back!" Magda shouted.

But Odie was already charging forward. The curious dog bounded up to the violinist, begging for attention at the start of each new measure.

Magda, embarrassed for pushing to the front of the audience, called Odie back from the tiny semi circle of crowd-members that had gathered to see the show. Odie turned to obey Magda, but as he did, his tail knocked over the violinist's tin can and the trinkets spilled out all over the street.

The boy instantly stopped playing, and the audience let out a series of gasps. They began whispering to each other:

"Why would she bring her dog outside?"

"Who does she think she is?"

"Let's get out of here fast."

Magda blocked out their whispers and turned back to the musician.

"Just give me a minute," he was saying frantically, rushing to pick up his payment. "I'll pick these things up, and we'll get back to the music!"

Magda rushed forward. "I'm sorry about my dog." She pulled Odie by the scruff closer to her despite his whimpers.

The boy looked at her curiously—it was clear he didn't understand her rushed Azuremi.

Magda switched to Flaustran, "I'm sorry."

Together, Magda and the boy began putting the money back in the tin can and the empty violin case.

"Don't worry about it," he shrugged. His accent was different, almost easier to understand. "I'm Ravi," he introduced himself.

"Ma—Dagmara."

He was about her age, with brown skin and a gentle smile. His wavy brown hair sat in a tousled mess on his head, coming down beyond his ears.

"What a mischievous dog," Ravi laughed, giving Odie an embrace, while Odie jumped up and licked Ravi's face with his tongue. "Brave of you to bring him out here."

"What are you talking about?" Magda smiled. "Odie comes everywhere. He's good." Then she cursed herself under her breath. Good? Why was it so hard to find the words she needed? Her Flaustran was definitely rusty.

Ravi glanced upward to notice that the crowd was already dissipating.

Magda also realized that he was losing his audience. The busy buyers and sellers were turning their limited attention back to the marketplace. "Let me make it up to you," Magda offered, searching for a bracelet or pin on her clothing that could serve as payment. She didn't have time to dig through her knapsack for the secret compartment. So she tore off one of her golden buttons on her sleeve, and was about to drop it into the violin case, when Ravi caught her hand around the wrist.

"I don't need your charity," he said.

Ravi's eyes flicked to the right and left, although his head hadn't turned, as if he was afraid of revealing where he was looking. "Stand and walk with me." He replaced his violin and bow in its case, and locked it shut.

Magda did as she was told, and the two began walking together through the busy streets. Odie circled behind them, wagging his tail furiously. Up ahead was a fork in the road. Magda knew one way led to the royal district and eventually the royal palace. She had no idea where the other fork led.

"I've been watching you as you made your way down the street," Ravi said. "You know you have members of the guild following you, right?"

"No, I don't," Magda protested. She turned to look over her shoulder, but didn't see anything out of the ordinary.

"You have to know who to look for and where to look," he answered her.

"I arrived here only an hour ago."

"The guild doesn't follow you for nothing," Ravi said. "Do you want to lose them or not?"

Magda turned back around. This time she was aware of two men that had seemingly shifted positions. They both wore small hats, decorated in bright turquoise, and she suspected they both had peacock pins pinned to their chests. They moved slower than the rest of the crowd, as if they weren't rushing to find the best deals, but waiting strategically to pounce. Did Ishani send men to follow her? All that she knew was that she had to make her way to the royal palace as soon as possible, and she couldn't get caught up in guild politics.

"Follow my lead," Ravi said.

Ravi pulled Magda across the road and ducked into a store, with Odie right behind them. There were no doors to the clothing-shop, just an open entryway leading into the rows of stands. It was full of day-time shoppers paying for fabrics and jewelry.

"In here," Ravi whispered, yanking Magda behind a thick curtain.

Magda stumbled behind Ravi into the dressing room. It was a small space, barely big enough for the two of them and her dog. Her body was pressed against his, and she had to turn her head away from his face uncomfortably.

Ravi pulled the curtain back slightly, peering outside. Soon, the two men with the turquoise and yellow uniforms continued down the road, passing by the shop. Magda breathed a brief sigh of relief. Sweat was pouring down her face, for she wasn't used to this heat—or being trapped in a tiny dressing room with a young man.

Magda didn't trust the violinist. Why was he helping her? She needed to lose him in this marketplace and make a run for the street ahead.

Magda gave Odie a quick scratch behind the ears, making sure he stayed with her.

"We lost them," Ravi said, breaking her thoughts. He stopped holding his breath, expanding his chest and pressing her into the wall.

"I don't even know for sure that they were following me," Magda retorted, pushing herself away from him and stepping out from behind the curtain.

"About time you two wrapped up in there," an annoyed patron raised her eyebrows. Then she tapped the wrist of her partner, "Look, a dog!"

Magda shook her head and walked briskly to a separate exit on an opposite road. To her annoyance, Ravi followed her. Now, she just had to get rid of him.

"Sir, we need some help here!" Magda yelled, pointing back into the store.

Ravi turned to see where Magda was pointing, and she quickly placed one of the store's hats upon his head, before sprinting in the opposite direction.

"Wait!" Ravi began to run after her, but the shopkeepers shouted at him.

"Sir are you going to buy that?" they asked, swarming him furiously.

Ravi screeched to a halt, turning back to the shop, and rushing back inside to find the correct stand to replace the hat. Then he was caught up in a fierce discussion with the shopkeeper, explaining how he didn't intend to steal the hat.

Magda and Odie finally reached the fork and tore to the left. She prayed she had gotten rid of the guilds—for now.

CHAPTER 18
Dagmara

Dagmara pushed open the door to meet the Mad King. She had expected to enter a room on the opposite side. Instead, she emerged onto a balcony. The vast space, lined with silver rails, looked out to the kingdom beyond. On one side she could see the rolling plains and vineyards, and on the other was the calm sea, brilliantly blue. Purple flowers twisted up the columns and ran along the railings, with a few petals dusting the floor. She barely noticed the four guards posted around the balcony, two watching the horizon and two with their gaze set at the table in the center of the space. One of them was massive, easily a foot taller than everyone around him.

The table was small and round, already donned with place settings and a bouquet in the center. There were only two chairs at the table, and the king was seated at one. He rose from the chair before placing his hand on his chest.

"Princess Magdalena, it is an honor." His voice was commanding, sending a chill down Dagmara's spine, and his Ilusaurian accent was captivating.

King Claude Mirage.

She had thought out every possibility for this encounter, but somehow she had missed this one. The king of Ilusauri wasn't a disgusting, scarred figure. He was stunning.

Only twenty-one years of age, the king was tall and slender with muscles in all the right places. He had a sharp jawline, and fierce, brown eyes. His skin was bronze and his hair was trimmed short. He was a picturesque version of a king, not resembling a monstrosity that had killed his parents at thirteen.

By the guardians, he was captivating.

She broke out of her stupor and curtsied clumsily. "Your Majesty."

She expected him to examine every inch of her, taking in his prey, but his gaze remained on her face, unbothered. He gestured to the empty chair. "Please, have a seat."

Immediately, one of the guards was moving from his post to pull out the chair, but Claude stopped him with a mere glance. Claude rounded the table and pulled the chair back to make room for Dagmara to sit.

If this was the man who had ordered Aleksy's death, she didn't want to have a casual lunch with him. Yet, she had no choice. This was all a game. She was only here to get close enough to Claude and find proof. For all she knew, she could find proof this evening.

She was an assassin, not an actress. However, she knew how to play a game of manipulation.

He, on the other hand, could be a great actor, presenting as kind until they were married and he had full access to Azurem. This would be a complicated dance.

Forcing a smile, Dagmara said, "Thank you." She approached the chair, aware of the distance between them closing, before she sat down.

He pushed her chair in, and she was surprised by his strength. A sharp, sweet cologne flooded her senses, but the king didn't remain near her long enough for her to truly take it in. He returned to his side of the table and took his seat, smoothing out the front of his shirt as he sat.

"Welcome to Ilusauri," he announced. "I hope the journey wasn't too arduous."

"Not at all." Dagmara folded her hands on her lap.

"To be honest, I'm surprised you agreed to my proposal," Claude began. "I know we haven't seen each other in over a decade."

She eyed the guards over his shoulder before answering, "I acknowledge many of our trading routes were cut off when our kingdoms broke ties with one another, and there are medicines here we simply don't have access to in Azurem. Marriage would repair all of that," she said.

His face flashed with an emotion that was gone before Dagmara could detect what it was. His lips curled downward into a frown too ugly for his beautiful face. "I see you only agreed for political gain."

"Why else did you propose this arrangement?"

"To protect one another."

"That sounds political to me."

The guard behind Claude shifted, and Dagmara sat up straighter.

"Don't worry about them," Claude said. "They're here for our protection."

Our protection or yours? Dagmara wanted to say. She held her tongue. That's when she noticed there were three wine glasses on the table. Would someone be joining them?

"Let us save politics for another time. How have you been since the coronation?" Claude said. She couldn't tell what she detected in his voice, but it put her on edge.

"I..." Dagmara's voice ran dry. How would Magda answer this question? Rather, how would Magda answer this question in front of her future husband who may have ordered her family's assassination?

"Forgive me, that was insensitive," Claude said. "My deepest condolences to you and your mother. Did you find out who was behind the terrible attack?"

Her body froze. Flashes of Aleksy's dead body flooded her mind, followed by the image of the assassin who escaped wearing Ilusaurian armor.

"No," she managed to say.

"Nothing at all?"

Dagmara eyed him incredulously. "I'm not sure what you want me to say. They were murdered, and our kingdom will seek justice."

Claude nodded before sitting back in his chair and motioning toward the door.

Dagmara could've sworn the side of his mouth twitched, almost as if he was repressing a smirk.

Moments later a servant approached the table with a pitcher in his grasp. The young man poured a sip of wine into the third glass on the table before drinking it himself. Then, he proceeded to pour the wine into both Claude and Dagmara's glasses in turn.

She would not be able to slip anything into Claude's drinks if the servants were required to taste them in front of the king. Any sleeping potions she had were useless here, and she wouldn't be able to use a truth serum.

"Your Majesty," the servant dipped his head before setting the pitcher down on the table, picking up the third glass, and leaving.

King Claude's safety protocols were meticulous.

Another servant emerged, repeating the same process with two small plates of what looked to be like a bite-sized quiche. She was unsure. The plates were set down in front of them and immediately Dagmara searched for what she needed. Salt. It was the one thing that helped her dizziness, and she over-salted all of her food. But there was no salt on the table.

Claude reached forward to take the stem of his glass, but he didn't drink yet. "As you see, I don't take any chances when it comes to protection." It was almost as if he was warning her not to try anything.

"Do you have salt?" Dagmara blurted out.

Claude's expression shifted, his eyebrows twisting on his forehead. "Probably. Why?"

She let out a sigh. "Nevermind."

Claude continued, "I understand you don't trust me, and I don't blame you. It is good to be cautious. I only want what is best for our kingdoms, and marriage would ensure that."

Dagmara took the stem of her own wine glass. "I also want what is best for my kingdom's people," she said, her mind entirely on Teos and the medicine he needed.

He gave her a subtle smile before raising his glass. Then he drank a sip of the wine, his throat bobbing, and Dagmara watched him while she drank her own.

The wine was sweet and aromatic, with a hint of bitter aftertaste that left her wanting more. She had to stop herself before she let out an audible sigh of pleasure.

"Is there anything you'd like to know about me first?" Claude asked, setting his glass down.

She wanted to know if he killed Aleksy. She wanted to know if he felt any guilt. She wanted to know why he invaded Celestaire and—

One thing at a time.

"There are many things, Your Majesty, but I don't think they are appropriate for our first meeting," Dagmara said. "Perhaps you can tell me what you love about Ilusauri."

And why the countryside seemed to be in a famine while the palace was overflowing with life.

Claude gripped his glass so tight she thought it would shatter. He shifted forward in his chair, his eyes now venomous. "I had hoped you weren't so susceptible to rumors, Princess."

"Which rumors are you referring to?"

He didn't entirely answer her question as he said with a growl, "You really believe I killed my parents when I was only thirteen?"

It wasn't a denial. Dagmara knew she was treading on thin ice and had to choose her next words very wisely. What would Magda say?

But she didn't have time to respond. Claude was no longer paying attention to her. The moment Claude peered over her shoulder, her blood turned to ice. The mood shifted, and any bit of hospitality Claude was displaying had disappeared. His expression turned hostile, and his eyes began to twinkle with silver.

The two guards behind Claude took a step closer to the table. She thought at first they were threatening her, but they only had eyes for their king.

Whipping her head around, Dagmara followed Claude's gaze. On the railing of the balcony, a blackbird had landed. The bird let out a single note, so piercing that it scraped against Dagmara's temples. The yellow ring around its eyes seemed fixated on her.

In one sharp motion, Claude rose from the table and chucked his wine glass at the bird.

Dagmara ducked, escaping the cup by inches.

The bird took flight as the glass shattered against the railing, the wine splattering the terrace.

It all happened so fast.

Claude yelled something in Ilusaurian before flipping the table. He was strong, and the table went flying.

Shrieking, Dagmara fell from her chair and dropped to the ground, covering her face with her arms as silverware clattered to the ground around her. Both the pitcher and the wine glass coated her in red liquid. The bouquet of flowers knocked her in the head before joining the broken glassware on the terrace. She scrambled backward, away from Claude, feeling the shattered glass under her palms.

An iron grip clasped her bicep, and someone yanked her to her feet before she could register any pain. It wasn't Claude grabbing her. It was one of his guards.

Another arm swooped around her middle, nearly lifting her off her feet and dragging her toward the exit.

She heard shouting, but they were speaking too fast for her to translate. Two guards ran to Claude, but before they even reached him, Claude merely glanced at them, and they crumpled to the ground like rag dolls.

Claude's eyes were pure silver.

Dagmara didn't know fear until Claude met her gaze.

She wasn't Magda. She wasn't royalty. He could get into her mind and project illusions or compel her. He was, after all, a Mind Guardian.

She squeezed her eyes shut just as the guard holding her rescued her from the room and slammed the door shut behind them. Another loud crack sounded out on the balcony, and Dagmara jerked upright, backing away until she crashed into someone.

"What happened this time?" Annette asked, grabbing Dagmara's shoulders and turning her until she was face-to-face with the advisor. Annette's question wasn't directed at Dagmara, but rather at the guard that pulled her to safety.

"I couldn't tell you, Madame," the guard said. He had a boyish face and dark ringlets.

Annette picked the glass from Dagmara's palm, her grip more painful than the glass itself, and switched to her native tongue. "What did she say to him?"

Dagmara struggled to interpret their words. Her body was still shaking. She normally wasn't afraid. But there was something about *him* that frightened her. The unpredictability. The look in his eyes...

"His parents, Madame," said the guard.

"She got him to speak about his parents in less than ten minutes?"

"Yes, Madame."

"It wasn't that," Dagmara blurted out.

Annette's eyes twinkled with curiosity, clearly not anticipating her to have understood their conversation in the foreign language.

Yanking her hand from Annette's, Dagmara continued, "After he saw the blackbird he...changed."

"Blackbird?" Annette echoed.

"Yes." Dagmara turned to the guard, waiting for him to explain.

The guard's mouth was slightly agape. "I...uh..."

"Speak, Pierre," Annette snapped.

"There was no bird, Madame."

"What?" Dagmara blurted out. "It landed on the railing."

"I..." Pierre gave Dagmara an apologetic glance. "If you say there was a bird then it must be so, Princess. My apologies."

Dagmara knew what she saw. One of the other guards had to have seen it.

Annette didn't hide her suspicion. "Let us give His Majesty space. I'll show you to your room now so you can clean yourself up. There will be water for your wound as well."

Then the weight of Annette's comment settled on her. *There will be water for your wound...*Annette was expecting Dagmara to heal the cut in her palm with Life Guardian magic. She couldn't do that.

She began to follow Annette. They turned to the mirror-filled entrance, and proceeded to exit the royal wing.

"Aren't I going to stay in the royal wing?" Dagmara asked, walking briskly to keep up with Annette.

"In the royal wing?" Annette laughed. "You're a guest, only *Ilusaurian* royals stay there."

"But...I'm marrying him."

"Eventually," Annette replied, with as much conviction as someone saying cats can fly. "But unless you are queen, you won't be anywhere near His Majesty's quarters, let alone in them." She fired her a sideways glance.

This was going to be more complicated than Dagmara thought. If she wasn't even allowed near Claude's chamber or study, how would she snoop around?

Maybe she had to go through with the marriage. What other way could she gain private access to the mad king's room? It had to be *her* room too. When they reached the chamber Dagmara would be staying in, she was utterly lost. Everything looked the same, and all the reflections caused her to get turned around. They had passed probably a dozen additional chambers full of mirrors, which didn't make any sense. The castle appeared perfectly symmetrical on the outside, but inside it was a maze.

Annette entered first before gesturing to a large bedroom. All of Dagmara's luggage was already inside, and Urszula jumped up from a chaise as soon as she saw the door open.

"Welcome," Annette said, unenthused.

"What happened?" Urszula gasped, seeing the wine stains on Dagmara's dress.

"She met the king," Annette replied before exiting the room and slamming the door closed.

"Are you alright?" Urszula asked. She took Dagmara's hand and examined the wound, still leaking crimson liquid. "Let's get you cleaned up."

She began pulling Dagmara toward the bathing chamber, but Dagmara jerked her hand back and said, "You don't have to take care of me the way you did with Magda. I'm not a princess."

Urszula frowned. "You don't have the authority to fire me. Besides, maybe being treated like a princess will help you act as one. Don't argue with me."

Begrudgingly, Dagmara followed Urszula to the bathing chamber. "Do you speak this way to Magda?"

"Absolutely," Urszula replied.

Dagmara didn't want assistance. Yet, after the water was boiled and Dagmara stepped into the soapy bath, she immediately felt better. She scrubbed the wine from her skin, feeling the sting of her hand against the soap. She would have to hide the new injury on her palm and wear gloves until it healed on its own. The scar on her collarbone was still fresh from the night she had killed Sabien, another mark she had to hide.

When the water turned cold and her feet were pruney, she finally exited the bath. She sat at the vanity in a plush robe, wrapping her hand in a bandage while Urszula brushed through her hair.

Then Dagmara remembered, "Did they find anything when they searched our things?"

A smile appeared on Urszula's face. "Nope." She exited the room briefly, returning with a case. She propped it up on the vanity and opened it, revealing a box of makeup and cosmetics.

However, it wasn't all makeup. It was everything Dagmara needed to make her potions.

Dagmara ran her hand against the box, feeling safer with the weapons in her grasp.

A plan was forming in her mind. Tonight, she was going to use the potions to find the proof she needed. Otherwise...the only other option was marrying the king and gaining free access to his chambers. She prayed it wouldn't come to that.

By the guardians...her thoughts rang. *Magda, where are you?*

She only recently met the malevolent Claude Mirage, and she already knew why he was nicknamed the Mad King.

CHAPTER 19
Magdalena

The sun had set by the time that Magda and Odie made it to the royal palace. After they had left the main marketplace, they had paid a carriage driver to take them all the way to the palace gates. The palace was outside of the city of Eloquas, set in the lush, green hills. All around the palace grounds were public gardens interspersed with statues of the royal guardians and majestic floral displays that could only have been produced with earth magic.

Magda entered the gardens, and the Flaustran palace spanned out before her.

It was much bigger than the Azuremi fortress, built in the shape of a rectangle from a mix of sandstone and marble. An outer wall enclosed a front courtyard. Brown double doors, which were framed by two windows filled with mosaic glass, blocked the entrance. The second story hosted massive, arch-shaped windows leading out to flat roofs on different tiers. On each corner of the roofs was a dome-shaped tower held up by small posts. A glow protruded from the torches, lighting up the ivory sandstone against the midnight sky.

Magda pulled her hood and scarf up over her face, even though the thick Azuremi fabric was making her entire body sweat. As she approached the outer gate, she was unsure of her strategy. The only way she would automatically be granted a meeting with the royal family was by revealing herself as Princess Magdalena. But, it didn't seem like a viable option to announce that the princess was in Flaustra, and not in Ilusauri. It would put Dagmara in danger. In addition, it could send another round of assassins after her. She could only hope there was another way to gain a meeting with the queen without revealing her identity.

Magda and Odie walked at a brisk pace through the main road of the gardens, until they reached the front gate of the palace, which was guarded by two men.

"Stop! Who's there?" an officer flashed a colored lantern in Magda's face.

"It's okay!" Magda yelled out from the darkness. "I've come to see the queen."

When the officer noticed she was Azuremi, he switched to Magda's language. "The queen isn't expecting any visitors this late. Do you have an invitation?"

Magda scrunched her face. "No, but..."

"No exceptions! There will be no admittance to the royal palace without an invitation. You can come back in three days when the queen will be taking public visitors and listening to their grievances," said the man.

"Three days?" Magda asked. What was she going to do in the city during those three days? She couldn't waste any more time. She continued arguing with him for a half hour more, telling him that the royal family in Azurem had sent her to speak to the queen, but he wasn't buying any of her story. It was clear Magda needed to be a better story-teller if she was going to get anywhere in this kingdom.

Distraught, Magda turned back around and exited the gardens, with Odie behind her. She decided that they would be back in three days' time, and then she would have to use every opportunity to talk not only to the queen but to Princess Kiran. Kiran would hear her out —Magda was sure of it.

When she got to the edge of the palace gardens, Magda paid her carriage driver once more to take them back to the city so they could find a place to stay for the night.

"I told you I should wait for you," the carriage driver grumbled. "No one gets in and out of that place."

"Not even for the day of grievances?"

"What?" the man piped up.

Magda cursed under her breath. The officer had lied. There was no public day where the queen was going to greet visitors from the village. What was she going to do now?

Once back in the city, Magda and Odie were again lost in a maze of small streets. The streets weaved in and out of each other, and buildings arched over the tiny alleyways like bridges. Magda's only hope was that they would be able to find an inn this late at night. She had no idea where to look.

A shadow reflected in the light of a colored-lantern, and she snapped her head to the darkness behind her. It was quiet and practically deserted in this area.

Somewhere in the distance, she heard the soft sound of music, but it didn't seem as if any of the storefronts were open at this hour. She continued circling the streets, Odie at her heel, wondering which direction to go next. Up ahead, she heard a few voices. Maybe someone would give her directions.

Magda emerged in a small town circle. Pathways spoked off in every direction, heading back into the maze of the city. In the center of the town circle, was a statue of Queen Sanyal.

She headed to her right, but suddenly a man in a hat stepped in front of her path. Behind him, a few companions pulled a large wagon down the road, and strange noises came from the tarp underneath it.

"Excuse me," Magda said.

The man placed his hand on her shoulder and stopped her. "What do we have here?" He also had a gilded pin on his chest; however, instead of a peacock feather, it depicted a strange beast.

Odie let out a soft growl.

Magda's heart fluttered, as the danger of the situation sank in. "I don't want any trouble," she said, stepping away from the man and holding out her hands in front of her. If there was ever a time to use magic—this would be it. Although she wasn't exactly sure how to use earth magic or what types of things were even possible with earth magic. Her eyes darted to Queen Sanyal's statue. It had to be created from some type of malleable stone, right?

Magda screamed as someone grabbed her from behind, wrapping his arms around her waist and holding her high in the air. Magda kicked and yelled as she helplessly watched the other two men throw a metal net over Odie, pinning him down on all sides. Odie snarled ferociously, but his bites were no match for the twisted wires that caged him.

"Stop!" Magda screamed. "Let him go!"

The man laughed and snapped his fingers, and like that, his group of friends dragged the net across the ground, before picking up the sides and throwing Odie into the back of their wagon. When they lifted up the tarp, Magda saw at least four other animals struggling to get free. But all too soon, the tarp was replaced and Odie was out of sight.

"He'll make a fine coat and bring in a nice profit," the burly man growled in her ear. "Hope I get to skin him myself."

"No!" Magda screamed hysterically, trying to wrench herself from the man's grasp. "Help! Please help!" she screamed until she was sure her voice would break from the strain.

The leader had already snapped his fingers, and the cart was rolling away. In a matter of seconds, Odie would be out of sight and lost to the city. Magda dug down deep, to the pit of her stomach, hoping to harness any magic to save herself and Odie. All around them were specks of dirt and sand lining the pathways, but she had no idea how to channel particles that were so minuscule. She turned her attention to the statue, but nothing came of it either.

Suddenly a figure jumped down from the rooftops, landing gracefully in a somersault next to the cart. They quickly pulled out the pin holding the cart door closed and pulled up the net. The dogs jumped down and out into the streets.

"Go, go!" the boy shouted at them.

The man holding Magda released her, going to grab the fleeing dogs. Magda stumbled to catch her footing and smashed into the mysterious savior of the animals. When she looked up, she recognized Ravi—the street violinist from earlier. He quickly grabbed her wrist and yanked her behind him, before facing three remaining men.

"How many times do I have to get you out of trouble today?" he asked through gritted teeth.

"You followed me?" asked Magda. She was about to ask another question, when she saw the lead man grab onto Odie's scruff, unsheathing a dagger in her pet's direction.

"No!" Magda shrieked.

The man stopped the knife's blade inches from Odie's neck. "Ah...Ravi Kalal," he spoke.

Odie whimpered, lashing in the man's grip, but the man's clasp on Odie's scruff was like iron.

"Give her back her dog," said Ravi assertively.

"It's nothing personal. Just business. Surely you would understand that."

"You did a nice job ruining my business today," Ravi retorted. "Not a single person came to my show when they heard you were in the district."

The man sighed. "Maybe it's time we end this little feud. I could use your skills. Street musicians are everywhere, under our noses, over them...the best ears anyone can buy. Be my ears, Ravi. In our world, information is the currency of kings, isn't it?"

"I won't spy for you, Vex."

Vex stood, shoving Odie into the direction of his henchman, before stepping aggressively in Magda and Ravi's direction with the sharp knife. The other two men held Odie back, for the rest of the dogs had escaped to the city.

Ravi put his hand out in front of Magda, pushing her further behind him.

"Luckily for you, Ravi, you're more useful to me alive than dead," Vex snarled menacingly, "Everyone has their price, and every secret has a buyer. I'm sure that there will come another time when you'll need your pockets full."

"I don't think so."

"So naive."

Magda cut them off, jutting in, "Get away from us! And if any of you hurt my dog there will be consequences."

"Feisty!" said Vex. "Now I know why she's made quite the stir amongst the guilds and why my people alerted me to a new dog in the streets."

"I'm hardly interesting enough," Magda said.

Vex got close to her face, saying, "Did you think a diplomatic representative of the kingdom of Azurem would slip into this city completely unnoticed? The Marauders Guild knows every individual or artifact that enters this city—including who they are, what gate they have passed through at what hour, and what business you have here. But it seems no one can figure out that last part." He began walking in a slow circle, back toward his henchmen, running his finger over the blade as he did so.

Ravi whispered, "We need to run."

"What?" Magda said. She looked toward Odie, who was still being held back by the two men.

Vex continued on his lecture, stroking the knife with his fingertip. When he nodded toward his two henchmen, Ravi grabbed Magda's arm and sprinted in the opposite direction.

"Not so fast!" yelled Vex, reaching out to grab Magda's wrist and swinging her around until she was facing him. His putrid breath blew onto her bare neck. "You're not leaving. There's someone willing to pay for your secrets."

Magda stomped down on his foot as hard as she could, pressing the sharp end of her boot into the soft part of his toes. "Ow!" Vex yelled, wincing and pulling away.

The two other henchmen reached out to grab Magda, but Odie was quicker. Odie leapt onto one of the men, smashing his teeth into the man's leg. He let out a squeal of pain that rang through the streets. At the same time, the other man slapped Magda across the jaw. Magda stumbled over, crashing into Ravi.

Then Ravi pushed Magda behind him and gave Vex a solid punch, while Odie took a snap at the remaining henchman.

Vex and his two hooligans were sprawled on the ground, holding various body parts in pain.

Magda shouted to Ravi. "Come on!" she yelled. "Odie!"

The three tore as fast as they could away from the town circle and could barely hear the shouting of Vex yelling, "Get them!"

They rounded the corner and turned onto the next block, but Magda had no idea where she was running. Most of the shops in this area were boarded up, and there were no houses or courtyards in the area where she could lose Vex and his companions. A flag flickered up ahead, leading the way into a small alleyway between two buildings.

"This way," Ravi yelled, beckoning her into the alleyway. They both sprinted into the small space, Odie slowing his pace to remain with them, before they realized they were in a dead end.

"You're going to get us both killed!" Magda yelled upon seeing the sandstone wall before them.

The shouting behind them was getting louder.

Magda didn't have time to wait for this young man to think of a better plan. She placed her hands on her thighs, bracing herself to feel weight against her shoulders. Then she shouted, "Odie, up!" as she motioned to the side of the building framing the alleyway.

In an instant, Odie charged towards the building, running slightly up the side of the building, before landing on Magda's upper-back, using her tall body as leverage before launching himself over the wall. Now that her pet was safely on the other side, Magda frantically searched for anything they could use to boost themselves upward. Next to them, was a large wheelbarrow on giant wheels. Ravi was one step ahead of her and heaved it over toward the wall. He spun it around on the wheels and used all his might to push it up against the wall. Then, Magda threw her leg on top of it and hoisted herself up. She reached up to the top of the wall, but the wheelbarrow teetered underneath her weight, threatening to tip back on its handles.

"I have it!" Ravi yelled, holding it steady.

Magda leapt up to grab the top of the wall. As she did so, the wheelbarrow slammed to the right. "I thought you said you got it!" Magda yelled, too angry to find the words in Flaustran, cursing Ravi's skills in broken Azuremi.

Magda felt Ravi grab onto her feet, pushing her up. She mustered all the strength she could and pulled herself over the wall. With all the strength she had left she pulled her feet over and jumped down on the other side next to Odie.

Ravi dropped gracefully beside her, as if scaling the wall had been no trouble at all. However, the shouting behind them still continued.

As fast as they could, the two began running alongside her pet. Magda was leading the way, but she felt like a ship with no destination. She didn't know if she could trust Ravi—for all she knew he was also working with the mysterious group who had tried to take Odie, even if he had been the one to release the dogs. She had no idea where to go or what was the next part of her plan. A few yards ahead, she could see shadows reflecting on and off the walls and bright lines bouncing around the corner of the alleyway. As they approached the next street, a loud shouting and the rumbling of music crescendoed.

They both emerged into a larger town circle, which was full of Flaustrans going to late-night restaurants, clubs, and stores. The streets were dotted with small carriages, whizzing by, and patrons shouting at merchants in the streets. Magda stopped to catch her breath, panting as her eyes dotted up and down the street.

"What's your plan?" Ravi asked her curiously. "Are you going to just run away from them all night—to the guardians know where?"

Magda had no idea what her plan was anymore. She was on the verge of tears. Not only was she exhausted, but she hadn't been admitted into Queen Sanyal's palace, and on top of that, Odie had almost been taken.

Ravi repeated his questioning. "Where were you heading when I found you?"

Magda continued panting. "I don't know," she said with a sigh. "I was trying to find a place to stay for the night."

"You don't have a place to stay?" Ravi asked, curiously. "Come with me."

Ravi began walking away, but stopped when he realized Magda wasn't following him. "Do you trust me?" he asked.

Magda hesitated. She didn't trust anyone right now. For all she knew, Ravi could have been associated with the assassins who killed her brother and father. Although she knew that was a ridiculous thought, for they were proven to have been Ilusaurian.

"Do you trust me?" Ravi asked, extending his hand to her. This time, the words flicked across his tongue in broken Azuremi.

Magda was so taken aback, she almost didn't know how to respond.

"I'll help you avoid those men," he continued in her native language, although grammatically incorrect.

Magda nodded. If anyone knew the streets of Flaustra, it would be someone like Ravi.

Behind her, she heard shouting. Magda snapped her head around to see Vex and his henchman on the opposite side of the large town circle. They had also climbed the wall.

Hesitantly, Magda extended her hand and placed it in Ravi's, and in a flash as quick as lightning, they all were racing down the streets of Eloquas once more.

CHAPTER 20
Magdalena

They circled around carriages and drunk patrons; Ravi moved quickly through the city, and Odie was easily keeping up. Soon they came to another dark alley, and Ravi yanked on the tassel of a curtain that was hanging on the outside of someone's house. Suddenly, a rope ladder rolled down from the roof ahead of them.

"This way," he said, heading up first.

Magda looked behind her before noting a stack of boxes in the corner of the alleyway that created a pathway to the roof. "Odie, up!" she commanded before heading up the rope ladder behind Ravi. While they climbed the ladder, Odie easily scaled the crates, jumping from each one skillfully. They all emerged on top of a roof, and Ravi gracefully jumped over a five-foot gap to an adjacent roof. "Come on!" he shouted, jumping onto the next roof. It all seemed too easy for him.

Magda exchanged a glance at Odie, and the dog looked back at her with his tongue out, panting. But two seconds later, the dog was charging towards the gap, launching his body to the other rooftop. If Odie trusted Ravi, maybe she should too?

Magda braced herself, lurching backwards before launching her body over the opening. When she landed on the other side, she finally allowed herself to take a deep breath. She followed Ravi's exact footsteps until they came to a bright-turquoise roof.

Ravi knelt down and opened a sun-window, leading down into the space below. He squatted onto the roof and held his hands out to Magda, saying. "I'll lower you down. It's a long way."

Magda's face squinted, but she realized she had no choice. It was apparent that the guilds slept in every corner of this city, and if they were searching for her, she needed a proper place to hide. So she reached out and locked arms with Ravi once more, before sitting down on the ledge of the sun-window and letting him drop her inside.

She landed in a musty room, and the only furniture was a double bed in one corner. On the floor and walls, were brightly colored handwoven tapestries acting as carpets and covers for the open windows. Across from the bed, were a series of clay jugs and trinkets, as well as Ravi's violin case. In the opposite corner of the room, was a spiral staircase leading downstairs.

Odie jumped down from the window onto the bed, before leaping to the floor.

Ravi dropped down next to her. "I know it isn't much," he admitted, before lighting a lantern on a shelf that hung over the bed. Then he crossed to one of the water jugs and grabbed two clay mugs. "Want some?"

Magda's throat clenched in thirst at the sight of the water. She hadn't eaten or drank anything all day. "Thanks," she said, reaching out her hands to grab the mug from Ravi. She took a sip before offering some to Odie, who lapped it up furiously. Then she stood there, silently, not knowing what else to say.

"I'm just glad I got there when I did," said Ravi, "Or else you might not have seen your dog again."

Magda shuddered. "Does Vex really kill animals for their fur?"

"Not exactly," Ravi answered, "Vex never kills his animals right away. He either sells them, or makes them fight in matches against each other at his gambling house."

"That's terrible," Magda shook her head. She knelt down, hugging Odie, realizing that she had almost lost another family member tonight. "What can I ever do to thank you?"

"Don't worry about it. I was pissed at Vex for ruining my show earlier." Then Ravi crouched down to scratch Odie behind the ears. "What's his name?"

"Odie."

Odie licked Ravi directly in the face, causing the musician to jerk back in alarm. Ravi smeared his cheek with the back of his hand and laughed. "You're welcome, Odie."

Ravi stood before crossing to a hook on the wall and removing his shirt, before hanging it up. He stood in front of her, bare-chested, in the dim candlelight.

"What are you doing?" Magda snapped.

Ravi shrugged his shoulders. "Getting ready for bed. Do you sleep in your outside clothes?"

"I'm not sleeping here," Magda objected.

"The streets are now lined with Vex's men. Inns are the first place they will look for a foreigner."

"I...," Magda's face reddened, and she couldn't find any words. She was too tired. She swung her knapsack off of her back, and dumped it down onto the floor. She only had one change of clothes.

Ravi crossed to the bed and sat down, before taking a large gulp of water. "Azurem's a long way to travel from...especially when you seem to have no family in the city. Want to tell me why the guilds seem to be after you? It can't just be because of your dog."

Magda let out a sigh and sat down next to Ravi on the bed, while Odie traversed the room, smelling each corner and staking out the area. "To be honest, you know as much as I do. I have no idea what they want from me. I just got here this morning."

"Why are you in Flaustra?" asked Ravi.

"To visit someone," answered Magda honestly, "but it seems like they have no interest in seeing me."

Ravi nodded. "Well, you've got guts, I'll give you that. But you have to be careful...you really stand out in the city."

"I need to blend in," Magda replied. She gestured to her outfit and her hair. "Any advice?"

"Your appearance and your accent do give you away," Ravi smiled warmly, "but it's not that. It's the way you stand your ground...it's the spark in your eye telling the world that no one can stop you. It's real bravery, and it's impressive."

"You got all of that in a few minutes?" asked Magda with a laugh.

"I watch people for a living. And when I saw you in the marketplace earlier today, I really saw you. I knew that you were in trouble. The run-in with the Marauders only confirms it," explained Ravi.

"Do you take it upon yourself to rescue every damsel in distress that ruins one of your street performances?" asked Magda.

Ravi paused, like he was thinking hard about the question. But then he said, "No, just you."

Magda blushed. "If you really want to help me, you can tell me the best way into the royal palace."

"That place?" Ravi scoffed, leaning back further onto the bed and looking at the stars through the sun-roof. Something had sparked interest behind his eyes. "Why do you want to get inside there?"

"That's my business."

"You just got me wrapped up into more trouble with the Marauders for helping you. I think it's my business too." Ravi raised his eyebrows.

Magda didn't know what to say to him. She couldn't let a random citizen from Flaustra have any indication that she could be a royal, but at the same time, she needed someone on her side—especially if she wanted to have any street-smarts in this city. So she gave him a mischievous grin, "I'm trying to find answers that could help my kingdom. As for why, that's a story for another day."

Ravi laughed, sitting up and taking the empty mug from her. Then he reached over her head to put it back on the high shelf. As he did so, he leaned in close. "You've definitely piqued my curiosity, Dagmara."

Magda swallowed, remembering she was hiding her identity. Everyone had to believe Dagmara was the real Magdalena. No one could know Magda was in Flaustra for both her safety and Dagmara's.

She continued, "Then will you tell me how to get inside the castle?"

"I can try," Ravi said. "I actually need to get into the castle myself."

"Why?"

"My own reasons," he shrugged, "but I'll help you. The only people that are getting in there are those that have an invitation to Princess Kiran's birthday celebration."

Magda perked up, excited. "Are you serious? When is it?"

"This month," Ravi answered, "but there's no way you'll get in without an invitation. So you'll have to steal one from someone that is already invited."

Magda thought about the plan, which could potentially be risky. Anyone who was attending the birthday celebration would likely be holding their invitation close—likely on their person.

"You'll need to steal one from a member of a guild," said Ravi, "They will all be going. But they aren't found easily."

"Where can I find them?" Magda asked.

Ravi stood up, and beckoned her toward one of the tapestries hanging on the wall. Magda followed, standing beside him as he pulled back the tapestry to reveal a gaping hole in the sandstone that acted as a window. As far as the eye could see were tiny, colored lights marking the dense houses, almost as bright as the stars in the indigo sky.

"There," Ravi pointed to the north, "is their district. But their hideouts change, and secret codes are passed through the city as fast as the wind."

"I see," Magda nodded, realizing how hard this was going to be. She stood there next to Ravi, looking out at the stars, taking in once more how much brighter they were here than in Azurem.

"You like them?" he asked, watching her gaze.

"Yes," Magda breathed a sigh of relief for the first time in days.

"In Flaustra, there's an old poem about the stars. They say that the stars aren't balls of fire, but they're the hearts of the guardians, looking down on us, and pulsing with the secrets of a thousand ancient loves and battles."

Magda smiled. For some reason, it was heartening knowing that her brother and father were looking down on her from their place in the heavens. It wasn't what Azurem believed, but it did bring her some comfort. She stared up at Ravi, suddenly overwhelmed with gratitude for everything he had done for her in the past hour. If it wasn't for him, Odie would have been gone forever. She wanted to thank him, or give him a token of her appreciation, but she didn't know how. Before she could respond, he said:

"We should get some sleep. I have to hit the streets early, and you have to steal an invitation."

"Right." Magda shook her head in agreement. Odie was already on the floor, his eyes barely remaining open as he struggled to remain awake.

Ravi gestured toward the bed, stating the obvious, "Only got one of those."

"I'll take the floor," Magda answered quickly and turned away from his gaze so that he wouldn't see her face turn bright red. He had done enough for her, and for some reason, was going to continue to help her. She wouldn't have him give up his bed too.

"No one has to sleep on the floor," said Ravi.

"Well, I'm not sleeping with you."

"What's going to happen while we're sleeping?" he asked.

Magda shot him a look, but he didn't reply. They stood in awkward silence for a long moment, until Ravi said:

"I'll take the floor—"

"No, I will," Magda cut him off. She didn't want to put him out of his way, or owe him anything.

"Suit yourself," Ravi shrugged, before tossing her the only blanket in the room, "but you might be cold. The days are brutal but the nights are worse."

"Thank you," Magda said, catching the blanket before laying down on the carpet on the floor. She adjusted her knapsack underneath her head as a pillow before curling up next to Odie. It was the first time she had slept on the floor, and for some reason, having something completely opposite of her life in the Azuremi fortress was what she needed at this moment. She didn't want anything to remind her of the life she once had, and the pain that it had brought her.

Ravi blew out the lamp before hopping into the bed, staring at the ceiling. A few moments went by before he said, "You're being ridiculous you know. Just come up here."

"I will not," Magda rolled over, facing away from the bed.

"We're not going to do anything but sleep."

Magda sat up. "Sleeping leads to other things."

"I can promise you that won't happen," Ravi said. "The floor is miserable, we can both be comfortable."

Magda let out a huff and lay back down, trying to close her eyes.

A few moments of silence went by. When she didn't respond, Ravi backtracked. "...not that I wouldn't want to...you're brave and stronghearted..."

"I know what you meant," Magda cut him off.

Ravi rolled over on the bed to face her. "You know, in Flaustran culture, people talk more openly. Relationships are not secrets. It's all small-talk. Needs and wants, that kind of stuff."

"I'll keep that in mind."

"Just trying to help," Ravi finished before laying back down. "You asked how you can blend in."

Magda sighed, but she couldn't help but grin. She did need to blend in, especially if she was going to get into Kiran's birthday celebration. She needed to steal an invitation from a guild member, one that was high enough to have earned the prestigious invitation. Magda had just the person, and she knew that this girl would most definitely be at the docks. It was the very captain that had brought her to Flaustra and helped her slip past the immigration guards.

Ishani.

CHAPTER 21
Dagmara

Dagmara didn't have access to the Mad King's royal chambers. However, there had to be some evidence pointing to Claude's involvement in the assassinations throughout the castle.

She was up late, mixing her potions that lay hidden in her makeup kit. A headache lingered at her temples, and a pain radiated through her upper back and shoulders, but nothing she couldn't handle. As she made her concoction, mist began rising from the vial, and she instantly capped it. She couldn't risk putting herself to sleep.

She crossed to the table and the teapot that rested there. She had called for tea earlier that evening, and it arrived moments prior. She hastily opened the top and dropped the vial in. Before the steam rose, mixed with the sleeping solution, she closed the lid.

Crossing to the door, she channeled her inner princess. She opened it to see Martine on guard, as suspected.

"This tea tastes funny, and it smells odd," Dagmara said. "What are you people giving me?"

Martine's brow furrowed. "What do you mean?"

"Smell it yourself." Dagmara held out the pot.

Martine took the teapot. The guard's expression was laced with suspicion, but she fell for the trap anyway. She inhaled the steam rising from the pot before closing the lid. "It smells..." her voice trailed off.

Dagmara caught the teapot before it shattered on the ground. Martine slumped against the wall before lowering into a sleep.

Dagmara returned the teapot to her room before taking off down the corridor. Rounding the corner, she attempted to retrace the steps she had taken with Madame Annette. She passed a neighboring hallway and froze.

There was a figure that disappeared into another room. There wasn't enough time to examine the figure, but the dark attire...the dark hair...the broad shoulders and tall stature...it was the Ilusaurian captain, Sabien, who she had killed.

Her heart lurched in her chest. Was her mind playing tricks on her? It was as if she was seeing ghosts. Fear fluttered in her chest, and she suppressed it before continuing down the hall. Turning the corner, she faced a dead end.

Inching closer, Dagmara ran her palm against the stone, but her hand traced thin air. While it appeared she was touching a stone wall, she wasn't touching anything at all. Gasping, Dagmara jerked her hand back.

Was this an illusion? She knew the Guardian of the Mind could conjure illusions, but why would they need a fake wall?

The answer hit her immediately. To keep her in. She was a prisoner here. The Mad King put up a false wall to prevent her from snooping, but she wouldn't fall for it.

Taking a deep breath, she walked straight through the wall. The corridor continued on the other side, and Dagmara smiled to herself. The only way to beat Claude was to be smarter than him.

A few guards were walking the hall, and she made an inconspicuous cross to turn at the next corridor. Passing some windows, lit with the moonlight and stars, she knew she had to be near the front foyer.

Then she heard voices. Frozen in her tracks, she began to follow them. The grand entrance was before her, and she peered around the corner.

Claude was charging down the staircase with two guards on either side of him. One was the large guard from the balcony and the other looked young and inexperienced, with a bow strapped to his back. She recognized him as Pierre, the guard who had saved her on the balcony earlier that day.

Madame Annette tried to keep up with the three of them on the stairs.

"Can't you clear it in the morning?" she asked.

"No, what if the hounds wake up?" Claude asked, not even hesitating to glance over his shoulder.

Dagmara had to lean closer. She was on the second floor, and the group was below her.

"You really think someone in Nouchenne is an assassin?"

Claude stopped. He whirled to face his advisor, the sword at his belt making an arc around his body. "I'm not taking chances with Magdalena here."

Annette was the first to admit, "I don't like her."

"You don't like a lot of people."

"Her mannerisms and language do not reflect that of royalty. I don't think she's a princess."

The king paused, and Dagmara couldn't breathe. She inched closer, trying to see their expressions without getting caught. It was hard to translate every word they were saying and follow the pace of their conversation.

Claude lifted his hand, waving away his guards. They obeyed, creating distance and moving out of earshot. Luckily, for Dagmara, she was directly above the king and his advisor, and she could hear nearly everything.

"Her father and brother just died, how do you want her to act?" Claude asked, his voice coarse.

"It's not about how she is acting. When I examined her hands earlier, they were calloused."

"So? Maybe they teach princesses to fight in Azurem."

"They don't," Annette responded, "furthermore, I know it has been years since that portrait, but she has filled out and doesn't have her mother's proportions at all."

Claude laughed. "I'm not going to question her figure." His voice shifted lower. "Even you can admit she's beautiful."

A strange, nervous feeling erupted in Dagmara's stomach upon hearing the complement.

Annette was relentless. "Her hair is dyed."

The feeling evaporated instantly, and Dagmara gripped her braid. How did Annette know?

"Give it a rest," said Claude. "Does it even matter? You know I don't intend to go through with the marriage anyway."

Dagmara craned her neck to hear better.

"I'm only suggesting to test her," Annette said.

"Test her?" Claude's voice became sharper. "I'm trying to gain her trust. You want me to ask for a display of magic?" He scoffed.

"Not a display," Annette replied. "Just a test."

There was a pause. "If she senses me trying to compel her, my plan is over."

"If she isn't the true princess then your plan won't work at all."

"Listen, somehow Princess Magdalena is still alive when she was supposed to die alongside her brother and father."

Dagmara covered her mouth with her hand, muting her gasp.

Claude continued, "Until you find any real proof, I will continue to believe the woman here is Princess Magdalena. I will use her to Ilusauri's advantage, find out what she knows, and then I can get rid of her." There was a pause, before Claude continued, "Annette, I'm so close. This is my chance."

Dagmara could feel her heart pounding against her chest. Tears began to well in her eyes. Magda was right all along. There was a list of royals to kill—the royals who already had their gift.

As long as he thought Dagmara was Magda, he would want her dead.

"What happens if she decides to return to Azurem?"

Claude's voice turned dark, rumbling in his chest. "She can't leave. Tell everyone she is not allowed outside the castle. Call more guards. I want more security around her room."

Dagmara had to get back to her chamber before someone noticed she was gone.

Annette was unfazed by the shift in his tone. "Well, you may have already scared her off with your actions this afternoon."

Claude responded, but his voice was too quiet, and Dagmara was unable to understand any more. She was distracted by a man approaching the king's guards, whispering something in Pierre's ear. Then Pierre stepped forward and spoke. "Your Majesty, there is news from Celestaire."

"See if you can contact Reon, I have to get to Nouchenne first before dealing with Celestaire." His footsteps pounded on the ground. "We need Sabien back to deal with this. Where the hell is he?"

He exited the room, Pierre and the large guard trailing him.

The door slammed, leaving Dagmara in near silence. The tapping of boots on the ground signaled Annette was leaving as well, no doubt to call for more security as the king had demanded.

Dagmara's breath was ragged, and her hands shook.

Claude had no intention of marrying Magda. He wanted information. Whether he wanted to know how she escaped his assassins, or if anyone else in Azurem could track it back to Claude, one thing was for certain—she couldn't tell Claude anything that she knew, otherwise, her life would be worthless to him.

She stood and raced back to her chambers. If they were increasing security to watch her, the only way to find proof of Claude's crimes would be if she was welcome in the royal wing.

I will use her to Ilusauri's advantage, find out what she knows, and then I can get rid of her.

She had to beat him at his own game.

She would marry him and search his personal room and study before he got any information out of her, whatever it was that he wanted.

And before he found out that she killed Sabien.

CHAPTER 22
Dagmara

The following morning, Dagmara woke with a jolt. Her time here would be limited, and she had to avenge Aleksy and Bogdan's deaths before King Claude was finished getting information out of her—or so he claimed.

Aleksy. The thought of him made her feel ill. He had been a friend her whole childhood, and was taken from her life too soon. Pushing aside those thoughts to avoid confronting her grief, as she had when her mother died, she focused on the task ahead.

Today, she was going to seduce a murderer, otherwise known as a Mind Guardian. She had to get Claude to like her enough so that he wouldn't kill her before she could access the royal wing. Easy, right? Meanwhile, he couldn't discover that she killed Sabien, or that she wasn't actually Magda.

Easy.

Urszula helped her get ready, making her look like a true princess. She was more careful to hide anything that made her stand out, opting for a long-sleeve dress to cover her arms, and pinning her hair up. Urszula had to add an extra coat of the silver dye, for it easily washed out in the bath water. The top of her dress covered the scar on her shoulder, but she chose one with a low neckline on purpose.

Additionally, she wore short gloves to cover the new scar on the palm of her hand.

Martine informed her that Claude was practicing swordsmanship all morning and would meet her for lunch on the front lawn. However, she wanted to run into him before lunch and decided to interrupt his sword practice.

"Why does he have to practice with a sword when he's a guardian? Can't he just kill people with his mind?" Urszula asked.

"I don't know, and I'd rather not think about it."

Dagmara exited her chamber, thanking Urszula, and went to the field. Martine, of course, accompanied her the whole way.

Glass doors led out onto a glorious walkway with a towering fountain. Beyond, the cobblestone ground turned to grass and stretched on for miles. The smell of ocean air and the countryside filled her senses. The trees were ripe with foreign fruits, and the vineyard on the castle grounds was overflowing with food. It was a stark contrast from the rest of the kingdom she had seen on the carriage ride here. Was Claude hoarding resources while the rest of his kingdom was starving? Everything he did was vile, and Dagmara knew she had to expedite this mission.

Not only would this marriage allow Dagmara to sneak around in the Ilusaurian royal quarters, but the medicinal trade routes could be reopened. Teos, along with all the other children suffering from zowach, would be cured.

Dagmara broke out of her thoughts when she reached the small field directly outside the castle. Her eyes were instantly drawn to the king.

Steel clashed against steel as Claude battled three of his guards at once. He wore a loose-fitted white shirt and trousers tucked into tall boots. His bronze skin glistened in the sun. He fought with one hand, the other pressed behind his back.

The way he moved was mesmerizing, each step both graceful and lethal. Every thrust of his sword was more powerful than the last.

Beads of sweat dripped from his temple, running down his sharp jawline and dripping to his collar. He was pure strength, the true embodiment of a guardian, and Dagmara had no doubt he could slice her to pieces with his sword.

He was frightfully good. It took him moments to disarm one guard before knocking the second onto the ground and pressing his sword to the third's neck. He spoke to them in his native language and broke into a laugh.

He looked so curious when he was laughing. It didn't fit his character, and certainly didn't fit the rage she saw yesterday.

Sheathing his sword, he reached his hand out to help a guard up. The guards saw Dagmara first. Claude was the last one to turn around and notice her standing there, watching him.

Then he jogged across the field, his sword at his side, and only slowed his pace when he was within earshot.

"Princess, I'm surprised to see you this morning," Claude said. His accent speaking Azuremi was still captivating.

"I seem to surprise you a lot, Your Majesty," Dagmara replied. She was acutely aware of Martine a few paces behind her. There was no doubt Martine was reporting everything to Madame Annette. That meant today she was going to be the perfect princess.

Claude used his shirt to wipe the sweat from his brow. As it lifted, Dagmara was briefly distracted by the rippling muscles in his chest and stomach. She had no idea there even were that many muscles in the stomach and chest. Her breath hitched, and she had to clear her throat.

"I have come here to discuss the wedding," she announced.

Claude's let go of his shirt, covering his body, and disregarded her comment. "Let me get cleaned up, and we can call for lunch. There's someone I want you to meet."

Dagmara didn't want to wait for lunch to speak with him. "How long after our marriage will the trading routes be reopened?"

"A week, maybe two," the king replied.

"And the medicines?"

Claude hesitated. "Can't we discuss this after lunch?"

"No," Dagmara replied, keeping her voice as soft and lady-like as she could. "I hardly know the schedule, and it is improper to not let a woman know her own wedding arrangements."

His expression twisted. "There are no arrangements. I wasn't certain how long the journey would take from the Azuremi castle."

"Then let's make arrangements."

Claude shifted his weight, analyzing her. She felt small under his gaze. "I won't lie, Princess, your tone is off-putting."

"And your inability to prioritize the proposal you made is off-putting."

His jaw clenched. "I have other priorities."

Dagmara bit her tongue. That was certainly too far. But if there was one thing she heard while eavesdropping last night, it was that he would make her stay to get information from her, no matter the cost.

I will use her to Ilusauri's advantage, find out what she knows, and then I can get rid of her.

"If you do not wish to marry me, Your Majesty, then I will return to Azurem."

"No," Claude nearly blurted out. He was quick to regain his composure. He let out a deep sigh, and a low laugh escaped his lips. "You are quite the negotiator. Fine. We will host the engagement ball this week, and we can schedule the wedding in three months' time."

Dagmara's eyes narrowed, and she forced herself to remain collected. "I will not wait that long. The wedding will happen this month."

"What?"

"This month," she repeated.

Claude objected. "Royal weddings don't happen overnight."

"I said this month, not tomorrow."

"There's lots of planning, and people have to travel in from across the kingdom."

"How many days does that take? This marriage is for the trading routes and medicine. I won't wait on those things."

"It...," Claude's voice ran off, a suspicious expression flickering across his face for a mere second before being replaced with indifference. "I will speak with Madame Annette. Perhaps we can send some medicine to Azurem in advance of the official marriage."

Confusion spread through Dagmara. This man was utterly unreadable, and she tried to piece his emotions together with what she had overheard last night.

"And will you speak to her about the date of the wedding?"

"If I so choose," Claude said through gritted teeth. His patience was wearing thin.

She added a flirtatious lilt to her voice to soften the discussion as she said, "Aren't you choosing to marry me?"

He took a step toward her, closing the distance between them. Her heart plummeted in her chest upon his close proximity. A palpable anger exuded from his entire body that sent a crashing wave of fear right through her.

"I'm choosing to ally myself with Azurem. Trust me, if I knew you had this demeanor then I may have thought twice about proposing."

She felt the words like a blow to her chest. However, after getting her condition, all she had left were her potions and words to defend herself. She couldn't remain silent. What she said and how she said it was her most trained weapon.

"Trust me, Your Majesty, that my presence here was *not* my idea. I am only here for the betterment of Azurem." *Seeking revenge would be an added bonus.*

He eyed her curiously, and she nearly saw the thoughts shifting behind his eyes. He finally spoke, "I will speak to Annette about the date. We would need at least a month to plan for the wedding..."

She opened her mouth to object.

"...but I will send a shipment of medicine to your mother in

Azurem this afternoon, and I will start writing up the documents to reopen the trade routes."

One month until she gained access to his private quarters. She could stay alive for one month. She simply had to watch what she said around him and not give him too much information about Azurem or the assassination.

"Done," Dagmara concluded before he had a chance to add on any addendums. "I hope you're a man of your word."

With a curt nod, she whirled on her heel, prepared to head back into the castle. She had to clear her head and plan what she would say at lunch.

The world froze.

A man was walking to meet them on the lawn. He was tall and broad, with tan skin and dark hair down to the bottom of his ears.

It couldn't be.

"Ah, just in time," Claude said, passing Dagmara's frozen stature to introduce the new guest. "My close friend and captain returned this morning. Princess, I'd like you to meet Sabien Renaud."

She locked eyes with him. He was supposed to be dead. She remembered driving a knife through his stomach and sending him over the bridge into the rocky waters. This wasn't possible.

"Sabien," Claude continued, "meet Princess Magdalena Krol."

Sabien Renaud.

Captain of the Ilusaurian guard.

Sabien's chocolate eyes twinkled with curiosity. He towered over her as he proceeded to reach her side. He took her hand and kissed the back of her gloved palm, his lips lingering. It took everything inside her not to pull away. She tried desperately to hold her composure.

"Princess," Sabien said, his sonorous voice rumbling deep in his throat. The side of his mouth raised into a smirk. "It's a pleasure to finally meet you."

CHAPTER 23
Magdalena

Once again, Magda found herself submerged in blackness. The desolate space was void of all noise, as if she had been sealed in a coffin. Not a single wisp of air rushed past Magda's ears. It was the same space she had found herself in only days ago in a similar dream.

The booming voice filled the void again. "Still running, are we?"

"Tell me who you are," Magda said, although she didn't believe for one second that this phantom of her imagination was actually a real person.

"Me? I'm surprised you don't know. You don't recognize my voice?"

Magda only grew more surprised. She didn't know the first thing about being a guardian, for her brother and father had passed away before they had the chance to tell her anything about the responsibilities of being a royal. Did Aleksy also have strange dreams?

"I'm not asking again. Tell me who you are," she demanded.

Then the voice said, "I was taken too soon from this world, without the ability to pass on my knowledge to you. You possess a rare spark of magic, one that transcends the ordinary—a rare piece of salt, raw and unrefined."

The metaphor akin to Azurem's culture was not lost on her. This time, Magda grew curious. Was that the voice of her father or brother, reaching out to her from the great beyond? Maybe they wanted to tell her what they couldn't before they died.

"Is that you, Aleksy?" Magda called out. "Dad?"

When the blackness didn't respond, Magda had her answer. She snapped back with a bitter tone. "Whoever you are, get out of my head."

A snarl went up around the room, as if the comment wasn't appreciated. "Come back when you want answers, Dear Princess."

Magda lurched upright, rubbing her back. Her entire body was sore from sleeping on Ravi's hard, wooden floor. The realness of the dream was still ingrained in her memory. For some reason, every breath she had taken in the void had felt real—like it was sucking the life out of her. She took a few deep breaths to steady her beating heart.

Next to her, Odie scrambled to his paws before proceeding into a big stretch.

Looking to Ravi's bed, Magda noted that he had already left. The space that once held the violin case was empty.

Magda refocused on her own mission. She had to speak to Queen Sanyal and ask her about being a guardian, and more importantly her strange dreams. Since she couldn't reveal that she was the princess publicly, she would have to steal an invitation to Princess Kiran's birthday party.

She crossed to a miniature spiral staircase and descended to the first floor. It was a small kitchen space, with barely any room to move around. Odie hopped down the stairs next to her, landing quietly.

Magda opened the door, stepping out onto the street. Now, during the day, Magda could see the expanse of the city, which stretched as far as the eye could see. In the distance, on the lush fields outside of the tan, urban sprawl, was the palace. In the opposite direction, lay the docks.

Ravi lived off a busy intersection shaped in a circle, surrounded by bars, nightclubs, and shopping centers. Vines and plants peaked through cracks in the walls, and weeds dotted the edges of the streets. It was a distinct enough area to retrace her steps to later or be able to ask for directions, if she needed to make her way back here.

Magda paid for a small breakfast before heading to the waterfront. She was certain that if Ishani had an invitation to the royal birthday celebration, the invitation would be kept on her person. The best place to find the leader of the Fowler's Guild would be on the docks.

Magda and Odie walked through the busy streets along the dock, searching the crowds of people for the Fowler Guild's leader. She remembered Ishani telling her that she lived on the ship, so Magda traced her way back through the busy marketplace and toward the coastline.

For a few minutes, Magda had considered leaving Odie behind in Ravi's apartment. Especially if there were people looking to kidnap dogs on these streets. However, Magda preferred not to let Odie out of her sight. All she could do was hope that no one would confront her during the day, when the streets were crowded with witnesses.

When Magda reached the end of the streets, she saw the Starway docked in the harbor, the wondrous turquoise flags moving in the wind as the vessel bobbed up and down in the clear water. Beyond the ship, a pink sunrise illuminated the clouds on the horizon.

Magda took in her surroundings before proceeding any further. She stole a side-eye at Odie, but his stance didn't indicate any danger. There were no guards at the immigration gate this time, and she suspected it was because there were no incoming or outgoing ships at this hour that were coming from other kingdoms. So they slipped forward, walking directly through the gate, before standing in the middle of the docks.

Magda made her way to the magnificent ship, Odie trailing behind her. She didn't know for sure that Ishani had received an invitation, or if she would keep it out in the open in her office. All that she had to go on was the information from Ravi, and she hoped it would prove true. She didn't have any more time to waste, especially if assassins were still searching for her.

From Magda's viewpoint, the ship appeared deserted. She was not able to make out any sailors on board. The harbor was still, and the air was void of commotion. It seemed as if she was one of the only people on the docks; however, Magda guessed that wasn't the case, and assumed that there were sailors either sleeping or preparing the ships below deck. Boarding the ship would be dangerous, and Magda had no idea if it was preparing to venture on the high seas today.

The gangway plank leading up to the ship was down. It would be too easy to head directly on board. Magda stepped carefully, one foot in front of the other, as she crossed the gangway and boarded the ship. Odie followed behind, sniffing the edges of the planks as he went. When she reached the upper deck, she noticed two sailors cleaning the floorboards. They hummed a tune in a foreign language under their breath.

"What are you doing here?" the older man asked. His eyes glanced toward Odie.

"I have a message for Captain Ishani," said Magda. The lie was quick. "She told me I could come see her at any time."

"And who are you?" the man asked.

"My name is Dagmara, and I'm affiliated with the royal court in Azurem. I came all this way, and I assure you that your captain will want to hear what I have to say."

The men exchanged glances, wondering whether to believe Magda's story or not. Finally, one of them said, "She's been expecting information from Azurem. You'll have to wait for her in her office. She's gone onto the Marauder's ship to speak with Captain Vex."

The sound of Vex's name—the man that had accosted her last night and tried to kidnap Odie—made Magda's heart jump. Suddenly she regretted bringing Odie along with her to the ship. She didn't know where Ishani's allegiances lied, and if she was also engaged in illegal dealings throughout the city alongside Vex. But she didn't want to show any hesitations or fear. That's not what Dagmara would do. Dagmara wouldn't let her emotions show, regardless of what she was feeling. Magda kept her face blank, channeling her best friend's persona.

"Perfect," said Magda. "Show me to her office. I can wait."

Magda and her dog followed the older man down a set of stairs on the right. They both passed through a door with turquoise stained-glass paneling. Inside, was a lush office, full of treasures and trinkets from the Starway's travels across kingdoms. On the right, was a painting of Ishani as a young girl next to a handsome captain, who Magda assumed was her father based on the age difference in the portrait.

"Wait here," said the man. "I'll get her. Don't touch anything."

Magda nodded before taking a seat on a velvet blue chair across from a wooden desk in the center of the room. Once the door slammed behind her, and she was sure that the man had gone, she leapt up from her seat.

"Odie, watch," Magda motioned toward the door. Quickly, Odie obeyed, bounding to the door.

Magda raced around to the other side of the desk, yanking open drawers and cycling through papers in a frantic manner. Her eyes were drawn to anything that looked like a royal seal coming from Queen Sanyal.

When she was sure she had given herself enough time to search the drawers, Magda scanned the top of the desk. All that was on the tabletop was a large map of the world, showing the kingdoms of

Celestaire, Ilusauri, Azurem, Flaustra. Interestingly, there were many Xs and scribbles drawn along the kingdom of Azurem. Circled towns were situated within the border of Magda's kingdom. What was this map?

Magda's eyes scanned the room once more. There must have been one hundred books on the varying shelves, scattered between two porthole windows, and a set of stained-glass paneling behind the desk. In addition, eight trunks were stacked in one corner of the room. There was no way that Magda could search this entire office before Ishani returned.

Magda's eyes caught a small side table underneath one of the porthole windows. On that table, was a golden letter opener. Magda's heart raced as she dashed over to the side table. Next to the expensive letter opener, was a stack of mail. Magda grabbed the large pile of letters and began sifting through them, looking for anything that appeared to be a Flaustran crest.

Her eyes widened when she stumbled upon the crest of Ilusauri. This was the seal belonging to King Claude. Letting her curiosity consume her, Magda opened the letter from the so-called Mad King, written in Flaustran. It read:

> *I don't care if your payment was delayed. The terms of our agreement still stand. Report back to me when you have anything useful to tell me about the locations we discussed. Otherwise, don't waste my time. If you think I care about your birthright, think again. There are many other captains that would take these contracts for far less. Think about that next time you report back with nothing.*
>
> *If I get information from Princess Magdalena before you get me anything, I'll have no use for you anymore.*
>
> *Claude*

Magda gasped, almost dropping the letter. What was the agreement referenced in the letter? Were the locations in the letter related to the map on the table? Why was a Captain of a Flaustran Guild speaking to King Claude directly? And why were they discussing the Azuremi Royals?

Magda had to get into the Flaustran palace immediately. She had to access the Scribestone and send a letter to Dagmara this instant. Her friend could be in danger—much more danger—than Magda ever thought before.

Odie growled at the door. That was her signal someone was coming.

Magda went to put the scattered letters back in their places as Odie scampered over to the desk. Quickly, Magda replaced the letter from Claude, and did a brief skim over the remaining pile. Queen Sanyal's crest flashed on one of the remaining letters. Magda snatched it in her hand, hoping that it was the invitation she sought out, before shoving it in her apron.

In her haste, she knocked over a vase of decrepit, blue flowers. The vase rattled, rolling toward the edge of the desk, but Magda leapt forward, grabbed it, and set it back on the table. As she did so, her fingers brushed the dying leaves. Her eyes widened as the once withering violets sprang forward, blossoming into a vibrant bouquet, this time in various shades of turquoise. The bouquet was almost twice the size as before, threatening to tip the vase over.

Magda gasped, but she didn't have time to waste. She steadied the vase and raced back to the chair in the center of the office. Just as she sat down, the door swung open.

"You have something for me?" The voice was direct.

Ishani circled around to her desk before she recognized Magda. Then she spoke in Azuremi with a thick accent, "Dagmara." Ishani's eyes brightened, before taking in Odie. "And your dog. What a nice surprise."

"Not your usual Azuremi messenger, am I?" Magda asked.

"No." Ishani unlatched both handheld axes and set them on the desk. The young captain was exactly how Magda remembered her from their trip together. Tall, fit, with beautiful, shiny black hair slicked back into a low bun. Today she wore a turquoise cape buckled tightly around her neck, overtop a leather corset; it pinched her waist and accentuated her breasts, which were dusted with gold sparkles and lightly beaded sweat.

Ishani continued, sitting down in her desk chair. "You've intrigued me, Dagmara. You've caused more commotion in this city than any other Azuremi visitor."

"I heard. I had a run in with Captain Vex last night," Magda said, hoping the mention of his name would make Ishani accidentally reveal what type of allegiances she had to him.

Ishani gave Magda a suggestive smile, "He's not the only Captain that's interested in knowing more about you." Ishani stared down at Odie once more.

Magda's face flushed, and heat radiated through her body. She wanted to keep the conversation focused on her, rather than her dog. So she said, "You never pressured me for information about myself."

"I don't care about guild politics. It's not why I'm in this position."

"So why are you in this position?" asked Magda, thinking back to the letter from Claude. Her eyes flicked down to the map scribbled with marked villages on the desk.

Ishani studied Magda's face before following her gaze to the map. Then she said, "Are you going to be a problem for me? Or will we agree to not ask each other any more questions that could get us both in trouble?"

"Agreed," said Magda. There was something that passed between them, but it wasn't trust—it was something different—something deep and emotional.

Magda changed the subject, "You won't have to worry about me for much longer. I'm headed back to Azurem and I need passage on your next voyage back," Magda lied once again. "That's why I'm here."

"I'm not headed to Azurem for another few weeks. But sure, if you can pay as much as you did last time, I'll save space for you."

"Thanks," said Magda, rising to go. As soon as she did so, Odie rose to his feet.

Deep down, Magda wanted to ask Ishani more about the letter from Claude, but she didn't want to risk revealing that she had been snooping around the office and angering one of the most powerful guild leaders. That conversation would have to wait for another time.

As Magda headed out the door, Ishani called out, "I'll save space for you and your dog on the next ship to Azurem. Stay out of trouble, Dagmara."

CHAPTER 24
Dagmara

Dagmara could hardly breathe. She wasn't certain anymore if it was because of her health, or if it was due to the fact that a ghost was standing in front of her. Shock rattled through her body upon seeing someone she had murdered come back from the dead.

Sabien Renaud.

The Ilusaurian captain stood before her, decorated in similar black attire as he had been dressed in the night at the tavern. The night she had killed him. His stature was still exquisite, and his gaze was just as captivating.

"Welcome home," Dagmara managed, hoping her voice wasn't as shaky as she thought it was. "The pleasure is mine. Excuse me—Martine," Dagmara gestured to her guard, "the heat in your kingdom is getting to me, might we find some shade?"

"Of course, Your Highness," Martine said, clearing the distance between them and giving a courteous nod at both the king and the captain. "There is shade at lunch. Perhaps we'll go over early?"

"Wonderful," Claude said. "Sabien, join them, I'll be over as soon as I finish cleaning up."

Sabien nodded before clasping his hands behind his back and giving an enticing glance at Dagmara.

While Claude returned to the castle, Martine took Dagmara by the arm and began leading her to the luncheon, a few paces ahead of Sabien and out of earshot. "Princess, you look as though you've seen a ghost. Are you ill?"

"It's the sun." Wavering slightly, Dagmara fought to remain presentable. She had been standing too long. She simply had to sit, have salt, and then she would be able to confront Sabien.

The man rose from the dead. If the stab wound hadn't killed him, the fall into the ravine would have. No one would have been able to survive the rapids below.

When they rounded the corner, a small, circular table came into view underneath a canopy. It was already set up for lunch, with plates and silverware, and a lilac bowl of fruit overflowing at the center. Martine led her to the table and Dagmara sat down, her heart rate no doubt at its peak.

"Thank you," Dagmara said.

"Can I get you anything?" Martine asked.

"No," Dagmara said, eyeing the fruit before her. "I'll just—"

Sabien grabbed her wrist before she had a chance to touch the fruit. His grip was like iron, sending a shiver down her spine.

"You should wait for the king before touching anything," he said, his voice low. He relinquished her like he would a child, and Dagmara didn't even meet his gaze.

"Water, perhaps, Martine?" Sabien directed his question to the guard.

"Of course," Martine replied.

Dagmara sat upright. "I'm fine, truly."

Martine froze.

"The water." Sabien commanded once more.

The Ilusaurian guard eventually listened to her superior, heading toward the castle to summon the servants. Dagmara could see them at the glass doors, but they were too far away. The other guards on the premises were yards away. She would be alone with Sabien until Martine returned.

Sabien casually pulled out the seat on her left, settling himself down at the table. She was unaware he had been invited to this lunch.

She could get out of this. Maybe he didn't recognize her? If he did, this would all be over.

"Have you enjoyed the Ilusaurian castle so far?" Sabien asked, his voice mysterious.

"Yes," Dagmara replied. She scoured her brain for anything to talk about that didn't give herself away. So she said, "Your kingdom is much hotter than ours." The weather? She scolded herself for being so stupid.

"I know," said Sabien. "I was in Azurem once."

Damn. Her weather comment gave him the intro he needed. What would Magda say if she was meeting this person for the first time? Magda was curious and unguarded, like there wasn't anything in the world to fear. Dagmara could pretend to be like that.

"Oh really?" Dagmara mused. "What for?"

"The coronation."

Dagmara studied him scrupulously. There was a way out of this. If he recognized her, she could simply brush it off and say that Magda was visiting the tavern for a short drink since she needed a break from royal life before the coronation. But then the fallacy of that plan came to her. If she made it seem like Princess Magda was at the tavern, Magda would be blamed for murdering her own citizens!

Sabien read her silence as surprise—or so she hoped. "Don't worry, we didn't meet there. Unfortunately, I didn't make it to the coronation. I was tied up in personal affairs."

Personal affairs? Dagmara had to get out of this conversation so she didn't slip up. Maybe he didn't recognize her. Maybe she was overreacting.

"Maybe it was better that way," Dagmara offered. "The coronation wasn't what we planned."

"My deepest condolences," Sabien said. There was something about his low, melodic voice that made her chest tighten. He was too close to her. If he shifted forward in his chair, he could touch her. One movement under the table and his leg could reach hers.

"Thank you," she said. "Maybe one day you can return to Azurem when you aren't caught up in personal affairs."

There was a tug at his lip as though he suppressed a smirk. "Maybe after this marriage I will be welcomed in Azurem. I wouldn't want to cause a scene."

"Nonsense. After the marriage and a new alliance, you would be welcome."

"A welcomed distraction, perhaps."

Like she had used him as a distraction at the tavern.

She met his gaze, holding steadfast as she said, "I guess only time will tell."

They were playing a game of cat and mouse. Dagmara just had to find out if she was the cat or the mouse.

She let her eyes wander, attempting to ignore his stare. That's when she noticed a row of purple plants dotting the cobblestone path. She nearly gasped. Was that leku? It was an herb used as a remedy for zowach. The herb that could save her brother's life was simply sunbathing at the Ilusaurian palace?

She could feel her fingers begin to prickle with anger. One more reason to detest King Claude. His country was lacking resources, Azurem was lacking medicine, and he had the audacity to flaunt leku like it was a common flower. Teos needed that. All she had to do was snatch a handful and send it home where an apothecary could turn it into medicine. A handful wouldn't be enough for Azurem to heal everyone, nor would it be enough to plant some of their own, but it would be enough for Teos.

"Do you like gardening, Princess?" The suave voice snapped her out of her thoughts but didn't diminish the anger boiling in the pit of her stomach.

Dagmara cleared her throat before returning her attention to him. "Not really."

Sabien leaned forward in his chair. "I saw you eyeing our leku. Are you into medicines...potions perhaps?"

Potions. He was testing her. "I was just admiring the view, Captain, nothing more." She flashed a half-smile, hoping she was channeling Magda's trained royal mannerisms somehow. Maybe she should sit up straighter?

"Well, in that case I'm also admiring the view." He let his eyes scan her bodice and her lips before returning to her eyes.

Warmth flooded Dagmara's entire body, and she felt her stomach curl. It took everything inside her not to let her mouth drop in shock. She was taken by his forwardness, but also taken by how quickly he transformed her emotions. He smirked, noticing the effect he had on her, which only made her heart rate increase. His face was beautiful enough, but that smile was deadly.

To her relief, she saw Martine returning to the table, but she wasn't alone. King Claude, Madame Annette, and an entourage of servants and guards were approaching. Two guards flanked Claude on either side. They had to be his main guards, just as Martine belonged to Dagmara. The younger one was recognizable as the boy who had pulled her from the balcony yesterday. Pierre. The other was massive, towering half a foot above everyone in the clearing.

Sabien was immediately on his feet, returning completely to his professional demeanor. Dagmara struggled to follow suit, feeling her entire body threaten to drag her unconscious as she stood in formality.

"I hope I didn't miss anything," Claude said, his tone even as he reached the table. He, for one, cleaned up nicely.

Servants pulled out the chairs for both the king and his royal advisor while Martine took up a spot on the edge of the terrace. She was spread out evenly with the other guards.

A glass was set down in front of Dagmara, filled to the rim with ice water. Then, a small wooden bowl was placed down next to the silverware filled with pink rock salt. Startled, Dagmara rocked back in her seat.

"I noticed you found my kingdom's salt lacking yesterday," Claude said. "This is straight from the salt mines."

"I can see that," Dagmara replied with a tilt of her head.

"Is something wrong?"

"It's just..." Dagmara noticed Annette's fixated glare.

Claude leaned forward. "You may speak freely, Princess," he growled.

"In Azurem, we usually shave it down to be more like a spice. To sprinkle on top."

"To...sprinkle?" Claude's eyebrows wavered, but he didn't have time to elaborate.

A servant approached the table with a large pitcher and a spare tasting glass. "Wine for the table." His nose was slightly crooked, and sweat beaded his brow.

"I don't drink while on duty," Sabien replied, flipping his glass down. He looked directly at the servant and said, "No wine today."

"I am too old for mid-day wine," Annette added, flipping her glass down as well.

"Never too old for that, Madame," Dagmara said with a laugh.

Annette's face insinuated that she was not amused.

The servant first poured a sip for himself in the tasting glass, struggling with the weight of the pitcher as he fumbled for a decent grip.

"Tell me, Princess, how is your mother?" Annette pried, loud enough for all to hear.

"She is well under the circumstances," Dagmara replied.

"And how many years has it been since you and Claude have seen each other?" Annette pressed.

"Eleven," Claude answered on Dagmara's behalf, switching his attention to his advisor. "Don't ask her a dozen questions."

The servant drank his entire glass. Dagmara couldn't help but notice Claude watching him diligently. This tasting must have been his idea.

"I'm not questioning her," Annette responded, "I'm getting to know her. Shouldn't you be doing the same?"

"I am," said Claude.

"Actually," Sabien mused, "I would also like to know more about the princess. Do you have any hobbies?"

Dagmara's throat went dry. "I ride every morning," she managed. At least Magda does. Magda always took her horse out to the waterfalls with Odie.

Sabien grinned. "Morning rides are my personal favorite."

"Since when?" Claude glanced at his captain.

There was a clatter of silverware as the servant struggled for a grip on the pitcher. "Apologies, Princess," he said under his breath, the sweat now running down his temple. He shifted his thumb and began pouring into her glass.

Casually, Sabien turned to address Claude. "I think we're discussing two separate hobbies."

The muscles in Claude's neck tensed.

The servant reached over and poured Claude's wine. The table was small enough that he didn't have to walk around to the other side. There was something about the pitcher that was utterly familiar.

Annette spoke next, "Tell me about your royal education."

Dagmara opened her mouth to speak, but was cut off.

"Don't make me regret inviting you both," Claude snapped. He grabbed the stem of his wine just as the servant finished pouring. He raised it to Dagmara. "To getting to know each other, in time, without a thousand questions."

Annette let out an audible scoff.

Dagmara raised her glass, giving Claude a smile, her thoughts elsewhere.

The servant turned away with the pitcher in hand, but something about that pitcher felt like home. And he shouldn't have struggled with his grip that much.

Claude brought the wine to his lips.

It was the same trick she had used in the tavern to poison her victims.

"No!" Dagmara screamed. She dropped her own wine glass, spilling it down her gloved hand, as she lunged across the table. She whacked the goblet firmly out of Claude's grip, and the contents splashed on the front of his shirt.

A collection of gasps broke out from the servants and guards around the table, Madame Annette's being the loudest. Sabien was already on his feet, and Claude shoved his chair back and rose.

"What was that?" Claude's voice boomed.

"It was poisoned." The words escaped Dagmara's lips before she had a chance to second-guess.

Was she sure? Did she see it correctly or was it all a slip of her imagination?

Claude's expression darkened, his voice barely audible. "Poisoned?"

That's when Dagmara felt the singe of pain. She looked down at her hand to see her glove coated in red wine and burning like hell. Wincing, she tore off her glove, throwing the fabric aside before wiping her hand on her skirt. She was familiar with the sting, but to anyone else who left it on a moment longer, it would easily leave scars.

Claude yelled what Dagmara could only assume was a curse word before tearing off his shirt, soaked in wine. Once it was off, everyone could see the inflamed skin on the center of his chest—the center of his very muscular chest.

Shouts rang across the terrace, and at one point Dagmara heard the word for 'doctor'. There wasn't time for all that. It just needed to be washed off.

Dagmara grabbed her glass of water and chucked it toward the king. The water splashed against his chest as the ice cubes bounced off in random directions.

Everyone went silent.

Claude froze, his expression indecipherable as his eyes flicked from Dagmara to the empty glass in her hand. His jaw ticked, anger flaring in his eyes. Beads of water ran down his chiseled body, over every divot in his abdomen. The water settled in the crevices between his taut muscles and low-rise pants.

She gave him an embarrassed grin.

In the silence, footsteps and panting were heard. The servant who had poured the wine was dashing up the terrace steps, the pitcher left behind on the ground, going for the escape. All of the guards had been too stunned by the outburst to grab him in time.

As if everyone jumped to action at once, the guards started making haste.

However, the guards didn't overtake the servant before the earth rose from the ground. Directly in the servant's path, the terrace split in a deafening crack, shooting upward to create a wall. The servant nearly collided with the wall, skidding to a halt and falling to the ground.

Dagmara gasped, stumbling back and catching herself against the table. She didn't even feel the terrace vibrate. Who had Soul magic here?

As the servant scooted away from the wall, trying to find his escape, an ember of fire ignited at the base of his pants.

Fire magic?

The servant let out an ear piercing scream as the fire imploded, reaching up his pant leg.

"Who sent you?" Claude's voice was louder than anything she had heard before. He started forward, silver magic dancing at his fingertips.

That's when it clicked. None of this was real. It was all in the mind. Claude was projecting all of this with his mind? Dagmara didn't even know that was possible.

"Who!?" Claude yelled, and the fire erupted, consuming the servant's entire body.

Dagmara could only watch in sheer terror as the servant threw himself at the ground, screaming to put out the flames.

"Claude!" Annette screamed.

Sabien stepped forward and placed a hand in front of Claude. His Ilusaurian was too quick for Dagmara to pick up amid the chaos, but she heard something about taking the servant for questioning.

Everyone on the terrace was frozen, watching the servant scream and thrash on the ground.

"Your Majesty," Sabien said.

With one wave of his hand, Claude dismissed the projections. In a blink of an eye, everything returned to normal. The terrace was untouched, no more wall of earth. The fire was gone. The servant's clothes weren't even burned.

It was all a mind game.

And it was terrifying.

Sabien was the first to move, charging toward the servant who was still squirming to put out the imaginary fire. A few guards followed, joining him to bring the servant to prison no doubt.

One servant mentioned something about grabbing the doctor, racing inside. Others crowded the table, asking if everyone was alright.

It was all a blur until Claude whirled toward Dagmara, a twinge of silver flecks remaining in his eyes as the magic disappeared. "How did you know?" he asked, his chest heaving.

Dagmara could hardly move. She felt her heart pounding against her ribcage, her hands shaking, and her knees about to give out. "I—"

Claude slammed both palms on the table, clattering the dishware.

Pure muscle rippled up his arms and shoulders. He was the embodiment of a guardian.

And Dagmara was the last thing from a guardian.

"How?" he screamed, startling Dagmara so that she staggered away from him.

"That's enough!" Annette yelled. She wrapped an arm around Dagmara, seeming to come to her aid for a surprise. Yet when Dagmara's body was pressed against hers, she could feel her quivering as well.

Claude hung his head. "Get out."

"What?" Dagmara's meek voice was barely more than a whisper.

"I thought I could protect you, and I can't. You have to hide. Somewhere safer than here." He lifted his head and met her gaze. There was something vulnerable there, hidden behind the rage. Dagmara could almost see it before it entirely vanished as he repeated, "Leave the castle now!"

CHAPTER 25
Dagmara

Dagmara bolted like she never had in her life. Nothing mattered. Not the deal she made with Magda, not the confidence she had in herself earlier that day. Not even her health could stop her as she raced up the terrace steps, tore into the east wing, and barged into her room.

Urszula gasped upon the sight of her, but Dagmara disregarded her. She fell onto the bed, catching herself on her hands and struggling to catch her breath.

"Are you alright?" Urszula asked, racing to her side. She rubbed Dagmara's back, waiting for her breathing to calm.

Dagmara's heart was beating far too fast. She felt like the world was going dark. She turned over, propping her feet up on the post that held the canopy, and let her blood rush back to her head. Finally her body seemed to settle, but her mind was still on full alert.

"We're leaving," she announced. "Now."

"Why? What happened?" Urszula asked.

"Start packing."

Urszula didn't argue with Dagmara, noting her urgency. She set to work right away. A few minutes went by as they collected their luggage, shoving all their belongings into cases, until finally there was a knock on the door.

"It's Martine."

Dagmara exchanged a glance with Urszula. "Come in."

Martine let herself in, and her attention immediately went to the luggage pile near the door.

"We're leaving," Dagmara blurted out before Martine had the opportunity to ask. "The king ordered me to leave."

Martine shifted her position. "The king asked to speak with you, Princess."

"Speak with me?" Dagmara asked.

Martine gave a nod and clasped her hands behind her back.

A laugh escaped Dagmara's lips. "No."

Martine's professional demeanor wavered for a moment as surprise flashed across her face. "You can't deny a meeting with the king."

"I'm a guardian. I can do whatever I please," Dagmara responded. She didn't know where this newfound courage came from. However, after seeing Claude's magic in full force that afternoon, she knew she stood no chance against him. She was scared, and the only thing she could do was pretend she wasn't. She and Magdalena hadn't thought this plan through. Especially now that Sabien was back and could easily blow her cover.

"I...," Martine tried to object, but her mouth hung open slightly, unable to find the right words to counter.

"Go tell the king I heard everything he had to say," Dagmara stated. "He made himself clear this afternoon."

"Princess—"

"Please, Martine," Dagmara said. "Don't make this more difficult than it needs to be."

With a nod, Martine turned and left the room.

Urszula wore an expression of shock. "This won't end well. He will find you."

"I know, so we have to leave right now." Dagmara rose from the bed and began filling the pockets of her dress with her most important potions. She slipped a few throwing stars into the slot on her corset, letting them hide behind the thick binding. She continued to instruct Urszula as she pulled on new gloves, hiding the wound from the first day on the balcony once more, "Grab whatever you can and get down to the stables. I have to get something first."

"No, you need to come with me. They won't let me go alone."

"I can't leave without something important," Dagmara stated. "Please."

After a few moments passed, Urszula finally nodded. "Hurry."

Following her instincts, Dagmara retraced her steps back to the terrace. It was one of the few places she was allowed to go in this castle, so she knew the way well enough. It had taken the remainder of the afternoon to pack, so the sun had set, leaving only the moonlight to guide her. The king gave her permission to leave, and she was taking it. She would have to find proof about his involvement some other way. It wouldn't matter if she ended up dead or if Sabien revealed who she really was. Now that Sabien was here, there were a lot more things that could go wrong.

Once outside, she spotted the leku plant. The only guards in sight were in the yard in the distance. Perfect. Dagmara skipped down the terrace stairs and dropped to her knees in front of the herb, marveling at its beauty. She had never seen so much in one place before. How dare he horde it all for himself.

She reached out to pluck a few strands. As soon as she picked one, it evaporated in her grasp. Shaken, she tried again, only to receive the same result. Was she going crazy? She picked another bush and plucked a stem, and yet within a blink of an eye, it was no longer in her gloved hand. She couldn't believe it. Using both arms, she scooped up full handfuls, yanking them from the earth. She could feel them in her palms for a moment before they dissipated once more.

"Taking a souvenir home with you?"

In one swift motion, Dagmara stood and whirled to face the voice. Her whole body tensed upon seeing the king. He didn't have the same malice in his face as he did the last time she saw him, but he frightened her to the core.

"Is this a trick?" Dagmara gestured to the ground.

"You know, I've never been denied when I request to see someone," Claude said, his expression stoic. He continued, "You would be the first."

"Maybe it's good for you to be turned down once in a while," Dagmara replied, unable to quell her fear. She was like a caged tiger lashing out at anything she could between the bars. "Now answer my question."

"You continue to surprise me, Princess. Walk with me." He turned toward the palace once more.

"No," Dagmara stated, nearly stamping her foot on the ground in protest. "Answer me first."

He paused to glance over his shoulder. "You know the answer already. But walk with me, and I will explain."

Deep down, Dagmara knew why the leku had evaporated, but she wished it weren't true. She wanted to go with him. There was something that drew her toward him whether it was curiosity or something else. If he was about to walk her to her death, so be it.

Letting out a sigh, she began to walk beside him, not missing the faint smile that crossed his lips.

"First I want to discuss what happened earlier," Claude said, much to Dagmara's surprise. He paused as they passed through a set of guards that were holding the castle doors open. "I am intrigued about how you saved my life," Claude continued. "That was supposed to be my job."

Dagmara suppressed her expression as they rounded the corner, heading down the north wing. Why was he being so kind to her? Suspicion gnawed inside her.

They walked side-by-side in the reflective hallway, passing through the row of sparkling mirrors—suddenly images of Claude flashed on all sides, even though he was right beside her. This, Dagmara knew, wasn't an illusion. If he hadn't been leading her through the expansive maze, she was convinced she would never find the exit.

"How did you know the wine was poisoned?" Claude asked.

That was the question she didn't know how to answer without giving herself away. Besides, she still didn't know why she saved him. Was it just instinct?

"It was the pitcher, Your Majesty."

"The pitcher?"

"It had a compartment I saw, and I assumed the worst."

"I didn't see a compartment," Claude replied. "You've seen pitchers like these before?"

Dagmara spared a glance up at him, but decided not to answer that question. Was she going to admit she has *used* these pitchers before? Absolutely not.

"I understand," Claude said, his voice low. "There is still a long way to go before you trust me."

"I don't know that I'll ever fully trust you, Your Majesty," Dagmara admitted.

Claude stopped in his tracks, grabbing her hand as he did. A chill ran through her at their contact.

"I didn't kill my parents," he whispered, but every word was filled with tension.

Dagmara didn't believe him, but maybe this was her way in. "Then what happened?"

"I...," he shut his eyes tightly. "I am not ready to relive that day."

Pulling her hand free from his grip, Dagmara gave him a curt nod. "It's fine to admit you don't trust me either."

His eyes fluttered open, and a flare ignited. "I neither trust you, nor like you." He pushed his hand onto a mirror, revealing a door, and led Dagmara out into a courtyard. She would never have noticed a door was behind the floor-length mirror.

Before her, was an interior courtyard and a path extending to a greenhouse. On all sides were arched columns leading into other wings of the castle, as well as a second-story balcony wrapping around the courtyard's edges. In front of Dagmara, was a sea-green pond bubbling with small fountains of water, and fuchsia flowers dotted the edges. In the center next to the greenhouse was a cherry-blossom tree, its pink buds in full bloom.

Two guards stood by the greenhouse entrance, and the king quickly ordered, "Leave us." They obeyed, and within moments, Dagmara and Claude were the only two present.

She felt her breath catch in her throat. This could be where he killed her. She had her chance to escape, and she didn't take it. What if he assumed she wasn't Magdalena? Although how could he kill someone in a place this beautiful?

"You asked if this all was a trick," Claude said, snapping her out of her scrambling thoughts, "and it is."

A silver light shimmered at his fingertips, and his eyes were aglow with silver specks. Everything around her began to decay. The flowers on the cherry blossom tree crumpled into dried petals, and deadly weeds snaked up its trunk, suffocating the life from its branches. The pond dried up, and the lively green plants became a decrepit shadow of what they once were. All around, the courtyard displayed signs of erosion due to wind and rain, and instead was choked with debris.

Dagmara couldn't help but gasp. She backed up, only feeling brittle grass crunch underneath her feet. "I...I don't understand," she stammered.

"Everything on the front lawn is a facade," Claude stated. He spoke as though this was rehearsed. It was simply facts for him, nothing more. "This is what is real."

She tried to take in the decay. It was hideous, and she felt sick to her stomach. A putrid smell of rotting plants filled her senses, making her gag. She covered her mouth, trying to hide her reaction from the king.

Everything that was glorious and beautiful about the palace...was a facade?

As she lowered her hand from her mouth, she looked at him. Truly looked at him. He was a few feet away, alone, in the center of a courtyard filled with decay.

"Why?" she whispered. "Why make such a false facade? People think you're hoarding resources from your own citizens."

"I'd rather them think me a monster than know the truth," he stated. "If they saw our entire kingdom was in a famine, there would only be fear. We would be vulnerable. The other kingdoms would think we were weak. I'd rather have my people angry than afraid."

Those words stuck Dagmara at her very core.

"This started after the death of my parents," Claude admitted. "Almost as if the death of the guardians began to drain away the soul of the kingdom. Don't you see, Princess? Your life is holding your whole kingdom together."

Magda's life. She was in more danger than Dagmara thought.

"But you're here," said Dagmara. "Why is your kingdom fading then?"

"I wasn't a guardian when my parents were killed. I wasn't crowned until years later," he explained. "I don't know how it works, but to the kingdom, the Guardians of the Mind may be dead. There were no guardians for years."

And if Magda truly has Soul magic...there are no Life Guardians left either.

Dagmara felt her stomach drop. She had to get news of this to Queen Bernadette, fast. What if Azurem started to perish like Ilusauri?

With a wave of his hand, a silver glimmer shone through the courtyards. A metallic hue glistened in his eyes, and the courtyard came to life once more. Foliage grew from the dust, and the tree sprouted pink flowers.

It was fascinating to watch. It was magic she had never seen before.

"I have one more thing to show you," Claude said before heading toward the greenhouse.

Dagmara didn't object this time. She followed his lead inside the glass room. Inside, was an overflow of greenery, with potted plants dangling from its arched roofs, held up by intricate ironwork between each glass panel. It was dark except for the moonlight, but Dagmara was still able to spot rows of herbs lining the walls, illuminated by the starry night sky.

She wanted to ask him if this was also a false projection, but she held her tongue as they walked into the structure.

Claude led her further into the greenhouse, stopping in a corner with his back to her. "Whoever killed my parents, whoever wanted Ilusauri to fall to dust, wants the same thing for Azurem. I don't believe they will stop until they kill you too," he said.

"If your theory is true, I am not safe anywhere," Dagmara stated. That, she knew for a fact.

He turned to face Dagmara. "After the assassination attempt this afternoon, I will double security. I know you don't trust me, but I vow to do what I can to keep you safe."

"Well, whoever it was did poison your wine glass as well."

A minor detail that made Dagmara question if Claude was really behind all of this. She wouldn't put it past a crazy murderer to poison themselves briefly if it meant killing her. She just wasn't sure who Claude was yet.

Claude shrugged. "I owe you for saving my life, and I don't do well when I have debts to pay. So ignore my previous remarks and stay here where I promise to do my best to protect you. Regardless of what we think about each other, this marriage would help our kingdoms. I don't need troops from Azurem. As you see, I need food for my people, and clean water, which your kingdom has an excess amount of. And, as I recall, you need medicine."

With a move of his hand, he gestured to a pallet behind Dagmara that held a wall full of leku. Out of instinct, Dagmara rushed forward to touch the leaves. She didn't have to pick one to test it, for she could smell the herb wafting from where it rested. These were real. These leaves, only native to Ilusaurian soil and climate, were right before her. She was both overwhelmed and lightheaded at the sight.

"We take special care to keep these alive, despite the famine. You can take a handful and return to Azurem, where I can't guarantee your protection, but you will be home," Claude said. "Or, you can sign the marriage contract with me, we can put on a good show for the engagement ball and the wedding, but live our own lives. Then our kingdoms can benefit from what we desperately need." The end of his sentence was breathless, as though it were a plea.

It was real. She stumbled back into an iron bench and took a seat, pressing a palm to her racing heart. Everything in the greenhouse was real.

But Ilusauri was dying. If this was to happen to Azurem, she would need all the allies she could get. How could the decay be stopped? What if he was behind it, and all of this was some ploy to get her to trust him? What if the destroyed courtyard was the real illusion?

Claude kept his distance as he watched Dagmara seated on the bench. His voice was low, but filled with intensity. "Aside from dropping to my knees before you, Princess, I don't know how else to beg."

The king on his knees in front of her? That would be a sight she would pay money to see. She almost asked for him to kneel down before her, but decided not to press her luck.

"I don't trust you," Dagmara began, "but I do trust that your need for resources is the motive for this marriage. As you know, medicine is at the center of mine. I will stay for the wedding and see to it that these arrangements are made for the betterment of both our kingdoms."

A soft smile caressed his face. It was beautiful, nearly taking Dagmara off guard.

"I am honored to hear that," he replied. "We don't have to like each other…this can be purely political."

"Purely political," she echoed.

"Then I will see you at the engagement ball at the end of the week."

"Wait—what?" she stammered, standing to her feet immediately. It was too fast, and darkness crowded the corners of her vision. She engaged the muscles in her legs, keeping herself upright.

"I'm sure you can feel the tension between us. There's no reason to try and make this relationship work if it isn't needed. We will see each other at the mandatory events."

Dagmara paused, her mouth slightly agape. Less time with the scary guardian and more time to herself to break into the royal suite?

She smiled at Claude. "Sounds wonderful."

A rapping at the greenhouse door alerted them both. Claude crossed the distance in swift strides, opening the door to reveal an older man in a dark robe. His wrinkled hands were clasped on a leather bound book, and two guards hovered behind.

"Coroner," Claude announced, a surprised tilt to his head.

"Apologies, Your Majesty, Princess, but I knew you would prefer I interrupt about this pressing matter." The coroner's voice was a high-pitched wheeze. Combined with the fact that he was speaking in Ilusaurian, it was difficult for Dagmara to understand.

Dagmara was quick to realize that even though she and Claude were alone, everyone knew where the king was in the castle at all times.

"Speak." There was something about the way Claude spoke in his native language that was much more authoritative.

"The perpetrator we apprehended today…is dead."

"What?" Claude's fists clenched. He pointed at one guard, "Find Martine to escort the princess back to her room. You," he pointed at the next guard, "stay with her until Martine arrives. Coroner, with me."

With that, Claude was exiting the greenhouse without so much as a glance in Dagmara's direction. The guards obeyed instantly, one hovering near Dagmara as though his life depended on it, the other rushing to find Martine.

Stepping out into the courtyard, Dagmara watched Claude and the Coroner walk toward the exit, both in furious discussion. She wanted to ask to stay with them, to hear what happened, but she knew her place.

"How did he die?" Claude asked, his voice as emboldened as his strides.

Just before they exited, Dagmara heard the Coroner's response. It seemed like a strange response, seeing as the servant was brought to the castle jail. Maybe she misinterpreted the words, or had the Ilusaurian verbiage wrong. But she could have sworn she heard him say, "He seems to have drowned."

CHAPTER 26
Dagmara

After hearing the truth about Ilusauri's deterioration, Dagmara knew she had to warn Queen Bernadette. Dagmara had to get to the Ilusaurian Scribestone somehow. Luckily, she was already in the royal wing, standing outside the greenhouse with the guard Claude assigned to her. This was the perfect moment to sneak off to the Scribestone.

Also, she wanted to ensure Magda had arrived in Flaustra safely. Magda had promised to send a message, but Dagmara hadn't had the opportunity to check.

Reaching into her pocket, she felt the vial of bilans she had grabbed while packing for their abrupt departure. She eyed the guard, but he seemed to purposely be watching the doors instead of her.

Turning away from him, she quickly withdrew the vial, dumping it into the palm of her gloved hand before hiding the vial back in the depths of her pocket. Rubbing her satin gloves together, she knew she had to be fast before the potion began seeping through the fabric.

"Excuse me," Dagmara said, lifting the pitch of her voice to sound innocent. She approached the guard and held out her palms. "I'm overheating, and these gloves are too slippery for me to take off. Can you help?"

The guard's nose twitched, a single question crossing his expression in the blink of an eye. "Martine can help when she gets here."

"I can't possibly wait that long," she persisted. "I wouldn't want to faint on your watch."

With that statement, he conceded. "Yes, guardian," he said before reaching out and removing her gloves with his bare hands. He did so carefully, as if attempting not to hold her hand at all. As soon as he had one off, he put it in the crook of his elbow, and then slowly began removing the next. Once the second one was removed, his expression changed after seeing the scar on her palm, but before he could ask about it, he stumbled slightly.

"Sorry, Princess, I think I'm lightheaded as well."

"Shall we sit?" Dagmara started for the bench before he had the chance to hand her back the gloves soaked in poison.

A loud thud echoed through the room as the guard dropped to the ground.

Maybe she had used a little too much in her haste.

She squatted beside him, using the fabric of her skirt as a barrier to pick up the gloves and deposit them into a nearby flower arrangement. They disappeared into the colorful array. Luckily, if the flowers were truly a projection of Claude's mind magic, the bilans wouldn't affect them. As long as no one saw the wound on her palm, questioning why she hadn't healed it as a Life Guardian, she would be fine.

Racing out of the courtyard, yet trying to look as inconspicuous as possible, she stopped a maid passing through the corridor. "Martine asked me to meet her by the Scribestone. Do you know where that is?"

The maid's face paled, clearly shocked that Dagmara was even speaking to her. "In the royal library, Princess," she said before gesturing to a stunning silver door.

"Thank you," Dagmara said before any more questions were asked. Luckily, she saw no one else in sight. She dashed to the library entrance and let herself in.

Shock rippled through her entire body at the grandeur of the space. The carpet was a patterned silver, and black banners hung from the rafters with the Ilusaurian crest. Bookshelves were stacked on either side, extending two stories tall. A few spiral staircases were spread throughout the space. The entire ceiling was a glass dome, allowing a pristine view of the starry night sky. The moon was aglow, so large that Dagmara questioned if this too was an illusion, or if the sky was really that beautiful.

On the other side of the library, across the entire stretch of the center alley, she saw a raised platform. It contained a different shade of bookshelves, spaced between floor to ceiling windows with silver curtains. In the center of the platform was a glass case with a silver book, resting on a circular table.

Dagmara raced forward, hearing her boots against the carpeted floor. There was seemingly no one else here, giving her the perfect opportunity.

Skipping up the stairs to the platform, she slid to a halt in front of the glass case. The book, glowing with magic, was the Ilusaurian Scribestone. She pressed her palms to the glass to slide it off, but it wouldn't budge. Examining the case more meticulously, she spotted a keyhole.

The Scribestone was locked.

"You need this to use it." A voice echoed through the room.

Whirling on her heel, she faced the door. Sabien was entering the library, shaking a ring with two golden keys. He had a smirk plastered to his face, as if he knew her plans were foiled and that he was holding the only solution. She watched as he slipped them into his back pocket before letting the heavy door shut behind him.

"What are you doing here?" Sabien asked.

"I could ask you the same thing," Dagmara replied, clasping her hands in front of her.

A dark laugh rumbled from Sabien's throat. He was still sauntering down the center aisle of the expansive library, approaching her.

He held up his hand, revealing a piece of parchment she hadn't noticed. "Business for the king," he said. "What's your excuse?"

"Waiting for Martine," said Dagmara. It wasn't entirely a lie.

He reached the platform and strode up the steps. Dagmara watched as he got taller and taller, until he finally reached the top of the platform. He approached her still, and she attempted to step away but felt the glass of the Scribestone against her back.

A grin creased on his face when he stopped only inches from her. "I like that I make you nervous."

"I'm not nervous."

"All the muscles in your neck just tensed. I would say you're nervous."

Swallowing hard, Dagmara tried to relax, but could practically feel the weight of his gaze as his eyes roamed her neck.

"As far as I know," he continued, "the king hasn't granted you permission to use the Scribestone."

"I was only looking at it."

His eyebrows raised. "Your lies may work on other people, but they don't work on me."

Her breath caught in her throat.

"See?" Sabien reached out and ran a single knuckle down the length of her neck. "It's a dead giveaway."

He shifted away from her, and his absence struck her nearly as much as his proximity. He approached the last bookshelf, pushing the billowing curtains aside as he grabbed a burgundy box off the shelf that rested next to a glass globe. She watched as he cracked the lid and hid the parchment he was holding.

Sabien had said he was here for official business. What exactly was on that piece of paper?

She had to find out.

But she had to warn Queen Bernadette about the famine that threatened Ilusauri, and what that meant for Azurem. If it were true all the Life Guardians were gone, Azurem could fall to the same fate.

Yet, if she convinced Sabien to let her use the Scribestone, he would undoubtedly watch over her shoulder. She had to get the key and use it without him watching.

There was only one way she could reach into his back pocket without him noticing.

She had seduced men before. How hard could it be to seduce the Captain of the Ilusaurian Guard who happened to be extremely seductive himself?

She shifted her corset slightly, feeling the throwing stars stitched into the ribbing, as she inched it lower. Then she approached him, leaning against the floor length window as he set the box back on the bookshelf, concealing the slip of paper inside. She took the curtain in her grasp, running her fingers against it. "So tell me, how does a..." she paused for effect, sizing-up his figure with her gaze, "...strapping man like yourself become the captain? You must be great at giving orders."

A muscle in his jaw ticked. He raised his arm, placing his palm against the glass as he leaned forward and began closing the distance between them. "I do more than give orders," said Sabien.

Dagmara let the curtain slip away as she cocked her head, inching closer. "Such as?"

Sabien lifted his opposite hand, tilting her chin up with his knuckles. "What are you up to?"

She could feel her stomach churning, her neck completely exposed as she was forced to look directly up at him.

"I'm bored here," Dagmara replied, "and you look fun."

He shifted closer, his lips nearly touching hers. His breath was warm as he said, "I am. Why don't you find out for yourself?"

This was her moment, and she took it. Her lips slammed against his, and he kissed her back with such ferocity it was almost all consuming. His tongue was instantly in her mouth, causing a soft whimper to escape from her lips. The noise elicited a sensual growl from him. His hands went to her waist, gripping her before pressing her against the glass window. She wrapped her arms around his neck, entangling her fingers in his thick hair. The kiss was relentless, and Dagmara nearly forgot the reason she had kissed him in the first place.

She slid one hand down his back, easily finding his belt. She lingered there for a moment, not wanting to draw too much attention to her maneuvers. One of his hands shifted, finding the back of her neck. He gripped the base of her hair, yanking her head back to deepen the kiss. His other hand traced her hip, finding every curve of her body.

Her fingers found the keyring in his back pocket and withdrew them, careful not to make a sound. Her mission was accomplished, but she could let him keep kissing her all night.

Then a memory flashed against the back of her eyelids. The last man she had kissed was Prince Aleksy. The thought sharpened in her mind, and she could suddenly feel every inch of herself. She felt the buttons of Sabien's shirt digging against her chest. She felt his teeth scrape her bottom lip. She felt his hand tighten around her thigh as he touched her body—no wait. There was something wrong about the way his hand felt her leg. He wasn't running it against her curves. He was grabbing clumps of her dress, and not in a way to lift it up.

The poison vials in her pocket clanked against one another as he found them through the folds of the fabric. If he reached into her pocket and withdrew one, her mission would be over.

He was kissing her for the exact same reason she was. He was trying to find out what was hidden in her pockets.

She shoved her free hand between their bodies and forced him away. He didn't back off gently, taking much more of Dagmara's strength to separate them than she would have liked. She slithered out from underneath him, creating space between them as she hid the keys behind her back.

"This isn't right," she panted. The way her body reacted said otherwise, but she forced that thought away. "I'm marrying the king." She was lightheaded, and wasn't sure if it was because of Sabien or her health. She quickly stepped closer to the circular table and leaned her weight against it.

Sabien laughed, running a hand through his hair to fix what she had messed up. "Whatever you say, Princess," he said, though there was a hint of sarcasm.

"I'm serious," she said, a new annoyance erupting inside her. First he kissed her to find out what was in her pockets—then he was laughing about it? "You should go."

He leaned his shoulder against the bookcase, crossing his arms. "You could've asked for the keys."

Shock rippled through her body. She knew he was feeling her up only to search her pockets—of course he would know she was doing the same to him. They were too like-minded.

His eyes darted to her neck again, seeing her muscles constrict, and a smile reappeared on his face.

"But then you wouldn't have had the chance to kiss me," she said, revealing the keys and playing with them in front of her.

His grin turned wicked. "As much as I enjoyed that, I don't enjoy being used."

She scoffed. "My hands weren't the only ones roaming."

"What's in your pockets?" he asked.

"Wouldn't you like to know?"

"Would you rather I wait until your clothes are fully off before searching your pockets?"

Heat flushed her entire body, and the sudden rush nearly caused her to drop the keys. She cleared her throat, controlling her emotions. "I would rather use the Scribestone to check in on my mother after weeks of travel."

Sabien gestured to the glass case, "By all means."

A shadow flashed across her face as a bird flew toward the window, landing on a ledge outside. Her eyes narrowed, inspecting it. It was the same bird she saw on the balcony the first day she met King Claude.

Sabien glanced out the window, following her gaze, before raising an eyebrow. "What are you waiting for?" His head inclined toward the Scribestone.

With another glance out the window, the bird had vanished.

"N-Nothing," said Dagmara. She crossed to the case and inserted one of the keys, having luck with the first try. The lock clicked open, and the glass case unfolded. She reached her hand out and rested her palm against the stone, letting the mystical book read her identity. To her shock, letters began to appear on the page.

One message from Teos Zosia, Azurem.

A gasp escaped her lips.

"Who's Teos?"

Nearly jumping out of her shoes, Dagmara whirled around to face Sabien. "A little privacy maybe?"

"It's alright," he said. "I don't mind that you have a man in Azurem. I like my women to be experienced."

"Ew!" Dagmara blurted out before she could stop herself.

A curious expression crossed Sabien's face.

What was she doing? She couldn't let Sabien know that Teos was her brother. "I mean...I didn't mean..."

He held a hand up, "None of my business, I'll give you privacy." He flashed her a wink before descending the steps, leaving her alone on the platform. She could still feel his gaze, but knew he was too far away to read the text.

She quickly turned back to the Scribestone, waving her hand above it to uncover the message.

I know I have to start this message telling you not to worry about me. It's still just a cough at this point. Until I'm bedridden, I'm going to help any way I can. Someone out there murdered Aleksy, and it's not fair. For all I know, you're with the murderous King Claude now.

I'm hoping you get this as soon as you arrive. I convinced Queen Bernadette to ask the border knights for a list of everyone that entered into Azurem the month prior to the coronation. Only three Ilusaurians crossed, arriving the day before the coronation. Mael Revel, Lyam Desco, and Samuel Arsenault. It fits—three Ilusaurians and three assassins. They're supposedly ambassadors, but Bernadette had never heard of them.

I analyzed the seal on their entrance papers, and it was a real ambassador seal. They weren't forged, which means King Claude signed off on these people entering Azurem whether they are fake aliases or not. Can you find out who they are?

I doubt it could be anyone else. Others who crossed would have had to pay a fortune to get their name removed from this official list. Perhaps that Ilusaurian who gave you the black eye paid to remove his name from the list, but he would have to have a lot of money, so he would have to be important—of a noble or a higher status. I'll try to find out if anyone received suspiciously large paychecks.

Hope you're safe. Queen Bernadette doesn't know you swapped. I think she sent a letter to Magda and will be expecting a response though.

Your favorite partner in crime, T

It calmed her slightly to hear Teos wasn't declining as quickly as other children, but he could be hiding the truth so she didn't worry.

Dagmara's head spun. She committed the names he listed to memory, repeating them over and over. She had to find out who they were.

She looked over her shoulder, seeing Sabien watching her from afar. "Do you have a guidebook of all the official ambassadors and appointed liaisons?"

"First of all we don't have liaisons, we have governors," Sabien said, "but yes. Why?"

"My mother suggested learning about them before the engagement ball so I can make a good impression. Seeing as I didn't even know you have governors, it is probably a good idea," she said.

"It's upstairs. I can get it," he stated. "But I'm watching you. Don't run off with my keys."

"Wouldn't think of it." She flashed him a smile before watching him disappear behind a nearby bookshelf.

Then she quickly returned to the Scribestone, summoning a brand new message.

Thanks T, I don't know what I'd do without you. We really do make a good team. Find out if they departed from Azurem.
I'm safe, will talk soon. Please take care of yourself.

She sent it to Teos only, watching the ink evaporate before her eyes. No new message appeared. Where was Magda's letter? Had she made it to Flaustra safely?

Concern trickled through Dagmara, but she pushed it aside. Magda was fine. She had to be.

Then Dagmara composed a new message.

Queen Bernadette,
Magda and I have just arrived in Ilusauri, and we are taking a long time to settle in. The king has been nice so far. He warned us that the guardians are connected to the land. Have you noticed anything different about Azurem? Magda suggested taking precautions for a rough winter just in case.
She sends her love.
Dagmara

It was the best she could do without raising too much suspicion. Dagmara sent it off immediately, not allowing herself to think twice about it. She could hear a creak of the floorboards above, and a shadow cast over the balcony. Sabien was still collecting the guidebook.

Glancing over at the bookshelf, Dagmara set her gaze on the box. She had to know what the parchment was that Sabien had stored away for the king. Racing over, she quickly peeled back the lid and pulled out the top piece of paper. Unfolding it, she revealed a map. It was drawn in charcoal, but the landscape was evidently Ilusauri. There was one, bold stroke of ink circling a city directly south of the castle.

Nouchenne.

Why was that city highlighted and the others weren't? And why did that name sound so familiar?

Footsteps alerted Dagmara that Sabien was descending the staircase. She quickly folded the paper, slipped it back in the box and covered her tracks. She returned to the center of the platform and began closing the glass case, locking away the Scribestone as Sabien approached with a book under his arm.

"Keys," he asked, holding out his palm.

Dagmara returned the keys.

Then Sabien held out the giant black book. "Here is the current administration."

"Thank you," said Dagmara, reaching out to take it, but he quickly withdrew.

"What do I get in return?"

Startled, Dagmara's expression withered. "I gave you your keys."

He chuckled, "No, I want something else." He took a step closer. "Show me what trinkets you have in your pocket."

"Don't be rude," Dagmara said. She reached out once more, but he held the book above her head. Her chest nearly smacked into his, and he took advantage of her proximity. He grabbed her chin, leaning closer.

"It's only fair to reciprocate generosity," he said.

She batted his hand away, jerking back. "I'm a guardian, of course I'm generous."

His lip curled into a vicious grin. "I see right through you. Who are you trying to fool?"

Her stomach plummeted. Her skin prickled, and she felt the shift in her breathing.

Then he grabbed her wrist, lifting her hand up to reveal her palm. "A little odd for a guardian with healing abilities to have a recent wound, isn't it?"

Dagmara tried to pull away, but his grip was too tight. "It's an old scar."

"Really?" Sabien shifted his grasp, digging his thumb into the center of her palm.

A gasp escaped her lips as pain surged through her hand, rippling up her arm. "Stop!" she shrieked, shoving his chest.

To both of their surprise, the library door opened, and Martine entered. "There you are!" Dagmara's guard exclaimed.

Sabien immediately relinquished Dagmara, stepping away.

Yanking her hand to her chest, Dagmara examined the mark. The cut had reopened, and a drop of blood was pooling in the center of her palm. She glowered at Sabien before hiding her hand behind her back.

"I thought I..." Martine's voice trailed off as her eyes flicked back and forth from Dagmara to her captain.

"Martine," Sabien said, his voice suddenly becoming authoritarian. "You have one responsibility: watch the princess. Care to explain where you've been?"

Her lips parted, but nothing came out.

"I told you I was waiting for her," Dagmara cut through the silence. She trotted down the platform stairs, escaping the captain.

"I thought you needed this?" Sabien called, waving the book.

"Martine will help me," replied Dagmara. Her steps quickened, almost thinking Sabien would chase her down. She didn't look back as she reached Martine's side and interlaced their arms. She nearly pulled Martine out into the hallway, not knowing if she was leading them in the correct direction.

"Are you alright?" Martine asked. "We found the guard and—"

"He fainted, and I went to get help."

"You're shaking," Martine noted.

"I'm fine," Dagmara's response was curt, but she wouldn't let go of Martine's arm, feeling a strange sense of security.

"Was Sabien—"

"I said I'm fine."

Martine nodded. She fell silent for a moment, and Dagmara eventually slowed her pace when she felt out of breath. Her heart continued to hammer against her ribcage even when she slowed her speed.

"What did you tell Sabien I would help you with?" Martine asked.

Dagmara glanced at her. "I'm glad you asked."

CHAPTER 27
Magdalena

When Magda and Odie reached the circular-shaped intersection, she knew they were free from Ishani and her officers. She found a dark alleyway and tore open the letter with Queen Sanyal's seal, praying it was an invitation to the ball. Magda's eyes scanned frantically over the contents.

Ishani,
    I expect you to be at Kiran's birthday ball. It is the least you can do. I know you are receiving these letters, and I don't know why you are giving me the silent treatment.
    If you won't come for me, at least come for the guilds. I have invited all of the guild leaders in an attempt to work out a new trade agreement that will benefit our kingdom.

The letter wasn't signed, but it was clear it came from the queen, for it was stamped with her crest on the outside.

Unfortunately, for Magda, it wasn't an invitation. She cursed under her breath, knowing she would have to either go back to Ishani's ship, or steal an invitation from another guild leader. At least this letter confirmed that *all* the guild leaders had an invitation.

She swung her knapsack from her shoulder, placing the letter inside, before putting it back on her back.

However, she had already wasted the day going all the way to the docks and back. Maybe Ishani's invitation was so valuable that it was kept on her person. Either way, Magda had to make a new plan.

It was already dark outside, and she didn't want to be out on the streets with Odie at this hour, especially with the dog-snatchers possibly around. So, Magda asked a storekeeper if there were any dog-friendly inns in Eloquas. Luckily, they mentioned a place named 'Mystic Sonata', known for its popular musical shows as well as its luxurious rooms.

Magda followed the directions she was given to another intersection. The city was vibrant in the evening, and even though the stars were already out, it seemed as if the population was just rushing to dinner. The narrow streets were packed with tables, where city-dwellers laughed over heaping plates of food and drink. In between buzzing restaurants were more shops where owners attempted to sell Magda fabrics, tea, and jewelry.

When Magda reached the Mystic Sonata, she could hear bombastic music and the shouts of a dozen people spilling out. She was grateful to stay in an inn tonight and get a good night's sleep—she was not sleeping in a random man's shack any longer.

When she entered, she looked past the desk and realized she had stumbled upon a wedding celebration. The otherwise simple building was full of brightly colored flowers, and a bride wearing a jeweled red and yellow gown danced in the center with her groom.

At the front of the large space, was a raised stage with seats for the couple, and in each corner, were musicians playing a lively tune. Much to her surprise, at the front of the string players—was the violinist Ravi next to a few other string players, although he didn't notice her. Why was he everywhere that she went? Magda didn't believe in fate, but it was as if the ancestral guardians were giving her a message.

"Can I help you?" asked a woman at the front desk.

"Yes, one room for me and my dog," Magda answered before giving her the coins.

The woman accepted the money before handing Magda the keys. Despite the inn being labeled as 'dog friendly', the innkeeper didn't seem too happy to see Odie. "Your room is upstairs. Number ten."

Magda thanked her, before stepping forward into the large music hall. She focused on Ravi at the front of the room.

He was cheerful as he took the lead for the next song, running his fingers wildly along the violin's neck as his bow danced along the strings in broad, slurred strokes. He added additional flourishes, his fingers gliding effortlessly towards the bridge as the notes ascended.

While he played, a joyful smile creased his face, and he spoke lively messages to lead the musicians behind him, allowing them to accompany him effortlessly. He also moved with the dancers, stepping forward and backward on the stage, even twirling around once as he stomped his feet, not missing a single bow-stroke.

At the end of the song, the room ended in exhilarated cries, cheering Ravi on in loud applause that enraptured the entire music hall. The bride and groom ended in a happy embrace.

While she watched the couple, Magda couldn't help but think of Dagmara, who was all alone in Ilusauri, putting on a marriage show to find out more information about Claude. She couldn't imagine that a wedding celebration to Claude would be this joyful. Magda wondered what would happen after this entire adventure was over, and if she would be forced to go through with the sham marriage and take Dagmara's place.

What's worse—Claude was investigating strange locations all over the kingdoms, asking Guild Captains to report what they had found out back to the Mad King. What was he searching for?

Someone placed a hand on Magda's shoulder, breaking her out of her trance. "If it isn't the beautiful woman from Azurem that has caught the attention of the entire city." Ravi greeted her with a smile.

"Don't give me that," Magda said with an annoyed tone, but she couldn't help but smile in return. "You were great up there."

"Thanks. I have a short break now. How about a dance?"

"I don't know any of these dances. Music is quite different here. I'm not sure I could get the rhythm right."

"All you need is the right partner," he offered. "Maybe the sound of our footsteps on the dance floor is just what this song needs."

"Maybe," Magda spoke. Truthfully, she wanted to dance with him more than anything, getting swept away in the music and forgetting about her problems and the guilt that ate at her from the inside. While she had met many people on her adventure to Flaustra, a deep loneliness was getting painful to bear, and anytime she thought of her family she risked breaking down in tears. As if sensing her emotions, Odie nuzzled against her knee.

Ravi noticed her change in demeanor as well, and changed the subject, "So, did you get the invitation?" he asked.

"Unfortunately not. I scoured Ishani's entire office, but it wasn't with her usual stack of letters."

"She probably keeps it on her person."

"My thoughts exactly," replied Magda.

"Alright. We'll get an invitation somehow. But first, are you sure you won't dance with me?"

Magda leaned her back against the wall, letting out a soft smile. "I think our relationship is better off the dance floor."

Ravi stepped closer to her, putting his arm on the wall next to her head and leaning close. "Oh, so you're saying we have a relationship then?"

Magda bit her lip. Something inside was intensifying, drawing her toward any type of comfort. All that she wanted was to be held, having someone validate her intense emotions and fears. But was that person Ravi, or could she be drawn to anyone in this moment as long as she could find some sense of release and respite?

"I'm not taking no for an answer," Ravi said. "If you're making me help you find an invitation, then I am demanding a dance." He grabbed Magda's hand, yanking her forward to the stage. Then he threw her bag up with his violin case, before shouting to one of his musician friends, "Hey, watch this dog for a minute for me. Your career depends on it."

Then Ravi dragged her out onto the middle of the dance floor. When they crashed into the bride and groom, they acknowledged them happily, and Magda realized that Ravi knew them both.

"You trust that musician to look after Odie?" Magda peered over his shoulder.

"Yes, we've been friends forever."

They jumped into the dance with the others, and Magda found herself drawing upon her elementary dance lessons where she had a private tutor visit from all of the foreign kingdoms, teaching both her and Aleksy about the world's dances. Some of the steps were vaguely familiar, and Magda did her best to watch and keep up.

For the first time since the attack at the fortress, she genuinely laughed as Ravi spun her around, pulling her body close to his in a tight embrace as they maneuvered between the other couples. She remembered performing these exact steps with Aleksy, but for some reason the memories weren't painful but joyous. There was something about being in Ravi's arms that helped her forget the pain, and the intense aching in her heart was redirected into a strange emotion that made her entire body flush.

When the dance was over, the guests around the circle let a huge cheer go up in the air. But she and Ravi stood—silent—as they looked at each other.

Ravi reached up and brushed Magda's hair out of her face, before letting his hand circle down to the side of her neck.

Magda pulled away. "I have to go."

"Go where?" he asked.

As much as she wanted to not be alone, she knew that if she gave into her desires now, it would quickly become impassioned rather than genuine. She said, "I don't know."

"Are you sure you don't want to stay? Maybe I know your favorite song and can play it for you," he said with a twinkle in his eyes.

"I can't."

Magda walked up to the stage, where she saw Odie sitting at the foot of Ravi's musician friend, watching Magda intently. "Come, Odie," she called him. Then she turned and headed towards the door, but she heard Ravi come up behind her. "Is something wrong?" he asked.

"I'm sorry," Magda said, turning toward him. "It's not you. It's just been a long day, and I need to get some sleep."

"Do you even have somewhere to stay?" he asked, raising his eyebrows.

"Yes, here actually," Magda smirked, knowing for once she had figured out something in this foreign kingdom. Then she added, "and my favorite song is the Azuremi Waltz."

"A classic."

"You should get back up there." Magda referenced the musicians on stage. "Please don't stop playing on my account."

Ravi smiled. "The music is brighter when you're here. You can stay a while longer if you want. It will probably be too loud to sleep anyways. And..." he touched her hair to brush it back behind her ears, and acted like he was going to say something else, but then stopped.

Magda reached up and brushed her hand against his. "We hardly know each other."

Ravi stepped forward, linking his arms at her waist, pulling her close as if they were on the dance floor once more. "What if I want to know more about you?"

Magda's heart fluttered, and something fiery and emotional pulled her closer to him. But a stronger voice in her head was saying no.

Suddenly, Odie jumped up on Ravi, knocking them apart, and

making the two burst into laughter. After calming down, Magda said, "I have to get some sleep."

Ravi seemed to understand. "Alright. Tomorrow I'll be on the streets again, and try to listen for any words of guild leaders that are going to the birthday ball. I'll be here playing the rest of the week. Just come down tomorrow night, and I'll tell you what I've found out."

Magda couldn't help a smile crease across her face at the thought of seeing him again, and her stomach turned with butterflies like it did with a new crush. "I'll see you soon then."

With that, she turned to head up the stairs, Odie at her heel. Soon Magda found room ten and used her key to open the door before locking it shut. It was a small space, with a bed and two side tables, as well as a table and chair, but the decorations and portraits on the wall were bright red and yellow, giving the room an aura of luxury.

Odie entered first, sniffing around the room with a wagging tail. Then he circled a few times before jumping up onto the bed.

Magda smiled. Odie always slept right next to her, despite Urszula's qualms that animals shouldn't be on the bed. He would always act like he was sleeping on the floor, before hopping into Magda's bed at the last second. Clearly, with Urszula in Ilusauri, Odie could do whatever he wanted.

Quickly, Magda pulled the chair over to the door, placing it against it, so that no one could enter. Then, she hung up her outdoor clothes over the bed frame, remaining in her undergarments. Finally, she spilled out the contents of her knapsack, counting her remaining money. She still had enough.

Then Magda laid back on the bed, staring up at the ceiling. Her thoughts ran wild, doubting everything. She knew deep down that she should head back to the Flaustran palace this instant, revealing herself as Princess Magdalena so she could speak to Queen Sanyal. However, she couldn't reveal her identity just yet. What if the assassins who killed her father and brother had followed her here? She couldn't announce she was in the city. And she couldn't let the word spread that Princess Magdalena was in Flaustra, rather than in Ilusauri about to marry King Claude.

Her hands reached across the bed, stroking Odie's fur. It was then Magda realized how homesick she was. Her father and brother were dead, and she had no idea when she would see her mother again. The loneliness ate away at her, and even though she heard the joyous music from the party downstairs, she couldn't have felt more isolated. It was as if she was in a different dimension—one that was entirely silent.

For a moment, she considered going back downstairs, talking more with Ravi, just so she wouldn't be without company. But she knew if she invited him up to her room she would surely do something she regretted, just to feel something—anything. Just to be held by someone.

Magda turned over and buried her face in Odie's fur, crying herself to sleep to the sound of the violin.

CHAPTER 28
Dagmara

"And you're certain?" Dagmara asked her guard.

"My answer won't change no matter how many times you ask, Princess," Martine replied. "To be on the royal guard I have to memorize all the appointments for security reasons. Mael Revel, Lyam Desco, and Samuel Arsenault don't exist."

Dagmara's brow furrowed, remembering the three men her brother had told her were on the border register. Which meant they were false aliases—but they had papers signed by the king himself. That had to be evidence that the king sent the assassins, right? She only had to confirm those three were assassins. Hopefully, Teos would find out more about them soon.

"Is there anyone with authority to grant citizenship or falsify papers?"

"Lionel Floquet, the governor of Sailonne, also manages border regulations, but none of our papers are falsified," Martine insisted.

Lionel...Dagmara would have to find out who that man was. If she could confirm that he had not created the aliases, then all leads pointed to King Claude.

"Why do you ask? Who are those men?" Martine interrupted Dagmara's thoughts.

"What do you know about the town Nouchenne?" Dagmara countered, avoiding Martine's questions.

Martine's head jerked back, her composure faltering for a brief moment. "Nouchenne was my hometown."

That's not what Dagmara was expecting. Her tactic shifted as she attempted to play into Martine's emotions. "How long did you live there?"

"Until I joined the guard at fourteen."

"And your family still lives there?"

There was a pause. "No." Martine replied.

"I've heard so much about it, and I would like to visit. Will you accompany me?"

Martine's brow furrowed. "Nouchenne was cleared by order of the king. That is why my family is no longer there but rather in the neighboring village."

Dagmara had heard the rumors that King Claude had eradicated towns throughout Ilusauri with no warning. Cleared? What did it actually mean?

"Why was it cleared?" Dagmara ventured.

"I don't know."

"You don't know?" Dagmara's mouth was agape. "You don't know why the king is clearing towns?"

"No."

"But Nouchenne is your hometown. Aren't you curious?"

"It is my duty to serve the king, not ask questions of him," Martine snapped. "Why are you so curious?"

"I know nothing about him, and yet, I am to marry him," Dagmara replied.

"He is an honorable leader."

"Well, you're trained to say that."

A change of emotion flashed across Martine's face, but it was gone before Dagmara could decipher it. Was it shock? Or guilt?

"I'm going to see the town for myself," Dagmara continued. "You can join me if you want. You can see your hometown for yourself, and maybe get your own answers as to why your family was thrown out."

"We're not allowed to go to cleared towns, nor are you allowed to leave the castle without his permission," Martine objected.

"I'll find a way to get there," Dagmara responded. "Either you can come with me, or not."

Martine folded her arms in front of her. "Will you use another sleeping potion on me?"

A cold shudder tore through Dagmara's body.

"That's right, I know what you did," Martine continued. "I am very suspicious of you, Princess, and so is the king."

And so was Sabien. Dagmara clearly needed to pick up the pace of this mission.

"You're not even the slightest bit suspicious as to why the king is clearing towns?" Dagmara asked. She added for effect, "Why was your family kicked out of their home?"

The wheels visibly turned in Martine's head. Then she finally spoke, "I'm only accompanying you to keep you safe, and to avoid more sleeping potions, not because I'm questioning why the king cleared out Nouchenne. Understood?"

Unable to suppress her smile, Dagmara nodded, "Understood."

The following morning, before the sun was rising over the horizon, the two set out to Nouchenne. Dagmara needed to make sure that she wouldn't be out when the sun was at its highest. There was no doubt it would drain all her energy, and she needed to save her energy for the upcoming engagement ball. Nouchenne wasn't too far from the castle, leaving them plenty of time to investigate. Martine had ordered the stablehands to prep two horses, and they set off south to the town. Dagmara had bandaged her hand and was wearing leather riding gloves, and whatever Martine may have seen in the library, she didn't bring up again.

They rode in silence for a long time, Dagmara racking her brain for the king's motive. Why was he clearing out entire towns? She hoped going to Nouchenne would give her answers. There was no doubt, although the guard tried to hide it, that Martine wanted to know the answer as badly as Dagmara, if for different reasons.

When they were well outside the castle walls and cresting over the top of a hill, the sun began to cast an orange glow along the brown grass. The air was filled with a morning fog, and Claude's castle had disappeared into the mist far behind them. The grass was withered, alternating between yellow and brown hues. Dust flew up underneath the horses' hooves as though it were a coating of ash.

When they reached the top of the hill, Dagmara yanked the reins of her horse, breaking his canter. He skidded, causing a spray of dirt to fly up from the ground, and tugged against the bridle in agitation. Yet Dagmara couldn't move, for her attention was fixated on the scene before her.

In front of them, at the bottom of the hill, was an expansive field. It was so large that it vanished into the murky fog, seeming to continue endlessly. The field was littered with bones—small bones, large portions of skeletons, and animal carcasses. Twigs and brambles unwound from the earth, and a thick layer of ash coated the area in a gray blanket.

Martine had turned her horse around and was approaching Dagmara at a trot. "You alright?" she asked, and her horse stopped with her back to the field.

Dagmara knew her expression gave away her surprise. "What is this?" she asked. However, she wanted to know if Claude was behind this more than anything. There were hundreds of bodies—thousands of bones. There was no way to bury all of these if someone wanted to.

"The Field of Valor," Martine announced. "I believe you have a sea of scarlet?"

Racking her brain, Dagmara remembered the poppy field Magda always went to on her rides, beside the waterfalls. The elders claimed the flowers were markings of the deceased, and the field was the gravesite for the fallen from the war for magic. The war was centuries ago, and Dagmara had always assumed the poppy field was more an abstract memorial.

"It used to be covered with irises," Martine continued, filling the silence. Her back was purposefully to the field, but Dagmara couldn't seem to look away. "The day King Percival Mirage—Claude's father—was killed, the irises began to transform to what you see here. It certainly makes you question if the stories about the war for magic were actually true."

Finally able to tear her eyes from the endless graveyard, Dagmara met Martine's gaze, surprised to find an expression of remorse. "Do you believe the stories? About the war against the First Prince?"

"His Majesty believes they are real."

"I asked what you believe," Dagmara countered.

Martine hesitated, fiddling with the reins in her grip. Her eyebrows narrowed as if she wasn't sure what her answer was at first, and she was simply trained to answer with the king's rules. After a long pause, she spoke, her voice timid, "It doesn't all add up. The First Prince wanted to kill his siblings before entering the trials, something against all sacred tradition. Then all the guardians teamed up to get rid of him. According to legend, the First Prince was the most powerful guardian to ever exist. So why would he try to kill his siblings before the trials if his win was practically guaranteed? And why are the guardians connected to their territory as though they are the land's lifeline?"

Dagmara looked to the field, littered in bones. She answered under her breath, "I don't know."

A few hours later, they arrived at Nouchenne. Dagmara's chest and lower back were wet with sweat, and she wiped her brow with the back of her wrist. She had brought everything with her to face the worst, her throwing stars, her stunning potion, and even the jasny light flash her brother had invented. Martine, on the other hand, had daggers lining her thighs, and a sword at her side.

The morning mist had cleared, and the entire village came into view at once. Dirt paths cut through gray, stone buildings, and their pointed roofs were interspersed by rain clouds. Around the two-story houses, were once healthy trees and flower beds that now were crippled with blight. Tan, scorched grass extended out into the fields, making the entire village a mournful color. There were no distinguishing characteristics—just rows of melancholy houses with tangled weeds, surviving in a thick coat of dust.

As they neared closer, the buildings grew larger, but the atmosphere remained quiet. At the border of town, Martine spoke first.

"Shall we dismount here, explore on foot?"

"No," Dagmara replied. For one, she wanted to conserve her energy. She couldn't walk long distances without easily exerting herself. Secondly, she didn't know what they would encounter and if they would have to make a hasty exit. "Let's keep going."

They ventured into the town, proceeding down the main road. The dirt road narrowed, turning into an alleyway. Dagmara pulled her horse forward in the lead, both sides of the road blocking her vision due to the thick, stone houses. Who knew how long it would take to find out why the townspeople were cleared of this area.

"What if it's an illness?" Martine asked, a new quiver in her voice. "What if we are exposing ourselves to something here?"

That hadn't crossed Dagmara's mind. It was too late, anyway, as they were already here. "It can't be," Dagmara denied. "That's too easy. Wouldn't the king have told people that reason? Besides, I'm sure the villagers would've been put in quarantine, not sent to a neighboring village."

Yet as they rounded the corner, turning into the center of town, the answer was directly before them.

In the main square, a gaping hole swallowed the central fountain and the rock foundation of another building. The cobblestone crumbled into the depths, and a line in the earth was drawn away from the hole, like a river running away from a lake.

"What is this?" Dagmara asked, dismounting from her horse and tying him to a nearby post. The sinkhole in the earth didn't look like it was created from an earthquake or natural disaster. It was eerily precise. It would've been a perfect circle if the broken cobblestone path didn't give it the illusion that it was uneven. On closer inspection, Dagmara saw that the line running away from the central hole seemed to extend deeper into the ground, as though it were a tunnel leading into the earth. And Dagmara wanted to know where it led.

"Come on," Dagmara said, approaching the crater.

"Maybe we shouldn't go down there," Martine objected.

"I want to know," Dagmara replied. "Are you coming with me, or am I going alone?"

Martine let out a sigh. "Let me go first," Martine said, having already dismounted from her horse. She approached the gaping hole and slowly descended. Her tactic was nearly a crawl, squatting and putting her hands on the ground before dropping to the next stable piece of earth below.

Following Martine's every move, down to her hand placement, Dagmara descended. Curiosity brewed deep inside her, and the same interest exuded from her guard. She climbed over broken chunks of rock, fumbled over the statue that was once at the center of the fountain, and even uneasily crossed boards and wooden planks that jutted out from the nearby structures. By the time they reached the bottom of the crater, she could no longer see the town. They were so deep in the earth, that all that was visible to them was the rubble they descended upon.

At the bottom of the crater, there was a small crevice in the wall. It was narrow enough that Martine had to turn sideways to shimmy through, but wide enough that she could slide through without touching either side. Dagmara turned her body sideways as well, and followed Martine. The crack in the earth at ground-level seemed far above them, but allowed the sunlight to cast enough of a beam for them to see their surroundings.

Martine's armor clattered as she stepped out of the narrow crack and into an open space. It was a tunnel that descended slightly downward. Relief flooded through Dagmara as she too exited the crevice. The two proceeded toward a light in the far distance. Then they emerged into a cave.

The cavern seemed to be the end of the underground space, since there were no other exits Dagmara could make out. The ground underneath them was stone, and another wide hole was in the center of the room.

Crossing to the hole, Dagmara peered down and only saw darkness. Even she was not brave enough—or stupid enough—to jump in and find out what secrets lay beyond.

The walls in the cavern were etched with various symbols. Dagmara scanned the entirety of the stone, her eyes landing on letters. Squinting her eyes, she saw a sentence written in large text. The words were strikingly similar to words in the Ilusaurian language, and she almost thought the sentence was in Ilusaurian at first. However, she couldn't translate it.

Dagmara's head began to spin. She reached out to the wall for support, then slowly sat. She could sense Martine glancing in her direction, but Dagmara ignored her guard. As long as she sat nonchalantly, maybe Martine wouldn't catch on that something was wrong with her.

Dagmara caught her breath, letting her vision refocus, and spotted a disfigured boulder against the wall. Her eyes narrowed, unable to make it out in the dim light. She rose slowly despite her throbbing head and neared closer, realizing it wasn't a boulder at all.

It was an animal.

CHAPTER 29
Dagmara

Darting over to the figure, Dagmara dropped to a crouch to examine it closer. "Martine!"

Martine was circling the perimeter of the room, running her hand against the stone to confirm there were no other exits. She halted, immediately at Dagmara's side.

On closer inspection, this animal wasn't anything Dagmara recognized. It was the size of a wolf, but its fur was an iridescent silver, and its underbelly was replaced with something scale-like. Its fur had a violet tint. Its jowls were gaunt, mimicking a skeleton, and its rib cage protruded from its chest at an awkward angle. Long talons extended from its webbed paws, and the creature's eyes were sealed shut.

What was this animal? Was it responsible for the crater or the clearing of the town?

"It looks dead," Martine noted.

She was right, of course. Its chest was unmoving.

"Then we shouldn't touch it," Dagmara replied, shuddering. She rose from the ground, returning her attention to the sentence on the wall.

"Martine, what language is this?" Dagmara asked.

Martine straightened, back on her feet. "It is a dialect of Ilusaurian, usually only spoken in the southern region."

"Any chance you speak it?"

"It is what we spoke in Nouchenne." Martine nodded, taking a step closer and squinting her eyes in the dim light.

Impatiently, Dagmara waited. It was no longer than eight words, so it couldn't be taking her that long to translate. What was taking Martine so long? Would she tell her the truth of what was etched into the stone?

Then Martine snapped her head to Dagmara, her eyes surprisingly wide. "Tell me again why you wanted to come here."

Dagmara startled. "What?"

"Tell me."

"I was curious."

"Enough of the lies, Princess," Martine demanded, her hand shifting to the sword at her waist. "Why?"

"I saw it circled on a map," Dagmara blurted out.

"A map?"

"Sabien said it was business for the king, and that's all I know," Dagmara said. She gestured to the wall. "What does it say?"

"It says 'The First Prince will rise.'" Martine's face was hardened like a soldier, but a glimmer of fear flashed across her eyes.

A pit formed in Dagmara's stomach. The First Prince. That is who the assassins were connected to. Why would King Claude have this city cleared? Was he the one who wrote the text on the wall?

There was a clatter of hooves above them, and both girls slipped into the shadows, away from the harsh light that cut through the opening in the earth. A shadow raced across the sun, and the loud hooves signaled that there were multiple horses above, moving fast.

"Are there others in town?" Dagmara whispered.

"There shouldn't be," Martine replied, withdrawing her sword carefully.

"Did you tell anyone we were coming here?" Dagmara reached

into her bodice, finding the edge of her throwing stars, ready to withdraw them.

Martine was quiet.

Snapping her head, Dagmara glared at her guard. "Did you?"

"Shhh," Martine held out her hand.

Suddenly Dagmara heard a faint noise. It was like a quiet shuffling on the cool floor, or a slight shift of fabric.

It was neither of those, however. It was the sound of the dead animal in the corner catching their scent.

With another sniff, the mysterious hound began to stir. The scales on its stomach seemed to radiate, and its eyes jolted open, revealing glowing circles beneath its lids. It pounced to its four massive paws, standing nearly four feet tall, its jaw opening to release a snarl. Drool fell from its massive canines before it launched itself forward.

Dagmara already held a throwing star in her hands and chucked it at the creature. It raked across the hound's cheek, causing it to stumble, but it didn't draw blood.

Martine launched herself across the cave, thrusting her sword underneath its neck. With a slick crunch, the sword went straight through the creature's throat. Martine kicked the hound to dislodge her sword, and it collapsed onto the stone with a harsh thud.

Martine reached down to pick up Dagmara's throwing star and examined it meticulously. "Where did you get these?"

Dagmara didn't have time to answer. She heard more snarls and her attention was pulled to the gaping hole in the center of the room. One by one, the massive hounds began to crawl their way into the open, their talons scratching against the stone. They clobbered into one another, each fighting for the surface.

"Run!" Martine yelled at Dagmara, widening her stance as she prepared to fight.

Nearly a dozen hounds were making their way out into the open, and it was impossible to fight them all. And yet, Dagmara knew she wouldn't be able to outrun them. However, it was either stay and be mauled to death, or run until her health gave out...then be mauled to death. She prayed her adrenaline would keep her heart in check.

"You can't fight them alone, come with me!" Dagmara screamed. "Run!" She withdrew the jasny bomb from her belt and chucked it at the center of the room. In one bright explosion, the cave shook, and a few hounds stumbled back into the depths of the pit.

Martine let out a shriek, but used the distraction to take off running toward the exit. They could both hear the thumping of the hounds' paws on the ground behind them. Dagmara severely underestimated their speed.

"Don't stop!" Martine yelled before turning around to face the nearest hound. It clobbered her to the ground in seconds. Martine crashed to her back, thrusting her sword upward, and it caught in the hound's massive jaw.

Skidding to a halt, Dagmara flung another throwing star at the hound who had Martine pinned. Her aim was true, this time lodging into a soft section directly behind its ear. It let out a loud cry before crumpling onto Martine in a heap.

The others were too close. Dagmara made eye contact with the nearest hound, seeing nothing but pure evil in its eyes. She stumbled back as the monster leapt for her, about to dig its talons into her chest. Moments before, a whiz of an arrow pierced through the air. It sliced through the scales of the hound, driving straight through its chest. The monster slammed against the wall and crumpled to the ground.

Glancing over her shoulder, Dagmara saw their rescuers. Claude stood in the center of the tunnel, flanked by his two guards. Pierre, the one who had pulled Dagmara from the balcony on the first day, was still holding the bow that saved her life. Claude wielded his shining sword, and the third man, his large size humorous in the narrow tunnel, wielded a longsword.

The king's eyes glowed silver in the dimly lit space, and three large dogs manifested.

"Get down!" Claude yelled, his voice booming.

Dagmara obeyed immediately, dropping to the stone as his three dogs leapt forward into the oncoming hounds. Watching in fascination, Dagmara noticed that they were merely a distraction. The monstrous hounds went after the dogs, but they were projections of Claude's mind and not a physical entity. The real hound's talons raked through the air, unable to make contact with something that didn't exist.

The burly guard raced into the chaos first, decapitating the first hound that leapt toward him.

Pierre fired an arrow into another violet creature's chest before skidding to the ground beside Martine. He shoved the dead beast off her and helped her to her feet.

Claude didn't race into battle. He strode into it. His dogs distracted the hounds so that Claude could slip behind one of the monsters and kill it in one blow.

Another creature leapt toward Claude, but he knocked it aside with his forearm before slaughtering it.

Blood splattered the walls, thick and black. The dozen hounds were eviscerated in moments. They stood no chance against the Guardian of the Mind and the Ilusaurian guards.

It was both horrifying and mesmerizing to watch how fluid Claude's motions were as he killed one after another. He wasn't even wearing armor, but voluntarily fought off the beasts. Dark blood splattered his clothes, his back muscles visible through the garment. Every thrust and stab of his sword should have sent pure fear through Dagmara, but there was an underlying attraction she didn't want to admit. By the guardians, the Mad King was a force to be reckoned with, and Dagmara wanted more.

After Claude slayed the final monster, the cavern fell silent. His two guards scanned for more threats while he stood still, eyeing the destruction before him.

"You alright?" Martine whispered, reaching underneath Dagmara's arm to help her to her feet.

"Fine," Dagmara responded, pulling away to stand on her own. As soon as she was upright, she met Claude's gaze.

He slammed his sword into its sheath before starting toward her. "What the hell were you thinking?"

Dagmara tried to step away, tripping over a dead hound. She had to think fast.

"I wanted to know why this town was evacuated," Dagmara admitted, hoping the truth would help her. She couldn't let him know that she had seen this town circled on Sabien's paper. Part of the truth was the best type of lie.

Claude's jaw ticked. "You didn't think to ask me?"

Dagmara's mouth parted but she quickly shut it. No, that had never crossed her mind. "Would you have told me the truth?"

"When have I lied to you thus far?" Claude countered.

"I..." Dagmara's throat tightened, her heart beating furiously inside her chest. Before she had a chance to respond, the king shifted his attention to her guard.

"And you accompanied her?" his voice roared.

Martine dipped her head, not meeting his gaze. "I'm sorry, Your Majesty."

"When a town is evacuated it means *no one* is allowed there," Claude stated. "I should have you removed."

"This isn't her fault," Dagmara insisted. "You could have told her why her family was evacuated."

Claude jerked his chin back as if the statement offended him.

"She's the one who warned me," Pierre blurted out from across the tunnel. "If it wasn't for Martine we wouldn't have made it here in time."

Dagmara's jaw dropped. She thought she could trust Martine to keep this a secret, but she instead chose to tell Claude's guard?

"Right?" Pierre asked in Ilusaurian, looking to the large guard for support.

The burly man was busy wiping off blood from his longsword. He shrugged, not even glancing up.

"I'll decide whether Martine keeps her position," Claude stated, switching the conversation back to Azuremi. "You two are lucky we were seconds behind you. The hounds seek out anyone who possesses magic. They wake up when they smell magic."

"They target...guardians?" Martine asked.

Dagmara felt her blood turn to ice. The hound didn't wake when Dagmara went near it, and she knew Martine had already made that connection.

Claude's eyes darkened. "They wake when they sense magic nearby."

He was under the assumption that Dagmara woke the hounds, and he arrived in time. The king had no idea that it was in fact him who had woken the hounds.

"You are not to leave the castle without permission." Claude pointed a finger at Dagmara. "You are not in Azurem, Princess. Ilusauri isn't safe to go anywhere you please. I didn't clear this town for my own enjoyment."

Then Dagmara noticed Claude's forearm. His brace was ripped off, revealing his flesh which was raked with a large scratch from the hound's talons. Claude noticed Dagmara's gaze, instantly seeing the wound for himself.

Claude cleared his throat and in front of Dagmara's eyes, the wound vanished.

Dagmara gasped, seeing his forearm perfectly smooth and free from injury. "You can heal yourself?"

"I'm not a Life Guardian," Claude snapped. "I'll take care of it later."

So he hadn't healed it like Dagmara had watched Aleksy heal his wounds. Claude was only masking the wound—showing Dagmara what he wanted her to see. Claude could hide anything he wanted from her, and she wouldn't be the wiser.

"Enough of this!" Claude bellowed. "Everyone back to the castle before more of them find us."

Claude stormed off, and his two guards instantly followed.

Martine approached Dagmara and extended a throwing star toward her.

Accepting the weapon, Dagmara tucked it into her bodice. "Thank you."

"Of course...Princess," Martine replied, as if the word was difficult to say.

Dagmara knew she was one mistake away from having her cover blown.

CHAPTER 30
Magdalena

Magda found herself once again in the void. She was alone, except for the eerie voice that raked against her temples, sending a chill down her spine.

"They're coming for you..." the voice said.

This time, Magda felt more physically present in the space. She looked at her hands, turning them over and taking in how real the dream felt.

"They're coming now," the voice repeated, this time more urgent. "You're in danger."

Magda jerked upright, hearing the sound of Odie growling in her ear. Outside her room she heard shouting between the innkeeper and a rough, male voice.

"What's going on?" Magda looked at Odie before leaping off the bed and pressing her ear to the door to listen in:

"I have one hundred witnesses putting that dog and the Azuremi girl at your inn last night. No one saw them leave. Where are they?"

Magda gasped. She recognized the voice. It could only be one person.

"You've never stormed my business like this!" the innkeeper shrieked.

"This is no longer business," Vex laughed, "Ravi and that girl let out a wagon of my dogs and humiliated me in the streets. You know how much that cost me? This is personal."

Odie grabbed onto the bottom of Magda's skirt, attempting to yank her back.

The footsteps grew closer, as if Vex was barrelling down the hallway.

"You can't go in there!" the innkeeper shouted.

Magda gasped, pulling away from the door before grabbing her knapsack. "Come, Odie!"

She ran over to the window, pushing it open, before staring at the street. All around the Inn's walls were thick vines. Just below her, was a tented awning covering a storefront. She could only hope it would hold her weight while she jumped down. Before she could stop herself, Magda jumped outside, onto the top of the tent. She landed onto the soft fabric, which dipped under her weight, before rolling to the side. Quickly, she shifted her body before grabbing onto one of the vines, using it as a rope to drop herself down to the street.

Above, Odie's paws were propped up against the open window, staring down at her. He let out a bark.

"Come on!" Magda yelled. She knew he was big enough to jump over the window sill and land on the tent. She hoped her demonstration of the maneuver was enough to convince Odie it was safe.

Odie barked twice more.

"Come on, Odie! You can do it!" she screamed louder.

Odie backed up, and prepared to jump through the opening. He began running toward the window, but just before he made the jump, something grabbed his hind legs and yanked him back. He let out a yelp as he disappeared.

Vex's face appeared in the frame. "Look who has him now," he chuckled. Then he vanished, no doubt taking Odie with him.

"No!" Magda yelled. She had to make it to the front door before they left with Odie. She pushed through the busy street, fighting against the crowd, attempting to make it there in time.

Suddenly, a man grabbed onto her wrist, pulling her back toward his shop.

"You think you can jump on the top of my store? Who do you think you are?"

"Please, let me go—I need to save my dog!"

"No one cares about your stupid dog," the man snapped in her face.

Magda's heart was pounding as if it was about to explode. She had already lost her father, and Aleksy, she couldn't lose Odie now. He was the only thing she had left, and without her dog, she would be lost completely.

"Let me go!" Magda screamed. She broke her hand away from the man's grasp, and in one swift movement, the vines attached to the side of the inn leapt from the wall, bursting forward and crashing into the man's tent. The awning tilted forward, about to crush them.

Magda and the man leapt in opposite directions, and the street was left in a disordered mess of vines and dust. Magda stepped over the fallen tent, as well as stands of fabrics and jewelry, running away from the scene. She hoped that no one had noticed the apparent display of Soul magic. Maybe, they would think the vines had moved by a gust of wind.

Quickly, she rounded the corner, and then the next one, heading to the front of the Mystic Sonata. Outside, she saw Vex closing a wagon door before yelling at the driver, "Get a move on, then!"

Magda tore as fast as she could, making her way toward Vex, but there were too many people in the crowd. He disappeared as fast as he had appeared, blending in with the plethora of citizens in the bustling town circle.

"Odie!" Magda screamed.

Magda reached the front door, putting her hands on her knees to catch her breath. Vex was gone, and so was Odie.

What was she going to do now?

That night, Magda attended the show at the Mystic Sonata. She had to talk to Ravi and tell him what had happened. He was the only person who possibly could help her rescue Odie. Just the thought of Odie being taken by Vex and his henchmen was gut-wrenching. What's worse, quite a few citizens had witnessed an unusual display of Soul magic. She was running out of time to get to the palace.

She stood in the back of the music hall, listening to Ravi play set after set. He often looked up at her, giving her a soft smile as she watched him, a smile she didn't return. The more she listened to his music, the more she realized how talented he was. In all of the festivities she had attended at the Azuremi fortress, she had never heard music quite like Ravi's.

When the night was over, Ravi approached her. "There you are," he said, "I have ideas about where you can get another invitation. There's Rachel, the head of the..."

Magda cut him off. "Vex was here today. He broke into my room and stole Odie."

Ravi's expression immediately changed. He reached out to Magda, "Are you alright?"

"I jumped out the window, but Odie didn't. I should have found another way...I don't know what I was thinking—"

"You jumped out the window?!" Ravi echoed, his voice rising.

Magda continued, the words coming out as quickly as they could in Flaustran, "Thank you for looking into other invitations, but I really can't think of anything else right now without knowing what is going to happen to my dog. I don't care about the palace or the ball if

I don't have Odie. Tell me everything you know about what Vex does with the dogs he takes."

Ravi let out a sigh as his eyes traced the floor. "It's not good. All of the animals are slated for fighting matches at Vex's gambling house—it's a fight to the death. It's a way for them to increase funding."

Magda gasped and fought against the stinging sensation in her eyes and throat. "No—Odie won't fight another dog! We have to rescue him."

"I don't know how that will be possible. The match will be heavily guarded. The only way to get in would be to place a bet on one of the animals."

"Money won't be an issue," Magda said.

Ravi gave her a curious expression, but continued, "If you have some money, I can get you into the gambling house where they are holding Odie. A bet will buy you an entry fee, as well as the exact time and day of the fight."

Magda nodded before slipping a few tiger-stamped coins from her purse and handing them over to Ravi. She couldn't lose Odie as well. He was a gift from her parents, and she and Aleksy had so many memories playing with him around the castle grounds. It would be too much to bear.

"Is that enough?" she asked.

"By the guardians!" he exclaimed with a laugh. "Of course it's enough. What did you do in Azurem again?"

Magda shook her head. "You have your secrets, I have mine."

"Alright. I'll do what I can."

"Please try, Ravi. You're my only hope to save Odie."

PART THREE

The Rescue

CHAPTER 31
Magdalena

During the days that followed, Magda sat in the tavern-area of the Mystic Sonata, pouring over books in Flaustran. It was the only way to keep her sane while waiting for news about Odie. The words she heard on the streets were significantly different from those she had been taught in textbooks by her private tutors, and she knew she needed to increase her vocabulary in order to navigate the city. Every day, she made her way to the marketplace and bought food so that she had an opportunity to interact with more Flaustrans, practicing how a real native would speak. While she was there, she trailed Ishani and her guild officers, trying to understand more about their daily routines so when the time came she could make another attempt at stealing an invitation to the birthday ball.

In the meantime, she asked the owners of the Mystic Sonata to bring a bouquet of flowers to her room, and she experimented with her magic. She crinkled the stems and petals, before instantly bringing them back to life. Pretty soon, she had mastered manipulating small plants.

She considered sending a letter to Dagmara, or to her mother, but realized it would be too dangerous without using the Scribestone.

Anything—even if it was written in code—could easily be intercepted. Especially since she had accidentally displayed magic in the city, she would just have to wait until she got to the palace.

A few days later, Magda was sitting in a booth at the Mystic Sonata, sipping the signature herbal tea while she poured over another book in Flaustran—this time about the guardians. She needed to know everything about Flaustran lore and Flaustra's perceptions of Soul magic.

"Thought I'd find you here," a familiar voice said as he slid into the booth across from her.

"Did you get it?" Magda's head piped up from her book.

Ravi slid an envelope across the table.

Quickly, Magda tore it open. It was a receipt confirming the bet that Ravi had made as an entry fee for Vex's upcoming gambling party. In addition, it confirmed the time and location—in two days time at the farthest dock from the marketplace.

"You did it," Magda said, nearly jumping up and embracing Ravi at her excitement. Somehow, she refrained. She could almost hear Vex's snarling voice cracking in her head: *"Everyone has their price, and every secret has a buyer."*

Then she asked Ravi, "What did you do to get this information?"

"It didn't cost me too much," he laughed.

"I don't want you to get in trouble," Magda responded sincerely, hoping that he wasn't putting himself in danger on her behalf.

"Don't worry about me," Ravi assured her. "I have a few friends in the Marauders." His response offered her a bit of respite, but she wasn't sure why she was letting herself put so much trust in this young man. It was too easy, as if they were already old friends.

"Why are you helping me?" she asked.

"Truthfully, I would like to accompany you to the royal birthday celebration at the palace. You know, with an official invitation you can bring a 'guest of the invited'. I was hoping you would bring me as your 'invited'."

"You want to be my date." Magda knew what he was asking. "You never told me...why do you want to get into the palace? Scouting out a new location to play your music?" she asked lightheartedly.

"Do you really think you'll get through the palace checkpoint and pass for a native Flaustran invitee?"

Deep down, Magda knew he was right, but he didn't exactly answer her question.

"I'll come to your room two hours beforehand, and we can leave from there," he finished.

Magda nodded. She was ready to get Odie back.

Magda and Ravi circled down the narrow streets of Eloquas, heading toward the district that housed the Marauders Guild. Vex's gambling party would be held on one of the docks that he owned, far away from the center of the city or the marketplace. In the night, tall ships could be seen, their masts reaching up to the heavens. While their sails were down, the area buzzed with quiet activity, signaling that they were in the right place for the upcoming gambling match. They were entering Vex's massive arena—about to be thrown onto the enemy's game board.

At the end of the dock was a warehouse, and connected to it, like it was some sort of special occasion, was a large tent. The sea-green tent connected back to the warehouse where Vex stored his contraband. Its outside layer flapped in the cool evening wind, and the doors were guarded by two officers, who appeared to be checking a list of guests.

"Follow my lead," Ravi said beside Magda.

He held out his arm, and Magda linked hers in his as they walked down the center of the pier, approaching the tent.

"Name," the man said.

"Ravi Kalal."

"Bet."

"Number 862. On the greyhound."

"Identification."

Ravi dug deep into his pockets before handing over the piece of paper. When the guard was satisfied, he looked to Magda.

"Name."

"She's not on the list," Ravi intervened quickly. "She's my investor, and she doesn't like nosy officers poking around in her business."

The guard nodded. "Seeing how significant of a sum you put down, we'd be happy to accommodate you, miss—"

"Dagmara," Magda said.

"Dagmara. Azuremi then?" the guard referenced her accent. "No last name?"

"No. And if you'll be wanting future investments from me for the guild, you'd best also keep my first name a secret. There's a lot more people and finances where I come from." Magda almost smiled. It was exactly what Dagmara would say, and it was working.

The guard nodded in understanding, before holding back the curtain for them to pass through and enter the match.

While the tent had been plain and inconspicuous from the outside, it was the exact opposite on the inside. Instantly, they were transported into Vex's cave of vices, ostentatious in its splendor, but reeking of illegal activity. All around were colorful tapestries and gambling tables running around the outside of the room in a semicircle. An ugly smoke clouded Magda's senses, as a foreign scent filled her nostrils. She could almost taste the sweet incense and the sticky sweat that lingered in the air from the heat and alcohol.

The guests present were wearing their finest clothes, and golden jewelry dripped from their hands and fingertips, as if they wanted to make the impression they had more money to spare. The air was thick with the clinking of glasses, laughter, and the symphony of dozens of languages.

In the center of the room was a cage with ceiling-high bars, meant for the fighting matches. Some of the guests stood close, cheering on the animals inside. Beyond the cage, toward the back of the tent, was a velvet curtain that led into the warehouse. The curtain was open, revealing a maze of crates and boxes that were stacked sky-high. Magda didn't know if it was stupidity or ego that caused Vex to display his wealth that way, revealing an opening directly into the heart of his entire operation.

"Keep a lookout for where they might be bringing the dogs in from," Ravi leaned close and whispered into Magda's ear.

"A drink for the gentleman and the lady," said a server, who passed a copper glass to both Magda and Ravi.

"Thank you," Magda replied.

"Don't drink that," said Ravi, when the server was out of earshot. "It's laced with truth serum. Vex doesn't only host these events for money, but for secrets. Look around."

As Magda did so, she noticed that every one of the guests was gushing over the drink, and in a deep conversation with officers that were manning each one of the gambling tables.

The duo moved forward, holding their glasses at their sides, and approached the center ring. Already, two vicious dogs were in a fighting match, their snarling teeth caked with dried blood. Even though a gate separated Magda from the match, she couldn't help but tense in fear at the sight of the hideous dogs. Their ghost-like eyes sent a spine-chilling sensation through her entire body.

She watched as they tore each other apart, and the death match ended with one of them in pieces on the side of the ring. All that was left was the remains of a mangled animal, laying in pooled blood. Magda wanted to look away from the ghastly sight, but if she was posing as an investor she had to stay calm. She closed her eyes to keep from gagging.

"Wait here," said Ravi. "I want to see where they bring out the next dog."

Magda looked away from the ring, scanning the surrounding areas. Vex was up on a raised platform, in a throne like one of the guardians himself, eagerly watching and calling out the winners. As he did so, more and more coins were dropped into buckets along the side of the room. She wondered if it was all Flaustran currency, or if they were also stamped with the elk, bear, and owl—representing the other kingdoms.

"Long live the First Prince!" someone shouted from the crowd, which caused Vex's face to turn red. All of the guests shrieked in a wild commotion as they watched the man scream.

"Long live the First Prince!"

"Get him out of here!" Vex said from his dais. "I'll have no blasphemy here!"

Instantly, two guards were upon the stranger, dragging him away from the crowd and outside a side entrance to the tent. He continued shouting as he was removed, "Long live the First Prince! He's coming back, and he'll set fire to all of you and your vices!"

Magda knew all about the stories of the First Prince, and the lore that dubbed him as the most evil guardian in history. At least Vex still had some morals.

Magda turned her attention back to the match. It was still empty. Damn it. Where were they bringing out the next dog?

"Couldn't stay away, could you?" a familiar voice sounded to Magda's left. She was surprised to see Ishani standing next to her, pressing her face against the bars as if she had no fear of the ferocious animals inside the ring.

"None of your business," responded Magda.

"I think you're starting to be my business," said Ishani, keeping her eyes on the match so it wouldn't seem like they were talking. "You shouldn't be here."

"Why is that?"

"You have too much money to go around. It draws suspicion. People want information soon, or they'll order your death. No one likes a wild card around here. Especially since you seem to be turning up at guild events."

Magda gulped. What would Dagmara say in this situation? She was only a few mistakes away from revealing her identity completely. The only way to keep up this charade was to keep everyone guessing.

"Let them wonder," Magda retorted.

Ishani turned her body toward Magda. "I looked you up in the royal records. Dagmara Zosia. Royal Assassin for the late Azuremi King, Bogdan Krol. Mother was a spy in the wars, former assassin, and was tortured to death. Sound familiar?"

Magda bit her tongue. "You're lying," she finally responded. "You don't have access to Queen Sanyal's royal records."

"You don't know the first thing about me," said Ishani.

Magda sighed, turning towards Ishani. "Because you've never told me. We're not even friends. Why do you care what happens to me?"

Then Ishani grabbed Magda's hand, pulling her close to her until she could easily whisper in her ear. Her breath sent a chill down Magda's spine, "Because I know a guardian when I see one."

CHAPTER 32
Dagmara

Before Dagmara knew it, the night of the engagement ball arrived. Supposedly, there would be nobles attending from all over the kingdom. Dagmara didn't know if they were there to judge her, or merely show their support to the king. Regardless, it was nerve-wracking. She tried to remain calm. Tonight, she had to play off that she and the Mad King were engaged—in front of the entire kingdom.

Madame Annette had given her clear instructions about the ball. The newly engaged couple would open with a dance, and then there would be a processional line as everyone paid their respects. Afterward, they would serve desserts and drinks while performers would take the floor. People wouldn't leave until it was well into the evening.

Dagmara wasn't a dancer herself. She knew the Azuremi Waltz which was performed often at weddings and King Bogdan's holiday balls. It was a romantic dance, one Dagmara had learned when she was a small child because she admired it so much.

Now, in Ilusauri, she was supposed to perform the Ilusaurian Lullaby and only had a few days to learn it. She and Urszula practiced for hours. Endlessly. Especially since Dagmara had to take plenty of breaks to account for her compromised stamina.

Urszula helped her prepare for the ball. She added fabric to one of Magda's dresses, creating a gorgeous ice-blue gown with a translucent cape that rolled off her shoulders and clasped around her neck. Her hair, dyed silver once more, was pulled half back and braided into a silver tiara. Long, crystal earrings dangled to her shoulders.

Finally, the hour of the engagement ball arrived. Martine and Dagmara walked side by side, past the whirling maze of mirrors. As they walked, Dagmara remained silent, her mind preoccupied.

"He's waiting at the second floor entrance," Martine said. "All the guests should already be in the ballroom. You two will make your entrance together and descend the stairs into the center of the dance floor."

Perfect. Starting the night like a show.

"Thank you," Dagmara replied. She had more to thank Martine for, ever since she had saved her life during the hound attack in Nouchenne. The monster didn't stir in Dagmara's presence, even though it only awoke when it detected magic, and Martine hadn't made a comment yet.

"I'll be here all night if you need anything," Martine added.

"Did learning the truth about Nouchenne change your opinion of the king?" Dagmara blurted out.

Martine inclined her head. "What do you mean?"

"Well, I forced you to come, and nearly killed you. But at least you found out why your family was cleared, right?"

"You didn't force me to come," Martine replied, "you're right, I did want to learn why His Majesty was clearing towns. If anything, it made me trust His Majesty more. I thought he was clearing them maliciously, but he was protecting civilians from the hounds."

"I suppose," Dagmara muttered. "Can I tell you a secret, Martine?"

Martine nodded, her eyes widening slightly.

Dagmara hoped Martine was trustworthy. Martine had already

kept it a secret that the mystical hounds didn't awake in Dagmara's presence. Now, Dagmara wanted to trust her.

"My father and brother were killed by men wearing masks with the symbol of the First Prince. In the cave...someone wrote *'the First Prince will rise.'* There has to be a connection between all of this."

"Maybe it wasn't written by *someone*, but *something*."

"What do you mean?"

"His Majesty has been clearing villages since his father died. These rifts must have something to do with the famine and decay spreading through Ilusauri."

They rounded the corner and arrived at their destination. Claude was waiting for her, flanked by his two guards, Pierre and the massive man Dagmara didn't know.

Dagmara stopped dead in her tracks. She hadn't seen the king since Nouchenne when he had been coated in blood. Now, he wore a regal, silver doublet with a cape down his right arm. His dark skin was gorgeous in the light, and his eyes radiant like a guardian's.

"You look..." Claude's voice trailed off. His eyes wandered at every portion of her body until he abruptly cleared his throat and fixed his gaze on her face. "You look presentable."

Her brow furrowed. "I would hope so."

"A moment alone," Claude demanded, and at once the guards left his side. They strode a few paces away, followed by Martine, until they were out of earshot but remained in sight.

Dagmara didn't know why she felt her stomach erupt in butterflies. The last time they were together, he slaughtered hounds to save her. Was there something about him rushing to her rescue that made her feel this way?

"Madame Annette is currently in discussion with your lead advisor, negotiating an equivalent trade for food and medicine until the routes are officially opened again. We will both have to sign off on the agreement when they write up the contract," Claude explained.

"However, I sent a small shipment of medicine to your mother in the meantime."

"Oh," Dagmara brushed her hair behind her shoulder. "Thank you."

"We can discuss territory and political implications later," Claude stated.

Dagmara only nodded. She never thought it would get so far as to discuss politics. That was something Magda excelled at, not Dagmara. How was she supposed to make decisions for the entire kingdom of Azurem? Was she even allowed to?

Noting her silence, Claude continued, "To be honest, I don't like this anymore than you do. I don't like the stunt you pulled going to Nouchenne, and I don't trust you," he said, catching her off guard.

Dagmara shrugged. "You haven't given me much reason to trust you."

Claude scoffed. "Well then I hope you are a good actress. The nobles and leaders have to think we're united. And they will object to two guardians marrying. It hasn't happened in centuries. So we must convince them we love one another."

"Convince them we're in love?" Dagmara let out, followed by a short laugh. "You could have given me some warning, Your Majesty."

He strode toward her, clearing the distance with three steps. His cologne wafted toward her, consuming her in its elegance. "Are you having second thoughts?" he asked.

"Not at all. I'm just not certain you can convince these people you're in love with anyone, let alone me."

"I appreciate your concern, but you don't have to worry about me."

She raised an eyebrow. "We will see about that. Is there anything I should know before meeting your people?"

"Nothing specific," he said. "We're supposed to perform a dance that is customary to Ilusaurian traditions, but don't worry about that."

"I learned the dance."

He blinked, his jaw slackening as he searched for words.

"You do know the dance, right?" Dagmara asked. "Don't tell me I learned it for nothing."

He cleared his throat. "Yes, I know it."

"Good."

He nodded toward the guards, and they approached, preparing to open the doors. One of them gave a special knock, notifying the guards on the other side that they were ready to make their appearance. A symphony of horns majestically rang in the ballroom, their sound only muted by the door. An announcement would shortly follow.

Claude extended his arm to her. "Shall we pretend we're in love for one evening? Then we can return to disliking one another."

"I said I didn't trust you, not that I dislike you."

"I knew from the moment you laid eyes on me that you loathe me. It's mutual if that makes you feel better."

Dagmara didn't want to argue. She couldn't without revealing that she blamed him for the death of Aleksy and Bogdan and was here to find that proof. Instead she stepped closer, wrapping her arm around his. "I can pretend to like you for one evening, Your Majesty."

"Claude," he said, his lips close to her ear. "Call me Claude."

Then he turned to the double doors. They stood there in silence, waiting for them to open and reveal the ballroom beyond.

He let out a sigh beside her, before whispering under his breath, "This is for the betterment of our kingdoms."

He was referring to the food supply Azurem would be providing, no doubt. He didn't want to marry her. All this was so he could feed his people. It made her question everything she knew about the Mad King.

Yet she was no different. She never intended on marriage. This was a quest to avenge Bogdan and Aleksy—but also for medicine. This was for her brother.

Her voice was a whisper as she added to his statement, "and the safety of our people."

His head whipped to her, meeting her gaze with ferocity. His eyes twinkled with an intensity she couldn't discern. She wished she could understand what was behind the wall of the Mad King. She wished she knew the truth behind all the rumors.

He watched her with as much intrigue, as if her words struck a different chord inside him. There was no doubt he was trying to interpret her intentions as much as she was. She didn't blame him. She was an imposter.

Neither of them realized that the doors had opened, and guests were watching them enraptured by one another.

The music to the Ilusaurian lullaby began, and both were startled back into reality. He led her out onto the balcony, pausing at the top of the staircase.

Dagmara froze, getting a glimpse of the ballroom. It was a lavish space, with mirrored panels covering the walls, ending in a glass window at the far end of the room. On the ceiling, hung at least a dozen chandeliers, their glittering lights reflecting on all sides and making the heavenly space seem more expansive than it was in reality. Instead of the gold paneling used in Azurem, the torches and decal were overlaid with metallic silver. Everything was pristinely polished, as if the platinum room was a purposeful distraction to the brittle fields outside.

There were nearly a hundred guests, and all eyes were upon Dagmara. They started down the staircase, and Dagmara prayed she wouldn't trip on her dress. She tried to keep a pleasant face, but struggled to remain amicable when she heard whispers ripple throughout the room. Were they judging her this early on? She hadn't even spoken yet.

At least she was going down the stairs. If these people had to watch her walk up them, they would know she wasn't a guardian.

Then she found Sabien in the crowd. He was taking in every

ounce of her body with his roaming eyes, a smirk on his face. She tried to ignore him, but her stomach curled with nerves.

When Dagmara and Claude reached the floor, the crowd parted like a ripple in a pond, creating space in the center. Claude shifted his grip, releasing her arm and taking her by the hand as he led her to the dance floor. With a tug at her fingertips, he pulled her close, her chest against his. She placed her free hand on his shoulder. Her wound had healed, but she hoped Claude didn't catch sight of the small scar in the center of her palm.

"Eyes on me," he said, his breath against her face. He wrapped his other arm around her, caressing her hip in the process. The sensation of his hand on her lower back sent a chill up her spine.

When the downbeat of the next stanza began, he started the dance.

It was nothing like practicing with Urszula. The king knew what he was doing, and he wasn't afraid to lead. With his hand on Dagmara's lower back, he nearly lifted her into the first movement. Her feet immediately remembered the choreography and matched his strides, afraid to step on him and embarrass herself in the process. She knew a turn was coming up, and she had fumbled through it every time, hoping the length of her dress would cover her footwork.

The music swelled, and she held her breath, feeling the eyes of everyone in the room judging her. When the moment came, Claude nudged her hip, sending her into the full turn. Her fingertips gently spun through his other hand, far above her head. At the end of the turn, he grabbed her by the waist, pulling her tight against his body once more.

He gave her a subtle smile, as though he were impressed. Meanwhile, she was breathless, feeling every inch of his body against hers.

She didn't know a dance could be so sensual. She certainly didn't know she could feel this level of attraction to someone she had despised for the past decade. Losing herself in the rest of the dance, she no longer had to remember the steps. Each time he guided her into the next section, her muscle memory snapped into place. All she had to do was keep her eyes on him, just as he had told her. She never noticed the small flakes of silver in the iris's of his otherwise chocolate eyes.

As the dance came to a close, the music ceased, leaving the entire ballroom in silence. Claude and Dagmara remained focused on one another a moment longer.

Then he cleared his throat, breaking the intimacy. He kept her one hand in his as he addressed the crowd.

"Thank you all for joining us this evening to celebrate the start of our union. I am pleased to introduce Princess Magdalena Krol. She is a Guardian of Life, and we plan to work together for the betterment of both our kingdoms. May you enjoy the festivities!"

The music began again as the ballroom erupted in applause. Claude pulled Dagmara toward him, shifting his hand behind her back as led her to the front of the room.

"I must say, I'm impressed," he said, his voice low so only she could hear.

"Honestly, so am I," she replied. "I thought you would have two left feet."

A soft laugh escaped his lips. "I've been dancing my whole life. You clearly underestimated me."

"I can't judge your dancing until you've performed the Azuremi Waltz. It's a tradition at balls and weddings."

"Hmm," he mused. "I'm sure it's easy."

She saw Martine, Pierre, and Claude's large guard standing a few feet away. Nearby, she also caught Sabien's eyes again. He was clapping his hands together, so slow that there was no sound. She forced herself to ignore him as she and Claude came to a stop at the front of the room.

There was already a line to greet the new couple like Annette had warned. Martine handed Dagmara her silk gloves that Urszula had prepared. She knew Claude was curious, but she wasn't going to tell him her reasoning. She knew she was capable of poisoning someone through touch, and she wouldn't risk one of the Ilusaurian nobles taking her hand and ending her life.

The first few guests said hello politely, introducing themselves and going on their way. She heard many questions and many condolences to her family.

One woman approached, giving a glamorous introduction, and saying she was from some village in the south, before asking Dagmara, "So how do you benefit Ilusauri other than birthing the next heir?"

Dagmara's face turned pale. She hardly knew how to answer that question, let alone her mind immediately shifted to her conceiving kids with Claude.

"Princess Magdalena brings her entire kingdom," Claude responded for her, his tone calm. "We are currently discussing all the benefits to this alliance, and there is no shortage from Azurem."

"Hmm," the woman replied, displeased.

Claude's voice dropped. "You will not speak negatively about Princess Magdalena in my presence again." His eyes glimmered silver in the light.

"Yes, Your Majesty," the woman said, and then disappeared.

Dagmara nearly gasped. Had Claude compelled her?

The next duo that stepped forward glanced at Claude with sheer horror before bowing at Dagmara and scampering off.

Forced to remain silent, Dagmara couldn't help but glance Claude's way each time a couple approached, but she didn't see the silver in his chocolate eyes again. She must have imagined it.

The line felt never-ending, and Dagmara started to lose energy. It was like her life had been sucked out of her, and she knew she had only been standing for ten minutes. Her heart pounded against her chest, threatening to do more damage. She needed to sit, but she couldn't make a scene.

Don't ask for a chair. Her thoughts were at war with herself. She couldn't seem weak.

Claude put his hand out, stopping the next visitors before he turned to Dagmara. His voice was barely audible. "You haven't spoken to the last three groups. Don't let their comments get to you. This is all for show, remember?"

The comments irked her, but that wasn't the problem. It would only get worse from here.

"May I sit?" she blurted out. "My shoes are killing me."

Claude's face twisted. "Yes..." he said. Then he snapped at his large guard behind him. Within moments, a velvet chair had arrived and was placed directly behind her.

She gratefully took a seat, immediately feeling the pressure release from her entire body. Her nausea began to subside, and before long, her heart would return to normal.

Then she felt a finger underneath her chin. Claude tilted her head so that she looked up at him, his fingertips gently caressing her neck.

"Better?" he asked.

"Yes," she replied. She didn't know if he was touching her this way for show or not.

Then he stood beside her, placing one hand behind his back and the other on the back of the chair. It looked like they were settling in for a painting.

A few more people introduced themselves, until one struck Dagmara by surprise.

She saw him approach, and there was no doubt he was Celesta. Unless he was an Ilusaurian citizen now...but his attire wasn't similar to those around him. Tassels laid against his chest, and his shoulder pads tilted into spikes. The red color of his clothing was too vibrant for the dyes on this side of the continent.

Ilusauri invaded Celestaire. What was a representative from Celestaire doing here?

The approaching man stepped before them, bowing. His jet black hair was slicked back into a thick bun, shiny underneath the light from the chandeliers. As he straightened, he revealed a young face, but it was worn from experience. He had to be a decade older than Claude.

Then he spoke, a smile on his face as he addressed the king and princess, and Dagmara realized in horror that she didn't know a single word of Celesta. Well, nothing more than hello, goodbye, and thank you.

But Magda was fluent.

Dagmara was supposed to be fluent.

She stared blankly at him, both surprised he was there and struck with fear that her secret would be exposed. Then Claude glanced in her direction, confused why she wasn't returning the greeting. "Princess?" he inquired under his breath.

There was no doubt suspicion lined his voice. This could be the moment he saw right through her.

CHAPTER 33
Magdalena

"*I know a guardian when I see one"* Ishani had said.

Magda's breath caught in her throat. Had she been too obvious? Did Ishani suspect that she had powers or was royalty?

Ishani continued, "You need to lay low. I can't lie to the other guild leaders forever."

"I'm not a guardian," said Magda strongly, but her thoughts ran wild. Did others suspect she had powers as well? And why was Ishani protecting her?

Ishani looked down at the glass Magda was holding, realizing it contained the truth serum. Then she scrutinized Magda suspiciously, as if she wasn't sure what to believe. Luckily, Magda hadn't taken a single sip of the intoxicating drink.

A bell rang from the other side of the ring, signaling that the next match had started.

Magda's eyes snapped to the ring. She cursed under her breath once more, for she hadn't seen where they had brought out the new animal to challenge the winner. The dogs were already going at each other, their bites scraping the other's skin. Already, the larger mutt had drawn blood.

When she turned to speak to Ishani again, the young captain had disappeared into the crowd.

Magda shuddered at the thought of a guild captain possibly knowing her true identity as a guardian. Had one of Ishani's men seen the apparent display of earth magic in the city? She knew that she had to be more careful than ever. Quickly, she walked away from the center ring, placing the glass down on one of the side tables.

A hand graced Magda's left shoulder, and she snapped her head around.

"Ravi," she let out a sigh of relief.

"This way," said Ravi, "They bring the animals from the warehouse. Through that curtain."

Magda and Ravi pushed their way through the crowd, squeezing between the various guild members as they shoved away from the fighting ring. They headed in the opposite direction of the crowd's flow, forcing them to push against the audience.

When they reached the curtain, they waited until the officer went to retrieve the next animal and the crowd was engaged in the match, before slipping through at the perfect moment.

Ravi pointed to a doorway toward the back of the warehouse.

"There," he said.

Magda could barely make out a doorway with a small sign. Four men guarded it, carrying hatchets. A maze of crates and cargo scattered the warehouse, providing some shelter from the officer's viewpoint. They could get close by maneuvering through the boxes, but it wouldn't be enough to run past the guards and through the door.

"Let's get closer," said Magda. She grabbed Ravi's hand and pulled him along, ducking between a set of boxes until they were within a table's length of the four officers. They pressed their backs up against the large crates and peeked their heads around the corner as they watched the four men lounge around the outside of the door.

Suddenly the door opened, and Magda let out a gasp.

One of the men led a dog. It was bloody and bruised, with a

brown and black fur coat. He limped along miserably as it was led to the fighting ring. It wouldn't stand a chance against the murderous dog in the fight that Magda and Ishani had just witnessed.

"Shh...," said Ravi, putting his hand over Magda's mouth and pulling her further back into the darkness. As the man passed directly behind their hiding place, the dog paused, letting out a bark. One turn of the officer's head, and they would be seen.

Magda stood perfectly still as the man and dog stopped short only paces from them. She was pressed closely up against Ravi's chest, and even though he held his breath, she could feel the rapid beating of his heart against hers. He kept his hand over her mouth, holding her close in the darkness.

"Randal, what's taking so long to bring the next dog?!" a loud voice yelled from the fighting ring.

Vex.

The man and the dog picked up the pace, heading out of sight.

Magda let out a deep sigh as Ravi released her.

"We need a distraction," he said.

"But what?" Magda scanned the scene, her gaze going to the open rafters in the warehouse roof. At different angles, a few tree branches had grown inside the holes that acted as windows, their leaves gently brushing the stacks of boxes.

Magda remembered the flowers in Ishani's office, and how she had manipulated them. Then she remembered the vines in the street. She closed her fist, focusing on the trees in the distance. She was distinctly aware of herself, and suddenly, before she knew it, one of the tree branches gently moved to the side, knocking over an entire stack of boxes. The boxes tumbled over each other, spilling out piles of treasures such as gold, artifacts, and scrolls. A shattering clamor rang through the space as the treasures crashed against each other.

The noise caught the attention of some of the attendees at the fighting match. They peered through the gap in the curtain. "Look, let's get some intel on Vex's goods."

"Let's get some for ourselves!"

A handful of guild workers headed toward the overturned boxes, and at the sight of them, the four officers rushed over, eager to protect their spoils and help one another restack the crates.

Magda stood, dumbfounded. She had really moved the tree. The thoughts circulating through her mind had manifested in real life.

Ravi broke her thoughts:

"Well, that was convenient. I guess the guardians are always watching," he laughed.

"You have no idea," Magda said under her breath.

"Come on, they'll be back soon."

Magda reached the door first, yanked it open, and was met by a set of stairs leading down. She descended quickly, with Ravi right behind.

At the bottom of the steps, a waft of musty air flooded their senses. They emerged into a wine cellar with arched, stone ceilings, as if they had stumbled into a cave. Before them was a long, wooden table. Leading into the darkness were rows of barrels and an iron-wrought gate leading into a secluded alcove. Covering the walls were racks of vintage wine bottles, covered in dust and cobwebs.

The sound of barking dogs echoed against the stone walls, coming from the gate ahead.

"Let's go," urged Magda.

They sprinted between the rows of barrels until they reached the gate and pulled it open. It was another room lined with shelves, but this time, the shelves held cages rather than glass bottles. Inside were dozens of shrieking and terrifying animals, with tangled fur and wasted bodies. Upon seeing Magda and Ravi, the barking and cries continued even louder.

"Help me find him—we don't have much time!" yelled Magda. She ran ahead until her face was against the cages, peering inside to find her dog.

"Right behind you," said Ravi, racing to the other side.

A loud, familiar bark sounded to Magda's left, followed by high-pitched whimpering. She snapped her head to the side to see the glimmer of fur.

"Odie!" Magda shouted, sprinting to the cage and dropping down to her knees. Her pet jumped up onto the bars, licking her face with his tongue. He shook violently from his overly wagging tail. "Ravi!" Magda called as she pulled up the latch and yanked the gate open. Instantly, Odie jumped into Magda's arms, and Magda squeezed tightly around his matted fur.

"You're alright, you're alright!" Magda cried.

Odie continued to whimper, his tail controlling his body, and his excitement and relief was palpable.

"Come on, we have to go," said Ravi. He laid a soft hand on Magda's back.

Magda stood up beside him, but her heart was breaking. "We can't just leave them."

"That distraction won't work for long," said Ravi, "and they'll be back soon to get the next dog."

"We have to try."

Ravi appeared fearful, but with one look in Magda's eyes, his expression grew more determined. "You're right."

While some of the dogs cowered in the back of their cages, others were vicious fighters, with the signs of blood on their teeth. Magda and Ravi were careful to only open the cages of the dogs that they were sure wouldn't rip them to pieces. They helped the majority of the smaller dogs escape, before turning to the larger dogs that were less menacing. One by one, the dogs raced out of the wine cellar and up the stairs, into the chaos of the fighting match above. Soon, shouts were coming from the story above.

Suddenly Odie yelped beside Magda, facing a cage. He stood in front of a fluffy, golden dog, almost as large as he was. Its ears were floppy and its demeanor quite friendly.

"Did you make a friend?" Magda shook her head with a laugh

before unlatching the golden dog's cage. It leapt out and raced around Odie, both of them playing for a brief moment.

Magda noticed Ravi out of the corner of her eye, reaching for a different cage. Something stirred inside her, and a terror paralyzed her body.

"Not that one!" Magda yelled towards Ravi, noticing his hand on the cage of a hound. The cage was massive—big enough for a full-grown adult to stand inside. The mysterious animal was unlike anything Magda had ever seen before. Its heaving breaths revealed shiny, violet scales on the bottom of its stomach. The hound's figure consumed the entire space of the cage with its muscular body, and bloody drool pooled in a pile under its sharp teeth. It slinked at the back of the cage, pacing back and forth.

"Shhhh...," Ravi quieted her. Magda stepped closer to him, hoping to pull Ravi back away from the cage. If the hound decided to pounce, surely it could break the lock with enough force if it wanted to.

When Magda stepped forward, the hound's eyes met hers, revealing glowing irises.

Odie and the new dog suddenly jumped up, positioning themselves in front of Magda and Ravi for protection as they snarled at the hound.

With a force that reverberated the entire wall of cages, the hound shot forward, its teeth smashing into the metal gate.

"Let's get out of here," Ravi yelled.

Suddenly a voice sounded at the end of the cellar. Four men were descending the stairs, pointing right at the pair.

"They're the ones letting out the dogs! Get them!" one yelled. One by one, they came barreling towards Magda and Ravi, holding hatchets and sprinting across the length of the wine cellar

"Do you trust me?" Magda asked.

"What's your plan?"

"Do you trust me?!" Magda shouted louder this time over the barking animals.

Ravi nodded.

"Get behind me," Magda said, and she reached forward toward the hound's cage.

"You're crazy!"

Magda opened the latch, and swung the cage door toward her, opening it all the way on its hinges so that both she and Ravi were smashed behind the bars.

The hound jumped out as soon as the four henchmen reached the cages.

In an instant, the hound was upon the men, biting at their feet and ankles, and ripping their flesh. The men retaliated, throwing hatches and daggers at the hound, but the animal was fierce and unwavering.

While the men were distracted, Magda yelled, "Quick, in here!"

She darted into the hound's empty cage, pulling Ravi behind her. Quickly, Odie and his new dog friend followed them inside, and Magda pulled the cage shut. For now, they were safe.

The hound made quick work of the henchman, and they crumpled to the ground, bloodied and bruised. Then the beast snapped its teeth back towards its cage. It leaped up onto the metal grate, threatening to yank it open.

"Help me!" Magda yelled, pulling back on the iron bars. She was careful not to get her fingers in the way of the hound's snarling teeth.

Odie and the other dog jumped forward, barking and snarling at the hound. They continued barking at each other until the hound seemed to still, calming down. Then, all of the sudden, it backed down, stepping away from the cage, as if something had passed between all three animals. Finally, it darted out into the wine cellar and through the barrels.

Magda let out a sigh of relief.

"Do you think it's safe?" Ravi asked beside her.

"I think so," Magda said, observing Odie. His tail was wagging again, and he was no longer on the defense.

She pushed open the cage, exiting first. Sure enough, the hound was nowhere to be seen. They stepped into the wine cellar, relief flooding through their bodies.

Magda let out a squeal of excitement, jumping up in the air. "We did it!" she yelled, turning to Ravi. In her excitement, she leapt onto him, encircling her arms around his neck in a playful but intimate embrace. He hugged her back, wrapping his strong arms around her until her feet dangled off the ground. For a moment, it was just the two of them, and she was distinctly aware of her body pressed against his and the closeness of his lips to hers.

Then Odie began to snarl, alerting them that their happiness was short lived.

A voice broke their lingering gaze.

"Well, look at what we have here," a booming man sounded. Vex came storming into the wine cellar, flanked by three of his henchmen.

Vex gave Magda a crooked smile. "You'll pay for this."

CHAPTER 34
Dagmara

"Forgive me," Dagmara said under her breath in Azuremi, praying that the Celesta man standing before her didn't speak Azuremi, and in the event that he did, her voice was barely more than a whisper.

She needed a reasonable excuse. Claude wouldn't believe her if she said she didn't remember Celesta. Her mind raced with excuses until one finally came to mind.

"I mainly learned Celesta with my father...and I..." the crack in her voice wasn't fake at least. The reminder of Bogdan's death was ever present in her memory.

Claude nodded, seeming to understand almost immediately. He returned his attention to the Celesta man, switching his language. "At least at this event, let us speak Ilusaurian." Claude's voice was beautiful in his native language, making Dagmara realize he nearly always spoke Azuremi for her.

"Of course," the Celesta man said in Ilusaurian, his accent thick, making it harder for her to translate. He repeated his introduction to Dagmara, "I'm Reon Ogawa, spearhead of the Celesta militia."

Not only was this man Celesta, he held one of the most influential positions in the kingdom.

"Thank you for coming," Claude said, without the slightest bit of malice. In fact, they both seemed amicable with one another.

Reon smiled. "If you need anything at all Princess, you have a friend in Celestaire."

"Thank you."

Then Reon shifted his attention to the king and said something in Celesta. They could say anything they wanted in front of her, and she would have no idea.

Reon gave Dagmara one more smile before he departed, making his way into the crowd. Dagmara didn't have a chance to ask what was said before another man approached.

"His Majesty, Claude Mirage," the stranger said, his voice boisterous. He was middle-aged, but his hair was pure white. He had a stocky frame, and a monocle hung from a pocket on his chest. "This is the longest you have remained in public for a long time. I see she is bringing you out of your shell."

"I am still in the confines of my palace, Lionel."

Lionel flashed him a twisted smile. Then he reached for Dagmara's hand. "Princess, I am governor of the southern province. The name is Lionel Floquet."

Dagmara was startled at the sound of the name. This was the man Martine mentioned...the only person other than Claude who could manipulate citizenships and create false aliases for the assassins that crossed into Azurem.

"One of four governors," Claude added, "A crucial position to the security of this kingdom, and a liaison between me and my provinces."

Dagmara knew Claude was informing her that this man was immensely important, and she was required to be on her best behavior. She let him take her gloved palm, and he placed a kiss on the back of her hand. "Pleasure to meet you, Governor."

"We are honored to have this alliance. I'm sure His Majesty has informed you about the food shortage?" Lionel asked.

In Claude's words, it was a famine that began when his parents died.

"Yes he has. My heart goes out to your people," Dagmara replied.

"Of course, the drought seems to stay away from the palace," Lionel continued. "You have plenty here."

"Do you have something to say, Lionel?" Claude asked, his tone stern.

"Nothing, Your Majesty," Lionel dipped his head, "simply that I look forward to Azurem's surplus of food. That is part of the alliance, is it not?"

"It is," Dagmara stated.

"And will the people be visiting the castle to retrieve their rations?"

"No," Claude responded.

"Hmm," Lionel frowned, "still can't show your face to your people, I see."

"That is not the reason," Claude said, a growl rumbling deep in his throat. "Only able-bodied citizens would be able to make the trek to the castle. I will not force my people to choose between their food and their safety."

Dagmara didn't know why Claude's reasoning surprised her as much as it did. She never thought about who would or wouldn't be able to pick up rations from the castle. Yet, Claude was already considering those with health ailments that couldn't make the commitment. Claude was considering people that didn't have money for a carriage and had to walk miles to reach the castle. He was considering people...like her.

"So only you will reap the benefits of Azurem's food, I see," Lionel said, his tone surprisingly jovial for the intensity of the conversation. "Hoarding it at the palace as you've been doing for the past decade."

Out of the corner of her eye, she saw Claude's hands turn to fists.

Dagmara rose from her chair, unfortunately too quickly. Dizziness threatened to drag her back down, but she ignored the stars dancing in her vision. "I don't believe this is the appropriate time for this conversation, Governor," she said, "but if you must know, we plan on delivering food to each province and letting the governors handle the distribution from there."

Lionel's jaw seemed to drop from his mouth. "Delivering? So you two will make an appearance?" His eyes flashed with wonder as he looked to the king for confirmation.

Claude seemed unable to respond, his fist beginning to shake.

Dagmara took his hand in hers, relaxing his fist and forcing him to interlace his fingers with hers—also using him as a crutch in case her dizziness intensified. "We are still working through the details, Governor."

If there was a way she could get to the capital of Sailonne and investigate Lionel under the guise of helping Ilusauri, she would do it. She had to find out more about the three Ilusaurian assassins who supposedly didn't exist.

"O-Of course," Lionel dipped his head. He glanced down at their intertwined hands. "We are abundantly gracious to you, Princess. You don't know how much it means to the citizens to see their king in person. It has been far too long. Ilusauri is indebted to you." With one last bow, Lionel excused himself, venturing into the crowd.

Dagmara tried to withdraw her hand, but Claude held onto her steadfast. "What was that for?" Claude said under his breath.

"I was helping you," Dagmara replied. She yanked her hand from his grip and sat back down, exhaling.

It seemed like a century before the line finally ended. Afterward, performers arrived, taking the center of the floor and performing dances and acrobatics. Dessert was served, which Claude adamantly denied.

"If you wait for the caramel tarts, they have salt on them, hopefully *shaved* to your liking. My chefs seem to be confused by your Azuremi customs," Claude said under his breath.

Dagmara shot him a confused expression. She accepted the chocolate tart, questioning Claude's denial. "You don't like dessert?"

"I don't like eating near someone who tried to poison me," he growled.

Dagmara nearly dropped the tart, shock rippling through her body. Did he think she was responsible for the poisoned wine the other day on the terrace? What happened to the facade they were putting on? He had seemed enraptured by her during their dance, and now he seemed upset with her. Was the dance all another illusion?

"Excuse me," he said before dismissing himself. His tone was still on edge. What had happened to the king from earlier?

She watched Claude carefully. He maneuvered around a few guests, entranced by the dancers in the center of the room. Then he found Reon, the soldier from Celestaire.

Claude and the soldier spoke quickly, their bodies directly facing one another. It was not a conversation they wanted other people to be a part of. Then, Sabien came out of the crowd and joined them. With a wave of his hand, the king ushered them to follow. The trio disappeared under an alcove and into the hallway beyond.

Rising from her seat, Dagmara made a straight path to where the king, the captain, and the soldier disappeared. She dropped her uneaten dessert in the hands of a servant. There was something strange in the way the king and the soldier interacted...there was something more between them. And what did the king and the captain have to tell someone from Celestaire in secret?

She could sense instantly that Martine was on her tail. Dagmara wished the guard would give her space, but knew if she asked, it would only seem suspicious. She slipped into the alcove, dodging the watching eye of Madame Annette.

She could hear the trio's footsteps receding down the corridor. She knew how to follow someone. Instantly tapping into her training, she slipped into the shadows, careful not to be caught. They were talking to one another in Ilusaurian, but they were too far away to hear. She continued to trail them, hearing Martine behind her, clearly not as skilled in quietly following someone. Then the trio disappeared into a room, closing the door behind them.

Dagmara dashed across the hall, pressing her ear against the wood, catching them in the middle of their conversation.

"Are they still in hiding?" Claude asked.

"Yes," Reon replied. "Guardian Sora knows someone is onto her."

Claude cursed under his breath. "But you know where she is?"

"Of course," Reon replied before adding, "Your Majesty, your troops can't proceed any further without raising more alarm. Let me handle it from here."

"You don't know what you're looking for," Claude countered.

"And you do?" Reon countered.

"Watch your tone, Reon."

"Apologies, Your Majesty."

A new voice startled Dagmara. "Princess." It was Martine, a few paces behind her. "I'm not comfortable eavesdropping on the king."

"Then go," Dagmara replied. "I didn't ask you to follow me."

"Princess—"

"Shhh!" Dagmara scolded, waving her hand at Martine. Then she pressed her ear against the door once more.

"Ilusauri is taken care of, we're almost through Celestaire, and Azurem?" Reon asked. "How is your progress there?"

"No territory under our control yet." That voice was Sabien's. He remained calm, as though he were required to be at this meeting. Was he a part of whatever scheme Claude and Reon were a part of? Or was he obligated to be there as Captain of the Ilusaurian guard?

"Wasn't that the point of this marriage?" Reon asked.

"I'm working on it," Claude countered.

"Have you at least gotten anything out of her?"

"Not yet," Claude replied.

"Why not?"

There was a lull in the conversation. Dagmara pressed her cheek against the wood, desperate to hear their words.

"Don't tell me you're actually falling for her," Reon said.

"Of course not. She's done nothing but create problems since her arrival."

"What about Flaustra?"

Dagmara felt a pit in her stomach. That's where Magdalena was. What was Claude's plan with Flaustra?

There was more silence. Had she missed something? Then she heard footsteps. They were coming toward her.

She quickly straightened her posture, reaching her hand up to feign knocking moments before the door flung open. Sabien stood in the threshold, eyeing Dagmara suspiciously.

"Oh, hello," she said, flashing a smile. She lowered her hand. "I was just coming to find the king. Is he in there?" She rose on her tiptoes, looking over Sabien's shoulder. She saw Claude, leaning over a desk, his head hanging.

"Now is not a good time," Sabien said.

She shoved past Sabien, ignoring him, and welcomed herself into the room. If they were going to talk about Azurem, she had every right to be there.

"You left me all alone out there," she began, trying to remain inconspicuous. She didn't want them to know she had been eavesdropping.

"I know you can handle yourself fine," Claude replied. He didn't meet her gaze, and she couldn't determine if he was annoyed by her presence or not.

"Reon," Dagmara noticed him, backlit by a moonlit window, wide open to let a cool draft in. "Lovely to see you. I must admit I didn't realize Ilusauri and Celestaire had such a strong alliance."

Reon dipped his head. "Celestaire is slow to accept relations with

Ilusauri, but at least Claude and my relationship is strong," he replied. "I look forward to getting to know you and the rest of Azurem."

Something flashed behind Reon. The outline was barely visible in the dark sky, but a figure manifested, flying in and landing on the windowsill.

Dagmara felt a wash of uneasiness as she stared at the blackbird. Its beady eyes pierced her soul, almost mocking her.

"Sabien," Dagmara said, "I think it's time Reon returned to the party. Could you escort him?"

Reon's eyes narrowed. He followed her gaze over his shoulder, unable to see the bird in the window, before looking at Sabien, confusion plastered on his face.

"That's inconsiderate, Princess," Claude said, looking up at her. His tone was strained, attempting not to argue in front of their guest. He was still angry at her for something, though she couldn't determine what.

Dagmara felt a pit in her stomach. "Martine," she ordered, raising her voice.

Martine passed Sabien, coming to stand beside Dagmara. "Yes, Princess?"

"Take Reon back to the party."

The room was strung with tension. Everyone remained utterly still, waiting for Claude to give the final word.

Then the blackbird let out a caw, its tone like a nail to Dagmara's temple. She winced, nearly covering her ears. Everyone saw Claude snap his head in the direction of the window, his demeanor shifting from annoyance to violence. He gripped the table, the papers on the desk crumpling under his fingers.

"Now, Martine," Dagmara commanded.

Suddenly on alert, Martine rushed forward, taking Reon by the arm. "This way, sir."

The blackbird took flight into the room, sweeping across the study toward a bookshelf on the opposite side. Claude covered his face, dropping behind the desk moments before the blackbird flew past his head.

The king picked up a chair, chucking it toward the bookshelf. It shattered against the shelf in an alarming snap, books and papers flying everywhere. "Get out!" Claude yelled. The bird gracefully flew from the top of the bookcase, rounding the outside of the room, sounding another ear-piercing screech.

Reon glanced over his shoulder. "Your Majesty?" he called in shock. Martine yanked him out of the room, and they disappeared into the corridor.

The bird would not land, circling the room like it was circling prey. It dove for Dagmara, and she didn't have a chance to defend herself in time. It raked its claws down her cheek, and an excruciating sting pierced her skin.

She grabbed her cheek, but there was no blood. There was no mark. Her skin was perfectly smooth. Was this all a trick of the mind too?

The bird dove for the king next, and Claude raised both hands, igniting the walls in flame.

Dagmara braced herself, collapsing to the ground and covering her face with her arms. The entire perimeter of the room was engulfed in flames. Fire stretched up the walls as though they were trapped in a circle.

But there was no heat. It was all a trick of the mind. He was trying to defend himself from the blackbird. She touched her cheek once more, feeling no mark. Was the blackbird real or an illusion?

"Your Majesty!" she called. This needed to end.

That's when someone grabbed her under the arms and lifted her to her feet. Sabien was pulling her toward the exit.

"Let go of me!" Dagmara screeched, yanking out of his grip.

The blackbird swooped toward Claude, threatening to peck out his eyes. Claude ducked once more before grabbing a broken leg of the chair and chucking it toward the soaring bird. It whizzed past Dagmara, clattering against the fiery wall, but never ignited.

"Claude, stop!" she pleaded.

Sabien wrapped his arm around her waist, picking her up. She couldn't fight him as he dragged her from the room and slammed the door behind them. He pressed her against the wall, blocking her from making an escape.

"You can't stop him when he turns into this," Sabien said.

Dagmara was trapped between his chest and the stone wall behind her. She could hear Claude's screams from inside the study and the crashing of more furniture.

"How did you know?" Sabien asked.

She wasn't listening to him. Her breathing was ragged as she cupped her cheek with her hand. Nothing. The bird left no mark even though she had felt the pain. She could *still* feel the pain.

Sabien grabbed her chin and yanked her head to look at him. "How did you know he was turning?"

"I didn't," she lied.

"You told Reon to leave the room. You knew before the king. How?"

"Didn't you see..." her voice ran dry when she saw his expression flicked with doubt.

"See what?"

Nothing. Nobody else could see the bird, which was made clear by Pierre who rescued her from the balcony on the first day. How was that even possible? Why was she the only other person that could see it?

She shook her head, yanking out of Sabien's grip. She shoved her palms into his chest, trying to escape. He backed away from her on his own, for there was no way she was strong enough to push him.

"What did you see?" Sabien repeated.

"Nothing," she said under her breath. She turned away from him, starting off down the corridor. She didn't plan on returning to the party. She wanted to disappear.

Fortunately, Sabien didn't follow her. He remained by the door, waiting for the king to calm down, letting the king fight his mind on his own.

Whatever afflicted the king seemed to torment her too. And if he was a Mad King...what did that make her?

CHAPTER 35
Magdalena

"Get them," Vex shouted at his officers to restrain Magda and Ravi.

As fast as lightning, he opened his palm and threw a white marble to the floor, which exploded in a burst of blue smoke. The choking cloud filled the entire space, causing Magda's hand to fly to her mouth. In the chaos, she felt herself being wrenched out of Ravi's arms, and her wrists being pinned behind her back. She wanted to scream, but her lungs were burning from the strange substance. All she could hear was Odie barking, mixed in with Vex's chilling laugh.

When the mist cleared, one man each held both Ravi and Magda. Their grips were like iron clasps, digging deep into Magda's forearms. When her vision fully came to, she noticed that the third henchman had placed another net over Odie and his new friend.

"Sit them down," said Vex.

Magda screamed as she was yanked through the rows of barrels and over to the table. The man easily shoved her down onto a wooden chair and held her in place. She stole a glance at Ravi, who was seated directly opposite of her, equally held down.

"Let us go!" yelled Magda. "All I want is my dog back."

"This goes far beyond your dog now," said Vex with an angry

growl. He leaned into Magda's face, his stinky breath flushing against her lips. "You released my hound, and I just had to kill it before it bore any more havoc on my guests. Do you know how much money I will lose?"

Magda gulped. It would not have been easy to kill the hound. Vex was more powerful than she had realized. What would Dagmara do to get out of this?

"I promise I will pay you more than you earned this entire night," said Magda strongly. "We can all leave here without any problems."

Vex laughed before sitting in a chair between them. "These games aren't about money. They're about reputation. About who can be trusted, and who will win the best contracts."

Magda stole a glance at Ravi sitting beside her, but he seemed equally as confused.

"What do you mean?" asked Magda.

Vex stood once again and clasped his hands behind his back. Then he began pacing as he spoke, "Together, the guilds are the most powerful corporation in history. We deliver goods around the kingdoms, and we're the main economic trading power in the world. Our pockets run so deep and our men so vast that we could have our own army. But there's one man who is more powerful, and he offers large contracts to any captain that not only brings goods back from uncharted waters, but full expedition logs."

"King Claude," Magda finished Vex's sentence, remembering the letter in Ishani's ship. "Why does he care about your logbooks?"

"Who cares," Vex laughed. "He asks for strange notes, information, topography, animals, words...presence of magic."

"He pays you greatly for this information I'm assuming. And you fight amongst each other to win the best information to bring back to Claude," Magda asserted.

"Precisely."

Ravi spoke up next. "We don't have any contracts for you to take. So what do you want from us?"

Vex removed a vial from his pocket, setting it down on the table. "The truth," he said. "I have a feeling that you have a secret King Claude will pay a lot of money for. For instance, why did the hound wake up when you approached?"

Magda recognized the truth serum. She knew that one gulp of it would reveal all of her secrets, jeopardizing not only her own life but Dagmara's. If Vex asked just one wrong question, Magda would be dead in an instant.

"The hound was already awake," Magda protested.

"No. It's been asleep since I smuggled it here months ago. It doesn't even eat or drink. One mysterious girl enters my basement, and suddenly it awakens? I'm sure this is one of the many secrets you hold, Dagmara."

"I swear I don't know anything—"

"Hold her," said Vex. He began unscrewing the bottle.

"No! Don't do this!" screamed Magda.

"Let her go!" yelled Ravi.

The third henchman pinned down the corner of the net before approaching Magda. Each one of them grabbed Magda's arms, yanking her out of her chair, and pulling her up onto the table. They slammed Magda down onto her back, one man on either side, and she banged her head against the wood, causing it to spin in confusion.

"You'll pay for this, Vex!" shouted Ravi.

Vex let out a laugh. "Ooooo I'm so scared..." he said sarcastically. "Don't worry, I have no use for you, Ravi. You can go back to playing your violin."

"If you let one drop of that touch her, I'll kill you."

Vex chuckled. "Don't waste my time with empty threats."

They held her down while Vex stood above her. Then Vex's hand caressed Magda's throat. He squeezed, tilting her chin back, and forcing her mouth open with his opposite hand. He shoved his fingers into her mouth, prying it open, while he attempted to pour the liquid down her throat.

Magda tried to fight back, but Vex's voice drowned out Ravi's, disorienting her even more. "You work in the Azuremi court, don't you Dagmara?" taunted Vex. "Claude has been quite interested in Azurem. Let's see what you can tell us now."

Magda dug deep, hoping that somewhere she could channel any magic. She was a guardian, after all. She screamed as every fiber of her being reached for any source of power, but she only created a splintering headache pulling her in all directions.

"Vex, I swear, if she suffers—"

An acidic taste lit her mouth on fire, and the potion ignited inside her, flowing through her nerves all the way to her fingertips.

Vex released the grasp on her neck. He stepped back and said, "Now, tell me—"

Magda kicked her foot up, smacking Vex in the chin with the heel of her boot. He staggered backward, and the man holding Ravi mistakenly went to reach for Vex. In an instant, Ravi was on his feet and had grabbed the chair. He swung it forcefully, and the wood fractured as it smashed into the henchmen's head, drawing blood before he collapsed.

The man on Magda's right released her and went after Ravi, giving Magda her arm back. She reached for a wine bottle on the table, smashing it against the man on her left. He staggered backward, holding his face as glass and a dark-red liquid splattered in all directions.

Magda rolled off the table and smashed onto the stone, taking in her surroundings. Ravi was going after Vex, but there were two more henchmen left. One grabbed Ravi by the arm and yanked him toward the barrels, before giving him a shove. Ravi stumbled backward, slamming against the wood. But the man didn't give Ravi an ounce of rest. He yanked on Ravi's shirt, pulling him close, before punching him across the face. The other one approached, grinning, and gave Ravi another punch. One time. Two times.

Magda scampered across the floor, reaching the net and throwing it off the dogs. "Go help Ravi!" she yelled.

She breathed a sigh of relief as the dogs went after the henchman, snapping at their legs and feet as they let out horrifying screams.

For a second Magda thought it was all over, but someone grabbed onto Magda's leg, dragging her back towards the table, and flipping her over onto her back.

Magda screamed but Vex was too quick. He slammed her head down into the stone, putting his arm up to her throat. Instantly, he was above her, straddling her body with his legs as he kept her pinned down.

"Now, where were we?" he asked Magda. He pressed his arm deep into Magda's throat, making her vision spin. His other hand stroked her hair before caressing around the side of her cheek. "Right. I think I was about to ask you some serious questions."

The fiery feeling ignited in Magda's entire body, and she was certain that the truth serum had not worn off. She knew she had to fight it as long as possible.

"Now, tell me who you are—"

Suddenly Vex was yanked back. He was ripped off Magda's body and pulled to his feet. Ravi grabbed Vex by the throat and slammed him into the table, before driving a broken glass bottle into Vex's stomach.

Vex gasped, stuttering as blood gushed from the wound, but he couldn't emit any words.

Ravi yanked Vex toward him by the collar of his shirt, whispering in his ear, "I told you I would kill you." Then he let Vex drop to the side, and his limp body crumpled into a wilted pile on the stone floor.

Magda remained on the ground, her entire body shaking uncontrollably. Small bruises and cuts were already forming on her upper arms. All around her lay piles of glass and seeping pools of red wine. Four dead bodies surrounded her, having been slayed by Ravi or the dogs.

Ravi raced over to her, kneeling down. "Did he hurt you?" he asked, helping Magda to a sitting position.

"No," Magda let out.

Ravi's lips and nose were dripping with blood, and his eye was already bruised. Magda reached up to touch his face, attempting to wipe away some of the staining. "You're hurt."

"It's fine," said Ravi, grabbing Magda's hand in his and removing it from his face. His hands shook as he held onto hers.

"Are you alright?" Magda asked.

"Yes...," Ravi stammered, his hands still shaking. "It's just, I've never killed anyone before." His eyes trailed to Vex.

Magda reached up and embraced him around the neck, pulling him close. "You saved my life."

Ravi let his arms encircle around Magda's back, tightening the hug. "I don't know what overcame me. It was instinct."

Magda let a deep sigh release from her body, and for a moment in his arms, she felt safe.

Then Odie and the golden dog scampered over to the two, leaping directly between Ravi and Magda. Odie jumped onto Magda's lap, almost knocking her over as he licked her face again. She gave Odie a tight squeeze as Ravi said:

"They're both fine."

"And that one?" asked Magda. "Does it have a name?"

"No, she doesn't," said Ravi, looking around the dog's neck for a collar.

"What should we name it?"

"Poppy," said Ravi with a smile.

Poppy gave a loud bark, before running out of the wine cellar, and darting out of sight, leaving all of them behind. Odie whimpered, but Magda stroked his fur whispering, "She has to go find her family too."

Ravi turned to look at Vex, and a look of dread spread across his face at the sight of the dead guild leader. But instead of sharing what was on his mind, he moved over to the dead body, searching inside of Vex's jacket.

"What are you doing?"

Ravi found what he was looking for, and held up a letter with Queen Sanyal's seal in his hands. He ripped it open. "An invitation to the ball."

Ravi passed the invitation to Magda. It was a turquoise and yellow gilded slip of paper, stamped with Queen Sanyal's seal. Shining letters read:

An invitation to the palace of the Guardians of the Soul to Princess Kiran Dhara's birthday ball. And one invited.

"Are you serious?" Magda beamed.

"Looks like you're my date now," Ravi grinned. "Let's get out of here."

CHAPTER 36
Dagmara

The engagement ball came to a close when the engaged couple never returned.

Dagmara sat upright in her bed, wearing nothing but her nighttime slip. She told Urszula everything. Luckily, Urszula didn't seem to judge her. She didn't even insinuate that Dagmara was going mad. She listened in silence, only asking follow up questions as needed.

It wasn't long before there was a knock on the door. Martine opened the door, and Madame Annette stood in the threshold.

"Princess," Annette said, her face in a scowl. "The king would like to see you in his royal chambers."

His royal chambers? Dagmara thought that she wouldn't be allowed to set foot inside until she was queen. Was this her opportunity?

She followed Annette through the castle. It was nearly the middle of the night, and all the guests had vacated the premises. She heard Martine trailing them, a few paces behind.

"Sabien tells me you were able to predict Claude's episode," Annette said. "How is that?"

"Sabien is mistaken," Dagmara replied curtly.

"Martine was there, weren't you?" Annette glanced over her shoulder.

Dagmara's blood turned to ice.

"All I remember is the king going into one of his episodes. The Princess was speaking to Reon at the time," Martine said.

Dagmara let out a sigh of relief, while Annette scoffed. Dagmara flashed a glance over her shoulder, silently thanking Martine. Her guard nodded, a suspicious yet sympathetic smile on her face.

They walked through the entrance of the royal chamber, once again surrounded by dozens of mirrors. Due to the night, it was darker in the room, making it feel even more daunting. Annette knew exactly where she was going, leading her through the mirrors and up a large staircase to a door inlaid with silver streaks.

She knocked before Dagmara could, and they all heard the faint, "Come in," from the king.

Steeling herself, Dagmara entered.

The royal bedchamber was expansive, with a study on one side of the room and a large, canopied bed on the opposite side. It was nearly pitch black aside from the moonlight streaming in through floor-length windows, hindering Dagmara's ability to examine every inch of the room.

The king stood by one of the large windows, his figure silhouetted by the moonlight.

"I'm surprised you didn't deny my request again," he said, his voice barely more than a whisper.

"Perhaps you can come to me next time," she offered, trying to keep her tone even. Her gaze wandered across the desk, seeing stacks of paper. She couldn't read anything from this distance. In the shadows, she caught sight of a blank canvas.

"You were very bold today," Claude said, his back still to Dagmara.

"Thank you."

"I never said it was a compliment."

"You never said it wasn't a compliment either."

The king shifted, turning over his shoulder to face her. His face was barely lit by the moonlight, but she could clearly see the weariness of his eyes. The silk robe was untied in the front, revealing his rippling muscles that disappeared beneath the trousers that sat low on his waistline. He held a goblet, decorated in gemstones.

"You're insufferable," he said, his voice nearly a growl.

Her eyes narrowed. "Excuse me?" From her recollection, all she did this evening was support him. She had even tried to prevent Reon from seeing his outburst.

"You overstepped," he stated.

"I was trying to help you. It's a good thing I arrived when I did."

"I'm not talking about the events in the study. I'm not going to even ask why you followed me," Claude said. "I'm talking about the rest of the evening. You thought you had authority to make claims today about my kingdom. Ilusauri is still mine, and how I decide to rule is my decision."

"I made no remarks about the way you rule, and never claimed Ilusauri was mine. You were the one who announced that Azurem and Ilusauri would be united, and you were the one who suggested that we put on a show," Dagmara said. "The entire night I was only trying to support you."

"You told Lionel I would personally visit the nearby villages."

She paused. The governor who asked about the rations?

"That's what this is about?"

Claude set the goblet down on the side table before approaching her on the other side of the room. His strides were wide and filled with anger. "I haven't left the castle in years."

"You came to Nouchenne."

"Only to save you," he growled. "I haven't visited a populated village since my parents died."

Dagmara was silent. She could feel the air in the chamber shift. "I didn't know that. Then tell Lionel it won't happen."

"I can't do that."

"You're king, you can do whatever you want."

"I can't!" his voice rang throughout the room, and Dagmara jumped. Her breath caught in her throat, and she felt frozen in her shoes.

The king seemed to notice her fear. He let out a deep sigh. "I will not go back on our word to Lionel. That is not a good look for either of us. It will only show we disagree with one another at the beginning of this alliance. But...I don't know how I can leave the castle."

"Why?"

Claude scoffed, turning away from her once more and pacing to the wall.

"I can't help you unless I understand why," Dagmara stated, finding her courage once more.

"You can't help me at all."

"I might, but I know nothing about you," she replied.

"And I know nothing about you!" Claude gestured at her with wide arms.

She took a step toward him. "A truth for a truth, is that what you want?"

He stared at her, heaving. His eyes twinkled with some masked emotion she couldn't quite discern. She wished she could. The muscles in his chest rippled as he clasped a hand behind his neck, breaking his eye contact with her.

"I don't know what I want anymore," Claude admitted. "I thought I had everything planned out before I met you, but you're very different than I remember. I know we grew up over the years, but I didn't expect to feel...," he hesitated. "I didn't expect your arrival to affect me this much."

Taken aback, Dagmara hardly knew how to respond. She had so many follow up questions cross her mind, and confusion settled in. A silence filled the space between them, and she struggled to form a sentence.

"This...situation...is not what I expected either." She fumbled, hoping she had conveyed some of her emotion. She no longer knew what she was doing. She was alone with him in his chamber, directly beside his desk which could contain the information she needed to incriminate him in the murders of Bogdan and Aleksy. Now, everything was turned upside down.

"I can't decide if I trust you," Claude stated. "What is a king who can't make a decision?"

"A thoughtful one."

His eyes met hers. His stare was intense, but not angry. No...it was something else entirely.

Dagmara's breath caught in her throat, and her stomach catapulted inside her body. She was startled by how much she was drawn to his eyes. They were hypnotic, magnetic, and consuming all at the same time. His gaze flooded her body with warmth, and her mind spun as though nothing else in the world existed but him.

And she didn't want the feeling to end.

"I guess we can't fully trust each other unless we know each other. A truth for a truth, if the offer is still on the table?" Claude asked, then quickly added, "For the betterment of our kingdoms."

"And the safety of our people," she appended, remembering what they had said to one another before entering the engagement ball.

His lips almost creased into a smile. Then he gestured toward the seating arrangement by the window, lit by the subtle moonlight. No, she was in his room now and was going to see what she could find, no matter the cost. She crossed the room to the bed and sat on the edge of it, folding one knee underneath her and letting her nightgown slide up her leg.

His jaw ticked, his eyes roaming for a brief moment. Then he gave her a curt nod as though she would have it her way before taking a seat on the edge of the bed. He leaned against the canopy post, facing her.

"You may go first," she said.

He pursed his lips, thinking of a question, before he finally spoke. "What is your favorite color?"

A smile almost immediately crested her lips. "Starting off difficult, I see."

"It is important to know if I can trust you," he mused.

She shook her head. "Turquoise. You?"

"Orange."

"Orange?" she echoed.

"Are you judging me?"

"No, not at all," she recovered.

His eyebrow raised slightly, a bemused smile crossing his face. "Best season?"

"Fall. What's your favorite book?"

"The Chronicles of Time."

"Oh, I've never read that one," Dagmara admitted.

"You're missing out then," he replied. "Favorite dessert?"

"Rice pudding. Beverage of choice?"

"Sailonne wine. A pastime you enjoy?" Claude asked.

"Cards. Who is your closest friend?"

"Sabien. Who would you do absolutely anything for?"

"My brother." The words slipped from Dagmara's mouth before she remembered who she was. She was supposed to be Magda. What was she doing playing this game? She couldn't be sharing information about herself and risking exposing who she truly was. She quickly reframed the answer, switching it from her brother Teos to Magda's brother. "Well, it was Aleksy. Now...probably Odie, my dog." She hoped her tone was believable.

Claude's expression shifted slightly. "I'm sorry about Aleksy. Why didn't you bring Odie with you?"

Dagmara bit her lip. It was time for this game to end. "It's not your turn."

A laugh escaped the king's lips, thinking it was a jest. "I apologize. Go ahead."

Then Dagmara asked the question she had been holding on to for too long, "Why haven't you left the castle?"

The conversation stilled. Once more, a blanket of silence cascaded down on them. Claude's expression fell, his smile vanishing. "I can't control when a spiral begins. I am afraid my people will see me as a Mad King. You saw what happened tonight."

The wall between them began to crack. For a brief moment, Dagmara felt sorry for him. Until his next question.

"Have you ever been in love?"

Dagmara didn't have an answer right away. Everyone she had been with in the past had been for fun. The men thought she was pretty, but never anything deeper. In fact there was never depth to any of her relationships. Aleksy was different...but their relationship had only just begun. In another world, she could have fallen in love with him, but in this world, she never got the chance.

"No," she replied. "You?"

"Young love, but not the real thing," he replied. He leaned forward on the bed, the mattress sinking under his weight. "Is there someone in Azurem?"

"Why would you ask me that?"

"I don't want you to despise me for taking you from your true love," he said. "And, I don't like sharing."

Dagmara shifted. "No. There's no one in Azurem."

"Then who is Teos Zosia?"

Silence filled the room as Dagmara stared back at the king, her mouth agape. The world was frozen in time as Dagmara's heart nearly stopped in her chest.

"Sabien informed me of the letter," Claude said. "By the expression on your face I suspect you intended to keep him a secret."

She couldn't tell Claude that he was her brother. And yet, she had to explain she didn't have an Azuremi lover. What if Claude asked her what exactly was in the letter? Her cover would be blown.

She had to back up her lies with some of the truth. That was what worked before, and it would work now. King Claude had the power to look into who Teos was if he wanted to.

"His mother worked closely with my parents before she was killed," Dagmara began. "We grew up together. Teos is unofficially adopted into our family, and one of the last people I have left. He's only fifteen, and he recently got sick. It's not fair that Ilusauri has been hoarding medicine that could help him."

"Oh..." Claude muttered. "Is that who you were stealing the leku for?"

Dagmara nodded.

"I'm beginning to see why you're invested in this exchange."

Dagmara knew she had to change the topic. She thought about her next question, feeling the stakes rise, before she dared to ask, "Have you ever killed someone?"

After a brief hesitation, he said, "Yes." He swallowed, the only indication that the question made him uncomfortable. "How did you know the wine was poisoned?"

Dagmara was silent. "I already answered that question days ago. I saw the extra pocket on the pitcher."

"I don't believe that is the only reason. It's because you've seen that trick before, isn't it?"

Dagmara knew her face was turning red. She pushed herself to her feet. "I've had enough of this game."

Claude was already on his feet and took a step toward her. "You've *used* that trick before, haven't you?"

"You're blaming me?" Dagmara gasped. She stepped forward, her chest nearly against his. "He was your servant. If anything, *you* were trying to poison *me*."

A sharp laugh escaped his lips. "Why would I poison you when I brought you here to protect you?"

"Protect me?" Dagmara asked. "No, you brought me here to finish what your assassins couldn't in Azurem."

His expression shifted as though Dagmara had stabbed him. "Why would you think that?"

Her chin was tilted up to meet his gaze. "The assassins were wearing Ilusaurian uniforms."

Claude's eyes narrowed. "Maybe they're framing me."

"That's convenient," she replied. "The Mad King playing the victim."

He grabbed her by the shoulders, making her heart skip a beat. His grip was firm, his fingertips digging into her skin. "If you believe I'm the villain, why did you come here in the first place?"

"Let go of me!" Dagmara slammed her palms against his bare chest, but he was as solid as a rock. He wouldn't budge against her hands.

"Why did you save me from the poison?" he demanded.

"Maybe I shouldn't have!" Dagmara yelled. "I should've let you die."

"And I should've let those hounds tear you to shreds!"

A shudder ran down her spine, and she gripped the lapels of his robe. "That would've been a better fate than marrying a monster."

One of his hands shifted from her shoulder to the back of her neck, holding her firm. "I can't stand you."

"The feeling is mutual."

"If I wasn't mad before, you will drive me insane," said Claude.

She rose to her tiptoes. "Gladly."

For a brief moment, they remained inches from one another. His muscles flexed against her, and she could hear her heart thundering inside her. His eyes glistened in the moonlight, filled with layers of emotions she couldn't interpret. She felt every inch of his naked chest through her thin nightgown, and there was no doubt he could feel her too. The silk didn't sufficiently cover her curves as she was pressed against him.

His fingers found the base of her hair, sending a shiver through her body.

Then he released her, turning his back as he walked away. "You're free to go."

Dagmara caught her balance, and her heart dropped when his body disconnected from hers. Too many feelings collided inside her that she couldn't interpret. Watching him walk away, she found indignation simmering in her stomach.

She frowned. "How kind of you to continuously summon me and dismiss me like a pet."

He froze, then turned over his shoulder. "I meant you're free to return to Azurem."

"No," Dagmara stated. "I will not continue this back and forth with you. We made a deal in the greenhouse, and we are seeing this through."

"That was before you accused me of murdering your family."

"The assassins were Ilusaurian, and they crossed into Azurem with false aliases that you personally signed," Dagmara said, unafraid that she was spilling secrets. If she got his confession, she wouldn't have to wait until she had access to his royal quarters for proof.

A muscle ticked in Claude's jaw.

"You have nothing to say?" Dagmara scoffed. "Let me know when you're ready to be honest." She whirled and headed for the door.

"The poison that was used at the lunch was Azuremi," Claude called out. "Smierc. Have you heard of it?"

Dagmara froze with her hand on the doorknob. That was impossible.

Smierc was what she had used to kill Jacek the day before the coronation. In fact, she used it often to take out her victims. Why was an Ilusaurian servant using it in the Ilusaurian wine? With the trade routes closed between Azurem and Ilusauri, there would be no way Azuremi poison could have made it to Ilusauri. Claude had to be lying.

"Nothing to say?" Claude imitated her.

No, she had nothing to say. She couldn't defend herself without revealing she was an assassin.

Instead, she escaped, leaving the king behind...abandoning her chances to examine his desk filled with proof of his involvement in the Azuremi royal murders.

CHAPTER 37
Magdalena

It was almost daybreak.

Ravi and Magda made their way back to his house, for it was the closest shelter that they could find. They were both covered in wine and blood-stains, and Magda didn't want to bring Odie back to the Inn where he had been taken. Secretly, Magda didn't want to be alone.

The stars overhead twinkled like sparkling candlelight, and even the busy music district had died down for the night. The air around them was eerily quiet.

Ravi and Magda entered his first-floor kitchen, followed by Odie. It was dark inside. Ravi lit a candle in the corner of the room before removing his jacket and hanging it up on the wall.

"I'll get Odie some water," he said, reaching up to a pitcher and bowl on the shelves above.

Magda leaned down, holding Odie against her chest. But this time she didn't cry. All she was filled with was an innate sense of gratefulness to have her dog returned to her.

"Good boy," she said, as she stroked his fur. Odie jumped up, running his slobbery tongue all over Magda's face.

"Odie," Ravi called, followed by the sound of clanking bowls on the floor.

Magda looked up to see Odie trotting away from her, rushing to the bowls of water and food that Ravi had prepared. Ravi had also laid out an extra blanket for Odie to sleep on in the corner of his kitchen.

Suddenly, she noticed Ravi holding onto his left hand, and a gash ran along his fingers.

Magda stood to her feet. "You're hurt!" she exclaimed.

"It's nothing." Ravi shook his head.

Magda crossed to him, examining his hand in hers. While it wasn't actively bleeding, it was badly bruised, and a red line ran across his palm. If only she had healing powers right now.

Ravi winced in pain, pulling away. "Ow!"

"That's your violin hand. Do you have bandages?"

"In the bathroom." Ravi cocked his head to a door at the side of the kitchen.

Magda crossed to the door, opening it and stepping inside. It was smaller than the kitchen, with a shower, sink, and cabinet. Odie followed her, barely separating from her knees. Magda reached the cabinet, removing alcohol as well as bandages.

When Magda turned around, she noted Ravi had followed her into the bathroom. "This might hurt," she said as she unscrewed the alcohol bottle, letting a whiff of the strong liquid clog her senses.

Magda looked sincerely at Ravi before taking his palm in hers, feeling his coarse calluses on his fingertips. Then she held his hand over the sink while she poured the alcohol over the wound. Ravi winced slightly, but didn't make a sound.

Then Magda used the cloth to carefully bandage his hand. All the while, she was aware of Odie, pressing up against her leg. When she was done, she replaced the items in the cabinet.

"Thanks," Ravi said, letting out a sigh of relief as he examined his hand.

"No. Thank *you*. For everything. How will I ever repay you?"

"You don't have to."

"But I almost got you killed," Magda confessed.

"Neither of us could have known what would have happened," said Ravi, "You got Odie back, and that's what matters." Ravi leaned down and scratched Odie behind the ear. The dog tilted his head into Ravi's palm, his tail wagging.

Magda beamed as she looked at Odie, who hadn't left her side since leaving Vex's hideout. He was dirty, with matted fur and blood sprayed onto his snout. Then Magda turned to the mirror above the sink. She too, was splattered with red-wine stains, blood, and dirt. Her silver hair was in a tangled mess, the half-back style almost fully undone.

"By the guardians, I need to bathe," Magda let out.

"Help yourself," Ravi gestured to the tub behind them. He grabbed a towel from a hook on the wall and tossed it to her.

Magda caught it abruptly.

"I'll be outside," said Ravi, heading into the kitchen before shutting the door behind them.

First, Magda drew the bathwater, which she assumed came from a communal tank for the surrounding houses. It wasn't as hot as she liked it, but at least it wasn't ice-cold. Then she took a sponge from the cabinet, dipped it into the bath water, before bathing Odie, ensuring that his coat and nose were a shiny color once again. She knew he wouldn't enjoy getting into the bath, and she would rather not make a mess in Ravi's house tonight.

Then Magda slipped out of her stain-ridden dress, letting it slip from her shoulders and onto the floor before removing her corset and other undergarments. She submerged her body into the bath, and the luke-warm temperature was refreshing in the sticky, Flaustran heat.

For a moment, she had an ounce of respite. Her fingers traced through the water, remembering the mystical waterfalls and fountain displays that her father and brother had always put on for show. The people of Azurem loved magic, and they loved the entertainment of it, as if it was a welcome distraction from the days in the mines and the illnesses plaguing the kingdom. As she soaked, she let her other hand fall to the side, petting Odie. He had his chin propped against the bath, his tail wagging, clearly never wanting to leave her side again.

When Magda had scrubbed the dirt from her body and hair, she got out of the bath, wrapping the towel around her bare shoulders. Then she remembered—she had left her knapsack and belongings at the inn, and she didn't have a single change of clothes.

Magda peaked her head out of the bathroom door, standing in the towel. "Ravi—do you have something I can wear?"

"On it," he called from upstairs.

"Odie, go fetch," Magda ordered her dog.

In a flash, Odie was darting up the spiral staircase. In an instant, Odie returned to the bathroom, a shirt and pants between his teeth.

"Good boy," Magda responded before shutting the door behind her pet.

Magda decided against retying her corset as an undergarment, for she wanted to be comfortable. Quickly, Magda put on the oversized shirt, and attempted to put on the pants. But they were not her size, and they kept slipping to the floor. Hanging the pants on a hook, she decided to use the shirt as a dress, although it barely covered her. She wrapped her hair up in the towel before exiting the bathroom.

She stopped short. Ravi stood in the doorway, his hand braced up against the doorframe while he leaned against it, as if he had been waiting to use the room. He was already stripped out of his dirty clothes, completely shirtless and wearing only his underwear. It was clear he had already washed the blood from the front of his chest, for it was glistening with droplets of water.

"All clean now?" he asked. His eyes glanced down to recognize that she was pantless.

"Yes...," Magda stammered at the sight of him.

"Good, otherwise you wouldn't be allowed in my bed," he said matter-of-factly.

"In your bed?" Magda scoffed.

"You really enjoyed sleeping on the floor?"

Magda hesitated, biting her lip.

"That's what I thought."

Fire surged up Magda's legs and through her body, and she backed up as to not act upon the magnetism between them. As she did so, she tripped against Odie, falling back into the bathroom. Odie let out a whimper, darting out of the way.

Ravi leaned forward, catching her around her lower back and breaking her fall. Their faces were close to each other, his lips inches from hers and his hot breath on her cheeks; his hand had grasped around her waist, snatching the shirt so that it now laid higher than it should, and his legs were pressed against hers. He held her for a moment while he reached up to the towel, pulling it off her head and letting her long, wet hair fall down, splashing wet droplets against the thin, white shirt.

"I'll need this," Ravi said, indicating the towel. "I only have one."

Magda's heart pounded against her chest as he released her, and she caught herself against the sink to steady herself.

Odie was beside Magda, tracing around her bare legs once more.

Ravi bent down to drain the bath, and refill it. As he did so, he said, "Just tell me, cause I need to know," he paused for a minute, as if he was unsure if he should ask the question or not. "Do you actually have a secret?"

Magda grew confused. "What do you mean?"

"Vex said you have a secret the Mad King will pay a lot of money for."

Magda's heart beat again, but this time it wasn't due to Ravi's proximity. "Do you believe him?" she asked.

Ravi sighed. "Honestly, I don't know what to think. You were right the other night when you said we don't know anything about each other."

"Then ask me what you want to know."

He stood up and faced her. "What do you do in Azurem that makes people think you have information?"

Magda answered as Dagmara would, "I live at the Azuremi palace, and I work for the princess."

He absorbed the information. "Then why are you really in Flaustra?" he asked.

"I can't tell you that."

Ravi's eyes flicked back and forth, as if he was thinking of another question. "Are you planning on staying here? Or going back to Azurem?"

Magda stopped short. It was another question she couldn't answer. How could she tell him that she was a princess, destined to go back to Azurem and rule? Destined to marry a royal or a member of the court? Her mother would never accept her falling for a boy from Flaustra, no matter how she felt.

Ravi stepped closer to her, and took her hands. His fingers brushed over her skin, caressing her hands in his.

"I see so much in your eyes. Pain, fire, something haunting you from the past. I just wish you trusted me enough to let me in. To let me share any of the thoughts that are going on in your head."

"I do trust you," said Magda, "I just...," she struggled to say the words that were on the tip of her tongue.

"Do you feel anything for me?" Ravi suddenly asked.

"I..." Magda couldn't put her feelings into words.

"It's alright if you don't. I just need to know."

"It's not that. I...I can't let myself fall for you. Honestly, I've been holding back each moment we spend together."

"Why?"

Magda confessed, "It's because I've been hurting, and I don't want to confuse this desire to ease my pain with something that could be real."

Ravi brushed her wet hair out of her face, and circled his hand around her neck. "We won't know if this is real unless we can acknowledge that there is something between us. Letting someone in is not a weakness. It can be your fortress, your resolve..."

"No," Magda said, pulling away from him. "I can't do this. I would be putting you in danger...," she paused, "...you don't understand."

"I can't be in any more danger than I was tonight."

"Yes you can."

"Then tell me. The truth this time."

Magda's heart was cracking. She didn't want to involve Ravi any more in this mess. None of the reality of being a royal or a guardian was anything he was used to. How could she explain her life in Azurem or the assassination of her family? How could she explain her true mission in Flaustra?

But for some reason, each moment she spent with Ravi was more emotional, more intense. It was as if a fire was burning inside her, begging to be let free, and would not stop blazing until she acted upon her feelings.

She looked at him, and his alluring expression was threatening to pull her deeper. She didn't know if it was his tall stature, toned body, or his perfect smile that had her enchanted, or if it was his charisma that had captivated her from the very beginning. Or if it was the way he made her feel safe. It didn't matter—she desired to be in his arms.

"My family was killed," Magda said, "and it haunts me daily. I'm afraid that the same people that killed them could be after me. That's why I came to Flaustra, and that is the truth."

"That's why you want to go to the palace?"

"I want to meet with Queen Sanyal. I think she'll be able to help me."

"I can help you. You can stay in Flaustra, away from whoever was after you in Azurem. Now that Vex is gone..."

"The people that killed my family are not like Vex. They're much worse."

Ravi nodded in understanding, running his fingers through his hair. He took a deep breath, before turning his body toward Magda's. She was reminded once again that he was standing only in his underwear, as another pang of heat radiated through her body.

He continued, "So what you're saying is, if by continuing to associate with you, I would be putting my life directly in the line of fire?"

"Yes," Magda answered firmly. "I'm so sorry. I've made a mess of everything for you. You'd be better off never having met me."

"That's not true," Ravi said. He stepped strongly to her, and cupped her face in his hands. "You've lit a fire in me. I can't explain it, but it's like I wasn't living until I met you. When I saw them, holding you down on the table and threatening to hurt you, it was like my entire life flashed before my eyes, and I wanted nothing more than to ensure you were safe. All I see with you is endless possibilities, and if I ask the earth for anything more, I know my heart would be daring into a territory where I could never turn back."

"You don't mean that," Magda said. She needed him to stop saying these things right now. Already, his words had seduced her, and in another second she wouldn't be able to stop herself.

"I do." He put his hand under her chin, tilting it toward him. The movement forced Magda to back up, until she found the wall at her back. She stood there, looking at him, his body against hers. His other hand found her waist, pushing her further into the wall.

Magda reached up to place her hands on his bare chest, feeling the smooth skin underneath her palms. "There's so much ahead of me that is in question and that I don't understand. I have too many battles to fight."

"Then I want to be the person you return to when your battles are over."

Magda's face softened. "No one has ever said anything like that to me. I feel like I'm dreaming."

"I don't want this to be a dream any more," he said.

Magda was on edge, as if her emotions were one big knot inside of her, about to explode and finally provide her with some release. All she wanted was his mouth on hers.

However, at the last second, Ravi pulled back, saying, "But until you're ready to tell me everything, I don't know if this is a good idea."

Magda's heart dropped to the bottom of her chest, as if his words had struck her with a knife. Disappointment surged through her veins, but she knew Ravi was right. Magda couldn't be completely honest with him, and she had no idea what lied in store for her at the Flaustran palace. Technically, she was engaged to King Claude. What would the Mad King say when he found out his fiancée was falling for a man in Flaustra? What's worse—how could she ever tell Ravi that she was a princess? Or that she was engaged?

"I...I agree," said Magda, even though the words stung.

Ravi let his hands drop away from her, before saying, "You can still stay here for as long as you like."

"Thank you," Magda stammered.

"I'm going to bathe," he announced, before turning away from her. He went to undress and—

Magda raced from the room, her emotions running wild. "Come, Odie." she said, heading up the spiral staircase while her dog followed.

When they got to Ravi's bedroom, Magda's eyes drifted to the floor, wondering if she would sleep there again tonight.

Before she could make a decision, Odie leapt up onto the bed before letting out a slew of barks.

"Odie, get down!" Magda laughed, before jumping up onto the bed beside him, attempting to remove him from the tangled sheets.

But Odie wouldn't budge. He nuzzled into the corner, looking up at Magda with begging eyes.

"Alright fine," Magda said, laying down in the bed and making herself comfortable, putting one arm around Odie and holding him close. "But only for one night."

Magda turned onto her back, staring at the ceiling. The sunroof was open tonight, giving a passageway to the outside world and a perfect view of the stars. She remembered what Ravi had said—that the guardians were gods that were part of the stars—and she wondered if that was really true. Was Aleksy guiding her?

She knew Ravi would soon be out of the shower. Before she could think anymore, sleep took her.

CHAPTER 38
Magdalena

"I see you still haven't found any answers."

The voice was back—this time, stronger. Magda was once again in the void. She couldn't discern where the voice was coming from or who she was speaking to.

"Who are you?"

"A friend," the voice answered. "Care to ask me about being a guardian?"

The space was unnerving, and Magda still didn't trust a voice that had never identified themselves. "I don't need your help," she retorted.

"The time will come when you do need it. I think that you will come running to me. In the meantime, this journey will be good for you. The more you discover, the more you can embrace the storm within you."

"What do I need to discover?"

"If I told you, you wouldn't have the chance to discover it."

Magda scoffed under her breath.

The voice continued, "By the time we meet, the magic burning inside you will be so great, that you'll be ready for the chaos."

"My magic will not contribute to chaos."

"Once you uncover who the guardians really are, and why I am here to help you, you will understand. New worlds can only be born from the ashes of the old…"

Magda's eyes burst open. She lay paralyzed on Ravi's bed, the starry night coming into focus through the rooftop window. A trickle of beaded sweat lined her brows and neck. What were these strange dreams? They felt entirely too real.

Her fingers grasped around Odie's fur, and she was relieved when she realized her dog was safe and sound beside her. His head shot upright, his ears perked in alarm while she ran her fingers through his fur.

"It's fine, go back to bed," she whispered.

Odie rested his snout on his paws, but kept his eyes on her.

"Are you alright?" Ravi's voice startled her.

Magda looked to the floor, seeing Ravi sleeping there, using the damp towel as a blanket.

"What are you doing?" Magda asked.

"You looked like you were sleeping soundly. I didn't want to disturb you."

"Don't be an idiot. Get up here," Magda said, scooting over on the bed. Odie reluctantly shifted, finding a new comfortable spot at the base of the bed.

Ravi reluctantly agreed, standing up and hanging the towel on the wall. He was still shirtless, but at least he had put on pants.

He slid into the bed next to her. "You had a nightmare?"

Magda turned onto her right side, facing Ravi with her back positioned up against the wall. She adjusted her pillow and sat up on her elbow. "I keep imagining I'm talking to someone in a dark space. It doesn't make any sense."

"Well, I haven't had any dreams tonight. I haven't been able to fall asleep once. Just been stargazing."

"What's on your mind?" Magda asked. She extended her hand slightly towards him, letting her fingers graze against his.

Ravi noticed the gesture and let his hand interlock with hers. Then he said, "Dagmara, what I did tonight...killing a guild leader...I could be sentenced for a very long time."

The name struck her, and she was once again reminded of the lies that she was spinning. "It was self defense."

"No it wasn't. We broke into the guild's lair. Technically, we were trespassing. If they find out it was me, they'll send me to Dreadmarrow."

"What?" gasped Magda, remembering the deadly prison.

He reached up and placed his hand against her cheek. Then he stroked her hair and said, "After everything that's happened, I just want you to know that—"

"Stop. Don't talk like that."

"It's the truth and you know it," said Ravi. He moved his hand, caressing around her neck and sliding closer to her. When their faces were inches apart he said, "Guild leaders are their own type of protected politicians here. They rule in partnership with the royals. All of Vex's officers will be after me."

Magda gulped at the thought of Ravi going to Dreadmarrow. It was on an island at the center of all four kingdoms where criminals went for the rest of their lives. No visitors were allowed. Most people died after carrying out only a few years of their sentence.

"I'm so sorry," Magda mustered. She slid her arm around his waist and burrowed her face into his chest, taking in every inch of him. His bare skin was soft underneath her fingertips. "I never wanted this to happen. I...," Magda' voice cracked as tears welled in her eyes. Right when she was getting close to someone else, he was in danger of being taken from her too. At least she was a guardian. Maybe she had some kind of weight in these decisions?

"I'd do it again," said Ravi, wrapping his arms around her and pulling her tighter to him. "A thousand times over."

A guilt spread through Magda's body as he held her. Ravi had put all trust in her, but she couldn't even bring herself to tell him the truth about who she was.

If Ravi was really in danger, she couldn't hide her identity for much longer.

Some secrets were meant to be told.

CHAPTER 39
Dagmara

A few days later, Dagmara was summoned by Claude. This time, she was told that a food shipment had arrived, and they would be making their first delivery to the provinces. It seemed awfully soon for the food shipment to have arrived from Azurem, but that gave Dagmara a newfound sense of hope. Maybe that meant Claude's shipment of medicine had already arrived in Azurem. Maybe with the leku, doctors would be able to start making the cure to zowach again. They had run out of it years ago, but now hundreds of lives could be saved, including Teos's life.

Dagmara gracefully tucked her dagger into a sheathe on her thigh and added her newly brewed potions to her belt. One was the flash bomb jasny from her brother, of which she had only one left, and another smoke bomb, also from her brother. It resembled the explosive he had set off the day of the coronation. Another was a simple, poison-free concoction of herbs that gave her energy when she needed it most. She knew today would include being out under the sun, and she still had to maintain the facade that she was a guardian.

Collecting her things, Dagmara headed to meet Claude.

Martine wasn't the only guard standing outside of Dagmara's chamber that morning. A young guard was standing before Martine, holding a small white box. Dagmara immediately recognized the young guard as Pierre. The two guards both whipped their heads to Dagmara, straightening their posture as if they had been caught in an uncompromising position.

"Good morning," Dagmara said, her gaze shifting between the two of them, curiosity gnawing inside her.

Pierre cleared his throat. "His Majesty has asked me to escort you both to the stables," the guard said. "I also brought this for..." his voice ran dry as his gaze lingered on Martine, his grip tightening on the small box. "For...Your Highness!" he blurted out, extending his hand rigidly toward Dagmara. "Caramel squares!"

Dagmara's eyes narrowed, a smirk subtly creasing on her face. "I am fine with you giving Martine a gift," she said, amused. Pierre was easily five years younger than Martine.

Martine's face turned red. "I cannot keep the box on my person, and I don't have time to return to my chamber," she paused, "as I already explained to Pierre."

"Then we shall keep them here until we return," Dagmara stated. She took the small box from Pierre's grasp, peeking a glance inside at the misshapen caramel squares, and reentered her room. She gave them to Urszula, who had heard the whole conversation, and then exited her room once more.

"Pierre is your name?" Dagmara asked.

The boy's face twitched as if it were a trick question. "P-Pierre Candide, yes, Your Highness."

"Nice to officially meet you, I'm Magdalena."

He gave her a smile and an awkward bow.

Martine said nothing, but gave Pierre a sheepish smile, which Dagmara certainly had never seen before. It made Dagmara grin seeing the two awkwardly interact.

"Shall we?" Dagmara announced, realizing the pair would stand together all day.

"Yes," said Martine, finding her professionalism once more. Then she proceeded to lead the group to the stables.

The morning was breezy, and the flowers that peppered the front yard created a calming ambiance, but a false one at that. Dagmara remembered that the beauty of the castle was all Claude's magic. He was leading a lie, falsely projecting wealth when he was as desperate as the rest of his kingdom.

Outside the stables was an entire entourage. Two carriages were ready to go, led by gorgeous stallions. One carriage was being loaded with crates, no doubt the food shipment. The other carriage, which could easily seat eight people, was left wide open, certainly for her and the king.

Madame Annette was barking orders at the servants. Meanwhile, Claude supervised silently, and he turned his attention to Dagmara as she approached.

The sunlight glistened against his skin, already coated with a thin shimmer of sweat. At least he was fully clothed today, but that didn't make him any less attractive. In fact, there was something seductive about the regal attire he wore and knowing exactly the handsome physique that was concealed underneath.

His expression turned suspicious. Did he still blame her for the poisoned wine on the terrace? A few nights prior he had accused her, telling her the poison was smierc. It didn't make any sense.

"Good morning," Dagmara said. "I'm surprised a shipment arrived so quickly."

"We all are," Madame Annette said, doubt laced in her voice. She fired a glance at the king before returning to bark orders at the servants. They seemed to be on their last load.

Claude remained silent.

"We're nearly ready to head out." The baritone voice sent a shudder through Dagmara. She saw Sabien approach, his deep voice loud enough for all to hear. "If you are ready, Your Majesty?"

"Yes," Claude said. Then he gestured toward the second carriage. "After you, Princess?"

Dagmara nodded before starting for the carriage. Sabien opened the carriage door for her before extending his hand to help her inside. She gave him a hesitant smile, remembering their kiss in the library, before taking his hand. His grip was firm, his thumb caressing her skin briefly enough so that no one else would notice, but it sent a chill down Dagmara's spine.

"Glad to see your palm has healed," he said, barely audible.

Her mind flashed to when he noticed the cut on her palm in the library, and it aroused suspicion that she didn't have Life magic. She quickly withdrew and took a seat in the plush carriage.

Claude joined her in the carriage, sitting on her opposite side. He adjusted the sword at his belt so that he could sit comfortably. Pierre, Martine, and Claude's other main guard joined them last. Before the door shut, Dagmara watched as Sabien started for the front of the entourage. There was no doubt he was accompanying them.

The carriage door closed, and Claude said:

"The shipment isn't from Azurem. It's from Celestaire."

"What?" Dagmara's expression flashed with surprise.

"Yes, Reon had it coordinated a long time ago, but it's the only shipment we received and will be receiving from them."

A call sounded outside, and the carriage jerked as they departed from the castle. Dagmara began, "I didn't realize you and Celestaire were in an alliance."

"We're not exactly," Claude admitted. "Again, this is a one time shipment. The council doesn't know about it, solely Reon and Guardian Sora."

The council. Dagmara was familiar with it. Celestaire seemed to do their ranking and governing differently. The guardian and her partner were solely figureheads for the country, mainly for show. It was the council that made governing and militia decisions, which was different from both Azurem and Ilusauri.

"Only the people in this carriage—and Sabien—know this shipment is from Celestaire as opposed to Azurem."

"What business do you have with Celestaire that their council doesn't know about?" Dagmara ventured.

"That is confidential. We will be telling everyone this shipment is from Azurem."

"Celestaire doesn't have the same produce that Azurem does, so no one will believe that."

"People in a famine won't question their food," Claude shot back.

Dagmara shifted in her seat. She glanced sideways at Martine, wondering if she knew about all of the illusions Claude was creating.

"The people at the castle know about the magic," Martine explained, nearly reading her thoughts.

That made enough sense. She couldn't imagine someone trying to harvest a vegetable and end up with nothing but air. However, how were all the servants and guards at the castle keeping such a large secret?

Claude continued, "This shipment will be going straight to Lionel, seeing as he was the one you announced our new agreement with. As soon as we start getting shipments from Azurem, we will travel to the other three provinces and then probably have to circle back to Lionel at some point."

"What province is Lionel responsible for again?" Dagmara had met far too many people at the engagement ball for her to keep everything straight.

"The Southern," Claude replied. "The capital of Ilusauri, Sailonne, is in that province, giving Lionel more responsibility than the other governors."

Dagmara knew that name and the reason she was here in the first place. She had to sneak away and find any proof that Lionel forged the three assassin's papers to cross over for the Azuremi coronation. If not, Claude was the only other person able to forge the papers.

"You said you haven't left the castle since your parents died, but did you visit the neighboring towns often before that?" Dagmara ventured.

"Yes, my father and I often went to the towns together," Claude replied. "We could play games in the open field, and my father and I would always race back to the castle. He thought it was important for the people to know their king. He didn't want to be an untouchable figurehead, he wanted to be a friendly leader. It's what he wanted for me too. It's what I wanted..." his voice trailed off and his face hardened. "It will be a long ride to the capital if you want to get some rest." In other words, he was done with her questions. The king went silent, shifting his gaze to the window.

The ride to the capital was long. By the time they reached Sailonne, the sun was already above the horizon. The landscape was gray, save for the sliver of blue in the sky, and the fields were dusted with ash, shriveled and decaying.

The carriage came to a halt at the edge of a sprawling city that was surrounded by a stone wall. Pierre and Martine were quick to shut the curtains, masking the royals from the outside. By the sound of it, there was already a crowd forming at the front gates.

"Let us speak with Sabien and assess the situation," Martine announced. She opened the door, and suddenly a plethora of smells and noises flooded the carriage. She exited, shortly followed by Claude's two guards. They shut the carriage door with a resounding smack, enclosing Claude and Dagmara in the carriage together.

"I'm sure I don't need to remind you how important this is," Claude said, "it is the first time my citizens are seeing us together."

The first time they were seeing him outside the castle since he was a child, but he didn't have to say that.

"What are we going for here?" Dagmara asked.

Claude seemed taken aback by the question, and his expression wavered with confusion.

Dagmara clarified, "What is appropriate in your kingdom? Do they want to see an alliance between two guardians? Do they want to see a couple in love?" Dagmara remembered the way Bogdan would show off with his magic. She remembered the fountain in the square before the coronation and how every child wanted a piece of the guardian's powers. The people of Azurem loved magic. She added, "Do they want a show?"

"No, not a show," said Claude, finally seeming to understand her question. "They loved how genuine my father was. They loved how close our family was. They like feeling as though we are one of them... not some higher being." *We* meant guardians. Dagmara was never a guardian, so acting as though she wasn't one would be right up her alley.

Claude's heel was still tapping on the ground, his knee shaking and vibrating the rest of the carriage. "I suppose they want to see honesty. I don't know if I can give them that."

Dagmara reached toward him, placing her hand on his knee. She wasn't sure if it was because she wanted him to stop shaking or because she felt for him.

He stilled against her touch, his expression shifting into something more calm.

"We can still be our genuine selves without revealing all our secrets," she said.

He cleared his throat. "We will keep the visit short, just in case."

In case they both were accosted by the blackbird. It wasn't only plaguing Claude's mind, making him a Mad King, but now it was in Dagmara's head too. They couldn't let the people see that.

There was a knock on the carriage door before it opened, revealing Sabien. "We're ready for you both. Lionel came to greet us."

Claude nodded and glanced at Dagmara. "For the betterment of our kingdoms."

A warmth spread through Dagmara once more. "And the safety of our people," she added, before they stepped out of the carriage to face the citizens of Sailonne.

Lionel Floquet stood at the entrance to Sailonne, his short, white beard seemed brighter in the sunlight, contrasting against his tan skin. His hands were interlaced against his stomach, waiting patiently.

Claude held out his hand for Dagmara, helping her step down out of the carriage. By the way Lionel's bushy eyebrows raised high on his forehead, it was evident he was surprised to see them both, despite the coordinated delivery.

The crowd that had gathered around the carriage suddenly fell silent, their eyes filled with anticipation and disbelief. Some of the children bounced excitedly in front of their parents and were scolded in a hushed tone. However, not all of them seemed happy to see the king and his new fianceé. A few teenagers and young adults bore grimaces on their face, their hands either folded against their chest or planted on their hips. The older generation was more happy to see the king than the younger. Was it because they remembered when Claude's father was around?

Past the archway, a stamped, stone road led into the city. The structures were similar to Nouchenne, but it appeared wealthier, and of a more grandiose size. The two-story houses were crafted of the similar gray stone materials with wooden, tudor-styles roofs. These houses were larger and more well-kempt than the ones in the other villages, giving the indication that they were for higher-class citizens. In addition, many administrative buildings, shops, and other structures were interspersed throughout the streets beyond. The entire city was built on a hill, and in the distance, a steeple with a large bell marked the top.

Stepping fully out of the carriage, Dagmara felt exposed to the onlookers. She expected Claude to release her hand after she was safely on two feet, so she was surprised when he only shifted his grasp, taking her hand so that his was in front as they approached the governor.

"Welcome to Sailonne," Lionel said, "It has been a long time, Your Majesty." Though the statement could have been a jab, there was no hostility in his voice. He approached the king while two people followed close behind.

Martine, Sabien, Claude's two guards, and the dozen others from the palace that made the trip seemed to spread out, their eyes on the crowd, blocking anyone from getting too close.

"I'm happy we were able to visit," Claude called. His voice had transformed, now boisterous and authoritative.

"We are honored to be the first province you are visiting," Lionel stated. "To be honest, I wasn't certain you would personally deliver the shipment," he added a laugh to lighten the air, "but we are blessed to see you here."

"It is my privilege," Claude replied, his voice loud enough to carry across the entire crowd, "but we have to thank Princess Magdalena. It is because of the alliance with her kingdom that we are able to be so generous."

Hushed whispers rang through the surrounding citizens.

"Yes, I understand," said Lionel. His attention shifted to Dagmara, glancing at their interlaced hands so briefly, that she nearly missed it. "Might I say, you are a wonderful influence on our king, and so generous, especially after your tremendous loss."

"I'm only so generous because of Claude." Dagmara added a smile. "Trust me, Ilusauri is benefiting Azurem plenty with the reopening of the trade routes, it is the least our kingdom could do."

She knew her Azuremi accent was thick as she tried to speak in Ilusaurian. She prayed that everything she said was grammatically accurate.

She felt Claude squeeze her hand slightly. Was he thanking her or telling her to stop speaking?

"But the personal delivery...we are beside ourselves that you brought His Majesty to visit when dropping off the shipment," Lionel continued. "Might I invite you back to my manor for a glass?"

This was perfect. It was exactly what Dagmara needed to snoop through his manor for information on the assassins.

"I would love to, but I'm uncertain what else Claude has planned for today," she said before glancing up at him, hoping he would agree.

Claude met her gaze. "I think we have an hour or two." His eyebrow raised at her as if he was wondering for himself how long he had in such a new environment with so many people around. Maybe that was what he needed. Maybe whatever was after his mind couldn't reach him here.

"Wonderful!" Lionel exclaimed. "My head of resources will be handling the rationing and distribution," Lionel gestured toward a woman on his right before gesturing to a man past her, "and my deputy will schedule the shipments to the surrounding towns."

"Our hope is to bring another shipment by the end of the month," Claude replied. "Captain Sabien Renaud can help coordinate with your leaders. He is familiar with everything we were able to provide."

Sabien bowed. "Of course, Your Majesty."

"Martine, Pierre, and Sacha, accompany us, will you?" he said. All three nodded—and Dagmara finally knew the name of his other head guard.

The citizens seemed to keep their eye on the king as he walked with Lionel through the city and to the manor. Many who hadn't come to the gates now lined the street, and others were leaning out of their windows to get a better look. Dagmara tried to acknowledge them, not paying any attention to what Lionel and Claude were discussing. She even waved at a little girl who bashfully hid her face against her mother's leg. However, the mother seemed pleasantly surprised that Dagmara had paid her daughter any attention.

By the time they reached the top of the hill and the steeple at the center of the city, Dagmara could feel her heart pounding in her chest and sweat collecting on her lower back. She was grateful Lionel hadn't asked her any questions so that she could save her energy and breath rather than trying to speak.

Inside the manor was a large staircase that caused Dagmara to slow her pace.

Claude caught her eye, curiosity edging his expression. She flashed him an uneasy smile and forced herself up the stairs. They reached the second floor hallway, passing an open door with a large desk—most likely Lionel's study. Soon they rounded out of the hallway and into the main room at the end of the corridor, and a bright parlor came into view.

Lionel's tea parlor was extravagant, with giant windows to overlook the city square. The steeple was directly across from them, the bell glistening in the sunlight. Martine stood near the table, Sacha by the entrance, and Pierre was making small talk with one of Lionel's servants.

Dagmara only had to find the perfect moment to slip away.

The conversation that proceeded was remarkably boring. Dagmara was forced to feign interest the entire time, but luckily, Lionel and Claude seemed to tumble into a variety of conversations about the province that Dagmara had no input on. Anytime she was involved in discussions with King Bogdan, it was about assassinations she was responsible for or conspiracy theories surrounding the castle. She found that exceptionally more exciting than taxes.

She didn't envy Magda. Certainly as a guardian, the silky skin, perfect health, and magical prowess were perks, but if she never had to discuss taxes another day in her life, Dagmara would be content. It must've been nice for Guardian Sora, the Celesta guardian. She was a Spirit Guardian, and didn't have a single political responsibility, for political duties were taken care of by the tower. Besides, the guardians didn't have much to guard for the last few centuries—according to the legend of the First Prince.

The First Prince will rise.

The haunting sentence carved into the cavern in Nouchenne caused Dagmara to shudder. Brushing aside the memory, she returned to the conversation at hand. Dagmara didn't know how she would be able to sit through these conversations for the rest of her life.

That's when she remembered—she was simply a placeholder. She was an imposter. She didn't have to think about the rest of her life. What would happen if Claude wasn't responsible for the murders? That meant, they would really go through with this marriage. What would happen when Magda returned from Flaustra and took Dagmara's place?

Dagmara was so convinced that Claude was the monster, that the wedding would be annulled, and that Ilusauri and Azurem would go to war with one another. She had never thought about the opposing possibility.

When the conversation turned to shipyards, Dagmara decided she had remained present for long enough. It was time to search the manor and find out if Lionel had anything to do with the aliases of the assassins.

"Pardon me, I must use the powder room," Dagmara said during a lull in the conversation.

"Down the hall, third door on your left," Lionel said with a smile.

She rose from the table and went straight to the hallway. As she rounded the corner, she immediately sensed Martine trailing her.

Glancing over her shoulder, trying not to sound suspicious, Dagmara said, "I don't need assistance in the powder room."

"I plan to wait in the hall. I don't know who is around here."

Trying to rack her brain for a decent excuse to get rid of Martine, she returned her attention to the hallway in front of her and slammed against someone. Looking up, she met the gaze of the Ilusaurian Captain.

"Hello, Princess," he said. "I'll take it from here, Martine, remain by the king."

"Yes, Captain," Martine replied without any objection and retraced her steps.

"This is familiar," Sabien said, his voice melodic.

"I don't know what you're talking about," said Dagmara. She bumped him on the shoulder as she passed, continuing out of the parlor and heading toward the powder room. When she reached the powder room, it was unlocked. Before entering, she eyed the door at the end of the hall, the woodwork more intricate than the other doors surrounding her. It was slightly ajar, revealing the desk inside. There had to be something in there. How could she get rid of Sabien?

Sabien spoke behind her, "I'm referring to how close we were in the library, when your chest was against mine right before we—"

Dagmara whirled around and lunged for the captain. She clamped her hand over his mouth, stopping him mid sentence. "Shh! What is wrong with you?"

She couldn't see Claude and Lionel from their position in the hall, but their faded voices alerted her that they might be able to hear them.

She felt Sabien smile behind her palm, and he reached to grip her hip.

A sudden warmth surged through her body. She batted his hand away before grabbing him by the wrist and yanking him into the powder room.

She closed the door behind them before glaring at him. "No one can know about what happened in the library."

"No one?" Sabien mused. "Or Claude?"

"No one includes Claude," Dagmara snapped. "Did you tell him?"

"Tell him that I loved the way his betrothed tasted on my lips? No, I did not."

Goosebumps ran down Dagmara's arms, and her stomach flipped. She calmed her nerves enough to say, "You told him I received a letter from Teos. How do I know you're not lying?"

Sabien let out a deep sigh as he ran a hand through his hair. "I only warned him in case your knight in shining armor showed up to win you back."

"Not that it's any of your business, but Teos is not a romantic interest."

"I appreciate the clarification, but I wasn't concerned," said Sabien. "The kiss was barely a sample of what I can do."

"Stop mentioning the kiss."

"Believe it or not, I don't tell my king everything. Including the secret you are hiding from him," he said.

"I don't have any secrets, you're just trying to get a reaction out of me," replied Dagmara.

"Oh, Princess," Sabien said as he took a step closer, running a single finger along her jaw until his knuckles reached her chin. "There are many things I would do to get a reaction out of you, but none require a single word." His hand found her hip again, slowly tracing the curves of her body. His lips inched closer to hers until she could feel his breath inches from her lips, causing her to tremble.

Then he withdrew, stepping away from her and lacing his hands behind his back like a soldier.

She felt his absence in a wave of emotion, her mind reeling.

A laugh rumbled deep in Sabien's chest. "I'll wait until you're able to admit you feel something for me."

"I'm marrying Claude."

"As you keep reminding yourself," Sabien replied.

"Even if I wasn't, you certainly would not be my second choice."

"I'm never a second choice. I'm always the first."

"Claude is the first," she snapped. "I mean, have you seen him?" She wanted to smash Sabien's ego for good.

"If only you knew the truth about him."

Dagmara's breath hitched. "What truth?"

"There's so much you don't know," Sabien said, his voice laced with pity. "And as soon as you find out, you'll be mine."

Dagmara scoffed before throwing the door open and storming into the hall. Her anger dissipated as she saw Martine waiting at the end of the corridor. Martine's eyebrows raised as the captain stepped out of the powder room behind Dagmara.

Exiting the powder room with the captain was worse than being caught snooping. She couldn't try anything now with them both nearby. Her attempt to search the manor without being caught was over.

She glared at Sabien over her shoulder, and by the smirk on his face, it was as if preventing her from snooping was the plan all along.

CHAPTER 40
Magdalena

Voices clamored in Magda's dreams for the next few nights while they waited for the date of Kiran's birthday ball. She awoke in a furious sweat, the sticky heat of Flaustra soaking into the bedroom. Magda jerked upright, realizing she was in Ravi's bedroom.

Ravi and Odie were both gone, so Magda leapt out of the bed and splashed cool water on her face from the pitcher on the high shelf. She dashed down the spiral staircase, coming to a halt at the bottom.

Ravi was holding a piece of meat above Odie's snout, teaching him a playful trick.

"Close the door," Ravi was saying.

Each time he said it, Odie pushed his nose against the bathroom door, slamming it shut. Then he did the same with the small, single kitchen cabinet.

"Good morning," Magda said from the staircase.

"Watch this," Ravi exclaimed, showing off the trick once more. "I taught him to close things!" he exclaimed.

"And how is that useful?" Magda giggled. She knelt down to stroke Odie's fur as he bounded over to her, as if wanting validation for performing the trick.

Ravi ignored her question. "I washed your clothes." He turned to the stovetop, pouring steaming tea into two mugs, before continuing, "They're hanging in the bathroom. You should get ready quickly cause I have a surprise for you."

"A surprise?" Magda asked. She couldn't help but grin as her heart fluttered. But quickly, she composed herself. What was she doing—playing house with Ravi? She quickly snapped out of it and rushed to the bathroom. Sure enough, her clothes were hanging on hooks. She changed into her dress and laced up her boots, before combing out her silver hair and twisting it halfback as usual.

When she exited the bathroom, Ravi had breakfast and tea waiting for them.

"Hurry and eat," he said between mouthfuls, "we don't want to be late."

Ravi led Magda and Odie to a small shop in the heart of the marketplace. It was a few blocks from the coast, down a side street that was a bit quieter than the main one. He made sure to lead them away from the main streets where Vex's officers spent their time.

Before them, was a window with three lavish, beaded gowns. They fell straight to the ground rather than poofing outward and were a mix of green, red, and orange—bold colors unlike the muted pastels worn in Azurem. The sign read: *Gilded Silks*.

Now that they had an invitation to Princess Kiran's ball, she had to dress the part.

Odie rushed to the doorway, putting his snout at the bottom of the frame and sniffing around the edges. His tail wagged happily behind him.

Magda walked up to the front door and paused. To her right, on the ground, was a spiraling green vine wrapping itself around the doorframe.

Ravi rapped on the door three times.

Soon, the door burst open, and a young girl, likely thirteen years old, stood before them. She had a pair of two long braids and wore a purple dress that fanned out just below her knees.

"Ravi!" the girl squealed.

Odie instantly jumped up, putting his paws onto the girl and knocking her backward.

"Odie, down!" Magda shouted, reaching out to grab him.

"Don't worry, I love animals," she smiled, turning back around to the fluffy, black and white dog. She knelt down, petting his head and back. "I'm Prisha!" She still held Odie in her lap, and giggled as she tried to speak while he lapped her face. "We're so happy to have you at our family's shop."

"Your family?" Magda looked at Ravi with a confused expression.

"Yes, my mom owns this place," Ravi explained, "and I knew she could fill an order at the last minute. Mom?" he called as he ventured into the shop.

Magda went to follow him, but as she did so, her fingers grazed the vine on the door frame. Three new leaves sprouted from its stem. Magda gasped, pulling back in alarm, before snapping her head in each direction—hoping no one had noticed the apparent display of Soul magic. Luckily, Prisha had already chased Odie deeper into the shop.

Magda stood outside and touched the vine again. This time, a force illuminated from her hand, shooting up the stem, and sending a refreshing shock throughout the leaves. Ones that were previously brown and wilted curled upwards, as if they had only sprouted seconds ago.

Magda shook out her nerves and entered the store. She was in a small space, full of beaded Flaustran gowns hanging on every wall. A table was set up with sewing equipment, where an older woman sat. At the back of the room, a small doorway led into what looked like a kitchen and the rest of the house.

"It's so nice to meet you, Dagmara!" the woman exclaimed from the table. "I'm Jasmine." She set down a piece of turquoise silk before standing up to greet Magda. "I'm sure we can find a beautiful dress for you to wear to the ball."

Magda gave her a small curtsy. "Thank you for your help. You're too kind."

For the next hour, Magda tried on dress after dress, trying to find something suitable for the ball that didn't need to be altered that much. It was only a few days away, and she needed to look the part as much as possible. Each style was the same, but the embroidered patterns, colors, and beading added unique flares to each dress. Some dresses had bangles and jewelry to match, providing golden accents to complement the overall look.

While she changed, Prisha played with Odie, taking old pieces of silk and throwing them in the air like whimsical ribbons. Odie eagerly bounded toward the ribbons, jumping high to reach them and keeping them from Prisha like a troublesome kitten.

Ravi just stood back, leaning against the doorway, looking mischievous as he watched her step out from behind the dressing room curtain and up onto the pedestal, displaying each one of the beautiful gowns. He gave a suggestive grin and raised his eyebrows, as if he was undressing her with his eyes and imagining the next gown.

Magda rolled her eyes, but couldn't help but twirl more, showing off the expensive fabric, before heading back into the dressing room. Her heart pounded as she thought of their interactions last night, and Ravi's lingering gaze took her emotions right back to those moments.

When she was sure she had found the right gown, both Prisha and Jasmine beamed in the corner of the room letting out exclamation after exclamation that she was the most beautiful girl they had ever seen.

"I love it," Magda said as she admired her appearance with a handheld mirror.

Jasmine smiled. "You could be a princess."

Odie let out a bark at her side.

Magda couldn't help but smile, for this moment reminded her of Urszula and Dagmara, choosing her coronation dress with her mother. The thoughts made her heart yearn to be back in Azurem. She knew she was running out of time—and getting to the palace was her first priority.

Ravi stepped forward from his spot against the wall, coming up behind Magda. "You look beautiful," he said. She caught Ravi's eyes in the mirror while he stood behind her, getting lost in them. She still had no idea why he was helping her this much. Why did he care about saving her dog, or going to a ball? He said he had his own reasons... but what were they? It was clear they were both still keeping secrets from each other.

Prisha let out a loud sigh.

Ravi broke his gaze from Magda's and stepped away, embarrassed.

"Let me help you get out of that," offered Jasmine.

"Thank you," said Magda. She stepped down from the podium before heading behind a small curtain and changing back into her normal clothes.

When she was finished, she handed Jasmine a few coins to pay for the dress and alterations.

"You can come pick this up the morning of the ball," Jasmine said, "I'm sure it will look beautiful on you."

"Thank you," said Magda.

"It was so great to meet you!" Prisha jumped up and hugged Magda. "This is the best day ever!"

CHAPTER 41
Dagmara

Just when Dagmara returned to the table, flashing a smile at the two unsuspecting men, the bell tolled outside. She jolted upright and peered out the window, seeing a massive group of men—and only some women—had gathered in front of the steeple. There were nearly fifty of them. All the men were shirtless, and the women wore trousers. On the third chime of the bell, the crowd let out a mighty roar and took off down the hill to the exit of the city at the front gates.

"What is going on?" Dagmara asked.

Claude leaned closer to her in his chair, getting a better view of the street below. "Ah," Claude laughed, "I remember that game."

Lionel smiled. "Soulaye."

"What is that?" Dagmara asked.

"A sport."

Dagmara's eyes lit up. She used to love playing sports with Aleksy before her health worsened. "With fifty people? How do you play?"

"More than fifty," Sabien said. He approached the table, peering out the window. His proximity made Dagmara's stomach curl.

Claude spoke again, barely giving Sabien a nod of greeting, "I'm sure Sailonne is playing against...Lousevve?"

"Correct," Lionel replied.

Claude continued, "The goal of the game is to bring the ball back to the city's steeple. Someone places a ball directly between the city centers, and on the third chime, it's a race to see who gets there first."

"That's it?"

A breathless laugh escaped his lips. "It's not easy. There are no rules, and it can get pretty violent. My father and I used to join, and the game would go on for hours."

"Sounds like fun." More fun than discussing taxes.

"It was."

Dagmara stood. "Then let's join."

Lionel let out a loud laugh. "I am far too old for that game anymore. My body does not recover the same way it used to. However, I'm sure they would love to see you two play with them."

Claude shook his head. "I would love to, but I don't want Princess Magdalena getting injured. I'm sure I'd receive a Scribestone from her mother, and I would be disowned before the marriage."

The governor laughed. "Let's not lose the best thing that has happened to Ilusauri over a game of Soulaye."

"I'm sure the Princess will surprise you," Sabien spoke. He had switched to Azuremi, his accent thick. "She is more...durable than you think, Your Majesty."

Claude gave his captain an incredulous stare. There was utter silence in the room, aside from both Pierre and Martine shifting their stance, as they understood the language.

Sabien was bold enough to let a smile crease on his face.

"What did you say?" Lionel asked in Ilusaurian, his eyes darting between the captain and the king.

Dagmara could feel the heat rising in her cheeks. "You don't have to worry about me, Claude," she blurted out. "How about I join while you three gentlemen finish up your conversation? It was lovely to see you again, Lionel."

His eyebrows were raised on his forehead, an impressed frown on his face. "It was my pleasure. Your Majesty," he shifted his gaze to Claude, "forgive if I'm overstepping, but it would be foolish not to accompany the beautiful girl in her first game of Soulaye. Don't crush her excitement. I certainly remember your excitement when you used to play with your father."

The last statement seemed to hit a nostalgic chord within Claude. "I'm sure we will see each other soon," Claude concluded before rising from the table. He turned to Dagmara. "Shall we?"

Dagmara bounded out of the room before Claude could change his mind. Martine was hot on her tail, while Pierre and Sacha were more hesitant to wait for Claude's approval. Sabien took up the rear, in no hurry. They burst out of the manor and raced down the hill to catch up with the crowd. Running down the hill was far easier than trying to walk up.

Azurem had nothing like this—a game between neighboring villages. Excitement was burning at Dagmara's fingertips. The wind soared through her hair, and she forced her legs to catch up with her body as she tore down the mainstreet, causing the people remaining in the city to stare at her. She saw the crowd wasn't too far away. Someone must have already seized the ball and was bringing it back toward Sailonne. There was a large forest across the open field, and Dagmara assumed Lousevve was just beyond that.

There were nearly a hundred people scattered across the field. Dagmara couldn't even see where the ball was, but she only assumed the tangle of bodies a few yards away was fighting over it.

Dagmara skidded to a halt beside a young boy who was trying to catch his breath. He was maybe nine or ten years old, his skin tan from the burning sun, and he had a round face. She was forced to catch her breath herself, bending over and using her knees for support. She stole the potion from her waistband and chugged it, knowing it was hydrating her triple the amount as water. Martine skidded to a halt on her left, and she heard Claude and his two guards slow their speed a few paces behind them. Martine wasn't even panting, making Dagmara realize the distance wasn't as far as it felt.

Dagmara turned her attention to the young boy. "Which village are you from?" Dagmara asked in Ilusaurian. The way the boy jerked back to face her made her feel like her accent was still awful.

The boy looked up at her, his eyes large. "Sailonne," he said. "Who are you?"

"Magdalena. And you?"

"Hugo."

"And this is Claude," Dagmara gestured to the king. "He's playing for Lousevve, but he's out of practice."

Claude's eyebrow rose. "I know this game better than you."

"Your Majesty!" Hugo exclaimed, straightening. He then took a formal bow. "I can't believe—is it really you? So you must be the new queen!"

"Well, we will see," Dagmara said, flashing Claude a glance.

"This is a dangerous game," Claude warned. His warning was followed by loud yelling from the crowd beyond.

"Are you scared?" she taunted.

His jaw shifted. "No."

"Then what's the problem?"

"We should be on the same team," Claude suggested.

"Where's the fun in that?"

"I get competitive."

"Oh good, me too," Dagmara said.

"Don't worry," the suave voice sounded behind them. Sabien approached the group, sauntering down the hill. "I can be on the princess's team."

"Against me?" Claude clarified.

Sabien shrugged, tugging his shirt out from his belt. "It's just a game." Pulling his shirt off his head, he threw the garment to the side, his tan skin already slick with sweat. "Right, Princess?"

Dagmara cleared her throat. By the guardians, he was attractive. "I don't care whose team you're on, Captain. There's no doubt Claude will beat you regardless."

Claude's eyebrows raised. Finally, he smiled, and gave in. "I'll take Sacha and Pierre, you take Martine."

"No," Dagmara replied. "Pierre and Martine should be on the same team. I'll take Sacha."

"That isn't necessary," Martine said under her breath.

"It's just a game." Dagmara smiled. "Sacha?"

The burly guard let out an affirmative grunt.

"Fine," Claude let in. "Pierre and Martine with me."

With one swift movement, Claude grabbed the bottom of his shirt and pulled it off. Dropping it to the grass, he revealed his broad chest. He kept eye contact with Dagmara as he did it, as if telling her this was what she had asked for. "Yes, I'm playing."

Butterflies erupted in Dagmara's stomach, and she forced herself to keep eye contact with Claude as opposed to staring at his accentuated muscles. It was beyond difficult. She thought Sabien was attractive, but there was something captivating about Claude that made her feel drawn to him in a way no one else had made her feel.

Claude started onto the field, and Dagmara and Hugo were quick to catch up with him, the guards trailing behind. Dagmara didn't miss the way Martine eyed Pierre as he stripped. She hoped the way that she had stared at the king hadn't been as obvious.

"We can't play against the king!" Hugo yelled.

All at once, the shouting and rough-housing died down. It was as if the entire field went silent. Everyone stilled and watched as Claude approached.

Everyone exclaimed his title before bowing.

Claude froze in his tracks.

A teenage boy with a bruise covering the right side of his face had the ball in his hands. He approached his king cautiously before throwing the ball. It was heavy, thudding to the ground and bouncing once before landing a few paces in front of Claude's feet.

Claude remained still. Dagmara wondered how long it had been since he had interacted with his people this closely. He had become the imaginary figurehead his father didn't want the king of Ilusauri to be. She assumed the late king of Ilusauri would want Claude to play Soulaye with his people, just as he had.

But everyone was scared of Claude now. There was no doubt that they watched him with fear.

Dagmara rushed forward, shoving Claude's shoulder with as much force as she could muster. It was time to prove that Claude was simply one of them. He only stumbled slightly, but it made her point. Dagmara raced forward, stealing the ball and yelling, "Let's go, Sailonne!"

The crowd erupted in cheers and cries as the game resumed, and Claude joined them, screaming, "For Lousevve!" An even louder cheer filled the air.

The game resumed, and Dagmara had the ball for mere seconds. The teenage boy clobbered her in the side, sending her crashing to the ground. The ball flew from her hands and was gone from her sight in a flash.

She knew her dress was already marked with grass stains and dirt from the hard fall. She pushed herself to a seated position, catching her bearings. Her shoulder was already killing her from the force of the blow.

Claude was standing before her. "You alright?" he asked, extending his hand down.

"You can't help the other team!" she scolded.

"I have her," Sabien said, cutting between them. Before Dagmara could object, he hoisted her underneath the arms, and she was on her feet in one swift motion.

The side of Claude's mouth lifted into a smile, his eyes only on her. "Fine, you asked for it. You already shoved me once."

She shrugged. "I'll do it again. Better be careful."

"Oh, it's on."

Hugo whipped past them, chasing the group. Dagmara couldn't keep up, for her brain was already spinning from exhaustion, but she let the boys have at it. Claude raced along after them, Pierre and Sacha hot on his trail.

Sabien stepped closer to her, his naked chest against her back. He leaned in to whisper, "Isn't it sexier when we're on the same team, and you're not fighting me?"

Dagmara jerked away from him. "If you don't stop the inappropriate comments I will start fighting you."

He smirked. "Noted." Then he left her side, chasing after the group.

Martine was the only one who remained nearby, her attention shifting between Dagmara and the captain as he retreated.

Instead of chasing after the group, already feeling her heart pound excessively against her chest, she chose to walk casually toward the shade of the trees. Martine followed.

"I can sit by myself," Dagmara said, taking a seat on the brown grass. "You can play."

"That's fine," Martine sat beside Dagmara, her eyes fixated on Pierre the entire time. "This is more fun anyway." She flashed Dagmara a grin, and Dagmara couldn't help but laugh as her own gaze traveled back to the men on the field.

The game was more violent than Dagmara thought. Sometimes, the ball would get lost in the middle of a pile up with more than ten men fighting for it. She could've sworn she saw someone break their wrist when they fell. There had to be some reward from this, right? Or was this what they did for fun?

Dagmara found it riveting. She remained in the canopy of the trees, seated. She hated that she didn't have the stamina to play and would risk becoming dizzy. Luckily, it appeared that she was only concerned about breaking a bone, so sitting on the sidelines wouldn't raise too much suspicion.

The game never paused for a breather. Pierre and Sacha used the opportunity to wrestle with one another, and Sabien and Claude even shoved one another. She had no idea who was on each team.

In one instance, Sabien collided with Claude, knocking him off course from the ball. Claude wasn't afraid to tumble with Sabien onto the ground. The two struggled against one another, both equally matched. They were both pure muscle and sweat, and Dagmara had to suppress the heat that raced through her body at the sight of them. When the ball was yards away and the two were still wrestling, she was uncertain whether it was for the sport or not anymore. Sacha approached, and the king and his captain broke away panting, both smart enough not to go up against the giant guard. She saw Sabien's lips move as he said something to the king, but he was too far away to hear, and she couldn't read his lips when he spoke Ilusaurian.

The group moved toward Sailonne, then back through the forest in the direction of Lousevve. The forest was the hardest area to play in. People knocked into trees and others dodged until the ball was at the center of another violent pile. Then, it slipped free, skidding in Dagmara's direction. Adrenaline lit through her body, seeing the ball's proximity. She would be stupid to not take this opportunity. She rose from the shade of the tree, finding her strength as she approached, the ball rolling closer.

Someone knocked into her side, derailing her. He grabbed her firmly around the waist as they fell to the ground, and he caught her with his other hand to lessen the blow as she fell onto her back. Claude was on top of her, grinning.

"That was not fair!" Dagmara objected.

The yelling from the crowd seemed to get distant. The ball must have been snatched away.

"I'm only getting you back for shoving me earlier," Claude responded.

She knew he was only bracing himself on top of her with one arm. She shoved his elbow, collapsing his arm before using the momentum to roll on top of him, pinning him down.

"I'm also competitive," she replied. She was straddling him, her hands against his bare chest holding him down.

The smile that creased onto his lips revealed that he was impressed.

Dagmara was keenly aware that Martine, Pierre, and Sacha were standing a few paces away, watching her. She could nearly feel the weight of Sabien's gaze on her as he approached. But for some reason, she didn't care. Her attention was fixated on the king she had pinned to the ground. Luckily, the crowd was chasing the ball toward the opposite side of the forest, so there were no other witnesses to the scene.

Then, the sound of wings flapping caught Dagmara off guard. She ducked as a blackbird swooped over her head and landed on the ground beside them. Its beady eyes with yellow rings seemed to stare into Dagmara's soul. She felt the muscles in Claude's chest instantly engage when he saw it.

Not now—not here!

Claude shoved her to the side with a force she hadn't witnessed before. She skidded on the ground, feeling the dirt scrape against her hands.

"Go away!" Claude's voice boomed. He picked up a handful of dirt as he stood, chucking it at the bird.

No, no, no!

Dagmara's thoughts screamed in her head. He couldn't act like this out here. This was the entire reason he didn't leave the castle. If the villagers came back this way—if he used his magic on them...

Pierre had her under the arms, pulling her to her feet, much like he had the first day on the balcony. "Run, Princess!"

"No!" she shoved Pierre off her.

Claude picked up a branch and swung it toward the blackbird. The bird took flight, soaring toward the canopy.

Sacha rushed forward to confiscate Claude's new weapon.

Claude whirled to face him, turning his back to Dagmara, and

Sacha crumbled to the ground. His massive body shook the earth as he landed. She couldn't see Claude's eyes, but she knew they were pure silver. She had heard what Claude said this time:

"*Sleep.*"

She had to stop this. He could terrorize the entire nearby village.

But how? If Claude turned on her and compelled her as well, she would collapse. If his compulsion magic worked on her, her secret would be exposed. Magic wasn't supposed to work on other guardians. It wouldn't work on the real Princess Magdalena.

"Princess!" Martine screamed.

The blackbird dove at Dagmara next, and she covered her face, remembering the way its talons seared across her cheek the last time. Then she saw the flames Claude was conjuring from his mind. Should she use a flash bomb? She couldn't leave him alone, not with the villagers so close...not when he would never leave the castle again if his citizens saw him like this.

She had to end this somehow, and only one idea came to mind.

She raced forward, grabbing Claude by his arm. As he rotated, he swung the branch at her. Dagmara easily dodged, expecting that much, before she grabbed his face, closed her eyes, and pressed her lips to his.

She had kissed men before, so kissing her fake fiancé on a whim should have meant nothing to her. However, she wasn't expecting her entire body to ignite, her stomach to turn inside out, and her breath to be taken away.

She heard a thud as the branch landed hard on the earth beside them. For a brief moment, Claude grabbed her by the hip and pulled her tight against him as he deepened the kiss. His tongue swooped inside her mouth and she let out a soft moan. Chills flooded her body, and she pulled him closer. Everything in the world seemed to vanish, and it was only him and her, their bodies against each other and their mouths unable to separate.

Then the king jerked away, releasing her as he backed up.

Dagmara felt as though he ripped something away from her. She faltered slightly, now feeling the fear return once more. When she met his gaze, she saw no more silver in his eyes.

He stared back at her in bewilderment, his mouth slightly agape. He was like a chiseled statue, his chest glistening with sweat.

Dagmara's lips tingled, and her heart pounded furiously in her chest, having nothing to do with her health.

"Pierre, ready the carriages," Claude said, his voice low. "Sabien, wake Sacha."

Pierre scampered away, charging at lightning speed back up the hill. Sabien approached Sacha on the ground, but kept his gaze fixated on Dagmara.

"I'm sorry," Dagmara said. "I didn't know what else to do."

"You shouldn't be the one apologizing. I nearly took you out."

She shrugged, knowing dodging the branch was the least of her concerns.

"This is what I was afraid of."

"I know—"

"And you stayed," Claude said, disbelief in every note of his voice. "You tried...to help me."

Dagmara knew what everyone else usually did. On the balcony, they left him alone. The night of the engagement ball, they left him alone to fight for himself. Had no one truly stepped in before?

"I know you think I'm a Mad King—"

"I don't know what to think anymore," she blurted out.

"But I am," he said, speaking no louder than a whisper. "I have had apparitions chasing me ever since the day my parents died."

"I see the blackbird too."

His expression shifted, his head inclining slightly. He took a step closer. "What?"

Her voice was barely audible, "I see it too."

Claude's eyes narrowed as though he were trying to see through a lie.

She continued, "I don't know how...or why. That's why I tried to send Reon away the night of the engagement ball. I saw it before you did."

He put the pieces together in his mind, remembering that night, and she could see that he believed her. "I don't understand how that's possible. The world shifts for you too? The Void?"

"No..." Dagmara admitted. "Just the bird."

Then Claude touched his fingers to his lips. "No one has done that for me before. No one has been able to pull me out of the other place."

"I would do it again," she said, much to her surprise. She could still feel her pulse racing.

He stepped even closer, removing the space between them. Her breath hitched, picturing his lips on hers once more. Then he lifted his hand slowly and placed it against her cheek. She could feel a slight tremor in his palm as he caressed her face.

"I don't want you to kiss me like that again," he said. His fingers trailed from her cheek to her neck. "The next time we kiss, I want to be completely sane, so I don't miss a single moment of it. I don't want any guards around either so that I have you all to myself."

If their kiss earlier wasn't a true kiss in his mind, she couldn't imagine what was. Her knees nearly collapsed underneath her, and the emotions rushing through her body were overwhelming.

"Yes," she replied, her breath shaky.

"I honestly didn't see more to this marriage than politics," Claude said, "but you're not what I anticipated. I never anticipated feeling... anything, let alone what I feel now."

She swallowed, unable to find her voice again.

He let his hand fall from her cheek before saying, "I'm so fortunate you're mine, Magdalena."

Magda.

At that moment, her emotions tumbled into a new form. The bliss and nerves that previously filled her senses were now cascading into devastation as she realized...she could easily fall for the king. And there was no way this would end well for her.

If she found solid evidence of his involvement in the assassination, the marriage would be over as quickly as it had come about. Azurem would declare war and Claude would be brought to justice.

However, if he wasn't at fault for the assassination, then the marriage would remain. But Dagmara would leave and Magda would take her true spot.

Either way, Claude and her would never be together. There was no Claude and her. It was always Claude and Magda.

And she would never be Magda.

CHAPTER 42
Dagmara

Following the game of Soulaye, Dagmara spent the entire next day recovering in bed. Everything in her body ached, and when she went to sit up, the world around her spun into darkness. Nausea overwhelmed her, making it impossible to consume anything but water. She couldn't even listen to Urszula as she went over new Ilusaurian vocabulary words.

It gave her plenty of time to stare at the canopy of her bed thinking about Claude. The Mad King who may have a heart. A heart that would never belong to her.

She was doing all of this for both Teos and Magda, and she reminded herself of that fact every day. She was protecting Magda's secret magic, and reopening the trade routes to cure zowach.

She hated how her illness dragged her down, and yet she looked well enough that no one knew she was struggling. By forcing herself to act well in front of others, she suffered for it when she was alone. Some days, she silently suffered in front of others. And yet, who was she to complain when there were people like Teos, his permanently injured leg from the accident at the cliffs confining him to use a crutch? On the outside, Dagmara looked fine, so she could pretend to be. Teos would never have that luxury.

It was alarming to call her hidden condition with no cure a luxury. However long she pretended to be Magda, she never would be.

At least what she was doing in Ilusauri would be worth it. Children in Azurem, including Teos, would be cured. Furthermore, no one had to know that Magda wasn't a Guardian of Life. She had to continue protecting Magda's secret. No matter how awful Dagmara felt, emotionally and physically, all of this was for the people she loved.

But for how long? Where was Magda? She was supposed to arrive in Ilusauri after speaking with Queen Sanyal.

After an entire day in bed, Dagmara knew she had to present herself the following morning, but she could barely make it to the washroom. The others in the castle probably assumed she was taking a day for leisure, having no idea that the day wasn't free for her. It was reserved for recovery, otherwise she would risk passing out in front of Claude, and she couldn't cause a scene.

Slipping on a thin nightgown, she stared at herself in the mirror, seeing dark circles under her eyes.

Her fingers traced the scar on her collarbone from the night Sabien slashed her. It was a reminder of her role as an assassin for King Bogdan. She wished she had asked him or Aleksy for the truth. Why was she assassinating Azuremi citizens if the people who killed them were Ilusaurian? Why was her mom hired in the first place, forcing Dagmara and Teos to move into the royal fortress? If only she could ask. But the only people who knew the truth were all dead.

Grief threatened to knock her over, so she exited the washroom to return to bed. As she was climbing under the covers, she heard a knock at the door.

"Come in," Dagmara said.

The door opened, and Urszula entered with a full tray. "Hello, Princess," she said, and Dagmara was surprised to see Martine enter behind her.

"Martine, I wasn't expecting you," Dagmara said.

"I have a special delivery from the king," Martine replied.

Urszula wiggled her eyebrows as she set the breakfast tray in front of Dagmara. "A special delivery," she echoed, her voice melodic. Urszula then made herself scarce as Martine approached.

"He heard you were homesick and wanted to give you a gift," Martine said. She extended a book toward Dagmara.

"Who told him I was homesick?"

Martine raised an eyebrow. "You missed lunch and dinner yesterday. If I told him you weren't feeling well he would have summoned doctors. As a guardian, I'm sure you wouldn't have liked that."

Ever since Nouchenne, Martine had become suspicious of Dagmara's identity. It was true, the hounds didn't stir in Dagmara's presence, only when Claude had arrived. Dagmara didn't know why Martine hadn't asked her blatantly about it, but she continued to make statements that showcased her suspicion.

"You're right," Dagmara replied. "Thank you."

Accepting the book from Martine, she read the cover.

The Chronicles of Time.

It was the book he claimed was his favorite the night of the engagement ball.

"And this," Martine pointed to a covered bowl on the breakfast tray.

Curious, Dagmara lifted the lid and revealed a pile of salt, perfectly shaven.

Salt. The one thing that helped her feel less light-headed when standing.

A smile creased on Dagmara's face. She suppressed a laugh before holding the book tightly to her chest.

"Can I pass along to the king that you are pleased?" asked Martine.

"Very pleased."

Martine clasped her hands in front of her. "Are you certain you're not avoiding His Majesty?"

Heat flooded through Dagmara's chest as she remembered the kiss with the king. She knew her face was bright red, and she tried to hide her expression.

"I am not avoiding him," said Dagmara. "I just need to rest this week. I'm sure you understand."

"I see." Martine nodded. She turned to exit, but stopped a few paces from the door. "If I may speak freely, Princess." She glanced over her shoulder.

Hesitantly, Dagmara muttered, "Of course."

"I do not ask what I don't want to know, for I am not allowed to keep secrets from my king," she said. "Despite his reputation, the king is an honest man and deserves honesty in return."

Dagmara swallowed the lump in her throat.

"Royals send placeholders all the time when they anticipate a dangerous situation. However, I saw the way you looked at each other in the forest. I don't believe you are a danger to his life, but you could hurt him nevertheless, and yourself in the process."

Dagmara was on the verge of breaking. Martine knew the truth.

"But I understand it may not be your choice. I mean, my entire life was given to protect you."

Was that what Dagmara's life was given for? To protect Magda? Dagmara was as much a guard as Martine was. And yet Dagmara was foolishly running around pretending to be a guardian.

Finding her courage, Dagmara responded, "I am not a placeholder, Martine."

Martine closed her eyes briefly. "Of course not. Forgive me, Guardian."

"And how about you and Pierre?" Dagmara changed the topic.

Martine's cheeks reddened. "I don't know what you mean."

Dagmara smiled before patting the bed beside her. "Come tell me."

Martine bit her lip before finally a smile broke out on her face, and she plopped down beside Dagmara, her professional demeanor breaking. "Where do I start?"

"Start at the beginning."

"So...when Pierre and I were put opposite one another in guard training and I nearly killed him?"

Dagmara burst out laughing. "I'm sure that's when he fell in love with you, so yes, start there."

The days quickly passed, and shipments arrived from Azurem. Dagmara traveled to the other provinces with Claude, meeting more governors and feigning interest in political conversations. Every moment was exhausting, and she attempted to bury all feelings that erupted when Claude met her gaze or took her hand. It was all for show.

Then the wedding preparations began. Dagmara was fitted into Magdalena's wedding gown, which Madame Annette noted was the wrong measurements. Her suspicious face did not help Dagmara's anxiety. Tapestries were being hung around the castle, and chefs were preparing tastings for the menu. The castle seemed flooded with servants and higher security. Everywhere Dagmara went, she felt a dozen eyes on her.

Luckily, Dagmara received permission to send her mother another message from the Scribestone. Sabien met her in the library, and Martine waited by the door, out of earshot.

Sabien unlocked the case around the Scribestone casually. "Messaging Teos?" he mused.

"My mother," Dagmara countered.

"Who is Teos anyway?"

"None of your business. Now, some privacy?"

Sabien nodded before stepping to the side, out of reach but remaining close.

Dagmara forced herself not to lunge toward the Scribestone.

Magda had to have sent a letter by now. They were days away from the wedding, where was she?

One message from Bernadette Krol, Azurem.

Dagmara,
  A slight earthquake caused a rift in the mountains and I sent a few knights to investigate. Otherwise, all in Azurem is well.
  Can you ask Magda to reply to her mother? I let her leave the kingdom, and she can't even respond to a single message.
  Bernadette

A rift in the mountains? Like the rift in Nouchenne? Dagmara's throat tightened. At least no one would get hurt if there were hounds there. The mountains were too remote, and no guardians would be going near the rift.

One message from Teos Zosia, Azurem.

I'm struggling more each day, but Bernadette said a shipment of medicine just arrived in Bergclow. Did you do it? Did you convince the Mad King?
  Mael Revel and Lyam Desco weren't reported to leave Azurem. As you remember, two assassins were killed. Suspicious? I agree.
  Samuel Arsenault departed the day of the coronation. One assassin escaped, so it must be him. I think we're onto something. We asked for a detailed description, and all they could give me was that he has a scar down his face and red hair with a beard. Have you seen anyone that fits that description?
  Furthermore—I know it gets more exciting—one border agent reportedly quit and went on a lavish trip right after the coronation. Seems like he received a large sum around the time of the coronation.

Looks like the Ilusaurian you shoved into the ravine paid to have his name removed from the border list. But why?

More sleuthing.

Just the coolest partner in crime, T

Why would Sabien pay off the border guards to have his name removed? Dagmara knew she couldn't ask him outright without informing him that she knew he was in Azurem, but the question lingered on her mind.

She flipped past her message from Teos and was left with a blank page. No messages from Magda. Now was the time to get worried. Had she even made it to Flaustra safely?

"You done?" Sabien asked.

Dagmara felt uneasy. She stepped away from the Scribestone and nodded.

Sabien returned to her side, closing the case and sealing it. He faced her, a smirk on his face.

"Whenever I'm in here, I think of the last time we were here together," he said.

Dagmara frowned. He was referring to their kiss. "I told you to forget it happened."

"I don't want to." Sabien inched closer, staring down at her. "So tell me, who is a better kisser? Claude or me?"

Dagmara's face went pale. She stuck her chin up before replying, "Claude." Even if she said it to get under Sabien's skin, she couldn't deny how she felt about her kiss with Claude in the forest. It had altered every emotion in her body.

Reaching out, Sabien placed a finger under her chin. "No need to lie to yourself."

Dagmara batted his hand away before whirling on her heel, returning to the entrance and where Martine was waiting. "I'm not," Dagmara replied.

"You'll see the real him soon enough," Sabien stated. "Then you'll come crawling to me."

She glanced over her shoulder and smirked right back. "Don't be jealous, it's not a good look on you."

Sabien's expression darkened, and for the first time, his smirk turned into an expression that could only be described as feral.

Walking back to her room, Dagmara's mind was running wild with thoughts. How she wished she was back in Azurem preparing for the coronation. Everything was better back then.

Or was it?

"Is there something going on between you and Sabien?" Martine said from beside Dagmara.

"He thought I was flirting with him when I wasn't, and now he won't leave me alone," Dagmara said briefly. "I'm trying to avoid him."

"Does the king know?"

"No," Dagmara was quick to reply, "and let's keep it that way. I can handle the captain."

Then a tune began to play in the distance that made Dagmara freeze. She recognized the music—she could sing it in her sleep. It was—

The music ended abruptly. Had she imagined it? Was the Azuremi Waltz simply playing in her mind?

"Strange," Martine muttered under her breath. "I wouldn't think the instrumentalists are practicing this late in the night."

"The Azuremi Waltz will be played at the wedding?" Dagmara gasped.

"I don't recognize the music," Martine admitted. "I don't know."

The music commenced once more. It was only the violin's line. Faint, but present.

Without thinking, Dagmara took off in the direction of the sound. Turning down a corridor, she found herself at the open doors to the ballroom. She and Martine stood at the threshold, peering inside.

The glossy floor was reflective of the dome ceiling, made entirely of glass. The stars were so bright, reminding Dagmara of the ceiling in the library.

Under one of the alcoves was a single violinist. His music was propped on a stand, and directly beside him was Sacha. The large man leaned against a column, his arms crossed. His expression was one of boredom, but that was how Dagmara was used to seeing the giant. On the ground beside him were Pierre's bow and swords.

In the center of the room, Claude and Pierre struggled to do a three-step turn. Pierre was on his tiptoes, clearly taking the female role in the dance.

Claude cursed loudly. That would be the next Ilusaurian word Dagmara learned.

"Stop!"

The violinist screeched to a halt.

"It's one, two, *three*!" Claude said, exasperated. Dagmara loved when he spoke in his native language.

"I thought it was one, *two*, three," Pierre replied, doing a jig on the ground that didn't look like the Azuremi Waltz at all. "Right?" He looked at Sacha.

Sacha uncrossed his arms, revealing a piece of paper. He was silent as he scanned it over, then he looked up and gave a shrug.

"You two are helpless," Claude said under his breath.

"I can help," Dagmara said from the doorway, announcing her presence.

The men jolted upright, Claude and Pierre taking a giant step away from one another. "I didn't see you..." Claude started, switching to Azuremi. "How long have you been watching?"

"Long enough," said Dagmara. "Pierre, why don't you dance with Martine, and I can steal the king from you?"

"Oh no," Martine said, "I'm a guard. I don't dance."

"I don't dance either," said Pierre.

"Yes," Martine nodded, her cheeks reddening, "that much is obvious."

A pout formed on Pierre's face.

"Come on." Dagmara grabbed Martine's hand and yanked her into the ballroom before she could object. They immediately moved into the two pairs. Despite Martine's objections, she eagerly put her arms around Pierre's neck to prepare for the dance. Pierre held her around the waist, keeping his distance as though they were teenagers dancing for the first time.

"No, no," Dagmara said, "like this."

She used Claude's hands to demonstrate, bringing one to her upper back so that she could rest her arm against his, and then taking his other hand in hers. Her breath caught in her throat as she met Claude's gaze. His proximity made her heart race. She hadn't been this close to him since she had kissed him. She saw his eyes flick to her lips, and she knew he was thinking the same thing.

Trying to forget the kiss in the forest, she proceeded to teach the choreography. Despite stepping on a few toes and slamming into Claude's chest every once in a while, Dagmara had the time of her life. By the end, her cheeks hurt from smiling so long. Her body was yelling at her, causing pain to ripple through every joint and she felt lightheaded, but she felt secure in Claude's arms. If she was going to feel miserable, she would rather experience bliss dancing the night away than sitting by herself.

When the violinist decided to join in, it was well into the night, and exhaustion wore down on Dagmara, her eyelids feeling heavy.

"You're a much better partner than Pierre," Claude whispered.

Dagmara glanced over Claude's shoulder, watching the two guards fumbling on a completely different tempo. Yet they didn't seem to care, their bodies moving at the same imperfect timing.

Dagmara smiled. "You're a much better partner than Pierre too."

Claude let out a laugh. "I told you I could dance. You didn't believe me."

"Next time..." Dagmara tried to hide her yawn, "I'll take your word for it."

Claude released her hand, bringing his palm up to cup her cheek. "I'm glad you challenged me. Otherwise, we probably wouldn't be here. And that would be a tragedy."

"Oh yes, because the Azuremi Waltz is certainly important for the betterment of our kingdoms."

"And the safety of our people." A smile formed on Claude's face, and it was beautiful. With his hand on the back of her neck, he guided her toward his chest. She let herself lean into his hug, her head resting on his shoulder, his leaning on hers. With one hand cupping the back of her head, and the other around her waist, Dagmara felt secure in his embrace.

They continued to sway under the starlit sky and she breathed in his soft cologne. The prior feeling of homesickness had vanished. For the first time, she felt safe in a place that wasn't home. The world around her blurred, the violin melody a nostalgic lullaby.

In Dagmara's mind, they were the only two that existed.

CHAPTER 43
Magdalena

Princess Kiran's birthday ball was only three days away. It was almost time for Magda to relocate to the palace. She had left some of her belongings in the room at the Mystic Sonata where she was boarding, and figured that it was time to pack up her books, money, and clothes.

That night, Ravi was playing another show, and Magda had a front row seat. The lively music filled the tavern, and despite Ravi's bandaged palm, he effortlessly displayed his advanced fingerwork like a true professional. After Ravi's performance, other musicians continued, and Ravi stepped off stage to swing Magda into a dance. They danced in each other's arms for hours, until it was quite late, and they had shared at least four glasses of ale.

When it was completely dark outside, the back doors banged open, and a large man barged into the tavern.

"What's going on?" Magda stopped dancing, looking curiously at Ravi.

"A proclamation," Ravi explained.

The messenger shouted over everyone, and upon seeing the man, the musicians screeched to a halt. Instantly, all eyes were on him as he waved a scroll in the air. "Royal news, royal news!

Everyone quiet and listen up." He cleared his throat as the music silenced.

Then he screamed over the antsy crowd. "News has arrived that a royal wedding between King Claude and Princess Magdalena is going ahead!" he curled open the scroll, continuing to read. "After a successful engagement ball, Azurem and Ilusauri have opened trade routes for medicine and food, and the royals will be wed in three days' time!"

Three days? Magda's heart almost stopped. She had thought she had more time than that. In an instant, her breath threatened to leave her and her entire body flushed hot with panic. Why did the news take this long to travel to Flaustra?

The man continued, "It is said the Queen Bernadette Krol approves of the marriage, despite previous tensions between the kingdoms. The kingdom of Flaustra has not yet released an official statement on the marriage. Thank you."

If the marriage was going ahead, and Magda's own mother approved, it meant Claude wasn't behind the assassinations. It meant that this was good for the kingdoms so that they could have medicine again. It meant that Magda would have to take Dagmara's place and in just three days' time she would be sharing a bed with the Mad King.

The thought made her sick. Not necessarily because of Claude, but because she only had three days until she was locked in a marriage forever. She had never fully accepted the possibility that Claude was actually good and that her kingdom would decide to go through with the wedding.

Suddenly, all around her, people began shouting:

"Will Azurem keep the medicine for themselves then?"

"That princess is stupid for trusting a Mind Guardian."

"I guess Queen Sanyal will be cutting off ties with Azurem now since Ilusauri is our enemy."

"Are you alright?" The voice was Ravi's. He was at her side, gently touching her shoulder. "You look like you're going to be sick."

Not wanting to be at the party anymore, Magda confessed, "I'm exhausted. I think I'll go to bed."

"You look upset at what the messenger said."

"Maybe a little," Magda shook her head, pushing her way past Ravi.

As she did so, she passed a drunken man who grabbed her upper arm. "Hey, Azuremi, would you marry King Claude?"

Before Magda had time to break free, Ravi was at her side. "Get your hands off her," he shoved the man back, and he stumbled into his friends.

"We want to hear her opinion on her kingdom's alliance."

Magda shoved through the guests, and Ravi followed her close behind, making sure no one else in the tavern badgered her. When they reached the stairs, Magda began ascending to her room at the Inn.

"Do you want to talk about it?" Ravi asked, yelling up the staircase.

Yes, truthfully she did want to talk about it. She had no other friends here, and no one else to confide in. In a few days, at least she would be able to use the Scribestone and send a message to Dagmara.

"Come upstairs," Magda beckoned him.

They both ascended and reached Magda's room. Pushing open the door, she noted her knapsack and belongings exactly where she had left them. Outside the window, the clear night was twinkling with stars. Magda hadn't realized how late it was.

"Are you sure Odie's fine with Prisha?" Magda asked suddenly. For the past few days, Ravi's sister had taken every opportunity to play with the dog.

"Of course," Ravi laughed, "I'm sure she would take him from you permanently if you let her. Are you going to tell me what's going on?"

"The news...," Magda shuddered, "...means I have to leave Flaustra." It was as simple as she could put it for the time being.

"You have to go back and serve your princess," Ravi seemed to understand, although he didn't meet her gaze.

"I'll have to go to Ilusauri too, and I'm scared."

"Why?" Ravi asked.

"Because from this moment on, with the new alliance and the marriage, my life will change forever."

"I'm sure it will be fine." Ravi crossed to her. "You will serve your princess, and you'll still be able to travel as you are now. It's not like you're the one marrying Claude."

"You don't understand."

"Then tell me. All I've ever been asking is for you to be honest with me."

Magda turned away from him, running over to the window. She didn't know how to confess everything now. She didn't want Ravi to look at her any differently, after her dozens and dozens of lies. Already, she would lose him when she married Claude, and she didn't want to taint the memories of the friendship they had.

Ravi came up behind her, sliding his strong arms around her waist. "You like the stars, don't you?" he asked sweetly.

Magda couldn't pull her eyes from the window. "Yes. I'll miss this place after I go back to Azurem."

Ravi was silent for a long moment. Then he said, "I always thought that could be a possibility that you would go back."

"I'm sorry. I wished we could have had more time together, but it's not my choice. I never planned to leave Flaustra so soon."

"Then let me come to Azurem with you. Or even Ilusauri."

"It would never work."

"Why?"

"Because I don't have the luxury of choosing who I can be with."

"What if I got down on my knees and begged you to stay? I can't give you much, but I could promise you a life of happiness and comfort. If you think this is real, which I think it is, would you consider leaving your place at the Azuremi castle?"

"I can't."

Ravi sighed. "I respect your decisions. I won't pressure you to stay then. Just tell me...will I see you again?"

Magda thought about it long and hard. Could she see Ravi again after she was married to Claude? Technically yes, but she didn't know if the Mad King would appreciate it. Given the way she felt about Ravi, there was no way any future husband would approve.

Ravi seemed to understand when she didn't reply. He deepened the embrace, closing his arms around her. Then he moved his lips to her ear, before tracing them down the side of her neck. The tingle of his breath ignited a fire inside her, and Magda closed her eyes so she could focus on feeling the soft movement of his lips brushing up against her skin.

"I should go," he suddenly said, but he didn't loosen his grip.

"Why?"

"Because if I don't leave, I won't be able to stop myself."

Magda slid her arms across his, pulling him tighter around her as they both looked out at the view of the city. "Then don't stop," she said. She let her head fall back against his shoulder, so that the bare skin of her neck was fully exposed.

He kissed her neck while his right hand moved up her body and caressed around her throat. His left hand squeezed tighter around her waist, pulling her flush against his chest, and reminding her how strong he was. Already, the heat from his body was radiating through hers. She was utterly helpless to move unless he decided to release her.

"But you're still going back to Azurem," he said.

"I don't want to."

"Then tell me what you want."

Magda knew what she wanted. Her emotions for him had only been building over the past few days, and Magda felt an overwhelming force pulling her to him. She wanted to be with him and only him right here and now.

"I want you," she answered.

"Are you sure?" his voice was barely a whisper. His body was rigid against hers, holding her in place so that his hips felt the curves of hers. "I've wanted you too."

"Since when?"

"Since I almost lost you," Ravi said. He kissed her again, moving his hand away from her neck. He gently pulled down the sleeve of her dress as his lips grazed her bare shoulder.

Magda steadied her breathing.

He continued, "The way I would make you feel if you let me..."

"Tell me." Magda cut him off. She wanted to hear him say it.

Ravi released her, and Magda turned around to face him. As she met his intense gaze, he leaned in closer, putting his hands on either side of her on the windowsill, restricting her movement.

He said, "I would kiss you all night long, holding you close to me and never letting you go."

Magda's entire body shuddered. Even his words were building anticipation inside of her. Her entire body flushed with heat, and her legs threatened to buckle.

"...and I wouldn't let you sleep for a second."

Magda couldn't take it anymore. She stared intently at his lips, hoping it would communicate an ounce of her longing.

In an instant, his lips were on hers, and Magda opened her mouth further. They kissed again, starting out slowly with one tender kiss after another. The raw taste of his mouth on hers and the tingling sensation on her lips took Magda to another place. She allowed herself to fully relax, forgetting everything it meant to be a Guardian, and her entire body melted into his.

Magda and Ravi crashed together, and his tongue was slick around hers, extending deep into her mouth. For a second, Magda pulled away slightly, lingering on his lower lip, before going back for more.

His hands found the back of her thighs through the dress, lifting her up onto the windowsill, while she clutched his shirt to pull him closer. Then he moved closer, standing between her legs.

Ravi gripped the back of her neck, pulling her into him and forcing her mouth to stay on his, while Magda did the same. She continued the impassioned kiss, every muscle in her body burning with frenzied emotion. Magda's palm spread across the back of Ravi's neck, running her fingers through his tousled hair, and entrapping him against her.

With every kiss she was more stimulated, and with every flick of Ravi's tongue, an unfathomable urge left her wanting. As they continued exploring each other's mouths, she could sense his increased arousal, for he moved faster on her lips, and pulled her tighter to him.

Soon, the lust threatened to consume her entirely. She moved her hands to the bottom of his shirt, before sliding her hands underneath it and feeling the smoothness of his skin. Under her touch, she could feel the lines of his muscles, and she let her fingers linger before she wrapped her arms around his back.

Ravi equally explored her body. His touch invigorated her, but all that Magda wanted was to feel nothing between them.

Magda furiously moved her hands to the bottom of his shirt. "Take this off," she ordered.

Ravi pulled away only for a second, to assist her with yanking the thin fabric over his head. He tossed the shirt to the side, letting it splay against the ground.

They locked eyes, and this time Magda truly looked at him. He was beautiful, with his brown skin and tousled hair. His bare chest revealed the contours of his muscles and the gleam of moisture on his skin in the starlight.

He said sweetly, "Even though you're leaving Flaustra, I want us to feel like we have all the time in the world."

The fire inside Magda was now in a full blaze. "Well, for some reason it feels like time has stopped," said Magda, moments before Ravi's mouth found hers once again.

CHAPTER 44
Dagmara

Two days before the wedding, Dagmara and Claude were set to return to Sailonne for another shipment. They had already made the rounds to the other three provinces, none of which hosted a game of Soulaye. Dagmara was looking forward to their trip to Sailonne. This was her last chance to find out if Lionel was behind the forged papers that helped the assassins cross the border. As head of the capital city of Ilusauri, he was the only one aside from Claude who was able to manage citizenship.

Upon arrival, the formalities and pleasantries remained the same. Lionel invited them to his manor for a cup of tea and a boring conversation. Sabien was coordinating the food delivery somewhere in town, but Martine and Claude's guards remained at their sides.

Dagmara glanced out the window, seeing the crowd form for another game of Soulaye. There was a flash on the horizon as movement surrounded the border of the town. Dagmara's eyes narrowed, watching as a barrage of horses flooded through the gate, the riders in crimson attire.

"Claude," she grabbed his arm, her voice thick with warning.

Both Claude and Lionel followed her gaze.

"What is going on?" Lionel asked.

Claude rose from the chair and pressed a palm to the window. "The Celesta. Why are they here?"

"I don't know. Stay here, I'll find out," Lionel said and immediately proceeded to the exit.

Rushing to the window, Dagmara joined Claude as he eyed the visitors. Shouting broke out from the streets between the opposing groups. There were a dozen riders a few paces from the large crowd preparing for Soulaye. These men were soldiers, equipped with weapons and full armor. The golden tassels glistened on their red shoulder pads, and their faces were hidden with helmets.

"What are they saying?" Dagmara asked, unable to understand Celesta.

"They're asking for Lionel," Claude replied.

As if on cue, Lionel exited his manor. The crowd parted as he walked through to face the soldiers.

"Why are you here?" Lionel called, his voice muffled by the glass.

The Celesta soldier at the front began speaking in his native language, and Claude let out an audible gasp.

"What did he say?" Dagmara didn't care that Magda should have known the language.

"He said Guardian Sora is dead," Claude whispered, his voice wavering.

It was as if the floor fell from beneath Dagmara's feet. Another guardian killed?

The voices on the street continued.

"And..." Claude paused, then met Dagmara's gaze, his face inches from hers. "They say I killed her, and they're going to burn Ilusauri to the ground."

Wordless, Dagmara stared back at the king. His expression was indecipherable, mixed with guilt and pain, but there was no fear. Was it possible? Had he sent assassins to kill Guardian Sora like he had sent to kill Bogdan and Aleksy?

Then, multiple events occurred in quick succession. A whiz of an arrow drew the pair's attention back to the street, and they witnessed the wood lodge into the center of Lionel's chest. Lionel fell to the ground, his head bashing into the cobblestone, and an immediate uproar began. Dagmara shrieked upon watching the death of the governor, and one of the Celesta soldiers spotted her in the window.

As the world returned to normal speed, Claude yanked her away from the glass. "You have to go."

"*We* have to go," Dagmara corrected.

"No, this is Ilusauri's war."

Dagmara yanked out of Claude's tight grip. "The kingdom needs you alive, and we both need to get out of here."

He studied her momentarily before he finally let in. "Fine. Martine, lead the way uptown. Sabien will be by the warehouse with the carriages. Pierre, Sacha, save as many citizens as you can." The guards nodded, all three withdrawing their weapons.

Claude grabbed Dagmara's hands. He said, "I'll create a distraction, and then I'll be right behind you."

"Don't lie to me."

"I've never lied to you."

A pang radiated inside Dagmara's chest. She nodded, and they raced downstairs and onto the street.

The streets were filled with chaos. Villagers were grabbing any weapon they could, completely unarmed against the Celesta soldiers. Dagmara realized in horror that the dozen Celesta soldiers she saw from the window was only the first wave. It was a massacre as arrows rained down from the sky, slaughtering innocent bystanders.

"Go!" Claude yelled at Dagmara before he stepped into the mayhem, outstretching his arms. His eyes were consumed in silver as he commanded his magic.

First, the cobblestone street near the entrance began to break, creating a gaping hole and stopping the oncoming riders from entering town. Then tiles cascaded down from the roofs, and billows of smoke flew up from the ground. The Celesta soldiers dove for cover while others fled. Silver snakes slithered out from the bushes, causing the horses to rear up in fright and knocking some of the riders to the ground.

Dagmara had to remind herself none of it was real before she tore off after Martine.

They wound through the narrow streets, skidding around corners. Dagmara collided into a fleeing villager, but immediately collected herself and was on the run once more. Her heart beat violently, and her chest tightened as she gasped for breath. She had no idea where she was anymore. All she knew was that she had to keep up with Martine.

At the next intersection, a soldier launched themself into the fray. Dagmara barely dodged his curved sword, skidding onto the ground. She could see two soldiers in the distance approaching.

Then the ground lurched underneath Dagmara's feet. A loud noise cracked the air, shooting through Dagmara's temples. It was as if an explosion had erupted on the adjacent street, and the building beside them began to crumble. A large piece of stone knocked the soldier out, and Dagmara dove for cover, feeling her palms skid against the ground.

Temporarily stunned, a high-pitched noise rang in Dagmara's head. She heaved herself to her feet. Smoke surrounded her on all sides, and her head spun as she regained her composure and took in her surroundings.

Her path was completely blocked off by the collapse of the building. The soldier's limbs poked out under the debris.

By the guardians, it was a real explosion, not one of Claude's mind projections.

When the deafening ringing began to cease, Dagmara heard the clash of steel. On the opposite side of the debris, Martine flashed in Dagmara's vision, swiveling under a soldier's blade and raking her own sword across his arm. When the soldier was unarmed, Martine drove the steel straight through his neck, finding the perfect opening between his armor and helmet.

"Run!" she yelled through the mountain of debris between them.

Dagmara obeyed. She withdrew her dagger and continued uptown, finding a different route. The Celesta had brought explosives with them? They had already killed one of four governors in Ilusauri, what was next? Claude promised he was right behind her, but was he safe?

Luckily the narrow alleyways widened and a large warehouse emerged in the distance. She knew it had to be where Sabien was working when she saw the two carriages parked out front. Sprinting across the cobblestone, Dagmara nearly collided with the carriage as she skidded to a halt.

"Sabien!" she called, but he was nowhere in sight. In fact, this far uptown she could only see a few townspeople darting across the street. But with the amount of surrounding buildings, someone could easily be hiding in the shadows.

A breeze swished past her ear, fluttering her hair, as a dagger flew inches from her head. It lodged into the carriage with a smack. Dagmara whirled around to face a Celesta soldier holding one more dagger in his grip.

There was no time to think of a plan. Tightening her grip on her own dagger, Dagmara withdrew a throwing star from her bodice. She flung it toward the soldier and it lodged into his breastplate. He stumbled slightly, but it only angered him enough to charge at her. His blade glistened in the sun as he raised it over his head.

Withdrawing a smoke vial, Dagmara thrust it to the ground, sending a blast of fog between them. It disoriented the soldier, giving Dagmara the time she needed to slide toward him and drive her dagger under his ribs. With one choke, the soldier collapsed dead.

"Nice move."

Dagmara whirled toward the voice, raising her dagger, and froze.

Sabien leaned against the carriage, his arms crossed in front of him. His casual demeanor starkly contrasted the screaming in the distance.

"You were watching?" Dagmara questioned, her heart rate an all-time high. Where had he come from? "I could have died."

"Don't be dramatic. I had a feeling you knew how to handle yourself," Sabien replied, his voice smooth. He eyed the fading smoke from Dagmara's bomb. "Interesting choice."

"There's no water nearby," Dagmara stated, lowering the dagger. "I practice other ways to defend myself."

Sabien shook his head, uncrossing his arms as he took a step toward her. "See, a Guardian of Life would never say that." He approached her slowly, but she would not back down. "There's water in the air...in the ground. There's even water inside people that you could draw from."

"What do you know about my magic?" Dagmara snapped.

He smirked. "More than you." He placed a finger under her chin. "Nice dagger, by the way."

Her heart lurched. It was the same dagger she had plunged into his chest the night they met in Azurem.

A shadow flashed behind Sabien, and a new fear replaced the one in Dagmara's chest. "Look out!" she screamed.

Both Sabien and Dagmara ducked the incoming blade, but it was aimed too far over their heads to have even made contact. The soldier was faster than Dagmara had ever seen before. He kicked Sabien in the back of the knee, knocking him off balance, before he grabbed Dagmara's wrist and yanked her toward his chest. Within the blink of an eye, Dagmara had her back pressed against the soldier's chest with his blade against her throat.

"Drop the dagger," he said in Ilusaurian, his accent hard to understand. He sounded so familiar, but Dagmara couldn't see him. When his curved sword pressed higher on her chin she obeyed, letting her dagger fall.

Sabien had his own weapon drawn, glaring at the intruder but keeping his distance. His jaw ticked in disgust. "Reon."

Reon Ogawa. The spearhead of the Celesta militia that had held the private meeting with Sabien and Claude the night of the engagement ball.

"I want to speak with Claude," Reon said.

"Release Princess Magdalena," Sabien ordered.

"I mean the princess no harm."

"Then release her."

"And let you kill me?" Reon asked. "Not until I speak with the king."

"You will do as the captain says!"

The voice boomed through the clearing. Dagmara recognized it immediately. She couldn't turn her head to see him approach, but could sense Claude rounding the corner. He came into sight, proceeding to stand beside Sabien. His sword was withdrawn, and his clothing was soaked in blood. His face was covered with dirt and debris, and his free hand clutched his abdomen. Behind him, Pierre had his bow ready and aimed at Reon.

Claude's expression was full of malice. "Let her go," he said, enunciating every word, "and I will consider letting you live."

"Was it you? Did you kill Guardian Sora?" Reon asked, not moving the blade from Dagmara's throat. But it wasn't until that moment that Dagmara noticed he held the flat part to her chin. His grip on her arm was light enough that she could break free. He didn't mean to harm her.

"Of course it wasn't me!" Claude retorted. "I warned you about this, Reon."

"I know," Reon said, his voice soft. Then he lowered the blade.

Dagmara didn't even stumble out of his grasp for he gracefully released her. She distanced herself, turning to face Reon, and felt Claude's hand at her lower back. Touching her neck, she checked for blood, but there was none.

Claude gripped her hip. "You alright?"

"Yes." Dagmara nodded.

The king then removed his hand and limped toward the Celesta militia leader. "What is the meaning of this?" he demanded.

Reon sheathed his sword in attempts to prove he wasn't a threat. "I didn't order this attack," he stated. "It was a reactionary attack to the news of Guardian Sora's death."

"Killing my governor is a declaration of war. What proof do they have that I'm to blame?" Claude asked.

"Everything," Reon replied. "You and Sora chose to keep your agreement a secret, despite my constant disapproval, so the council believes you invaded our lands without permission. They believe you sent assassins."

"Then tell the council the truth," Claude said. "We kept it a secret because Guardian Sora wanted to. I respected her wishes. Now you must tell them the truth."

"The council won't listen to me," said Reon. "Rumor has spread that Ilusaurian assassins executed the Azuremi royals."

"That is not true."

Reon shook his head, exhaling. "It doesn't matter if it's true or not."

"So that's it then?" Claude's voice broadened with anger. "Celestaire and Ilusauri are at war?"

Reon's brief silence was enough of an answer.

"Aren't you the spearhead of the militia?"

"Yes, but I can't influence the council," Reon replied. "They will simply have me replaced. As your friend I came to warn you. You must know this is not what I wanted."

"I don't have time to go to war with your kingdom, Reon!" Claude yelled. "Take my kingdom as an example! This decay happened when my father was killed and my powers weren't honed yet. There was no Mind Guardian for five years, and that branch was severed. With Guardian Sora gone, Mind and Spirit are dead. Life and Soul are the only two branches still standing!"

Dagmara could feel the weight of the truth on her shoulders. If Magdalena had Soul magic, not Life magic, that could mean that all the Guardians of Life were gone. That could mean Soul was the only one that remained.

Guardian Sora's assassination was greater than Claude knew.

"I understand!" Reon replied. "You warned me to heighten security around Guardian Sora, and I did. I have no idea how anyone reached her, and I have no idea how anyone could kill a Guardian of Spirit."

Claude shook his head, distraught. "I warned you how, Reon," he growled. "I warned King Bogdan too, and clearly it wasn't enough even with his assassin."

Dagmara's blood turned to ice. "What did you say?" She stepped closer and gripped Claude's arm. "What about King Bogdan and his assassin?" She completely forgot her role as Princess Magdalena, forgetting that Magda would have said father. But suddenly none of that mattered. King Bogdan kept the reason behind the assassinations she was carrying out a secret. Did Claude know why she was assassinating certain people?

When Dagmara took Claude's arm, she felt him waver, slightly off balance. His eyes looked fatigued and sweat dripped down his temples. "I will tell you in private."

Dagmara didn't want to wait. She wanted to know everything.

"You haven't told her?" Reon questioned.

"No," Claude scowled, "because until recently I haven't trusted her."

His words felt like a dagger through her chest. She didn't know why it hurt to hear them, because she had been hiding her identity from him this entire time. He had every right not to trust her. But why wouldn't he tell her about his correspondence with King Bogdan?

Reon let out an audible sigh, breaking the silence. "I can't prevent this war, Claude, I simply came to warn you and let you know I will continue what you and Guardian Sora started. I will let you know if I find it, but by the original guardians, I pray I don't."

Claude winced, but didn't respond.

Bringing his fingers to his lips, Reon whistled. Within moments, a black stallion exited the narrow streets and came to Reon's side. With one swift movement, Reon mounted the horse.

"Get your soldiers out of this town," Claude growled.

Reon frowned. "Those who are still alive, yes."

"And hold your men until after my wedding."

Reon lingered, his horse stamping its hoof impatiently. "I will try to speak with the council, but I make no promises."

"Reon," Claude didn't raise his voice, but it was filled with malice. "Don't ruin my wedding."

The Celesta soldier merely snapped his reins, and the horse bolted out of the clearing, toward the smoke rising from downtown.

"Claude," Dagmara insisted. "I must know what you told King Bogdan." She took his hand and instantly felt a sticky substance. Looking down, she could see nothing, but felt warmth on her palms.

"We have to get back..." Claude's voice trailed off as he began to lean against her.

Dagmara barely caught him, his weight nearly knocking her over. His sword clattered to the ground.

"Sabien!" she screamed.

The captain rushed forward, catching Claude before he hit the cobblestone. When the captain cradled Claude, Dagmara saw the blood.

There was so much blood.

It oozed from a rip in his shirt at the center of his stomach, turning his clothes a deep red. The blood on her hands appeared like magic, dripping onto her clothing and collecting under her nails.

Dagmara felt bile rising in her throat, and she swallowed it down, suppressing the nausea.

"Pierre grab water!" Sabien yelled and the guard obeyed immediately.

Dagmara dropped to her knees, her hand going to the back of Claude's neck to prop him up. The king's eyelids fluttered and a raspy breath escaped from his lips.

"He used magic to hide the wound from Reon," Sabien said, his tone expertly calm as he examined the wound on Claude's stomach. "There's no shards or debris, it must've been a sword."

As Claude began to slip into unconsciousness, his mind magic wore off, and the amount of blood he was hiding increased tenfold. Then, like a stroke of paint, a scar etched down the side of Claude's face. His left eye became discolored, intersecting the large scar perfectly. The mark was a shade lighter than his skin, and the one side of his face transformed into a gruesome wound.

Gasping, Dagmara yanked her hands away.

"I'm sorry..." Claude choked before his eyes shut completely and his head fell limp.

Sabien scoffed. "Never seen a scar before?"

"No, I—" Dagmara searched for words that never came. Her brain tried to process this new image of the king. There was no denying the giant scar across half his face. "He hid himself from me."

"He hid his face from everyone," Sabien said. "If people called me an ugly monster I would have done the same thing."

Dagmara felt like her chest was being ripped in half.

Then Pierre interrupted the moment, landing on the ground beside them with a clumsy thud. He held a pail of water, splashing half the contents as he extended it toward Sabien. "Here!" he panted.

Sabien claimed the pail immediately. "You need to heal him."

It wasn't until Dagmara met Sabien's gaze did she realize the captain was talking to her.

"The king doesn't have time, it needs to be now," Sabien ordered.

Then the realization struck her. He was asking her to use the Life Guardian's healing powers. Powers that both Aleksy and Bogdan possessed, but she didn't. Neither did Magdalena, but no one was supposed to know that. How could she reveal the truth in a moment like this when Claude's life depended on her?

Claude's life. Looking down at him, his face half disfigured, all the memories flashed before her. If she wanted to, she could let him die. He could be the reason Aleksy and Bogdan were killed. But something inside her fought against the urge. She didn't want him to die. She didn't want to admit the feelings she was starting to have for the Mad King.

"Princess!" Sabien yelled.

Her voice was barely audible as she said, "I can't."

"P-Princess," Pierre stammed. "Please save my king." His voice sounded so innocent. If only she could express that this wasn't her choice. She *wanted* to save him, but she couldn't.

"Magdalena," Sabien said, his voice guttural. She met his gaze, and his chin angled down, his eyebrows raising. It was almost as if he meant to silently communicate something, but she was in too much distress to interpret it. "I know you've never healed someone else before, but you must now. I know you, I've watched you, and I know you can. Just channel it."

Tears began to well in her eyes. "Sabien...I—"

With his free hand, Sabien lunged forward and grabbed her by the wrist. He slammed her palm against the bloody wound on Claude's stomach. She wanted to pull away, the warmth of the blood making her sick, but Sabien placed his hand firmly on top of hers, holding it in place. She wanted to gag, her nausea overpowering her, and it took everything inside her to disregard the feeling of the wound against her skin.

"Close your eyes and channel now!" Sabien yelled as he poured the pail of water over their hands.

Dagmara squeezed her eyes shut, feeling tears drip down her

cheeks as the water rushed through her fingers. She prayed to anybody that could hear her, begging the guardians to save Claude. She remembered when he saved her from the hounds. She remembered dancing with him at the ball and sharing truths about one another in his chamber, the way he remembered her request for salt and learned the Azuremi waltz for her. Then there was the kiss in the forest where she felt emotions she hadn't for anyone before. All of her feelings for him heightened in that moment, and she knew with horrid certainty that she was helplessly falling for him. No matter what secrets he held about King Bogdan, no matter what scars he had hidden from her, she was falling in love with him. She couldn't lose him now.

Her palm began to tingle, a warmth spreading through each one of her fingers. A shudder ran up her entire arm, reaching her chest in a blaze that ignited the rest of her body. For a brief moment, everything inside her felt healed. No grief, fear, or pain. A jolt of magic blasted through her hand and entire body.

"Thank you, Princess!" Pierre exclaimed, his voice that of awe.

A wave of emotions returned as an onslaught. Dagmara's eyes shot open, and she yanked her hand back, clutching it to her chest. Through the rip in Claude's shirt, underneath the leftover blood, was smooth skin. The injury was gone.

The pail clattered to the ground as Sabien chucked it aside. "I told you," he said, a proud smirk creasing his lips.

Dagmara looked down at her palm, her hand shaking uncontrollably. Her fingertips prickled with leftover magic.

What had she done?

PART FOUR

The Wedding

CHAPTER 45
Dagmara

After the attack in Sailonne, Claude was unconscious the entire ride home. When they arrived back at the castle, he was quickly taken in by the royal nurses, making it impossible to ask him any questions. That evening, Dagmara washed away the battle, sitting in the tub until the water went cold. Every limb hurt, blood pooled in her feet making them a shade of purple, and she could feel her head pulsing. She would've fallen asleep had she not been preoccupied staring at her pruning fingers. She examined her palms as though they were foreign to her. How was any of this possible? How could she heal people and what did that mean?

Skimming her fingertips on the surface of the water, she tried to clear her head enough to think about the potential. Was it possible she had Life magic? She had watched Aleksy and Bogdan manipulate water time and time again. She had to find out, but her body was too exhausted. As she traced her hand against the surface of the water, nothing happened.

What was she doing? She should stick to what she knew. Her potions would bring her comfort. That was something she was decent at.

She exited the tub, put on a nightgown, and was combing through her wet hair when there was a knock at the door.

"Yes?" Dagmara called.

"Princess? It's Claude."

The voice instantly changed Dagmara's mood. She dropped her comb on the nightstand and raced to the door. She threw it open to see Claude in the threshold.

He was alive. Her magic had healed him. He stood before her, dressed in a billowing white shirt that was tucked into loose trousers. The shirt was rolled up to his elbows, revealing his muscular forearms. His face was clear, and there was no more scar.

"Claude," Dagmara said, breathless. She ignored Pierre and Martine that hovered in the hall behind him.

"Hi," he replied, his voice quiet. His accent was still as gorgeous as the first day she had met him. "I know it's late, but I had to see you."

Dagmara nodded. "I'm glad to see you're alright."

"Thanks to you," Claude replied before a laugh escaped his lips. "Again." He rubbed his hand along the back of his neck, glancing sideways at the guards before asking, "Can I come in?"

"Oh, yes," Dagmara muttered, opening the door wider.

Claude stepped inside and closed the door behind him, purposefully leaving Martine and Pierre in the corridor.

Suddenly Dagmara felt like her dress was too thin, and the air was hard to breathe. She crossed to the bed and sat down, pulling her dress farther past her knees.

The king approached, but stopped a few paces away. He leaned against the post that held up the canopy, shoving his hands in his pockets. "I was nervous that I scared you away because of my...my appearance. I should apologize for lying to you and hiding the real me. I should have told you before."

"You didn't scare me," Dagmara spoke. "I understand why you kept it from me. People keep secrets for a multitude of reasons." *I'm also lying to you.* She wanted to add, but bit her tongue.

"You don't see me as a monster?"

"I don't think of you any differently."

"Well," Claude said, a lilt to his voice that almost sounded like a laugh, "this was far easier than I expected. I had this whole monologue prepared to save our marriage. Pierre said you saved me, when you could've let me die. You saved me from the poison on the terrace, you're helping rebuild my kingdom, and you even saved me from myself in the forest the day we played Soulaye. I don't know what I did to deserve you."

Dagmara inclined her head, gazing at the king. "Is it that hard to believe someone likes you?"

His gaze was chilling. "It's hard to believe I'm more than what people say I am. A Mad King."

Dagmara spoke, "We are not defined by our titles, our appearances, or our..." she paused, thinking of herself, "...or our illnesses. We are defined by the actions we take, and the difference we make in this world, no matter how small." She waited for his response. Her words settled in the air as even she mulled over them. It was so easy to encourage someone else and not take the advice for herself. But, there was something about the way the words spilled out that had her questioning if she could someday accept herself, illness and all.

She was never going to be Magda, and she knew that. She was a daughter of an assassin, a girl with a condition the nurses couldn't name, and she just wanted someone to love every part of her, not only the outside appearance.

She had taken Magda's name, but Dagmara was the one who had accomplished everything up until now. The first day on the terrace with the poisoned wine...Magda would never have noticed the abnormal pitcher. That would have been the end of Magda's life. Even with her health, Dagmara had been the one to save both her life and Claude's. As a result, an alliance was formed, and trade was beginning again.

Whether Claude was involved with the assassinations or not, one truth was still clear: he was sending medicine to her kingdom, and Azurem was sending food to Ilusauri. They were helping thousands.

And maybe that was enough.

Claude's chocolate eyes roamed every inch of her face, the small specs of silver catching the light, as a faint grin began to form.

"May I ask what happened?" she ventured, referencing the scar which was now invisible to her eyes.

Claude's smile wavered. He cleared his throat as he took a seat on the bed beside her. The mattress shifted under his weight as he made himself comfortable. "It was the night my parents died," he paused.

A pang of sympathy filled Dagmara's chest.

"Mind Guardians can't project illusions if they can't see what everyone else is seeing. Luckily, I still have one eye," Claude explained. Then his expression darkened. "I haven't told this story to anyone."

Dagmara reached forward and placed her hand on his.

Claude jerked back, but then he slowly shifted his palm and intertwined his fingers with hers. "For the first time in my life, I want to share my story with someone."

"And I'm here to listen," Dagmara replied. She needed to ask him what he knew about King Bogdan. He mentioned being in contact with the king regarding the planned assassins. She had to know the truth.

"Why don't you tell me about yourself?" Claude countered.

Unease crept through Dagmara. She thought she could finally get him to open up. Discover the real him. Now he was shifting the attention back to her. Her mind flashed to the first night in the castle.

"I will use her to Ilusauri's advantage, find out what she knows, and then I can get rid of her."

Yanking her hand from his, Dagmara rose from the bed. "I'm tired," she announced, hoping he would take the cue and leave.

There was a flash of disbelief on Claude's face, but it was gone in an instant. The king rose from the bed. "What are you hiding from me?"

"Nothing," Dagmara answered.

He took a step toward her. "You haven't been honest with me about everything. There's something you aren't telling me, but I simply can't figure it out."

Tilting her head, Dagmara stuck her chin in the air. "You're the one that still holds secrets about the night your parents died. I don't think you've been completely honest with me."

"I don't want to be honest with you!" Claude said, his voice filling the room. "I don't want to admit the way you make me..." his voice trailed off, fire blazing behind his eyes.

"What?" Dagmara urged.

Claude's expression darkened. "You have invaded every single thought," Claude stated. "I can't see medicine without thinking of your dedication to your kingdom. I can't walk by flowers without thinking how nothing could compare to your beauty. I can't even look at any color resembling turquoise without wondering the exact shade of your favorite color. I had forgotten the sound of my own laughter until you reminded me how to laugh again. So now, I can't even hear laughter without you crossing my mind." He let out a deep sigh. "Since the moment you arrived, no matter how much it initially bothered me, you have spoken to me as though I am not the Mad King, but just a man. It's as if this madness isn't my only defining characteristic. Because of you, I am irrevocably doomed, but somehow...I relish this destruction."

In one moment, he was a foot away from her, his expression indifferent. The next, his palms gripped both sides of her face and he pressed his lips to hers. The kiss was powerful and all-consuming, threatening to make her knees buckle under the sheer intensity. A fire ignited inside her, and she wanted more. Desire coursed through her body, hotter than the first time she kissed him. Now, he was in control, and it was undeniably attractive. He slipped his tongue between her lips, searching her mouth, and she couldn't help the moan that escaped her.

Then he yanked back, stumbling away and letting his eyes consume every ounce of her. His chest heaved as he panted, as though the kiss had left him breathless.

Her lips ached, her heart pounding against her chest. She wanted him. She wanted more.

"We agreed this would be purely political," he said. His voice was low, almost guttural, sending shivers through Dagmara's entire body. "Sailonne needs me to appoint another governor after Lionel's death." He smoothed out the front of his shirt. "Goodnight, Princess." He turned to leave, but Dagmara wasn't done with him. She lunged forward, grabbing him by the wrist and stopping him in his tracks. She wasn't strong enough to pull him back to her. He willingly halted, curious.

She wanted to tell him she didn't want to keep this purely political. She wanted all of him, the Mad King, the Guardian, both the good and the bad. But she couldn't bring herself to tell him that. If he wanted it to be purely political, she could find a way to quell the intense emotions she held for him.

At least that's what she told herself as she kissed him again.

There was no hesitation on his part. His arm wrapped around her lower back, pulling her body flush against him. Her chest pressed against his, only thin fabric separating them. His hand found the back of her neck, his fingers curling through her hair and tilting her head to kiss her deeper.

Her body burned with need, and she wanted to feel his skin against hers. She gripped the collar of his shirt, tugging at the fabric that blocked her from running her hands down his naked chest.

He obeyed her request.

Taking his hands off her for a brief moment, he gripped the bottom of his shirt and tugged it over his head, discarding it to the side.

She used the brief pause to catch her breath. She scanned his body, taking in every ounce of him. Every rigid line, every curve of muscle. By the guardians, he was everything she wanted and more. Yet, he was still hiding his face from her.

Before she could speak her mind, his lips were once again on hers. His hands roamed down her backside until he reached her thighs. He gripped her tightly and hoisted her in the air. She immediately wrapped her legs around his waist, their kiss unrelenting. He took a few steps toward the bed before guiding her down on her back. She scooted back on the bed, and he followed, climbing over her until he braced himself with his elbows on either side of her head. He let his body settle between her legs, and every part of him pressed against her. Heat flooded her core, and it took every ounce of her strength to break the kiss long enough to say, "I want to see the real you."

He paused, his face inches from hers, and his eyes burning with desire. "I...don't usually show people that."

Her hands cupped his face. She felt an indent on the left side of his face, but she couldn't see it. "You can't scare me away, Claude," she said.

He nodded, letting out a shaky breath. Then his face began to transform. The right side remained chiseled and perfect, while the left revealed a giant scar. His eye turned a shade of gray, the scar running directly through it from his eyebrow to his chin. The scar was a shade off from the rest of his skin, the surrounding area rough and marked from a healer's attempt to fix it.

Dagmara ran her thumb against his cheek, somehow feeling more attraction to the man before her. She didn't have words to express her emotions. Instead, she pulled him toward her, needing his lips on hers once more.

His hand traced the side of her body, following every curve. He reached the hem of her dress, and the moment his fingers touched her bare thigh, her breath hitched. He kissed her jaw, tracing all the way to her neck. His lips met the soft spot under her ear, and as his hand trailed higher, another gasp escaped her lips. A shiver raced down her spine, and she tightened her grip around him.

"You're so beautiful, Magdalena," Claude whispered through kisses.

Dagmara's body froze. Ice course through her veins, and despite the burning in her core, she was thrown back to reality. What was she doing? Claude would never be hers and she knew that. It didn't matter how much she was falling...none of it made a difference. He was betrothed to Magda.

Claude pulled back, touching her cheek to turn her face to his. "What's wrong?"

Everything.

"Nothing," Dagmara muttered. "I don't think we should go too far tonight." The words tasted bitter in her mouth.

Claude seemed unfazed. "That's fine."

Dagmara shifted underneath him, trying to escape, and he sat upright.

"Are you alright?"

"Yes," she lied.

He nodded, his scarred face full of concern.

This is not what she wanted. She wanted him and all of him. But she also wanted him to want her...the real her. She hated lying to him.

"I'm tired," she tried to cover her tracks. "But...can you stay?"

The concern faded from his face. "I should really appoint a new governor...but I can stay until you fall asleep."

She smiled. That was enough for her.

Climbing under the covers, Dagmara shifted to the side to make room for him. He slid in beside her, pulling the blanket up to their shoulders. He wrapped his arm around her waist, drawing her toward him until she was snuggled against his chest.

"Remember how I said if I wasn't mad before that you would drive me insane?" he asked.

"Yes," she replied.

"Well you've driven me mad, for I'm falling madly in love with you."

A smile formed on Dagmara's face, her entire body settling in his embrace. She closed her eyes to fall asleep before answering in a whisper, "I suppose we're both mad."

CHAPTER 46
Magdalena

The evening of Princess Kiran's birthday ball came sooner than Magda expected. Leaving the Mystic Sonata, she made her way to the *Gilded Silks* in the afternoon, to pick up the dress that Ravi's mom, Jasmine, had created.

When Magda put it on, she had never felt more beautiful in her life. The dress was flowing silk and chiffon fabric, in the color of a soft pink rose. The long sleeves naturally fell off of Magda's shoulders, exposing her collarbones. Golden embroidery was stitched along the sleeves, coming together in a sweetheart neckline around her breasts. The dress cinched at her waist, exposing her midriff through pink lace, before fanning out in an a-line shape.

Ravi's mom had styled Magda's silver hair halfback, fastening it with a sparkling pink hairpiece in the shape of Flaustran flowers. They matched identically colored earrings that hung from Magda's ears.

"You look beautiful," Jasmine stepped back and admired the dress on Magda.

"Thank you for everything," Magda stepped forward, giving Jasmine a warm hug.

Then Prisha dashed into the shop, holding a ribbon high in her hands. She swirled it around, and Odie lay down on the floor, before rolling over. When Prisha turned the ribbon once more, Odie rolled over again. "Look what I taught him!"

Magda turned to Odie who was wagging his tail, "That's amazing Odie, but you have to say your goodbyes."

Odie jumped up, lapping Prisha's face. Since Magda planned to stay with Queen Sanyal and Princess Kiran from now on, Odie would be coming with her to the castle.

Tonight she was getting into the palace and would finally have answers. She would finally have access to the Scribestone with the opportunity to get in contact with Dagmara. It had taken her this long, but there had been no other choice. If she had made any other decisions on this trip, Odie would be dead, and she would never have been able to forgive herself. She only hoped she got there in time to send a Scribestone to Dagmara and ask her to delay the marriage just a few days.

A bell alerted the trio that the door was opening.

Ravi stood at the entrance, wearing a long-sleeved pink shirt with golden stitching. On top, he wore a patterned vest. "The carriage is here," he announced.

When Magda met his eyes, her heart lurched in her chest, and anticipation rose inside of her. It was the first time she had seen him since they had spent one long night together.

"Get going so you aren't late!" Jasmine broke the silence before pushing Magda toward her son.

Magda grabbed her things, and they all scrambled out of the doorway. Ravi opened the carriage door for Magda. "You look..." For once, he was at a loss for words.

"You look handsome," Magda said first.

"You ready?" Ravi clutched Vex's royal invitation in his hands. It was still strange to Magda that Queen Sanyal invited criminals to the palace for a birthday celebration, but it occurred to her that perhaps they weren't criminals in the queen's eyes, rather necessary for the functioning of the kingdom. Turning a blind eye to some of Vex's vices was better than complete economic collapse.

"Yes. Time for me to find Queen Sanyal," answered Magda.

"Don't forget, you're *my* 'invited'," Ravi smiled, waving the invitation in front of her. "You will owe me a dance at some point."

Magda grinned. "Agreed. We know the plan?" she asked, referencing Odie.

Ravi nodded.

Then she grabbed onto the door before stepping into the covered carriage, Odie jumping in behind her, for they were on the verge of being late. Then Ravi shut the door before getting in the front to drive the carriage.

They took the long trek on the outskirts of the tightly-packed city, heading outside of the urban area and to the lush, dark-green fields that lay beyond the dirty, gray buildings. The carriage fell in line with numerous others, making their way slowly up the path to the palace.

When the carriage screeched to a halt, Ravi spoke to the men at the gate, sounding like he had shown the invitation. Then, the carriage was directed to the left to be parked in the outer gardens next to a row of other carriages.

Soon, Ravi opened the door, extending his hand to Magda before helping her down onto the stone walkway that led up to the palace. When her hand was in his, he caressed his thumb over the back of it, assuring her that he wouldn't let her fall.

Magda looked back at Odie, giving him the command to stay silent and calm. "I'll be back with Princess Kiran soon," she said.

Then Ravi and Magda turned to a line of guests heading through the outer gardens toward the palace. The Flaustran palace was still as magnificent as ever, with its domed roofs and outer wall leading into the gardens beyond. When they reached the gate to the inner courtyard, a guard blocked their path, holding out his hand for the invitation.

Ravi passed Vex's invitation to the guard, remaining silent. They had decided he was the best one to pass for a guild member, due to Magda's Azuremi accent when speaking Flaustran.

"And this is your 'invited'?" the man turned to Magda, breaking her thoughts.

Ravi turned to Magda with a twinkle in his eyes. "Yes. My fiancée."

Magda had to keep her mouth from dropping open.

"You're telling me your fiancée is Azuremi?" the man asked.

"Yes," Ravi said. Then he took off his outer vest, putting it on Magda extra slowly while he simultaneously flashed the inside pattern toward the guard. The inside of the vest revealed the beast symbol—the insignia of the Marauders guild—sewn inside.

Magda examined the insignia. When did Ravi have time to get that made?

Then Magda guessed it probably took Jasmine all of five minutes to embroider a pattern inside the vest. It was clear his family knew what he was doing—impersonating a guild member—and Magda was startled that they didn't have a problem with it.

After draping the vest over Magda's shoulders, Ravi lingered with his arm around her, and Magda had to suppress her emotions. This was all a ruse to get inside.

"Any other questions?" Ravi asked the officer, but his gaze was focused on Magda, his face so close to hers that she could rise to her tiptoes and kiss him.

"Enjoy the party," the guard said, handing back the invitation before gesturing inside.

Ravi and Magda passed through the large, double doorway and entered into the interior courtyard. It was a large space, full of pristine, green patches that were lit up with glowing lanterns all around their plots. The sandy, orange walls contrasted a pink sunset.

All around, were sandstone-colored arches and domed towers, projecting an orange glow on the fountains and flower beds around them. Candles marked their path as they walked around a central gazebo and to the front door. Vines and plants snaked around the tan walls, marking every inch of the palace with Soul magic.

"Your fiancée?" Magda said snidely as they walked arm and arm through the gardens.

"You need a serious date to get into the palace."

"I thought you said relationships were casual here."

"Exactly," said Ravi. "They're so casual that I need to make it seem like you are someone more than that to me. Or else they wouldn't have let you in as my 'invited'."

"So what about the other night? Was that just casual?" Magda grinned.

Ravi turned to her, brushing the back of his knuckles gently across her cheek. "I know you're leaving, but there was nothing casual about that night to me. It meant something much more."

Magda could feel the heat rising in her cheeks and had to break their eye contact. She went to take off Ravi's vest, but he stopped her.

"Keep it. It looks better on you."

Magda laughed. "No it doesn't. It's a man's vest."

He leaned closer. "Well, what can I say? I also like that the other men will know you're with me."

"With you?"

"As my invited."

She wanted to argue, but she simply couldn't. She secretly liked wearing something of his too. Her stomach curled with butterflies as she remembered the night prior with Ravi, and if they weren't in broad daylight, she was certain she would have kissed that sheepish grin right off his face.

"I'll wear it. For now."

The sound of music alerted them that activities were beginning in the ballroom. The guests were being herded toward the front door, and the duo followed the others across the wide garden. Magda knew she had to find Princess Kiran immediately.

They passed under the central archway, leaving the garden and emerging into the wide, open ballroom. The ballroom was expansive, in the shape of a perfect circle. The floor was a colorful mosaic pattern, marked by blue titles and tan-colored stones. The intricate carvings on the titles extended up the light-stone walls, and every archway surrounding the circular room was detailed with minuscule carvings. Large turquoise and yellow banners hung from the ceiling, interspersed between lanterns.

Magda guessed it made sense that the entire ballroom was made of stone—she was in the land of the Soul Guardians, and if they ever needed to wield, they could pull right from the palace walls.

Up ahead, on a raised dais, sat Princess Kiran and Queen Sanyal.

For her birthday celebration, Kiran's curly hair that normally fell to her waist was pulled half back, and her brown skin was accentuated with heavy make-up. She wore a red, long-sleeve dress that exposed her stomach and was covered in beaded, gold embroidery. Instead of wearing a crown, a decadent choker necklace hung from her neck, shining with metal, golden-plated leaves spanning outward and down her chest. The necklace perfectly matched her bracelets and earrings.

Suddenly, a lively music started, with a distinct rhythm that Magda had never heard before. Women of all ages passed their drinks to their partners, before dashing to the central area. Princess Kiran stepped down from the dais and made her way to the front of the group of girls.

When the music picked up, they began stomping their feet as they moved into a triangular formation. Their arms flowed to the rhythmic music, their sharp hand-movements falling perfectly in sync with one another.

"You should get out there," Ravi encouraged beside her.

"I've never seen this dance before," said Magda.

"It's easy. You just follow the leader—in this case it's the princess."

Kiran was in the center of the group, spinning quickly with her hands spread out around her. As she twirled, her long, vibrant dress fanned out across the stone floor. Soon after, the other girls mimicked her movements.

When the music crescendoed, the choreography included lively jumps to the beat of the music. The girls moved in a circular formation, with their bodies positioned to the center of the circle while their wrists expressively rotated above their heads. They spun on their own axes while they maneuvered around the outside of the circle, showcasing the exquisite fabrics they wore.

Unlike in Azurem, their faces were particularly expressive, with Kiran glowing in the joy of the dance from the middle of the circle.

Suddenly, Kiran's eyes caught Magda's, and for a moment, she almost paused in the dance. It was clear that Kiran recognized her.

Magda gave a small wave by Ravi's side. Magda remembered she had sent Kiran a message from the Scribestone, so in some ways, she was expecting her.

Kiran whipped her hair over her shoulder, and twirled her arms about her head, her wrists curling around each other. As she did so, her golden jewelry clinked. She cocked her head, as if motioning for Magda to meet her off the dance floor, to the side of the dais.

Magda nodded in return.

Then Kiran gracefully bent backwards, leaning so far that her hair almost brushed the floor. Then she raised back up and continued into the next section of the dance, grabbing her skirt in her hands so she could move her hips to the beat.

"Those look like guild leaders," Ravi said at Magda's side. His eyes were toward one of the arches. "I'm going to check it out."

"Alright. Meet back here afterward."

Ravi agreed before heading back toward the entrance.

When Kiran met Magda's gaze once more, Magda slyly pointed to the entrance. Then Magda turned around and pushed her way off the dance floor, heading toward the outskirts of the room.

From this distance, the music was fainter. When it came to a complete halt, the guests burst into applause. Almost immediately after, another song sounded, and the men took center stage.

Magda only had to wait a few moments before she noticed the guests were parting, making way for someone approaching the front entrance that led out to the gardens in the interior courtyard.

Princess Kiran was coming to speak to her, flanked by two officers.

"Magda?!" Kiran's eyes were wide. She squealed at a high pitch and clasped Magda's hands. "Is that really you?"

"Yes, it's me!"

They both leapt into an embrace.

"Come here! It's been forever!" Kiran said, jumping up and down in the hug. She pulled Magda outside, and they stepped into the sticky air, approaching the central gazebo. The officers followed them, but Kiran waved them away, and they spread out in the gardens.

"First," Magda stopped her. "I brought Odie, and he's in the carriage."

"Who's Odie?"

"My dog," Magda said bashfully.

"Are you serious? This is the strangest night yet. It's too hot out here for dogs," said Kiran. She snapped to her officers, ordering them to go to the outer gardens where the carriage was parked and bring Magda's dog up to her room. They nodded, quite confused, before heading under the gate.

Kiran continued, "I don't understand. I heard you were marrying King Claude! I was considering writing you a letter since I wanted to know what it was like to get betrothed. They're thinking of betrothing me to a man in Celestaire, and I wasn't sure whether to go through with it, or what it would be like being with a man you don't even know if you're compatible with..."

"Kiran!" Magda let out a laugh.

Kiran's eyes trailed to Ravi's vest that Magda still wore over her gown. Her fingers trailed the fabric and she raised her eyebrows suspiciously. "What man's clothing are you wearing? Wait, does Claude know you're here? Is he going to be upset? Is he really as 'mad' as everyone says?"

"Well..."

"Is he *good*?" Kiran raised her eyebrows. "I was always into the brooding, mysterious fighter type." She circled her finger around one of the curls framing her face.

Magda said, "I really want to catch up, but I need to use the Scribestone and speak to your mother. It's important."

"I got your message saying you were coming. What was so important to come all this way that you couldn't talk to her through the Scribestone?"

"It's a long story," said Magda.

"How did you even get in?"

Magda smiled. "That's an even longer story."

"Oh, gosh," Kiran shook her head. "This sounds like we need a full-on gossip session. Don't worry, I fully expect you to stay over. I'm so excited to see you. It's nice to see another peer—another guardian. And my mother will be so surprised." Kiran grinned. "She was shocked that you decided to get married right after the assassination attempt, and she was even planning on attending the wedding so that your mother would have someone to sit with."

Kiran squeezed Magda's hand again. "Let's go find my mom. I think she's in her office having an important meeting. But I have to warn you, we've been on thin ice since the trials."

The trials where Kiran undoubtedly fought her siblings and won the guardian magic for their generation. Magda couldn't remember how many siblings Kiran had, and felt too embarrassed to ask.

"Thin ice with your mom?" asked Magda.

"Yes, another long story for our gossip session tonight. Let's go."

Suddenly Magda noticed Ravi all the way on the other side of the courtyard. He was talking to someone from the Fowler's Guild—Ishani's Guild. Weren't they trying to avoid all guild members? As quick as lightning, the two men exchanged hands, and Magda was almost positive that she saw Ravi drop a few coins in the hand of the officer. In exchange, Ravi stuffed a crumpled piece of paper into his front pocket. After another second, Ravi gave a nod to the guild member before disappearing inside a side door to the palace.

What was he doing?

"Kiran...," Magda stopped walking through the crowd. "Where does that door lead?" she asked.

"To the other wings of the palace," she announced like it was an obvious answer.

Magda was suddenly on alert. "You go find your mom. I'll catch up with you."

Kiran's expression drooped, but she said, "Alright. Come sit at our table during the meal."

Magda agreed.

Magda slipped around the gazebo, past the open door into the party. Their laughter slipped into the background, as Magda focused on the side door ahead of her. Where had Ravi gone?

Suddenly, a bark was let out behind her.

"Madame, your dog is being brought to Princess Kiran's room." The officer had returned, and next to him was Odie. In an instant, Odie was racing to Magda, jumping up on her.

"Madame, I can't leave the Princess's side for this long." He seemed annoyed.

"Then go, I'll find someone else to help me soon. Thank you," Magda replied.

The guard shrugged, picking a piece of Odie's fur off his suit, and disappeared back into the party.

"Odie," Magda said. "Find Ravi."

His ears pricked up and his head tilted.

"Ravi," Magda repeated.

Then she had an idea. She quickly removed Ravi's vest, and presented it to her dog. Odie sniffed it furiously, taking in the scent, while Magda repeated Ravi's name a few more times. Then, while

Magda put the vest back on, Odie began circling a distinct path in the garden. He wagged his tail by the side door. Magda grinned, before pushing it open.

It led to a hallway that disappeared around a dark corner. Magda and Odie dashed forward, rushing through a stone arch and into another passage, which was dimly lit by hanging lanterns. There were three directions, and Odie chose the one to the left. At the next fork in the hallways, Odie chose the one to the right.

"Good boy," Magda said.

Ahead, Magda heard footsteps against the stone floor, and she rapidly picked up her pace. Then she turned the corner to see two guards on patrol, who were walking away from her. Magda stopped short, flattening her back against the stone until they had left. Odie followed her instincts, jerking instantly to a stop at her knees. As soon as they had gone, a door opened further down the hallway, and Ravi peaked his head out, looking right and left before continuing in the direction of the guards. What was he up to?

Magda pushed forward, following him. She was careful to step quietly on the stone and remain paces behind him. If he was more than a musician, he certainly wasn't very good at noticing when he was being trailed. Odie obediently followed Magda's every footstep, remaining quiet.

Suddenly Ravi stopped dead in his tracks.

Magda held her breath, hoping that he wouldn't turn around and see them standing directly behind him.

Ravi reached into his pocket, pulling out the crumpled piece of paper, and unraveling it in his hands. He scanned it over a few times, before looking left and right in the hallway. Finally, he decided to head to the right after checking the paper again.

Directions. He had paid the guild for directions. To what?

Magda and Odie picked up the pace, careful to stay a long distance from Ravi. She watched him intently as he followed whatever was on the piece of paper, checking it numerous times before making decisions on the next turn. They ventured down a set of stairs, around another bend, and finally through a stone, curved corridor that was darker than the last. Barely any lanterns were lit here, signaling that it wasn't frequented often.

Ravi made one more sharp turn to the right, before coming to a halt at the end of the passageway. Before him, was a turquoise and yellow banner with the emblem of a tiger. He looked right and left once more, before pushing the tapestry out of his way and opening a heavy door into a room beyond.

Magda only grew more curious, and she urged herself to continue her pursuit. This time, Odie was a few paces in front of her.

Why was Ravi sneaking off into secret rooms? Was he after something? Was this the real reason that he wanted to come to the ball and why he had been helping her all this time? She had to find out.

As soon as she pushed aside the tapestry, Magda felt stone under her shoes, and heard the faint dropping of water from deeper down the hallway. She realized she was in a tunnel, with slick stones descending slightly downwards. Already, she had lost sight of Ravi, who had disappeared in the darkness. Here, the light was even less prominent, and the door was closing rapidly. As soon as she let the tapestry drop behind her she used her fingers to catch the door before it shut.

Magda exchanged a glance with Odie. Were they really following Ravi into a secret, dark tunnel?

Odie seemed to answer when he pushed his nose against the frame.

Magda gave in and pushed open the door, careful to let it close quietly behind them.

A lock clicked.

Magda's stomach dropped, and she pushed up against the door, but it didn't budge. She shoved her shoulder against the wooden frame, but she was no match for the strong bolts. Now, there was no way out but forward.

Reluctantly, Magda stepped deeper into the tunnel, Odie at her side, straining to hear any sound of Ravi's footsteps in the distance. When she didn't hear a sound, she walked more briskly, careful not to slip against the stone.

At the bottom of the corridor, Magda was met with another gaping door, which was cracked open. On the ground, in front of it, were two guards slumped on their sides, completely unconscious, and unmoving. A set of keys lay beside them on the ground.

Odie began sniffing the scene, examining the bodies.

Hastily, Magda dove to the ground, reaching to the officers' necks to feel for a pulse on each one of them, and luckily, it was still there. There was a hint of residue on the floor and Magda's mouth fell open. Bilans? The potion that knocked people out? Dagmara had tried to teach her all about potions for protection. Leaving behind this much residue was quite a sloppy job. More of the potion was on the floor than was likely on the guards.

"Odie, get back," she whispered, yanking on his scruff so that he didn't accidentally lap up the potion.

Magda's heart only beat more rapidly against her chest as she looked up at the door in front of her, still slightly ajar. What was inside?

She examined Odie's demeanor before she pressed it open.

Inside were rows of boxes and barrels, and beyond that were a series of jail cells against the wall. The dozen or so cells were lined with sleeping prisoners, their chests barely heaving.

Ravi knelt in front of one of the cells, his arms extending through the bars and clutching desperately onto a girl who was locked inside. He brushed her hair out of face and kissed her on the forehead, before embracing her again as best as he could through the bars.

"Don't leave me again," she said in his arms as she knelt beside him.

"I won't. I love you, Laila."

CHAPTER 47
Magdalena

Magda felt as if a knife had been plunged through her chest. She left the heavy door cracked open and moved behind a tall stack of crates, hiding herself as a wave of crippling horror shot through her body. She couldn't bring herself to intervene as she watched the scene unfurl before her eyes. Her fingers found Odie's fur, clutching onto it to steady herself. Then she gave Odie another command to stay and be silent.

Magda pressed her shoulder to the stacked crates, peeking around the side to get a better view. The jailed girl hadn't noticed her entrance because she was too busy being comforted by Ravi.

"I love you too," Laila returned the words. From her voice and demeanor, she appeared to be Ravi's age, maybe slightly older. "How did you even get down here?"

"Princess Kiran is having a birthday ball. I got an invitation and snuck my way in here just so I could come see you." He smiled.

"Don't tell me you're doing more tasks for the guilds," she laughed. "By the guardians, I missed you." She let out a breath of relief, but she didn't take her hands off him.

Disgust flared through Magda's entire body, and for a moment she felt the gold magic sparkle at her fingertips. Quickly, she shook out her hands, refocusing on the scene as she suppressed her emotions.

"No, this time I found someone else to help me find my way inside the palace," he answered.

Her. He was talking about Magda. She was the person that he worked with to get into Queen Sanyal's palace.

"And everything is okay? With your violin playing?"

"Yes."

"And Prisha? The store?" Laila continued.

"Everyone is fine," he assured her, bringing her in for one more close hug. "Gods, I thought I'd never see you again."

"How long has it been?" she stepped away from him for the first time. This time, Magda saw her face. She was only slightly shorter than Ravi, with bronze skin and shiny-black hair with a slight wave that fell to her waist. Her hands were stained blood-red. She was very thin, likely from not being fed well in the jail cell. Besides being caked with dirt and grime, she was absolutely stunning.

It only made Magda despise her even more.

"Ten months," Ravi answered.

Laila nodded.

"Did they hurt you?" he asked, staring at her hands.

"No, nothing like that," she admitted, "it's not mine."

Ravi gave her a stern look.

"Stop it. I've had a lot of time down here to think. If I had to go back, I'd do it all over again."

"But none of this was your doing."

"I wouldn't leave yet anyways even if I could. I think the other prisoners have more answers than I do."

"I don't like this, and I won't make you stay here alone."

"What was your plan, anyways? Break me out of here and commit treason?" she asked. "Get locked up right beside me?"

Ravi stared at her. "I didn't think that far ahead."

"Typical. Of course you didn't," Laila rolled her eyes and threw her hands in the air, but her expression remained playful.

"I just had to know if you were alive. Not a day goes by that I don't think of you or of what happened the day you were taken. If we hadn't gone to Azurem, none of this would have happened…"

Azurem? Magda's thoughts were running wild. When did Ravi and his mystery girl travel there?

"Don't remind me," she shrugged. "Promise me you won't do anything stupid, and you'll leave this place right now."

"I…,"

Suddenly, there was the light sound of footsteps echoing off the walls of the tunnel. Someone had come through the doorway and was heading for the dungeon. They would see the unconscious guards, and Magda would be spotted as soon as they entered the jail.

Someone had been following Magda.

Laila's voice was urgent, "Hide."

Before Ravi darted away, his hands lingered on hers. He looked at her with a strong gaze, as if he was silently promising to return, before whipping around and heading to a hiding spot—Magda's hiding spot.

Ravi dashed behind the boxes, and terrified to face him, Magda jumped back as to not be seen. However, her foot kicked over a pail, sending a clattering noise through the stone jail and spilling water onto the stone floor. Ravi, startled by the abrupt echo, instinctively pushed her figure up against the tall crates. He had one arm pressed against her throat as he yelled:

"Who are you?"

His face melted when he recognized Magda. "Dagmara, what are you doing here?"

Odie snarled, growling at Ravi as he pinned Magda against the boxes, and immediately, Ravi released her. "Odie, it's just me," he said.

Magda tried to steady her beating heart. The fact that he didn't even know her real name was like another blow to the face. She didn't know what to do, and she felt as if her emotions were in one big knot that was about to explode. Before she unleashed her anger, she said, "Get away from me."

"Please let me explain," Ravi pleaded. "I never meant for you to find out about this."

"Because you thought I was leaving for Azurem?"

Odie continued growling, his aggressive stance focused on Ravi.

"Ravi, they're coming!" Laila called from her cell.

Magda and Ravi were once again alerted to the officers racing down the corridor. In a matter of seconds, they would see the unconscious guards and investigate. They were barely hidden behind the crates if the officers decided to enter the jail.

Ravi continued, "Keeping this lie from you has been killing me inside, and I'm so sorry I didn't tell you sooner."

Magda's stomach twisted. She wanted to cover Ravi's mouth before he could admit anything and taint her image of their entire relationship together. She couldn't believe that he would have any terrible, dark secrets. She didn't want to believe that he could betray her. And above all, she didn't want to believe that another woman had his heart.

"Who is she?" Magda demanded. It was the only question that mattered to her at that moment.

Voices could be heard directly on the other side of the cracked door.

"Shhh...," Ravi said, pressing Magda's body against the crates and covering her mouth with his hand so she couldn't speak. His other hand pushed her stomach into the wood, preventing her from moving.

"Don't touch me!" Magda yelled, pushing him back against his chest, causing Ravi to stumble back from their hiding spot, and clatter against even more pails. At the same time, Odie snapped at Ravi, causing Ravi to scamper farther away.

Magda wasn't afraid of getting caught. She wasn't afraid of facing

Queen Sanyal or Princess Kiran—she was a guardian, and she wouldn't let anyone intimidate her. Ravi had used her.

Suddenly three officers barreled into the room, running toward the sound and spotting Magda, Ravi, and Odie. "Hold it right there!" they yelled. "This room is strictly off limits!"

Two officers moved to grab Ravi, yanking him away from Magda and wrenching his arms behind his back. "Let me go!" he shouted as they twisted his shoulders so that his arms were unmoveable.

Another officer grabbed Magda by the upper arm, yanking her toward the door. "You both are charged with trespassing on the property of the Guardians of the Soul and with poisoning two officers."

Odie began barking, not knowing who to attack first.

"No, Ravi!" Laila screamed from behind the bars.

"Get your hands off me!" yelled Magda.

The officer didn't budge. "You both will rot in the dungeon until after the ball when the royals decide what to do with you."

Magda looked at all of them with fire in her eyes. No one could suppress her incredible fury in this instant.

Then another officer grabbed Odie, picking him up. "And you... we'll see what to do with you, as dogs are not welcome here."

Absolutely not. After everything Magda did to get Odie back, she was not losing her dog again. All at once, the rage consuming her heart and mind threatened to release in all directions. She gave into the magic, letting the golden flurries sparkle at her fingertips, and the yellow haze spread across her irises.

"No!" she screamed, throwing up her free hand.

Suddenly, the stone floor in front of her buckled. Flying out in the direction of her fingertips, the stones that were covering the ground were flung from their places in the earth, as if she had cut directly forward into the rocks with a sharp blade. Some of the rocks flew upwards in the direction of the cells, pitifully smashing against the iron bars and cracking into dust.

What was that?

The gold power lingered around her shaking hand, until it withered into nothing.

"You have Soul magic?" Ravi's eyes widened.

Upon seeing the display of magic, the officer holding Magda only became more violent, yanking her arms behind her back. "I'm bringing her to Queen Sanyal. Lock him up with the dog for now, and run some tests to make sure he doesn't have magic either."

"No, please, don't hurt him—" Magda screamed, attempting to not be separated from Ravi. But the officer was already dragging her away, pulling her out of the jail before she could wrench one of her hands free from his grasp to unleash the magic once more.

"I—" Ravi called out to her.

But the rest of his words were lost as the door to the dungeon slammed in his face.

CHAPTER 48
Dagmara

The wedding day had arrived.

Dagmara checked the Scribestone every moment she had, but there was nothing for her. No word from Magda, and nothing else from Bernadette or Teos. She decided to send a message directly to Magda, asking her to respond before she went through with the wedding. Only Magda would be able to read it if she even made it to the Flaustran Scribestone. The note was a little desperate, but so was Dagmara.

She had one last minute fitting with the wedding gown, after all the alterations had been made. Dagmara stood in front of a floor length mirror, letting Urszula and two other handmaidens lace up the back of the gorgeous gown. Meanwhile, Dagmara was muttering under her breath, practicing her words in Ilusaurian before she would have to say them at the ceremony.

There was a soft knock on the door.

"Come in," Dagmara said, and the door opened, revealing Madame Annette.

"You look beautiful princess," Annette said with a smile that didn't reach her eyes.

"Thank you," said Dagmara.

"I have a visitor for you."

In the mirror, Dagmara could see the entrance to her chamber. She watched as Annette opened the door wider and Queen Bernadette stepped inside.

After the initial wave of shock, comfort flooded through Dagmara to see such a familiar face. She shooed away the handmaidens so she could turn and get a better look.

Queen Bernadette's face was unamused. "Where's my daughter?"

A pit formed in Dagmara's stomach. "I-I know mom," she stammered, "I hardly recognize myself either." She ended in a forced laugh.

Bernadette clasped her hands in front of her dress, waiting for the explanation.

"We will give you some privacy," Madame Annette said. She fired a suspicious glare at Dagmara. "Come." She gestured to the handmaids and Urszula who quickly scurried out, bowing to Queen Bernadette as they left.

The door closed, but Bernadette waited for the footsteps to recede before raising an eyebrow. "What is going on?" Her tone was frighteningly calm.

"I can explain."

"I hope so."

Dagmara heaved up the wedding dress before stepping down off the rise. "Magda decided it was safer for me to take her place, worried that Claude was behind the assassinations. If she arrived and Claude tried to have her killed, I would have died in her place."

"That is exactly why I told her not to go through with the betrothal in the first place."

"Yes, but how could we find out if he was behind the assassinations if someone wasn't here to discover that information?" Dagmara blabbered on, trying to defend their stance. She couldn't tell Bernadette half of the truth: Magda had magic belonging to Guardians of Soul and if she accepted Claude's proposal, she could have easily exposed herself.

"And where is my daughter?"

"With Queen Sanyal."

"Who is protecting her?"

Dagmara winced. "Odie?"

Bernadette glowered at her. "Have you heard from Magdalena? You know she's safe?"

Dagmara nodded. "She's much safer there than here." It wasn't a complete lie. She prayed Magda was safe. By the guardians, why hadn't Magda sent a message?

Bernadette let out a large exhale, shaking her head. "Why didn't you tell me?"

"It was Magda's decision."

"Well, have you found proof about King Claude's involvement yet in the death of my husband and son?"

"Not yet," Dagmara replied. "I can't be in the royal chamber without being watched until I'm legally wed."

"So you're going to consummate the marriage tonight? And expect the man won't notice when you and Magdalena switch places?"

Dagmara opened her mouth to object, but found no words. She hadn't thought that far.

Bernadette saw her hesitation. "I see. You're hoping to find proof that he is behind the assassinations, and neither you nor Magda will see him again."

"That was the original plan."

"Well, that is the stupidest plan I've ever heard," Bernadette stated. "Let us call it off. We can leave now for Azurem. Better yet we can leave for Flaustra and meet Magda."

"Leave?" Dagmara asked. "But I don't..." she stopped herself before she finished the sentence.

"You don't want to?" Bernadette eyed Dagmara with a knowing look. "Dagmara, honey, it's not safe here. I saw the way that woman glowered at you, I'm sure others are also suspicious. How are you even going to stand for the whole ceremony tomorrow?"

"How did you..." Dagmara muttered.

"Aleksy told me," Bernadette replied. "The nurses also mentioned they were wasting resources trying to figure out the source of your condition."

Dagmara felt the statement like a blade to her chest. The nurses always thought she was making it up. They never gave her a diagnosis.

Bernadette continued, "If the king finds out about your condition, he will not marry you."

"Don't you think I know that?" Dagmara snapped. "I just..." her voice trailed off, her mind returning to the king. Her body flushed, remembering the way he held her and how his skin felt against hers—

"Oh, honey," Bernadette said, "I'm certain falling for him wasn't a part of the plan?"

Embarrassed, Dagmara shook her head. She couldn't meet Bernadette's gaze.

"I need to speak with Magda. Let us delay this," Bernadette said.

"If we delay this, the king will know something is wrong."

"Something *is* wrong," Bernadette said. "Why would Magda do this? Why did she go to Flaustra?"

Dagmara didn't know how to answer that question. Magda went to Flaustra because she had Soul magic. But Magda didn't want her mother to know. It wasn't Dagmara's place to tell.

"Dagmara," Bernadette insisted, "I need you to be honest with me. I want to help, but I can't unless you tell me what is going on."

Dagmara's voice was barely audible, "You can't say *anything*."

"You have my word."

"Magda...doesn't have Life magic," Dagmara whispered. "She has Soul magic. And we can't let anyone find out, otherwise, the future of Azurem is at risk if there's no Life heir. That's why I'm here, and that's why she went to speak with Sanyal."

Bernadette was silent for a long moment. Her face flashed with a multitude of indecipherable emotions. "But the coronation..."

"That was Aleksy's magic."

"By the guardians..." Bernadette said under her breath. "How is that possible? She's Bogdan's child."

"I don't know how it's possible," Dagmara admitted. "But you understand why no one can know, right?"

"Of course I do, but it doesn't mean I like what you girls did to try and hide it. We didn't have to go through with this marriage at all."

"We had to find out if Claude killed the king and Aleksy," Dagmara stated.

Letting out a long sigh, Bernadette crossed to the edge of the bed and sat down. "Alright. We're here now, we will see this through. I will work with my councilors to ensure there are clauses in the marriage treaty so we can get Magda out of this if anything goes wrong. You must search the royal chambers before the night is over, but after the legal vows."

Shaken, Dagmara felt the shift in the conversation. "What?"

"After you are legally wed, before the night is over, say you want to freshen up and prepare in his room. Use the time to search his study and his room—check for false backs of his closets."

Dagmara couldn't help but laugh. "Your Majesty, I'm surprised."

Bernadette shrugged elegantly. "In this world, being a queen requires intelligence and tenacity."

"What then?"

"If you find the proof, we will make a hasty exit. I will have a carriage ready. And if not..." Bernadette paused, "well I hope you can decide for yourself if you want to pursue a marriage night with someone who will be yelling another woman's name."

"Your Majesty!" Dagmara gasped, covering her mouth.

A smile creased on the queen's mouth. "I do not envy your position Dagmara. But I also know I cannot be mad at you as you were only following orders. However, I am ready to wring Magda's neck." She ended in a laugh. "I wonder what Bogdan would have made of this." Her laugh stilted, then she shifted her attention to straighten the wrinkles in her dress.

"Your Majesty," Dagmara said, approaching the bed. She took a seat beside the queen. "Claude mentioned he warned King Bogdan of something...something that led to the assassinations. Is that true?"

"I tried to stay out of that messy business."

"But you must know something," Dagmara urged.

"Your mother was employed long before King Claude reached out to us," Bernadette said. "But yes, it is true. A few months after King Percival Mirage and his wife were killed, King Claude sent a Scribestone to Bogdan. He said his parents were killed by an assassin with Mind magic. He warned King Bogdan to keep an eye out for citizens with magical abilities, saying they could come for the throne."

"Claude's parents were killed by an assassin with magic?" Dagmara gasped. "Why didn't you tell anyone?"

"Come now, magic from people that aren't guardians? I thought it was an excuse or a false alibi. I didn't believe it for a second."

"But King Bogdan did?"

Bernadette's eyes softened. "Not until your mother's death. When we found her body, her heart had been removed, but she had no injuries, not even a scar. Whoever killed her must have sent her through rounds of torturing, harming her and then healing her again and again. Evidence she was killed by someone with life magic, no doubt. And a mark of the First Prince accompanied her."

Dagmara had stopped listening. She felt the onset of tears. "Why didn't you tell me?"

"We couldn't have news spreading that other people in the world had magic besides the guardians. You must understand, that would threaten the guardian's legitimacy."

A pang radiated from Dagmara's chest. She glanced down at her palms, remembering the power of magic that flooded through her in Sailonne—when Claude's wound was magically healed. She still didn't believe it had happened.

"What if there are other people with magic...who aren't guardians?"

"Well..." Bernadette paused, "those are the people Bogdan sent you to take care of."

A sudden terror coursed through Dagmara's veins. She was killing people...with magic? Or people that may have magic? Were they actually against the throne, or simply a threat to the guardians?

She was sent to assassinate people...like her?

"With this new news about Magda's abilities, I don't know what to believe about the magic of this world anymore," said Bernadette. The queen reached out and placed her hand on Dagmara's knee. "Don't worry about that now. It is time to focus on the wedding. Teos couldn't make the trip, but he wanted me to tell you he's thinking about you."

"Is he alright?"

Bernadette sighed. "He's staying strong, but he is very sick and will need many doses of the medication. But King Claude was very generous with his shipment of medicine. There was one that arrived a few days later specifically for the *'Royal Family and any Adopted Members.'* Was that from you?"

Dagmara could feel heat rising in her cheeks. "No," she said, knowing this was the first time hearing of such a shipment. "That was all Claude."

CHAPTER 49
Magdalena

Magda was dragged down a back hallway toward Queen Sanyal's royal study. The officer didn't dare bring her through the ballroom and threaten to disturb the party. The entire time, Magda was preparing for a scolding from Queen Sanyal, as if she was being brought to her own mother. However, her mind was spinning. Ravi had lied to her about his entire intentions for coming to the ball tonight. He had never wanted to help her, he had only wanted to see his lover who was locked away in the castle.

What was Laila's crime? And why did Ravi use Magda as a placeholder?

Soon, the officers opened the doors to the study, forcing her to step inside.

It was a spacious room, with a large desk in front of a mahogany bookshelf. The walls and floor were stone, with a patterned tile mosaic in the shape of a flower in the center of the floor. Around the mosaic were three velvet couches, and matching banners hung in the windows. To the right, was an expansive balcony.

Before her, sitting on couches across from each other, were Queen Sanyal, Princess Kiran and...Ishani? What was she doing here? All three looked deep in conversation, as if they were in the middle of a fight.

The biggest officer stepped forward, interrupting their conversation. He had to raise his voice even louder than the three to be heard.

"Your Majesty, this imposter was caught in the dungeon," said the officer. He pushed Magda forward toward the Queen.

"In the dungeon?" Kiran blurted out, shooting a glare at Magda.

"Queen Sanyal, let me explain...," Magda switched to Azuremi.

"Princess Magdalena?" Queen Sanyal rose to her feet, stepping closer to her. However, upon recognizing her, she didn't smile. "Leave us," she ordered her officer.

"But, Your Majesty, she has magic—"

"I know. You may go."

The officer seemed reluctant, but exited the room.

"Now Magda," Queen Sanyal continued, "You will sit on this couch right now and tell me why you're here, and why you stupidly disobeyed my instructions for you to stay in Azurem."

The queen's words took Magda aback. Finally, she was in the palace and in a meeting with Sanyal. This is how the queen was reacting?

Nevertheless, Magda needed to focus on her mission, finally taking responsibility like the princess she was. It was her opportunity to ask two guardians about the true meaning behind the magic. Magda had so many questions for them, she didn't even know where to begin. From her family's deaths, to the guardian's oath, to her own powers, to her strange dreams, everything was muddled in her head.

"Please, you have to tell me everything," Magda blurted out desperately. She crossed to the couch, and sat down next to Kiran. "It's been a nightmare getting here and searching for answers. I've been completely in the dark for weeks after the assassination of my family, and I have no idea what it means to be a guardian or use my powers. There's no one else I can go to but the two of you..." Magda hesitated and stared up at Ishani, who sat across from her on the couches. What was she doing here anyways?

Queen Sanyal noticed Magda's gaze. "Anything you say to me can be said in front of Ishani."

"I don't care about this anyways," Ishani shrugged, standing up and walking over to one of the walls. She pretended to be admiring a banner before leaning up against the stone, her axes on full display.

"I care," said Kiran, reaching out to lay a soft hand on Magda's.

That's when Magda noticed that Kiran and Ishani were exactly the same height, with the same shiny dark hair, although Kiran's was curly. Something about them was strikingly familiar.

"How do you know each other?" Magda asked.

"This is my younger sister," Ishani admitted. "You didn't know that Flaustra had multiple heirs?"

"I did, but I didn't know it was *you*," said Magda, "Why did we never meet growing up?"

"I refused to come to any of the royal meetings. I wanted nothing to do with being a guardian."

"But you're the older sibling," said Magda, putting it together. "Kiran would've had to challenge you for the powers."

Ishani rolled her eyes. "Precisely. I had my powers fully manifested for five years after my coronation."

"Yeah, and you threw the challenge," Kiran said with an annoyed tone. "You did it on purpose."

"I did not."

"You did too. We all know it's the only reason I'm the guardian. I can't fight like you, Ishani!"

"Girls!" Queen Sanyal quieted her two daughters. "There are many reasons as to why the Flaustran trials went as they did, and that conversation is not for today." Queen Sanyal walked behind her desk, her fingers clasped behind her back. Then she let out a deep sigh. Her voice was laced with anger toward Magda as she said, "I intend to send a message to your mother via the Scribestone, telling her that you are safe and sound in Flaustra."

"What?" Magda let out a gasp. Her mother would not be happy when she heard the news that she wasn't in Ilusauri about to be married to King Claude.

"Magda, what were you thinking?!" Queen Sanyal yelled forcefully, slamming her hands down on the desk. "It's dangerous out there. I told you not to come."

"You weren't giving me any answers, and my mother wasn't letting me leave the fortress!" yelled Magda. "The only way I could convince her to leave was by faking a marriage to Claude."

Ishani scoffed, and Kiran shot her a glare.

"I don't believe that's true." Queen Sanyal shook her head.

"I came directly to the palace, and I wasn't let inside."

"We've put up more protections since the assassination attempts," offered Kiran. "There was no way the officers would let you in even if you were one of the gods themselves."

Queen Sanyal threw up her hands, disregarding Kiran and continuing to yell at Magda, "You are a disgrace to the guardians—you could have put everything in jeopardy if something happened to you!"

"And that's why I had no choice but to come to you," said Magda, on the verge of tears once more. "I have no idea what it means to be a guardian. I've been utterly and hopelessly lost since my dad and brother died, and I don't know where I'm heading. All I know is that you are the only person that might have one answer for me. And I'm begging you to be honest so I understand the real danger we are in!"

The words came out in a forceful yell, and Magda stopped suddenly. She instantly felt ashamed for screaming at the Queen of Flaustra, but she didn't know who else to turn to. If she didn't get answers soon, she feared as if she would break down completely. And time was not on her side.

Kiran scooted closer to Magda. "Don't worry, we're here to help. We're all in this together."

"What does that mean?" Magda persisted.

Queen Sanyal took a deep breath, before taking a seat at her desk.

Sanyal began, "All the guardians have the same mission. Guardians have existed since the beginning of time. They take care to protect their sacred form of magic, and tap into the winds and the earth to keep our connection with the magic that flows through this land. Without the guardians as vessels to channel the magic in our world, nothing would exist. Crops wouldn't grow, water wouldn't flow down from the glaciers, mathematical theory couldn't hold true, and the sun wouldn't rise each day."

"So we are like scholars, destined to understand and connect with nature," said Magda.

"In some ways," said Queen Sanyal. "Your father was responsible for understanding the natural balance of water, from the oceans to the rivers to the atmosphere. So much so that he could channel the power of water himself."

Magda asked, "If guardians hold the land together, why are assassins trying to kill them? Surely killing a guardian and ruining the land would be bad for humanity."

Kiran leaned closer. "Do you know the tale of the five?" she asked.

"Yes," Magda answered. "There were five siblings—the original guardians. The oldest brother was excluded from the trials because he was more powerful than all the rest. In turn, he destroyed his siblings. It's a schoolyard story, meant to teach children to stop bullying each other."

"No," said Queen Sanyal firmly. "The Blaide family was real. They guarded the fifth branch of magic we no longer have today, and their oldest brother wielded powers unlike anything recorded in our entire history. The First Prince, unlike his family, had the ability to control all elements of magic: Life, Soul, Mind, Spirit, and the Void."

Magda gasped. There was a person in history that wielded multiple forms of magic? What did that mean?

Kiran continued the story, "But the other remaining families of guardians feared he was too powerful, so they destroyed him."

"They didn't destroy him," Ishani corrected the princess, her tone cold.

Queen Sanyal nodded. "He was too powerful to be killed, so the remaining guardians trapped him in a tomb, sealed with four magical locks that are each controlled by the current kingdoms. The lives of the guardians today are connected to those locks. As long as the guardians live, the tomb cannot be opened."

Magda couldn't believe her ears. Suddenly, she was scared to reveal to Queen Sanyal and Princess Kiran that she had Soul magic. Did that mean all the Life Guardians were dead and that lock her family had been protecting was broken? Regardless, how was the First Prince in a tomb and no one had told her about it?

"Where is this tomb?" asked Magda. "Is it actually a physical tomb or is it abstract?"

"No one knows," said Kiran with a shrug, and somewhat of an eye-roll. "Apparently, the guardians destroyed all records of its location."

Magda could read through Kiran's expression, and she turned to ask Queen Sanyal the question that was on all of the younger girls' minds. "If you've never seen this tomb, how do you know that this ancient story is actually true?"

"Because," Queen Sanyal shook her head. "I felt the magic rescind when Bogdan and Aleksy died. I felt a crack in the core and a loosening of great power. It's the same thing I felt when Claude's parents were murdered."

"Mom," Kiran objected, "you know that people say the tomb—the heart of our world—is a myth. A story to scare everyone into thinking that the guardians should always hold this power and be treated like gods."

"I don't care what you think about our politics."

"Why should we continue this autocracy? It's not good for anyone."

"Stop this, Kiran," Sanyal snapped. "You have much more to learn."

Kiran grew silent.

While Magda let the tension die down, her thoughts drifted again to her family. "So the assassins are killing the guardians to break the locks on the tomb? They want to release the First Prince?"

"Correct. If you die, Magda, the lock bound by Life magic will be broken, and we will be closer to unleashing evil than ever before. You must go back to Azurem and stay safe. Do you have any idea who did this to your family?" asked Sanyal.

"We think the assassins came from Ilusauri," confessed Magda.

"King Claude Mirage," Sanyal mused, "Yes, killing his own parents would have broken the Mind magic seal, as he wasn't crowned yet. Someone in the family blood line can always be re-coronated as a guardian and tap back into the powers of the land. This would have happened with Claude when he was crowned after his parents death. However, it doesn't change the fact that the bloodline and lineage was temporarily broken, removing the lock."

"And you believe Claude was behind this?" Magda asked.

"It would be foolish to ever trust a Mind Guardian. He wrote to me claiming his land is dying—but is that what he wants people to see so he can steal my kingdom's food?" Queen Sanyal asked, her tone bitter. "Also, according to Ishani and other guild Leaders, he's paying them for information. He's looking for the tomb, no doubt."

"The tomb of the First Prince?"

"Yes," Ishani confirmed. "He's written multiple letters about his search to me and others I trade with."

Sanyal continued, "And why else would he need to find the tomb if he didn't want the First Prince to return?"

The question hung in the air, and Magda gasped. She had to get

Dagmara out of there. It wasn't safe. Her mind flashed back to the letters she had found in Ishani's ship days ago. If Ishani had proof in all of his other messages that Claude was searching for the tomb, that was enough.

"So Claude broke the mind seal. Killing off Aleksy, Bogdan, and Magda would break the Life seal," explained Kiran, "...in theory..."

"Leaving just Celestaire and Flaustra...," Magda's voice trailed off as a brooding feeling caused goosebumps to travel up both her arms. It was time to tell them that she did, in fact, have Soul magic, and this would create an even bigger problem for them all. Suddenly, the voice in her head was back, this time as clear as day:

Destruction is but a prelude to creation, Dear Princess...

"I haven't been honest with you, Queen Sanyal," Magda blurted out.

Sanyal placed her elbows on the desk, leaning forward. "About what?"

"The reason I came here instead of seeking guidance from Guardian Sora is because..." Magda hesitated. This was the moment of truth. "I have Soul magic."

"What?" Kiran blurted out.

Sanyal held up a hand to silence her daughter, her attention remaining fixed on Magda. "That's not possible."

"Look!" Magda sprang up from the couch, darting to the balcony. Vines weaved across the open doorway and through the banister. Focusing on her magic, Magda tried to make the vines move. She had practiced this. Slowly, the vines curled, thorns protruding from the greenery.

Both Kiran and Sanyal gasped, while Ishani said under her breath, "I knew it."

"You suspected me at Vex's hideout," said Magda, turning back to Ishani.

"Of course I did. It was so obvious."

"Because you were once a guardian yourself?"

"Precisely. But also, I saw the flowers in my office that you magically brought back to life."

"You're a Soul Guardian!" Kiran squealed, covering her mouth with her hands. "What does this mean?"

Sanyal was studying Magdalena. "You only have Soul magic? Nothing to do with water?"

"Nothing," Magdalena admitted.

"Is that possible?" Kiran continued. "Could Magda be our cousin or something? It has to be Uncle Ivaan!"

"Who?" Magda asked.

"Kiran," Ishani snapped. "Does she look like our cousin?"

Kiran froze, her nose scrunching as she examined Magdalena more thoroughly. "No."

"This is why I'm here," Magdalena said. "No one knows about this, not even my mother. I don't know anything about being a guardian let alone honing Soul magic! I need to look into your records, I need to understand my past. I need your help, Queen Sanyal, please don't send me back to Azurem. How do I have Soul magic?"

Sanyal was horribly still, her expression indescribable. "There's only one explanation."

Dread flooded through Magda's body, and a cold wind pricked her skin. It was the same unease she had felt during her dreams with the unknown voice.

"By the guardians, Magdalena," Sanyal said, breathless, "I never thought this day would come."

"Please, tell me—"

Sanyal held up her hand, silencing Magda. The room went still.

"What is it mom?" Kiran asked.

"Shhh," Sanyal silenced her. She rose from her chair, her head inclining as she listened.

That's when Magda heard it too, stone scraping against stone. It was faint, but the noise sent a chill down her spine.

Sanyal approached the glass doors to the balcony, and Magda countered, stepping away.

Then Magda saw a figure scale the edge of the balcony, using the vines to hoist themselves onto solid ground. The figure was dressed in black with a white mask.

Magda's body went numb. She recognized the mask immediately, including the symbol in the center of the forehead. It was the same mask the assassins wore that had killed Bogdan and Aleksy.

The assassins had found her.

"Get back!" Sanyal yelled before commanding the earth to obey her. With a single raise of her hand, the vines instantly grabbed the assassin by the neck and yanked them backward off the balcony. A single cry pierced the air as they fell to their death.

But they weren't the only ones. Two other assassins scaled the opposite end of the balcony.

Sanyal whirled on them, her eyes glowing gold. She reached out, commanding the vines to grab the assassins, but the vines froze, moments away from their targets.

Magda watched in awe as the vines shook, unable to reach their targets. What was going on?

Sanyal looked equally in shock. Then the vines turned on the queen and lunged for her throat. They whirled around the queen's neck and hoisted her into the air.

The earth was turning against the Soul Guardian.

"Kiran, what are you doing?" Ishani yelled.

"It's not me!" Kiran cried. She collapsed to the ground, cowering behind the couch.

"Magda?!" Ishani screamed.

Magda was frozen. She had no idea what was going on. All she could see were the assassins charging toward her. There had to be something here.

The tiles on the wall. They were stone. Stone would listen to her.

Magda thrust out her arms and the tiles burst from the wall, flying toward the two assassins like shattered glass. They both ducked, skidding onto the ground.

Ishani appeared from behind Magda, her two axes in hand. She used one, throwing it upward at the vines that strangled Queen Sanyal. The vines snapped as the axe tore them, and Sanyal dropped to the ground instantly, her body smacking to the stone floor.

Then Ishani whirled on the assassins, skidding through the open doorway. She threw her other axe before the assassins had gotten back up from the ground. The axe circled in the air before landing perfectly in one of the assassin's chests. Blood spurted from the wound, and the assassin collapsed a moment later.

There was only one assassin left.

"Magda!" Ishani yelled before racing to recollect her axe.

Magda stared back at the last assassin, the white mask reminding her of her father and brother's deaths. She would kill this girl, whoever she was. She wanted revenge.

Magda reached out, summoning the remaining vines that twirled over the balcony, but the assassin took one look at her dead comrade and fled.

The vines barely reached her, wrapping around her wrist and digging into her jacket.

The assassin was fast, pulling her hand from the sleeve and slipping out of the jacket entirely. She swung her legs over the railing and disappeared.

Ishani was panting, standing with an axe in hand. She looked at Magda, fear written on her face.

Kiran crawled over to her mother, shaking her as tears streamed down her face.

She looked up, her eyes bloodshot, and screamed, "She's dead!"

CHAPTER 50
Dagmara

Dagmara's heart pounded in her chest. This was the moment that she had dreamed about in childhood—getting married to her future husband. Not once in her life did she think it would be like this.

The doors to the ballroom remained closed, waiting for her grand entrance. She simply had to make it up the top of the staircase where they set up an altar so that everyone in attendance could see them on the balcony.

Bernadette had told her to legally marry the king, then immediately search his room. If things went wrong, she would be waiting with a carriage. This was now a direct order from the queen, and Dagmara had no choice but to go through with it. She prayed everything would go as planned.

Where was Magdalena? Dagmara hadn't heard from her friend at all. Was Magda on her way here to Ilusauri? Had something happened to her in Flaustra? Did she decide not to come at all?

If you're going to arrive, Magda, it's now or never.

"You look beautiful, Princess."

"Thank you." Dagmara smiled at Martine, as she flattened her hands against the dress.

Her wedding dress was a full-length gown with a striking, fitted bodice that accentuated her waist, before curving up into long sleeves made of only sparkling beadwork that covered her breasts, shoulders, and arms. The back plunged into a deep v-shape, while the skirt flared out dramatically in mixed layers of silver and white, The heavy fabric was embellished with intricate silver embroidery that fanned out into a long train. Her silver-dyed hair was left hanging loosely around a diamond-studded crown.

"You also look nervous," Martine noted, letting a smile form on her face.

Dagmara sighed. "I didn't think I would be so nervous. I thought this wedding would be a formality. But...by the guardians, the way I feel for him..." her voice trailed off, embarrassed.

"You're falling in love with him." It wasn't a question.

Dagmara nodded.

The fanfare began, and it was time to enter. She fixed her crown, feeling the sharp points of the diamonds nearly like daggers. She felt awkward not holding anything in her hands, but in Ilusaurian tradition, her hands needed to be free for the ceremony.

The doors opened, and white light poured onto her. She forced her feet to move down the makeshift aisle of people standing in groups on either side of the ballroom. There were tables set up for the dinner later, and a large area of the floor remained open for her dance with the king. Queen Bernadette had a special location to watch the wedding on the balcony, surrounded by Azuremi guards and her advisors. The musicians were on the other side of the balcony, their notes echoing through the room. The sun was setting, and rain began to fall, tapping on the glass windows beyond the chandeliers.

Then Dagmara saw him. He was at the top of the staircase, his hands clasped behind his back, in white attire. A white cape fluttered behind him, stitched in silver. He looked like a knight in shining armor. Or rather, a king.

Her king.

The world faded away, the music a distant lullaby. She ignored the hushed voices of the crowd, unable to take her eyes off Claude. She had never seen him more handsome. His expression softened when he saw her, expressions of pride, lust, and yearning crossing his features.

She ascended the stairs, willing her health to be kind to her for once in her life. She needed to get through today. That was all.

She felt her heart rate increase with each step she took, but she was nearing Claude, and she focused solely on him.

When she reached the top, Claude took her hands, and it was as if electricity rushed through her body. By the guardians, she wanted to grab his face and kiss him then and there. He had hidden his scar once more, but she would've preferred to see his true self.

"You're stunning," Claude whispered as the maidens fixed Dagmara's dress.

"Thank you, but you're...you're stunning as well."

A soft laugh escaped his lips. His smile was captivating.

The officiant proceeded with the ceremony, starting with a long list of what they should and shouldn't do in marriage. Then the ceremonial caster arrived, the Azuremi tradition, and Claude and Dagmara interlocked their hands before reaching them into the liquid. As soon as it molded around their grasp to later become a sculpture, another maiden washed the excess of the casting liquid off their palms.

At that point, Dagmara knew she had been standing for too long. She could feel darkness dancing in the corner of her vision, her stomach roiling with nausea. The world began to tilt.

"Are you alright?" Claude whispered. The officiant could hear, but none of the guests in attendance did.

"Lightheaded, but I'll be fine."

"It's a good thing we all kneel for the next portion of the ceremony."

"We do?"

Claude glanced at the officiant. "Right?"

Initiating the sequence, Claude knelt, leaning back on his heels to face Dagmara. Dagmara followed his lead, and her maidens frantically rushed to readjust her gown. She hadn't read about this anywhere, and deep down she knew Claude was doing this just for her.

The officiant let out a scoff before clumsily taking one knee, guiding them into the vows.

"My partner, my better half, my queen," Claude said in Azuremi for her. "I will put you first, keep you safe, and never leave your side. Whatever the world may bring, we will face hand in hand." Then he extended his palm toward the officiant. The man pricked Claude's finger, extracting a single drop of blood. It landed in a concave spot on the backside of a ring. The diamond gemstone was then closed, concealing the drop of blood inside. Claude took Dagmara's hand and put the ring on her middle finger. "With my blood, I am yours."

Dagmara was about to proceed into her vows. She was binding her life to this man, whether she remained married to him or not. There was no turning back. If she and Magda switched places now, even if no one noticed, it would always be Dagmara's blood inside Claude's wedding ring. A piece of her would always belong to Claude somehow.

"My partner, my better half, my king," Dagmara began her side of the vows, hoping her Ilusaurian was intelligible. By his smile, she couldn't tell if it was awful or if he found her accent adorable. "I will put you first, keep you safe, and never leave your side. Whatever the world may bring, we will face hand in hand." She repeated the same Ilusaurian tradition. The prick of her finger stung, but she didn't mind. With a drop of her blood in his ring, she guided it onto his finger. "With my blood, I am yours."

"For the betterment of our kingdoms," he whispered.

She smiled. "And the safety of our people."

He stood first before helping her to her feet. She felt secure with his guidance. Then they descended the staircase, hand in hand, before the music shifted to the Azuremi waltz.

They danced with one another, their bodies moving perfectly in time, his cape fluttering behind him. Her chest was pressed against his, and his arms supported her. She was lost in his eyes, and it was as if no one else existed.

As the song came to a close, they remained in one another's arms, unable to break apart.

His hand shifted from her back to her neck, cradling her head. Leaning closer, he rested his forehead against hers. She closed her eyes, breathing in his cologne and knowing there was no other place in the world she would rather be.

"I want to respect your Azuremi traditions," he whispered, "but why must I wait until midnight to kiss you?"

"By the guardians, that is the worst tradition ever," she laughed. She opened her eyes, meeting his gaze. Their noses were touching. "I want you to kiss me."

"I will kiss every inch of your body, and more," he said. "I would take you right now in front of all these people."

Heat rushed through her body, her blood pulsing. "What's stopping you?"

"I am a king, and I respect your kingdom's traditions," he said. "Besides, your mother is watching."

She laughed. "If she wasn't?"

"You'll find out tonight when I have you all to myself."

The music shifted into another tune, and a guard made an announcement as they brought out the table for the married couple, raised on a platform so they would be higher than everyone in attendance. Claude held out his hand to Dagmara, and she accepted it. He led the way over to the table, Sacha, Pierre, and Martine falling into step around them to separate them from the guests.

"Forgive me, your Majesty," Pierre whispered. "There is something you should see."

"Right now?"

"Yes, it's about..." he hesitated, "it's important."

"Alright," Claude said.

Claude led Dagmara to the front, stepping up on the riser their table was on, and pulled out her seat. As she sat, he laid a finger under her chin and lifted her head to him. "I'll only be a moment."

"Is everything alright?"

"I don't know. Maybe the other governors are questioning why Lionel isn't here. I'm hoping it has nothing to do with the Celesta."

Then Claude proceeded up the staircase, flanked by Pierre and Sacha. He exited the room, leaving Dagmara by herself.

"You can eat," Dagmara told Martine, feeling her presence.

"I'll eat later," Martine replied, her hands behind her back as she surveyed the crowd.

Dagmara, on the other hand, wouldn't risk eating too much. If she ate too big of a meal, she would become fatigued. Another symptom of her unknown condition.

Everyone settled for the dinner, taking a seat at the banquet tables. There was a special table reserved in the back for Queen Bernadette.

Briefly, Dagmara caught Sabien's eye as he sauntered across the back of the room, whispering to each guard he passed. He maintained an attentive gaze on the crowd, taking a post by the grand windows. The rain pelted the glass behind him, night finally falling. He looked up at Dagmara, and she quickly averted her gaze.

She saw a bowl of salt already at her table, and she once more felt at peace. She knew Claude had put it there.

"To our new queen!" a voice rang through the room. It was from Madame Annette. She was standing in the aisle, not seated at a table.

"We are grateful for the union between Ilusauri and Azurem, and we are glad to have another guardian on the throne to protect us." Her voice was sweet but filled with contempt. "We would love nothing more than to see your power in action."

Ice coursed through Dagmara's veins. Two guards brought out a large bowl of water and set it down at her table. They bowed before walking away.

"What is this?" Dagmara asked, shooting a glance at Annette. She tried to keep her voice even, but was keenly aware that everyone's eyes were on her.

"If you truly are the Princess of Azurem, you wouldn't mind showing us a bit of your magic? Like you did at your coronation, right?" Annette's eyebrows were raised on her forehead. It was evident she no longer believed that Dagmara was the true princess, if she ever had believed it. "Wouldn't we all like to see?" She addressed the crowd.

A thunderous round of applause echoed through the room.

Everyone applauded except Queen Bernadette, who inched forward in her chair, prepared to intervene.

But Dagmara could do this. She remembered the way the magic had coursed through her body when she healed Claude in Sailonne.

"Alright," Dagmara announced, standing from her chair. She refocused her attention on the bowl of water as the room fell completely silent. She tried to draw from within, her gaze set on the water. Something was different about her. She had felt it in Sailonne. She had healed Claude.

She had magic.

Time seemed to lengthen as she waited to feel something. She waited for the magic to tingle at her fingertips as it had before, but nothing came. A dead space seemed to fill through the room as the time dragged on, everyone waiting.

Maybe she had no magic at all.

Then the water stirred. Her body went numb.

She watched as the water levitated before swirling in the air. The room let out a collective gasp, covering the sound of Dagmara's own gasp. The liquid molded into a wolf. The blue liquid rippled as the wolf figure let out a silent howl.

Applause rang through the room at the show.

Dagmara couldn't move. Her eyes were transfixed by the magic before her. This wasn't her own doing. She felt no magic coursing through her like she had when Claude was healed. But then, how was this possible?

There was only one answer. This wasn't her. She remembered how Aleksy had tricked everyone at the coronation, making everyone think Magda had Life magic. Now, someone was doing the same thing, but this time, they were saving Dagmara.

She shut her eyes quickly, hoping no one could see that they had not transformed into the icy-blue color. She waited, feeling a mist from the water before her, until she knew the display was over.

The thunderous applause rang through the room.

"How dare you!" The booming voice echoed through the dining hall and caused Dagmara to jump in her shoes.

The applause stopped.

Dagmara whirled around, her body alight with fear. Her eyes widened at the sight of Claude, storming down the staircase. His white cape fluttered behind him, and his brow was furrowed. But he wasn't looking at Dagmara. His gaze was set on Annette.

The room was utterly silent as the king reached the bottom of the stairs. He pointed his finger at Annette. "Magdalena doesn't have to put on a show for you. If you ever question her integrity again there will be consequences."

"My King, the Princess—"

"She is your *queen*." Claude cut her off, his voice so threatening it sent a chill down Dagmara's spine.

"My apologies," Annette stammered. She curtsied low to the ground, dipping her head to the king. "It will not happen again."

"Do not bow to me," Claude scolded. "Bow to your queen."

Dagmara's breath hitched. Although he wasn't looking at her, Dagmara searched Claude's expression. His eyes were still dark without a hint of silver. He wasn't compelling Annette. He was ordering her. It was almost worse that he was forcing her to bow out of her own will.

A tense silence filled the room. It felt like an eternity before

Annette met Dagmara's gaze. Her eyes were wide with fear. Any distrust or condescension in her expression had been wiped clean.

"My Queen," Annette said before dropping into a bow.

Then Claude stepped onto the platform beside Dagmara. As he approached her, she forgot how to breathe. When he took her hand, her blood turned to ice. He pressed a kiss on the back of her palm, his lips soft and gentle against her skin.

"I am a man of my word, and today I made a vow." His whisper was barely audible, meant for only her to hear. "I will always put you first and keep you safe." His tone was sincere. Then he looked at her, his eyes glistening.

Dagmara was too stunned to think about the expression on her own face.

Claude's regal tone resurfaced as he stated, "You are now Queen of Ilusauri. Serve our people, and I, in return, will serve you."

He lowered himself to his knee in front of her, still holding her hand, and dipped his head.

Realization dawned on Dagmara like a dagger. He was bowing.

The Guardian of the Mind was bowing to *her*.

In unison, the entire room rose from their chairs and dropped to a bow, following their king.

The world began spinning around Dagmara. She wrenched her gaze away from Claude and looked out to the guests.

Emotions flooded her body. They shouldn't be bowing. She wasn't Princess Magdalena. She wasn't Queen Magdalena. She was a false queen. A fraud.

Every guest in attendance was bowing to her. Even the soldiers lining the room followed their king. Even Queen Bernadette inclined her head. Everyone except—

Dagmara's heart stopped. One person remained standing at the back of the room, barely visible in the shadows. His hands were poised behind his back as he stared at Dagmara with a smirk plastered to his face and ice-blue magic shimmering in his eyes.

Sabien Renaud.

He tilted his head ever so slightly, and the water in the bowl rippled.

Thoughts rushed through Dagmara's mind like a tidal wave as everything made sense. *Sabien* was the one who healed Claude in Sailonne, not Dagmara. His hand was over hers the entire time. She was never the one with magic. She was horribly ordinary and Sabien was...he was...

A Guardian of Life.

CHAPTER 51
Dagmara

Dagmara felt like she was going to faint.

Claude rose to his feet. In unison, the rest of the audience straightened. Even Annette stood, her face red with embarrassment.

"Let us eat!" Claude yelled, though his voice was muffled. He was miles away from Dagmara. She couldn't tear her eyes away from Sabien, and the Captain of the Guard wasn't backing down either as the magic faded from his eyes.

Music flooded the room once more, and the clattering of plates and utensils turned into a cacophony of noises.

"Are you alright?" Claude placed his hand on Dagmara's lower back.

"Y-Yes," Dagmara stammered. "I just need some air." She yanked away from Claude. Hiking up her wedding dress, she raced out of the room through the closest door.

Once the door had slammed shut behind her, she nearly collapsed into the wall, leaning her shoulder against it to keep her upright. She felt sick to her stomach.

It was him. Sabien Renaud. He had created the wolf figure in the air. He had water magic. There was no other explanation. She remembered their first interaction in Azurem and how he commented on the wolf sculptures in the tavern. She remembered shoving him into the rapids—

It made perfect sense now that she saw him for who he was. The rapids had healed his injury. He must have commanded the water to bring him to safety. That was the only explanation for how he had survived.

Then why would he step in and create the scene in the banquet hall? Why let everyone think Dagmara had magic? He made it seem like she had healed Claude, and then he put on the show with the wolf figure in the water. Why didn't he let the truth be exposed? It didn't make sense.

"Princess."

Dagmara whirled at the voice, coming face to face with Martine.

"Are you alright?"

Breathless, Dagmara nodded.

"What happened in there?" Martine asked, her eyes full of concern.

Dagmara leaned her back against the stone wall, clutching her chest. She avoided the direct question. "You followed me?"

"It is my job to watch you," Martine said. She took a step closer, taking Dagmara's free hand. "But I am not only your guard. I would like to be a friend."

Another pang radiated in Dagmara's chest. She was lying to everyone, even Martine who *knew* she wasn't a guardian.

"You are a good friend, Martine. There are things I wish I could tell you, but you are still Ilusaurian."

"I may be Ilusaurian, but that doesn't make us enemies. As your guard, everything I do is for your safety. And as your friend, everything I do is because I want to help."

Dagmara smiled. "It feels good to have a friend again. I—"

Another voice interrupted them.

"Hello, Princess, or shall I say, Queen."

Dagmara's head snapped up to meet Sabien's gaze. He approached them, his chocolate eyes burning with ferocity.

"Martine, a moment with my queen," Sabien ordered, not even glancing in her direction.

Instinctively, Dagmara gripped Martine's hand tighter.

"I..." Martine started to argue, but Sabien cut her off.

"By order of your captain, I command you to leave us."

Martine straightened her posture. "I don't answer to you anymore, Captain."

Sabien's brow furrowed. "What did you say to me?"

Dagmara released Martine's hand. It was time she spoke to Sabien alone. "I'll be alright. Thank you."

Martine gave a curt nod. She fired a suspicious glance at Sabien before leaving.

Dagmara was alone with Sabien, and he stared down at her expectantly. This was the man who caused the scene in the ballroom, making everyone believe she had water magic. It was exactly like what Aleksy had done on behalf of Magdalena during the coronation.

This man was a Guardian of Life.

Sabien took a step toward Dagmara, and she immediately countered. "Stay away from me," she said under her breath, holding her hand out defensively in front of her.

Sabien's expression darkened. "That is no way to thank me."

Dagmara let out a sharp, short laugh. "Thank you?"

"They would've torn you to shreds if they knew you were an imposter."

Dagmara could feel the heat rise in her cheeks. She glanced around the hall to be certain they were alone before she stuck her chin in the air.

"How dare you accuse me of being an imposter," she scowled. "And how dare you let me believe..." she stopped mid-sentence.

How dare you let me believe that I was special? She thought she was the one who had healed Claude in Sailonne.

"Pierre was watching," Sabien said as though he could read her mind. "Otherwise, we could have had this conversation much sooner."

"Who are you?" asked Dagmara. "How do you have Life magic?"

Sabien shrugged casually. "I don't know."

"Liar."

"Why do you think I was at the coronation?" he asked.

Dagmara froze. "What does that have to do with my question?"

Sabien stepped closer, dropping his voice to a whisper.

"I went to the coronation to find out why I have these abilities," Sabien said. Although his voice was quiet, it was sharp. "I thought that I could be a bastard king to the Azuremi throne. I went secretly to speak with King Bogdan, and nobody was supposed to know. The coronation was the perfect time for a chance to speak to him without explaining myself to all of his knights. But he was murdered before I had the chance."

Dagmara's mind ran wild with thoughts. If he were telling the truth, she had to keep Magda's powers a secret now more than ever. If the world knew Magda had the magic of Flaustra, and Sabien had the magic of Azurem, he would have a claim to the throne.

This was worse than Dagmara ever imagined.

"Then I came to find out Claude and Bogdan were working together to assassinate anyone with magic who wasn't a guardian. It meant they would come after me and kill me. So, I paid the Azuremi border knights to have my name removed from the border list. I couldn't risk there being a record out there, or to have someone question why I went to speak with Bogdan," Sabien continued. "Can you imagine what would happen if Claude found out about my magic?"

"Claude would never have you killed," Dagmara objected.

"How are you so sure?" Sabien asked.

Dagmara wasn't sure. She wasn't sure about anything anymore. Everything she thought she knew had been shattered.

"Now," Sabien's voice brought her back to her senses. "I told you who I am. I feel it is only fair for you to tell me who you are."

She narrowed her eyes. "I am Queen Magda—"

He came toward her in a fury. Before she knew it, he pinned her to the wall, his body flush against hers, and his hands on either side of her head. She could feel his hot breath against her lips when he growled, "Stop lying."

"I'm not lying!" She tried to squirm away from him, but it only created friction between their bodies. Her heart lurched in her chest as she felt his muscles stiffen. He was like a rock against her. And he was staring at her lips.

She froze once more, her breathing shallow.

No...he wasn't staring at her lips. He was staring lower.

His fingers trailed her neck, sending shivers through her body, and grasped the fabric of her sleeve. Slowly, he pulled the shoulder of her dress to the side, revealing her collarbone and the scar. With one shoulder of her dress hanging, she knew her bodice dropped dangerously low.

"I knew I recognized you." His breath was warm against her face. He traced his thumb over the scar. The scar he had given her the night she shoved him off the Azuremi bridge.

He smiled. "Hello, Dagger."

Her mission had officially been compromised.

Dagmara was suddenly aware of how firm he was against her and how her curves were pressed against him. She recognized the warmth flooding through her body and the bottomless pit of emotion in her stomach. She couldn't let her mission be compromised now. She finally had access to the royal chambers.

"You're wrong," Dagmara said.

"I know the face of the woman who tried to kill me."

Heat rose in her chest. It was all over.

Then a thought struck her.

"I'll tell Claude about you."

"Blackmail?" He let out a sharp laugh. "Claude will never believe you."

Was that true? Dagmara knew she wouldn't have believed it if she hadn't seen the magic with her own eyes.

But if she told Claude about Sabien, she would have to confess how she knew. She would have to admit that Sabien was the one who had created the wolf out of water and that she didn't have magic. She would have to confess who she really was.

Sabien seemed to read her thoughts as though she professed them out loud. He gave her a smirk. "Don't worry, I'm very good at keeping secrets."

"What?"

Sabien fixed the shoulder of her dress, covering her scar. Then he took a step back, finally giving her room to breathe. "I have no intention of outing you, Dagger."

"Then why confront me in the hallway?"

"I figured I should explain that I have magic, and you don't," Sabien said casually, "and I wanted you to admit you're not Magdalena. Very risky move by the way. Why go through with the wedding and not kill Claude earlier?"

"I have no intention of killing Claude," Dagmara said.

He crossed his arms. "Sad excuse for an assassin then, aren't you?"

"I'm here to find proof that he killed King Bogdan and Prince Aleksy, nothing more. If you knew I was an assassin, why not tell everyone to protect Claude?"

"I...was mad at him for killing Bogdan before I had the chance to discover the truth. And I told you, Claude and Bogdan were using assassins to kill people with magic. Claude is the type of king who would kill me if he knew I had this magic."

Dagmara tried to read Sabien, but his face was a mystery to her.

"Fine, don't believe me, see if I care," Sabien shrugged. "But at least let me help you."

Dagmara hesitated. "Why?"

"I need to know who I am and why I have Life magic," he said. "If I help you, maybe you can get me an audience with Queen Bernadette? Or Princess Magdalena? They have to know something. I need to know who I am."

Dagmara didn't like anything about this. Her top priority was maintaining Magdalena's secret. No one could know she didn't have Life magic.

"You and I are on the same side," Sabien continued, taking a step toward her. "Claude killed King Bogdan moments before I was going to discover the truth about my magic. We both need the truth."

"Do you have proof Claude was behind the assassination?" Dagmara questioned.

"I'm not positive but..." Sabien paused. "No, it's nothing."

"Tell me."

He let out an exaggerated sigh. "I know it may be unrelated, but he signed some false documents a few days before the coronation."

False documents? Those had to be the three identities Teos had told Dagmara about.

Sabien continued, "And one time I thought I caught him with...a mask."

"A mask?"

"Maybe it was nothing. But I could've sworn it was the symbol of the First Prince."

A sick feeling rose in Dagmara's stomach. Her mind flashed back to the day of the coronation and the assassin who had killed Aleksy. The man had stared her down in the center aisle. The man had worn a white mask with the symbol of the First Prince.

It couldn't be.

"If Claude was responsible, why hasn't he tried to kill me by now?" Dagmara asked.

"Well why would he before tonight?" Sabien countered. "He wants to claim Azurem. First he killed your family to convince you to marry him. Now that you're legally wed he can kill you and take Azurem for himself…"

"Magdalena!" The call came from around the corridor. She recognized that voice immediately. Claude was approaching.

"Where is this mask?" Dagmara asked in a whisper, suddenly in a hurry.

"Has to be in his room," Sabien's voice was quiet. "I can sneak in—"

"No," Dagmara cut him off. "Leave it to me."

Then Claude appeared at the opposite end of the corridor, jogging into sight. "There you are!" he exclaimed, approaching at a slower pace. He glanced once at Sabien before returning his attention fully to Dagmara. "Are you alright?"

"A little overwhelmed," Dagmara said, forcing a laugh. "Your captain wouldn't let me escape."

Claude shifted his gaze to Sabien. "I appreciate you trying to help, Sabien, but I can take it from here."

"I admire your confidence," Sabien replied. "I would be humiliated if my bride ran from me at my own wedding."

"Sabien," Dagmara scolded, no more than a whisper.

Claude's jaw ticked. "For you to have a wedding, Captain Renaud, you would need a bride first."

"Yes, well, at least I know I can find one who isn't simply marrying me for my title."

"That's enough!" Dagmara snapped. "Leave us, Captain."

"Of course, my Queen," said Sabien. Then he gave Claude a sidelong glance. "Your Majesty," he finished before disappearing down the corridor.

As soon as he was gone, Dagmara spoke first. "I wasn't running," she blurted out. Sabien almost ruined her entire plan, and now she had to cover her tracks. "I was overwhelmed and needed to breathe."

Claude cleared his throat and shifted in his stance. "I'm sorry it's overwhelming," Claude said. "What do you need from me?" The tenderness to Claude's voice surprised her. She nearly didn't recognize him. Was it true he had the mask the assassins wore?

She needed to know now.

"I think I need a moment to rest to touch up my makeup and loosen this corset slightly. Just twenty minutes before returning to the party. Everyone's eating now, so I'm sure they wouldn't notice."

"Of course," Claude said. "Do you want me to come with you?"

"No," Dagmara said, a little too quickly. She paused for effect, then added, "but Urszula said they were moving all my things to the royal quarters now. I don't know where to go."

"You can rest in my chamber," the king said. Then his face shifted, and he added, "If you're comfortable with that."

"Are you sure?"

"Yes, let me walk you," Claude said. Without waiting for an objection, he took her hand and began escorting her around the corridor and toward the large staircase that led them to the royal chamber.

"You don't have to," Dagmara said, hoping she wasn't sounding too suspicious. "I know the way."

"I know, but Martine isn't here to keep you safe," Claude replied, "And..." he paused to sweep her off her feet.

Dagmara's heart lurched in her chest as Claude swiftly picked her up into a cradle. She instinctively wrapped her arms around his neck, a shriek of shock slipping from her lips. "Claude!"

"...I know how much you dislike stairs," he said as he proceeded to climb the large staircase. He made it seem effortless, and his breathing was barely labored.

"I don't dislike stairs!" Dagmara objected, but she could feel the warmth in her chest and the smile cresting her face.

"I watch you glare at the steps every time we go to Lionel's manor," said Claude.

Dagmara felt like her heart was about to break. This couldn't be the man who ordered Bogdan and Aleksy's assassination...how could a ruthless monster hold her so gently? Unless this was all part of the act. As Sabien had said, Claude could still be planning to kill her tonight.

He set her back down on her feet once they reached the top of the staircase. Dagmara selfishly didn't want him to let her go. She wanted him to carry her all the way to his bed, and then stay there with her.

They arrived at his chamber too soon, which was blocked by two guards.

"I know you want a minute alone," Claude said before softly caressing her cheek. His hand was gentle against her face, and his thumb brushed against her skin. "But if you're gone for too long I'll come find you. I don't want to be away from you tonight."

She nearly melted at his words. She tilted her head against his palm. "I just want to freshen up," she said, quoting Queen Bernadette.

He nodded, his eyes lingering on her lips. "By the guardians, this Azuremi tradition of waiting until midnight on the wedding day will be the death of me. Soon," he promised. He addressed the two on guard. "Make sure she remains safe."

Then he turned away from her and disappeared down the hall, returning to his subjects at the wedding.

She tried to bury her feelings for him as the guards let her pass into the royal chamber. The time had come to finally find proof.

Proof that would seal her future forever.

CHAPTER 52
Magdalena

Queen Sanyal was limp, her body laying on the ground at an awkward angle. The vines not only strangled her, they were full of thorns that shredded the queen's neck.

Magda stood over the queen alongside her two daughters.

By the guardians...she was really dead. It couldn't be. Why had her magic turned against her?

Kiran was sobbing beside her mother, unable to catch her breath. "Why did they kill mom!?"

"I'm here." Ishani engulfed Kiran in a warm hug. She squeezed her tightly and did not let go.

"I'm so sorry." Magda couldn't bring herself to look any more.

"They tried to kill us too," Kiran said in between sobs.

Magda said, "They were wearing masks identical to the assassins that came after my family."

Ishani held her sister intensely, not releasing Kiran until she pulled away. Then Ishani shook her head before her hands clenched to fists. She looked as if she was about to explode from anger, and Magda couldn't blame her, for she knew how it felt to lose a parent.

Ishani grabbed one of her axes that was on the floor and said, "I'm going to kill that assassin."

"What?" Kiran said, reaching out to her sister.

"Don't stop me," Ishani pulled away.

"Don't leave me." Kiran wept.

Ishani's face was stoic. "You're in danger...both of you. It's clear that all the guardians are being attacked. I received word from one of my contacts that Guardian Sora was also killed, and Celestaire is planning on taking out Ilusauri."

"What?" gasped Magda. "It can't be." Dagmara was in more danger than ever before.

Kiran tried to wipe her eyes, but she could still barely talk through the emotion, "But why would this happen to mom?! Of all people!"

Ishani turned away so the other two wouldn't see her wiping her eyes.

Magda knew the assassin would run back to her superiors and report that Kiran was still alive. Also, they could report that Magda was in Flaustra, if they recognized her. They had also seen Magda use Soul magic. Letting the assassin go free was a mistake.

Also, if Prince Claude got word Magda was in Flaustra, and found out that he had been deceived this entire time, it would be disastrous. It could mean a possible death sentence for Dagmara. And what would happen once everyone found out that Queen Sanyal had been killed?

"We have to go after the assassin," Ishani seemed to read Magda's mind.

"And we have to protect Kiran," Magda said. "She's the only remaining guardian from Flaustra."

"And you from Azurem," Kiran said softly.

"So, in theory, if what your mother said was true, and we're tied to the land, there's only three true guardians left with magic. Me, Kiran, and Claude," said Magda.

"But your branches of magic have been severed," Ishani pointed out. "Claude's was severed when his parents died, Guardian Sora's must be cut off now, and you...," she trailed off.

"You don't have to say it," Magda said.

"Meaning...," Kiran perked up.

"You're more important than ever," said Magda, reaching down to hug her friend, "and more people might come after you."

"And you," Kiran sniffled.

Ishani stared at them both, her anger boiling, until she said to Kiran, "I should've never let you take the powers."

"Then you would be a target and not me," Kiran said.

"Better me than you," said Ishani. "Not a single guardian is prepared for this!"

Magda realized that she had a point. Never in her life had she actually been worried about imminent danger. She had always gone out into the poppy fields, racing with her horse and with Odie. Sometimes, Magda would run away for days on end, exploring until the ends of the coasts, and never once had her father or brother shown any fear.

But Dagmara had been doing some sort of undercover work for her father. What had really been going on behind closed doors?

Glancing over her shoulder, Magda saw the jacket the assassin discarded, wrapped in vines. She approached it, tearing it from the thorns and examining it. On the inside of the jacket was an embroidered insignia of a beast.

"We can't let her get away," Magda said assertively.

"How will we find her?" Kiran asked.

Magda flashed the inside of the jacket to the two princesses.

Ishani froze. "The Marauders."

"That doesn't make sense though," Magda muttered. "The assassins that came after me were Ilusaurian. Now they're Flaustran?"

"They could easily be taking on disguises," Ishani said. "Or, Claude realized sending assassins in his kingdom's attire was a poor choice, and so he sent these disguised as Flaustrans."

"We'll do it together," Magda told Ishani.

Ishani nodded, before giving her sister a hug, and saying that she would order fifteen of her men to not take a single eye off of Kiran. Until Ishani came back to the palace, they were ordered to stay locked in a bunker on the second floor.

"Fine, I'll go hide. But promise me nothing will happen to you," said Kiran.

"I promise. I'll come back here, and we'll bury mom properly."

Kiran held back tears, turning her face away from Magda as she dashed out of the room.

Ishani approached Magda. "Up for another adventure to Vex's hideout?"

"Another?" Magda questioned.

"Don't be so naive. I know you killed Vex."

"How did you even find out—" Magda started, but Ishani cut her off.

"You're gonna have to keep up if you're one of the three remaining guardians left in the world."

The words stung, but Magda changed the subject, "How do you know the assassin will be there?"

"I don't. But where else should we start looking?"

"Fair point. But first I need to talk to someone, and for that to happen, I need you to release someone from jail. His name is Ravi Kalal. The officers just locked him up a few hours ago even though he didn't commit any major crimes."

"The boy that you hang out with all over the city? Sentencing is now Kiran's decision as the reigning guardian," Ishani shrugged.

"That doesn't matter," said Magda, "As a guardian, I outrank you."

"Princess, I think I'm a much better partner to take on a mission to hunt down an assassin."

"What, jealous much?"

"Not really. Are you sleeping together?"

Magda's face flushed bright red. She didn't have to answer to Ishani...in fact, she didn't have to answer to anyone. "That's none of your business."

"By the guardians, it's not that big of a deal. Tell me."

"In Azurem, you only talk about those things with people you're close to."

"Well, we'll be spending a lot of time together from now on," said Ishani with a twinkle in her eye.

"What makes you think that?" asked Magda.

"Princess," Ishani shook her head in annoyance, almost in the exact mannerism as she had to her sister, "because I'm the only person left on this planet that actually knows how to use Soul magic."

"Just get Ravi," Magda rolled her eyes. "And my dog."

"Fine," Ishani laughed, sauntering away. "Let me go fetch both your pets."

"And Ishani," Magda called. "I need to send a Scribestone to Ilusauri. It's urgent."

Magda hugged Odie for as long as she could when she saw him again. He was safe, and in her arms, wagging his tail with so much excitement that his entire body wiggled. He was one of the few family members she had left, and she would not let him be taken from her again.

She brought Odie with her to the Flaustran Scribestone, knowing time was running short. The Scribestone was raised on a gorgeous pedestal covered in vines and flowers. The stone book was a vibrant turquoise, resting in an archway decorated with more greenery. She placed her palm against the blank, magical page, and words appeared.

One message from Dagmara Zosia, Ilusauri.

The wedding is today. I have no idea where you are, and I'm praying you didn't die on your way to Flaustra. Are you safe?

I have yet to find any proof of Claude's involvement, but if I'm legally wed, I have access to his royal chambers. By the guardians, I don't know what I'm doing. Both the Captain and my guard are onto me.

Yeah, the Captain? He's alive, and he's here.

Also, I found a cave with monstrous hounds and a note 'The First Prince will Rise.' There's something going on that's bigger than the both of us.

Magda felt her blood turn to ice. The Captain...Dagmara claimed she had killed him the day before the coronation. He could blow her cover!

Magda hastily wrote a reply:

I hope you get this before the wedding. Get out of there, it's not worth it to search his chambers. Queen Sanyal says he's hunting for the tomb of the First Prince, and I believe her. He's been in communication with guild leaders.

Queen Sanyal is dead. Assassins were here wearing the same masks as the men who killed my father and Aleksy. They will stop at nothing to kill the guardians which means posing as me is putting your life in danger.

The assassins were wearing Flaustran attire, but honestly, I didn't realize how powerful Claude's magic is. He can make people see anything he wants. Anything. I underestimated him.

Get out. Come find me. We will figure this out together.

She prayed Dagmara would read it before it was too late.

THE MAD KING AND THE FALSE QUEEN

Magda waited in the courtyard of Queen Sanyal's palace, anxiously pacing back and forth while she waited for Ravi to be brought to her. It was dark now, and the clear sky revealed a dazzling display of bright stars. The full moon cast an evening glow on the gardens and domed towers.

She was alone in the courtyard except for a few straggling officers, for she had told Ishani that she wanted to speak to Ravi by herself.

Even though he had only spent a few hours in a holding cell, she was sure that he would be furious with her for keeping secrets from him. The fact that she was a princess...the fact that she was a guardian...the fact that she had exhibited Soul magic...

At the same time, she was angry with him for concealing the real reason that he wanted to get into the palace. Why spend so much time with Magda in the first place? Did he not think he could secure an invitation on his own?

"Dagmara," his voice sounded from behind her. Firm, but not angry. "I was..."

"Let me stop you right there," Magda cut him off, whirling to him. Immediately, she was met with his innocent eyes. She wanted to embrace him, feeling his touch against hers, but she stopped short.

"My name's not Dagmara," Magda admitted. "It's Magda." For a second she felt guilty with such a cold statement, but she didn't care. Especially after she had stumbled upon him confessing his love to another woman.

"Magda," he mused, but he didn't make the connection. "Why did you feel like you couldn't be honest with me about your name?"

"You're one to keep secrets," Magda snapped.

"You didn't even let me explain what happened in the jail," Ravi said.

"What could you say that would make it any different? Do you really have another lover? Why did you lie to me about why you wanted to come to the ball in the first place?" Magda blurted out.

"You've got it all wrong," Ravi stepped toward her to embrace her, but when Magda pulled away, he stopped short. "Laila is my sister."

"What?" Magda asked, suddenly extremely confused. "Why is she in jail?"

Ravi sighed, "My sister Prisha got sick a few years ago. When the trade routes were cut off from Ilusauri, medicine became very expensive here. I knew Vex had the highest quality potions and herbs from Ilusauri that he traded on his black market, so Laila and I started making friends with the guilds. I traded secrets to get close to the guilds so that we could steal the medicine from Vex. Luckily, Prisha got better. However, when Vex found out that we had stolen from him, he wanted someone to punish. Laila took the blame and the entire fall for the goods we stole in order to protect me and the rest of our family. Vex manipulated the officers, and she went to jail for smuggling goods and the handling of illegal substances from Ilusauri. Which is ridiculous cause Vex was the one who brought those things to the kingdom in the first place."

He paused, as if the story was getting to be too much for him.

"I'm sorry," said Ravi.

"Why didn't you just tell me?" asked Magda.

"Because it sounds crazy, and because I didn't want to get you wrapped up into trouble that could cause you to get thrown in jail as well. I knew Vex was looking to punish me again one way or another. Please forgive me."

"I do," said Magda. She suddenly felt terrible for keeping all of her secrets from him. He had wanted to break into the jail to see his sister, and it was a noble endeavor. And all this time, she had kept her entire identity from him. She wanted to make it right.

"I'll ask Princess Kiran to release your sister," said Magda, "It's the least I can do."

"It's my word against Vex's," Ravi shrugged, "and if I bring it up again, people will find out...," he lowered his voice to an extreme whisper, "...that I killed him. I'll be shipped off to a much worse place than the palace dungeon."

"Trust me. You have my word she'll be free."

"How?" Ravi asked.

"Because my name isn't just Magda. I'm Princess Magdalena Krol, heir to the throne of Azurem." She let the words hang in the air, worried about his reaction.

For a second, she thought Ravi wouldn't believe her. He stared at her with a dumbfounded expression, as if he was putting the pieces together, and then he finally said. "So you are a guardian?"

"Yes."

Ravi's face broke her heart. It was as if he no longer recognized her. Or maybe he finally understood why they would have no future together. "I guess that explains all the secrets, and it explains the magic. But you wielded Soul magic in the dungeon?"

Magda continued, "I'll explain everything, but first it's my turn to apologize. I'm sorry for lying to you. I'm sorry for not telling you who I was when I came here originally. I know this hurts tremendously, and I don't have a good excuse. I kept telling myself that it was too dangerous to confide in others, but at a certain point I think I secretly wanted to keep up the charade so I wouldn't risk losing you completely. It was never my plan to meet someone like you in Flaustra."

Ravi spoke intentionally, "Are you done?"

His words cut through her like a knife. Of course he was mad at her.

Magda nodded.

"Good," he said, "Because before you started accusing me of having a secret lover, I was rushing out here to make sure you weren't hurt. Ishani said you were almost killed, and that Queen Sanyal was assassinated. And before that, all I was thinking about in the jail was you...that and hoping Odie wouldn't bite my hand off," he laughed.

"Every second that went by I was furious with myself for betraying your trust and possibly losing you forever."

Magda couldn't believe his words. "You're not mad?"

"I'm furious how these secrets almost made us look at one another completely differently," Ravi said, "and how they threatened everything between us. But you underestimate how I feel about you. I told you before that when I saw you in the marketplace, it's like one song was ending and another symphony was starting. You've made me feel alive again, and for once, I feel like I can have hope in a brighter future."

"You've made me feel alive as well," said Magda, "in ways that I don't know if I can truly put into words."

"But, I guess, the fact that you're a princess does change things between us."

"It does."

"You're betrothed to the Mad King."

"It's true."

"That doesn't make any sense," said Ravi. "The Ilusauri royal wedding is taking place now. How can you be in two places at once?"

"...Because I sent my assassin in my place."

Ravi's hands flew to his head. Then he crossed to one of the walls surrounding a flower bed, and sat down on it. "By the guardians, Dagmara...Magdalena...whatever your name is...I don't know how many more twists to this story I can take."

Magda crossed to the wall and sat down next to him. "You can call me Magda."

"Magda," Ravi repeated, looking intently at her. "I can't believe you're the Mad King's betrothed! If Vex was bad, now the Mad King himself is going to try to kill me."

"Don't worry. He'll never find out."

"You still have to marry him, I guess?"

"I tried to call it off, but if it doesn't work, then I don't know what will happen."

"By the guardians," Ravi shook his head. "I can't believe this. I can't believe I'm falling for King Claude's soon to be wife. I know I'll never have you again, but I don't think I'll ever be able to get you out of my head."

"You're falling for me?"

"Madly," he replied, "I don't understand it, but I don't want it to end."

"So you don't hate me?"

"Hate is the opposite of what's burning inside me right now. I'm happy you're safe, I'm relieved you don't hate me, and I loathe the fact that I couldn't be there to protect you."

"I'm alright," Magda reassured him.

"But the thought of you..." he hesitated, before reaching out and tentatively taking her hand. "The thought of the assassin succeeding scares me to death. I know you can take care of yourself, you're brave and intelligent...and now you're a guardian!" He let out a soft laugh that took Magda's breath away. "But life is short. I want to live in the moments while I have them. I can't imagine if I never had the chance to do this."

Magda blinked. "Do what?"

He smiled. "I think you know."

Then he slid his hand to the base of her neck and pulled her toward him. His lips met hers, and butterflies erupted in Magda's stomach. The world fell away around her. All the fear, guilt, and grief died, and for the first time in a long time, she was happy. She had no idea what future she had with Ravi, but she knew he was right. Life was short, and she wanted him now. Why not act on her feelings for him before someone else tried to kill her?

She laced her arms behind his neck, pulling him even closer. His tongue swooped inside her mouth, deepening the kiss, and warmth flooded through her entire body. Her pulse quickened, and she wanted more of him. She wanted to forget everything and spend the entire night with him.

But she couldn't. Not until the assassin was caught.

Magda pulled away, her breath heavy and her emotions alight inside her. She ran her hand down his chest, keeping her forehead pressed to his.

"I don't care if you're engaged," he assured her.

"I know. I wish we could do this all night," she said, breathless.

He grinned. "But...?"

"The assassin is out there. They're connected to the First Prince and the assassins that killed my family."

Ravi pulled back so he could meet her gaze. "I'm coming with you."

"It's too dangerous. Ishani's a trained fighter, and I have Soul magic...which still doesn't make complete sense."

"Don't do this to me again," said Ravi, "You have to let me in."

"I don't want you to risk your life for me, especially if I belong to another man," said Magda.

"I don't care about a political promise to Claude. I want to be the world you return to every time you come back to Flaustra, and maybe one day, titles won't stand between us."

His words overwhelmed her, and her heart beat faster. She said, "Alright, but this is not your fight. It's mine. These are the people that killed my family, and are killing all the guardians. They won't stop until we're all dead...until I'm dead."

"If you're dead, then I'll have nothing to live for," said Ravi, "I know we fight different battles, you and I, on different fronts. But I'll be there for you, no matter the cost. No matter if I have to stand on the sidelines."

Magda smiled, before moving in for another kiss.

CHAPTER 53
Dagmara

The Ilusaurian royal chamber was nearly the same as Dagmara remembered, the only difference was a trio of canvases in the corner. Two were landscapes, exquisitely detailed, and one was a painting of the hounds from Nouchenne. A shudder ran down Dagmara's spine at the sight, and she quickly redirected her attention to the desk.

Shuffling through the papers at the top, she found nothing useful. Everything was written in Ilusaurian, and she could only decipher half the words. Opening one drawer, she came across a letter to a woman named Ishani with a guild seal. What did Claude have to do with Flaustra? There was an entire stack labeled to this person. What business did they have together? If only Dagmara could read Flaustran.

Then the doorknob rattled.

Dagmara stumbled away from the desk, her heart pounding as the door opened.

"Hello, Dagger," Sabien said, stepping into the room with a smirk. "I love when I make you nervous."

"You could've knocked," she retorted. "How did you get in here?"

"As Captain of the Ilusaurian guard it isn't difficult for me to tell two guards I am taking over their post," he said. "Find anything?"

"Nothing."

Dagmara wanted to object or kick him out, but she knew two people searching would be more efficient than one.

Without giving him another moment of her precious time, she returned to the desk, pulling out the next drawer to shuffle through it. She could practically hear the imaginary clock that signaled her time was running out. Pouring rain beat against the large windows, mimicking the pounding of her heart.

She sensed Sabien's approach before he reached her. He stood behind her, his chest touching her back, as he reached around her to pick up one of the letters written in Flaustran.

"Do you read Flaustran?" he asked, leaning against her until her hips met the edge of the table, her body trapped.

"No, you?" She turned her head to look at him over her shoulder, suddenly aware of how close he was to her.

He hesitated, his eyes examining her like she was his prey. "For you I can."

"A little space, maybe?" Dagmara snapped, elbowing him in the chest, but he wouldn't budge.

"Is that a request or a command from the new queen?" he asked.

"It..." her mind whirled upon hearing the title of queen, "it's a request," she muttered.

"In that case...no," he leaned closer, his lips inches from her neck. "Also...do you outrank me now?" His eyes glanced at the shimmering crown on her head.

Shoving her shoulder against his chest, this time with as much force as she could muster, Dagmara slipped out from between his body and the table. "Technically, I always outranked you." She readjusted her crown to make her point.

"As Magdalena, maybe," Sabien replied. "But now you, Dagmara Zosia, are legally the queen of Ilusauri."

Dagmara felt her chest tighten. She didn't want to think of the legalities of any of this. She also didn't like the way her stomach curled whenever Sabien touched her. She decided to finish looking through the desk when Sabien wasn't standing over it. Turning on her heel, she went to the armoire.

Opening the door, she searched the entire closet, even using Bernadette's advice to check for a false back. Crossing to the seating area, she searched both side tables, once against finding nothing of value.

She could hear Sabien rattling around at the desk, searching each drawer thoroughly and making an awful ruckus. If everyone wasn't at the wedding, and the rain wasn't so loud, she would have scolded him for causing too much noise.

Then Dagmara crossed to the bed, struggling to kneel in her wedding gown. Dropping her cheek to the ground, she looked underneath. There was nothing but shoes, weapons, and a lot of dust.

"Um...these letters are suspicious," Sabien muttered under his breath.

"What do they say?" asked Dagmara, careful to rise to her feet slowly to avoid a dizzy spell.

"Seems like His Majesty is corresponding with an assassin in Flaustra to find and kill anyone with a hint of magic," Sabien said. "Much like what you were doing in Azurem for King Bogdan."

"Was that what Claude and Guardian Sora were doing in Celestaire?" Dagmara asked. "I heard that he was working with her to look for something...not someone."

Sabien shrugged.

Dagmara returned to the desk. "Did you find anything else?"

Shaking his head, Sabien replied, "Only a stamp he uses to sign documents and more paperwork." He returned his attention to the handful of correspondence with Flaustra.

A stamp to sign documents...or maybe to sign false aliases for the three assassins?

"Did you check for false bottoms?"

The captain glanced up from the stack of letters he was holding, a twinkle of amusement in his eye. "I love the way you think."

Brushing aside the compliment, Dagmara proceeded to open each drawer, examining every inch of it. Sabien continued to flip through the pages. She was grateful for having him here so that he could read the correspondence in Flaustran.

Reaching the final drawer, she almost lost hope. Then she felt a latch, as small as an earring. She pressed against it, but nothing happened. Twisting it, she heard a click. Another compartment cracked open perpendicular to the drawer. Holding her breath, Dagmara slid it open.

The world stopped as Dagmara's mind went blank. Fear coursed through her veins as she stared down at a mask. It was pure white, with a dent on the chin and a scrape on one cheek. On the center of the forehead was a black symbol. The symbol of the First Prince.

Her heart began to pound in her chest. She wanted to reach out and pick it up, to make sure it was real, but her hands were shaking. The last time she saw this mask, it was on the face of the assassin who killed Aleksy—the assassin who made it out alive.

There was one other item in the drawer. It was an orange bottle, half the size of a perfume bottle. Dagmara picked it up and swirled it, examining the contents.

She could guess what it was by the color. Very few liquids were bright orange.

Popping off the lid, Dagmara brought it to her nose.

Smierc.

This was the poison that was used on the terrace. How Claude had acquired an entire bottle from Azurem, she had no idea. All she knew was that this was plenty of poison to use on the terrace and later frame her for the incident.

"I think this is the evidence we need," said Sabien, waving a piece of paper in the air. "I guess he planned to send it after the wedding."

Clutching the bottle in her palm, Dagmara waited for Sabien to read. The thunder rumbled outside, increasing in intensity as the panic rose in her chest.

"*Ishani*," Sabien read the letter, translating from Flaustran. "*Now that Princess Magdalena is my wife, I have full access to Azurem. We can finally remove her from the picture.*"

Dagmara's stomach flipped. Did Claude know Magda was in Flaustra and that was why he was writing to a woman named Ishani? Or was Claude planning to kill Dagmara tonight now that they were legally wed?

Sabien continued, "*Finally the entire Krol line will be gone. I've done my part with Azurem as promised, now it's time you did yours and handled the Flaustran Guardians. Stop wasting my time, otherwise, I'll get rid of you too.*"

Dagmara could barely stand. She backed away, sitting on the bed to keep herself from falling. The betrayal ripped her apart from the inside out. She had fallen in love with Claude, only to discover what she had believed from the beginning...he was the murderer behind it all.

Sabien knew better than to console Dagmara. He placed the pages on the desk and waited for her to meet his gaze. "He still believes you are Princess Magdalena, so he will kill you. And it is only a matter of time before he discovers I have magic, and will execute me too. We have to get out of here."

His words barely registered. She gripped the vial of poison in her palm. "I can't believe it."

"Is it really that hard to believe?" Sabien countered.

No. It wasn't. That was the problem. She had wanted to believe Claude was innocent. Maybe she missed all the signs because she was blinded by her emotions.

"But there's still an assassin out there," Dagmara objected. "Teos said the assassin who escaped after the coronation had a description of a man with red hair and a beard."

"Couldn't it have been Claude himself?" Sabien asked.

"No, I said—"

Dagmara froze. It *could* have been Claude himself. Whoever was behind the mask — whoever she faced off in the cathedral could have been Claude. She had watched him disguise himself time and time again. The wound he received in Nouchenne he hid from her, he hid his wound from Reon in Sailonne, and not to mention the scar down half his face. Who is to say he didn't make the knight at the Azuremi border see what Claude wanted them to see?

She was so foolish. All the signs were there and she had missed them all.

"By the guardians..." Dagmara said under her breath.

Then there was a brisk knock at the door. "Magdalena?"

It was him.

The Mad King.

Snapping out of her daze, Dagmara jolted upright. "Hide," she commanded, her voice a whisper.

"You're going to face him by yourself?" Sabien shot back. He closed the false bottom, concealing the mask, before slamming the drawer closed.

"You're not supposed to be here!" Dagmara's whisper was sharp.

The doorknob rattled, and Sabien obeyed. He swiftly disappeared, concealing himself behind the massive silver curtains that hung in front of the floor length windows. He was still large, causing the curtains to billow around his figure, but the shadows of the room concealed his location.

As the door began to open, Dagmara turned away instantly. She hadn't prepared thoroughly. She hadn't thought through what she was going to say. Deep down inside, she had wished Claude was innocent, but the insurmountable evidence was undeniable. How could the man she came to know be behind everything?

"Magdalena," Claude said. The door closed. "They think Celesta troops are nearby—that is what I was called away for earlier. I didn't believe them but..." Claude's voice quieted. "Magdalena?"

His boots on the ground alerted Dagmara that he was approaching. She felt her breath hitch, the pit in her stomach making her nauseous.

Then he reached her. The moment his hand touched her arm, she felt a jolt surge through her body. Her adrenaline spiked, a sudden fear coursing through her veins. This was the man who murdered Aleksy.

She whirled to face him. "Don't touch me!"

The king threw his hands up defensively, his palms open. "I'm sorry," he muttered, backing up. Then his eyes found the vial in her hand.

She raised the bottle up higher. "I found this," she said.

"What is that?"

"It's smierc. A deadly poison. But you know that already."

A muscle ticked in Claude's jaw. He let his hands fall slowly to his sides. "What is going on?"

"You tell me," Dagmara countered.

His head inclined. "I've never seen that bottle in my life."

Lightning flashed outside, the room brightening for a single moment.

She shook her head. "You're lying. I found the poison next to a mask with a First Prince symbol."

The king's eyes narrowed. "You were snooping through my room? I thought we finally trusted one another."

Dagmara scoffed. "I was a fool to trust you. I also found the letters to Ishani."

"I don't..." he paused to shake his head, "So?"

Anger surged through her body. She ran her hand across the table, sending the letters scattering to the ground. "You admitted to killing Bogdan and Aleksy. You planned to kill me tonight."

"Kill you?" Claude echoed. "What are you talking about?"

"Stop lying to me, Claude. I've had enough."

"I've never lied to you, Magdalena—"

"Stop calling me that!" Dagmara yelled. "That's not my name!"

A deadly silence filled the room. Dagmara could feel the blood coursing through her body, her heart pounding in her chest. She would not drop his gaze, both of them staring intensely at one another.

Claude's hands flexed before curling into fists. His low voice was calm, making it even more menacing. "What do you mean that's not your name?"

"I'm not Princess Magdalena. I came in her place," Dagmara said.

"You're not...Magdalena?"

"No."

"Then who are you?"

"It doesn't matter. You've already lost, Claude, because you won't get to kill the real Magdalena tonight."

Claude was silent. His mouth was slightly agape, his eyebrows raised on his forehead in surprise. He was unwavering, as still as a statue until he yelled, "Guards!"

Within the same breath, the door burst open to reveal Sacha, barely fitting in the frame. Pierre was directly behind him.

"Seize her," Claude commanded.

Dagmara's blood turned to ice. She would not let this be the end.

Using the only weapon she had, Dagmara chucked the bottle of poison directly at the king. Claude threw up his hands, and the glass shattered against his forearms. He let out a shout, the poison splashing in all directions.

Before Dagmara could make a run for it, Sacha had already grabbed her wrist. It was impossible fighting him. As tall as she was, she barely reached his collarbones. In two seconds he gripped both her arms behind her back. Pain surged through her shoulders, but she fought through it, tears welling in her eyes.

However, Pierre remained by the door. He hovered next to Claude, his expression confused.

Claude tore off his shirt before the poison could seep through the fabric. He thrust it to the side, revealing his naked chest. He was all muscle, and his body was tense with anger.

"What was that for?" he yelled.

"Just let me go!" Dagmara screamed, struggling in Sacha's grip. It was no use. Fighting Sacha was like fighting a stone wall.

"Let you go?" Claude's voice boomed through the room. "You've impersonated a guardian, and our marriage is a fraud! And if I didn't know better, I'd say you just attacked me!"

She didn't have any words to counter him. She hadn't thought this marriage could be considered treason on her part.

Claude panted, gazing at the scattered poison and papers on the ground as he caught his breath. His face twisted with a multitude of indecipherable emotions. Then he raised his head.

"Everything..." he cleared his throat, "It was all a lie? You were using me the whole time?"

"I..." There were no words. None of her feelings for him were a lie. She suppressed her anger long enough to admit, "It wasn't *all* a lie."

Claude took a step toward her. Glass crunched underneath his shoes. "So what part was real?"

Tears threatened to course down her face. Her lip quivered. She didn't want to answer. She didn't want to admit it.

"It doesn't matter anymore," she said.

"Where is Magdalena? The *real* Princess?"

"You'll never find out." Dagmara scoffed.

Claude nodded, then froze with a jerk. "But if you're not a guardian...how did you use magic?"

Dagmara glanced in Pierre's direction. Did he have any idea that it was Sabien who cured Claude during the attack in Sailonne? Would he expose Sabien's secret?

"That means..." Claude started. "You're an assassin."

Dagmara didn't answer, unsure how he reached that conclusion so quickly.

"So you're here to kill me?" Claude asked, backing away. His hand went to his bare stomach as though he were injured, his skin glistening in the dim light. "Well, no need anymore, because it feels like you already drove a stake through my heart."

Then, in the distance, a horn rang out.

"The Celesta," Pierre blurted out. "They've reached the front gates, Your Majesty."

"What is your name?" Claude asked, ignoring Pierre and the alarm.

Unable to look away, Dagmara held Claude's pained gaze. She hated the way her heart broke to see him in despair. Why did he look so broken? He was the one who betrayed her. He was the murderer.

"Your Majesty," Pierre continued. "The Celesta—"

"I need to know the name of the woman who ruined me!" Claude roared, never glancing at Pierre.

"Dagmara." A tear coursed down her cheek.

Exhaling, Claude closed his eyes as though the name confirmed her betrayal. "Dagmara," he repeated, and the way he said her name caused her stomach to erupt with butterflies. His eyes opened, finding hers immediately. "I gave you my heart, Dagmara, and you mutilated it. I didn't know an emotional pain could be this visceral," his voice wavered, and he didn't attempt to hide it. "I painted a whole picture of my future where you were the center of it. Now what am I to do?"

"Claude..." she breathed.

"You don't deserve to say my name," said Claude. "You will address me as 'Your Majesty'."

Another piece was torn from Dagmara's heart.

Claude turned to Pierre. "Lock her in here, I can't deal with this now. I have to defend my kingdom."

Then the Mad King disappeared from the room.

As soon as Sacha released his grip, Dagmara fell to the ground with a hard smack. She hadn't realized Sacha was holding her up.

Immediately, tears started racing down Dagmara's cheeks and she clutched her chest, feeling more pain than ever before.

Sacha vanished, heading to defend the castle from the oncoming Celesta, but Pierre lingered at the door. Before long, he left, and the door slammed closed. The sound of a bolt echoed through the chamber, signaling a lock.

She knew Claude was the murderer. She had all the proof. Why did it feel like her chest was being ripped apart? Why did she want to chase after him and beg for forgiveness?

Someone was lifting her off her feet, and Dagmara was hardly aware of her surroundings. They were blurred by the tears.

"We have to get out of here," Sabien said. She had forgotten he was hidden behind the curtain the entire time. He had heard everything. "I wasn't expecting you to out yourself. They'll have you executed for deceiving the king, impersonating a guardian, and sabotaging a royal alliance. We have to go."

Taking her wrist, Sabien yanked her in the direction of the corner. Dagmara stumbled after him, barely able to stand. Everything hurt. Everything felt wrong.

Sabien pressed a panel against the wall, and a door popped open. "It can only open from this side," Sabien replied. "Once we're in the passageway we can't get back into the castle."

His voice was only words. Dagmara was too broken to think about the hidden passage. She fell in line beside Sabien as they entered the hidden corridor, the passageway sealing behind them. They descended into the secret halls underneath the castle, Sabien leading the way.

"First, we get ourselves to safety, and then we should make sure Princess Magdalena is safe," Sabien said.

"She is," Dagmara replied, her voice hoarse as she held back a sob.

"Are you certain? Claude knows you aren't Magdalena so he will go straight to Azurem to find her."

"It's a good thing she's not in Azurem then," she snapped.

"Where is she?" asked Sabien.

"It doesn't matter," Dagmara replied. After all this time protecting Magda, she still wouldn't disclose her location. Then a thought struck her. "Queen Bernadette said she would be waiting with an escape carriage in case something went wrong. We have to find her."

They picked up speed in the tunnels, but her mind was replaying the confrontation with Claude.

She could still hear his broken voice. She could still hear his lies that he had never seen the bottle before. He was so lackadaisical about the letters, it was as if his admittance wasn't written plain as day.

And how did he make the connection that she was an assassin that quickly after asking how she had magic? It was as if all people with magic who weren't guardians had to be assassins.

Her mind flashed to her conversation with Queen Bernadette about Dagmara's mother.

Her heart was removed, but she had no injuries when they found her...evidence she was killed by a Life Guardian...and a mark of the First Prince accompanied her.

Dagmara's mother had been killed by people with Life magic—the same people she had been ordered to assassinate.

Claude had told King Bogdan his parents were killed by an assassin with Mind magic. Was it true that somehow the First Prince was rising...and that he was sending assassins with magic to take out the guardians? Was there anywhere in the legend that stated the First Prince could grant people magic?

Dagmara and Sabien rounded the corner, and a door appeared at the end of the dark hall. "That's our exit," he said.

Dagmara froze in the center of the hallway.

If Claude was the one she faced off against on the day of the coronation, how did he return to Ilusauri so quickly to send the proposal Scribestone to Magdalena? It couldn't have been Claude who had faced off with her in the throne room.

The captain was forced to come to a halt. He turned over his shoulder and eyed Dagmara curiously. "What's wrong?"

"It was you," Dagmara said under her breath. "Claude's father was killed by an assassin with Mind powers. You have Life magic, which means you were sent for the Life Guardians. That's why you were in Azurem for the coronation. Why else have you kept my identity a secret and tried to get close to me? You've just been waiting for me to tell you where Magda is so you can kill her and finish the job."

Sabien shifted his weight, planting one hand on his hip. He let out a laugh, "It took you long enough."

CHAPTER 54
Magdalena

Heading back to Vex's hideout, Magda knew there would only be one way to find the assassin.

Odie.

After Ravi and Magda joined Ishani and Odie, they headed directly to the docks, the streets far less crowded than during the day.

If only the people knew their guardian was dead.

Shaking the thought from her mind, Magda tried not to think about Queen Sanyal, but she couldn't remove the image of her death from her mind. Why had the earth attacked her? The thorns slit her throat while the vines strangled her. If Queen Sanyal had Soul magic, why did it turn against her? Magda was certain it wasn't her own doing, and Kiran was unable to function let alone channel her magic. Kiran wouldn't have taken her own mother's life.

The only logical answer was that the assassins had Soul magic. But that solution was equally illogical. Only guardians had magic.

When they reached the docks, the salt on the wind clouded Magda's senses. Ishani led the way to the warehouse, her steps silent as she moved with grace, her two axes on either hip. Ravi brought along a knife, and Magda felt completely exposed with nothing on her person. Then she remembered, nearly everything around her could turn into a weapon. Plants, roots, rocks, sand...it all answered to her. She still didn't know why.

The trio reached the warehouse, Odie padding along beside them. He remained close to Magda, glancing up at her every few paces.

The sea-green tent was closed. The entrance flapped in the wind, completely unguarded. Had the Marauder's scattered when Vex died?

Ishani glanced over her shoulder, placing a finger to her lips to tell them to remain quiet, before she parted the curtain and disappeared into the darkness.

Magda exchanged a glance with Ravi. He nodded at her encouragingly, and they both followed after Ishani.

The tent seemed larger when no one occupied it. It was completely empty save for the tables and tapestries. The arena was coated in dried blood, and the space still smelled of liquor.

"Alright," Magda whispered, kneeling beside Odie. She extended the jacket that the assassin had left behind toward her dog. "Go find," she ordered.

Odie sniffed the jacket, his ears perking slightly. Then when Magda withdrew the jacket, Odie's nostrils flared, picking up the scent. He bent his head to the ground, his snout scouring for the trail as he started padding around the room.

He led the way past a few tables, through the benches at the edge of the arena, and toward the other end of the room. He reached the back corner of tables, still littered with empty bottles and mugs. Odie crossed over an alcohol-stained rug, heading to the edge of the tent. Then Odie paused, retracing his steps, narrowing his search until he stopped at the center of the rug. Looking up at Magda, Odie sat down, his tail wagging.

"I guess the assassin didn't have anywhere else to go," Ravi said.

Magda was equally confused, initially thinking the assassin would have gotten as far away from Vex's hideout as she could, but she wasn't going to argue.

"Good boy," Magda exclaimed, rushing over to Odie and running a hand down his back. She tossed the jacket to the side before saying to Ishani and Ravi, "It's here."

Ravi nodded before peeling back the edge of the rug. Magda summoned Odie out of the way, and the rug folded up to reveal a trapdoor.

"Hmm," Ishani mused. "Care to work for the Fowler's, Odie?"

Odie's head tilted, his ears flopping as he looked up at the guild leader.

The trapdoor creaked loudly as Ravi opened it, revealing a steep staircase.

"I'll go first," Ishani announced, nearly pushing Ravi out of the way. She withdrew one of her axes before descending into the room below.

"Come, Odie," Magda said, heading down next. She arrived at the bottom, stepping into a cave-like room. From first glance, it appeared to be a study. There were bookshelves scattered through the area, and maps on the walls, but both the wall and the ground was made of dirt as though the room had been dug out. A single tunnel revealed a narrow staircase, descending further into the ground.

Odie struggled down the steep stairs, hopping the last few to land in the dirt beside Magda. When he reached the bottom, his lip curled and a low growl rumbled in his throat.

"Shh, Odie, it's alright," Magda said. She headed into the shadows, rounding a bookshelf and reaching the table Ishani was at. On the center of the table was a single white mask, the black emblem of the First Prince in the center.

Magda's mind flashed back to the coronation. Fear coursed through her body as she pictured the assassins and her father's death. She hadn't seen her brother die, but she remembered the numbness that overcame her when she found out. The sadness that replaced her denial was all-consuming.

Now, she was angry. She wanted whoever was behind this to pay.

A hand gently touched her lower back as Ravi appeared at her side, looking over her shoulder at the mask for the first time.

"I've seen that symbol before," Ravi said.

"The First Prince," Ishani stated.

Odie's growl intensified. His ears perked and his tail was upright. Magda glanced down at him, noticing his focus was set on the shadows behind one of the bookshelves.

"The First Prince has been dead for centuries," Ravi said. "Why is a group of assassins using his symbol?"

"Not any group of assassins," Ishani corrected. "They're killing guardians."

"Ishani," Magda silenced her. The shadow was moving.

Odie barked, but his warning was too late.

The assassin stepped out of the shadows, two rocks in hand. She wasn't wearing a mask, her face younger than Magda anticipated.

Wait...the rocks weren't in her hands. They were levitating above each palm.

Magda's jaw dropped open. The assassin had Soul magic? How was that possible?

The assassin hurled the rocks at them. Magda dropped, covering her head with her hands as one of the rocks flew over her head and smashed against the table. The other rock flew toward Odie, barely missing his paws as he scrambled out of the way.

The assassin smiled as she said, "Looking for me? I was waiting for you." Then she cocked her head to the side. "Why didn't you bring the other princess?"

"You'll never find her," Ishani snapped.

Magda's hands curled into fists. "Who are you? Who are you working for?" she demanded.

The assassin scoffed. "Save your breath, girl. You won't get a word out of me. I'm going to kill you all, or die trying."

The assassin's eyes glowed yellow in the dim light of the room as she summoned Soul magic.

CHAPTER 55
Dagmara

Deep underground, Dagmara stood face to face with the man who murdered the Azuremi Guardians.

Captain Sabien Renaud.

She could hear the pouring rain pounding against the door at the end of the corridor. Sabien said the door they had passed through didn't open from this side. That meant she couldn't turn around and make a run for it, and the door at the end of the hall was the only exit. She had to make it to Queen Bernadette.

"I must admit," Sabien spoke, his voice rumbling deep in his chest, "I thought you were on to me much sooner. I guess you were preoccupied with the idea that I knew who you were from the moment I laid eyes on you."

"The day I met you...the night before the coronation—"

"The night you drove a dagger through my chest and shoved me off the bridge," Sabien added.

"You were there to kill the royal family."

"Correct. I wasn't there to speak with them about my magic, I knew exactly where my magic came from. The First Prince."

"And you framed Claude for the assassinations?"

"It wasn't hard seeing as he was already known as the Mad King."

"But he was the one who signed off on the assassins' false identities," said Dagmara.

"You mean his royal seal? The one sitting inside his desk? Sorry to say, but he doesn't sign every document. I have access to it, and I made those aliases with no problem."

"But one assassin escaped."

"That was me."

Horror came crashing down. Dagmara stumbled away from him. He was the one in the aisle the day of the coronation. He was the one she stood up against. He was the one who killed Aleksy.

"I was the third assassin, Samuel Arsenault, who entered Azurem under a false name and then escaped. I still paid the border well to alter my description for the records. However, the mask you found wasn't mine. That at least was Claude's," Sabien said. "The assassin who came for his parents left it behind as she fled for her life."

"And the poison..." Dagmara's brain raced with thoughts, "you found the false bottom of the drawer when I was searching elsewhere. You planted it in the drawer for me to find."

"I love how intelligent you are."

"Why did you poison us on the terrace anyway?"

"The servant was only supposed to poison you, but I guess I can't trust anyone these days to do one simple task. I had already made arrangements with the servant before I arrived on the terrace and met you," Sabien explained. "I thought the real Magdalena would be arriving, and I didn't have time to call off the assassination attempt on your life."

"But the letters to Flaustra on Claude's desk—"

"You think I can read Flaustran?" He let out a bark of laughter. "I made all of that up. Nearly everything I've ever told you has been a lie."

"Why?" Dagmara asked. "Why kill the guardians?"

Sabien inclined his head. "For the First Prince."

Dagmara swallowed her fear. "The First Prince from the legends? The one who is dead?"

A crooked smile appeared on Sabien's face. "Yes. He's locked in a tomb by four branches of magic. Mind, Life, Soul, and Spirit. He needs the branch to be severed for each lock to break, and in order for the branch to be severed, the guardians must be killed," Sabien explained. "The Mind lock was broken when Claude's parents died. I'm responsible for the Life lock. With Magdalena still alive, I haven't killed all the Life Guardians. I need to kill her to break the Life seal."

"Aren't you a Life Guardian now? Don't you have to die for the seal to be broken?"

"No." Sabien laughed. "I was made a guardian, I have no blood connection to the founding guardians, so my blood doesn't bind the lock that holds the First Prince."

"How can you be made a guardian?"

"The First Prince can do anything."

"But why are you working for him?"

Sabien laughed. "Why not? He is the most powerful guardian of all time. He is the only one who can hold the fifth branch of magic: the Void. Besides, he made me a guardian. Who wouldn't want to receive the gift of magic?"

"He gave you the magic to assassinate guardians, Sabien," Dagmara argued.

"You're an assassin. You of all people should know it's just a job. Instead of money, I get to be a guardian."

"Why would the First Prince choose someone like you?"

"For starters, you were assassinating everyone he planted in Azurem, so that's why he offered it to an Ilusaurian," Sabien said. "It's not hard for him to reach people through the Void. You simply have to witness someone you love be killed. Or, you can kill them yourself. That's what I did."

"You murdered someone you love for the First Prince?"

"I killed her to be a guardian. Serving the First Prince is only part of that."

Shaking her head, Dagmara stepped away from him. "You're despicable." She stole a glance at the end of the hall, seeing her escape within reach.

"And yet we are so similar." He smirked.

Dagmara glowered at him.

"Don't act like you wouldn't want to be a guardian." He pointed his finger at her, moving toward her. "You've already taken someone's life. All you'd have to do is kill a guardian, and you would keep the powers the First Prince grants you. Why not kill Magdalena to have the life of a guardian?"

"I would never hurt her."

"Is she so different from the other lives you claimed?" Sabien countered. "Why is she special?"

"She's like a sister to me."

"And you've never assassinated someone's sister?"

Anger began to simmer in Dagmara's stomach.

"Besides, I've noticed you have an...ailment," Sabien said, his eyes narrowing. "You're not as good at hiding it as you think."

Dagmara's hands curled into fists. "So?"

"Life magic can't fix that, but perhaps there is a slim chance..." he grabbed her by the chin, tilting her head higher, "...that becoming a guardian would fix you."

Dagmara knocked his hand aside and swung hard, slapping him across the face. The noise rang through the corridor, and Dagmara felt her palm stinging from the blow. "I don't need to be fixed. There is nothing wrong with who I am."

After a moment, Sabien shifted his jaw, running his thumb across his lip. "My sweet Dagger, you really shouldn't have hit me." His eyes began to shimmer, and a blue tint edged his pupils.

Dagmara bolted toward the exit. She had nothing on her. All her weapons had been left behind before the wedding ceremony.

Sabien lunged toward her, missing her body but catching the train of her wedding dress. She tripped, slamming face first onto the ground. The impact caused her crown to break free from her hair, clattering to the stone in front of her. The world began to spin, stars dancing in Dagmara's vision and threatening to obscure her entire sight.

A hand gripped her hip, rolling her onto her back. Sabien hovered over her. He extended his arms, his large hands binding around her throat.

She couldn't breathe.

"Tell me where Magdalena is!" he growled, his grip tightening. "We can work together."

Dagmara reached above her head, blindly feeling the stone to find her crown. As soon as she caught the edge, she used it to her advantage. She thrust the pointed diamonds into Sabien's forearm with as much strength as she had.

Sabien yelled, reeling back. It gave her the leverage to thrust her knee into his groin. He screeched an Ilusaurian curse word she didn't know, but rolled off her, yanking the crown from his forearm.

Scrambling to her feet, Dagmara ignored the dizziness that threatened to pull her down. She hiked up her dress, charging for the escape. She turned the handle and flew through the door. She battled a canopy of vines concealing the entrance before she burst into the night.

Rain immediately soaked her, streaming down her face and chest. Screaming could be heard in the distance, and muted explosions shook the ground from the attack by the Celesta. A lightning bolt flashed overhead, barely illuminating the forest that laid beyond the exit to the passageway.

She had to get to Magda before Sabien did, but what about Claude? Would he ever forgive her?

Sabien's arm latched around her waist, yanking her off her feet. She screamed before he slammed her against the rock wall concealing the door. Her breath was instantly stripped from her as her back collided against the wet stone. The Ilusaurian captain was relentless, using his forearm against her throat to pin her in place as she gasped for air. Her head was spinning, and she could feel her heartbeat racing at an all-time high. She tried to kick free, but her attempts were futile. Without her potions and explosives, she had no leverage against his brute strength. She was weak. He was a guardian.

Sabien raised his free hand, summoning the raindrops to him. They transformed in a magical blue hue, congealing together into a dagger made of ice.

He drove the dagger into her stomach.

The immediate surge of pain was overwhelming, taking over every ounce of her senses. She gasped and gripped his arm before he could yank the dagger free and expedite her death.

"It hurts, doesn't it? Being stabbed?" Sabien growled. "It's not so fun when these roles are reversed."

"Sabien..." Dagmara gasped.

Thunder rolled through the air. Water poured from the sky and Sabien basked in it. A smile creased his cheeks as he closed his eyes, feeling the rain cascade down his face. He let out a breath as the water brushed over his skin, immediately healing the wound she had punctured in his arm from the sharp point of the crown.

Then he looked at her, his eyes icy blue.

"I could heal you. You can join me. Think how easy it would be for you to walk right up to Magdalena. What is one more life when you've taken many before?" Sabien shifted closer, and Dagmara let out a shriek of pain as the dagger shifted inside her. His lips were inches from hers. "Or I can let you die."

"Just let me go," Dagmara said, her voice barely audible.

"That wasn't one of the options," said Sabien. "I need to know where Magdalena is."

"She's hiding in Azurem."

"You forget I can tell when you're lying."

Within a flash, he withdrew the dagger of ice and plunged it into her side.

She screamed, blood pouring from the first wound. The pain was unbearable. Her mind began to fall numb.

"Tell me where she is, and all the pain will stop," Sabien said, his baritone voice hauntingly melodic.

Dagmara assumed she was strong enough to bring her secrets to the grave, but in this moment, she was breaking. Her mind flashed to her mother. Was this the fear her mom felt when she was tortured to death? This was the moment she was afraid of. This was the scenario she desperately wanted to avoid. If Dagmara died, who would be left to take care of Teos?

"Heal me first," Dagmara choked.

"You're not in the place to make demands."

"How do I know you won't kill me anyway?"

"You're the princess's best friend. I plan to use you to lure her to her death. That is, if you cooperate now and tell me where she is."

Dagmara knew that exposing Magda's location would be like killing Magdalena herself. She would never take the life of her best friend, regardless if Magda's life was connected to keeping the First Prince entombed. But dying by Sabien's iceblade now wouldn't help her save her friend. Dying now meant the end of everything Dagmara had worked for. She would never return to Azurem to see Teos. She would never see Claude again.

Claude. She had been so wrong. She blamed him for murders he had no part of. She had hurt the man she loved, and for what?

Tears welled in her eyes. With Claude on her mind, Dagmara knew she wasn't ready to die.

Dagmara choked. "She's in Flaustra."

"Where?" asked Sabien.

"I don't know!" Tears streamed down her face, dripping off her chin with the rain. "Truly. She never sent me a message when she arrived."

Sabien tilted his head. "Hmm. I suppose we will find her together. That is, if you want to live."

"Yes, I do. Heal me."

A crooked smile appeared on his face. "I want you to beg."

The world was beginning to blur. The stone rumbled as another explosion rang out in the distance. The sound of the pouring rain and the screams of war began to fade away.

Dagmara's voice was barely audible. "Please save me. I'll do anything, Sabien, I'm begging you."

Sabien removed his forearm from her throat and held her by the chin. A smirk creased on his face as he said, "Good girl."

Then he ripped the magical dagger free, eliciting another shriek.

Dagmara fell against his chest, every inch of her soaked either from the rain or her blood. Sabien knelt as her body collapsed in his embrace. The mud sloshed underneath them, rain continuing to beat down from the midnight sky.

First, Sabien ran his hand through her hair, slick from the rain. "There she is," he said. The silver tint was washing out in the torrential rain, returning her hair to her natural blonde. Then Sabien's hand roamed down her body before finding the wound in the center of her stomach. "I'm stronger than you," he growled. "I won't hesitate to bring you to the brink of death time and time again just to prove who holds the power."

A heat began to radiate from the wound, magic seeping through her and sealing her injury. But she was out of energy, and there was too much pain. Thinking of Claude, she wanted to weep, but she had no more strength. Her head fell back, the blackness consuming her.

Before she lost consciousness, she felt Sabien tighten his grip around her, leaning closer to whisper, "You're mine now, Dagger."

CHAPTER 56
Magdalena

Ishani chucked one of her axes at the assassin, but the woman dodged easily. She thrust her hand at the ceiling, and dirt broke off, cascading down on Magda and her friends, and momentarily blinding her.

Odie charged at the assassin, leaping for her arm and biting down hard. She let out a scream before summoning roots from the earth, littered in thorns. The roots gripped Odie around his hind legs, piercing his skin and yanking him to the ground. He let out a howl of pain.

"Odie!" Magda screamed, rushing forward. The assassin was already fleeing down another staircase, running deeper into the earth, Ishani hot on her trail.

Ravi withdrew his knife, "Go after her, I'll save Odie!" he yelled.

Magda trusted him. She turned and raced down the staircase, finding herself in a narrow tunnel. When she reached Ishani's side, the tunnel began to rumble. Suddenly, both girls were thrown to either wall, landing with a hard thud on the earth.

"Watch out!" yelled Ishani, rolling deeper into the tunnel.

Magda looked up to see small rocks falling down on her. As fast as she could, she rolled out of the way. Large stones collapsed from the ceiling, blocking the entrance to the stairs. The staircase leading above was fixed on the other side of the cave-in, providing no escape for either Ishani or Magda. There were a few gaps between the rocks, but it was clear they would have to find another way out if they wanted to survive.

"Get ready," Ishani was at Magda's side, pulling her up to her feet. "She's here somewhere."

As Magda regained her footing, she looked around at the space before them. It was a small, enclosed tunnel lined with pipes that wove in and out of each other before disappearing into the ceiling and walls. This had to be a hotspot for the city's water system. It wasn't a large area, but some of the pipes were thick, and shadows lined the narrow space.

Ishani gripped her axe, walking forward, her eyes peeled.

Magda tried to summon her Soul magic. She had watched the assassin conjure roots from the ground, surely she could make something happen here? But nothing was coming to mind. Magda had the powers to command both rock and earth, but she couldn't feel what she could pull from in this space.

The assassin had somehow commanded the earth in this space, for she had caused the cave in, hoping she wouldn't be followed. Now, all three were trapped on this side together.

A gust of wind was heard behind them.

Ishani and Magda turned around.

The assassin appeared from behind them, summoning the earth toward Magda. Before she could react, roots laced around Magda's stomach like rope, hoisting her into the air. The thorns dug into her like nails, and she screamed.

Ishani lunged for the assassin, her axe missing and instead made contact with one of the old pipes, causing it to burst. The water sprayed the assassin in the face, causing her to stumble.

Digging deep, Magda found her earth magic. She commanded the roots to release her, and she dropped to the ground with a hard thud. Looking up, she watched as a pile of dirt cascaded from the ceiling, blocking Ishani's vision. The assassin dislodged a portion of the ground beneath them, and a large rock was thrust up toward Ishani. It collided with her head, and she fell back, her skull banging on one of the pipes before she collapsed to the ground, unconscious. Her axe skidded from her grasp, landing in front of the assassin.

"No!" Magda screamed.

Standing to her feet, she used the roots the assassin had summoned and grasped them with her magic. She thrust them at the assassin, hoping and praying they would bind around her enemy's throat. The roots listened to her, circling around the assassin's neck and nearly imbedding her skin with thorns before they froze.

The assassin had her hand raised, ordering the earth to listen to her.

"A Soul Guardian?" the assassin asked, her voice hard to hear over the water gushing from the pipes. "But you're not Princess Kiran."

"No, I'm not," Magda snapped. She raised her hand, willing the roots to listen to her.

But the assassin was too powerful. The assassin had trained with Soul magic, and Magda hadn't. The assassin was the one who had control of the earth.

Then the earth turned against Magda. New roots snaked out from the wall behind her, latching onto her wrists.

The assassin picked up Ishani's axe from the ground and started toward Magda. "The First Prince will be so pleased with me." She raised the axe, ready to bring it down onto Magda's chest.

Magda screamed. She was a guardian. She was more powerful than this assassin. She demanded revenge for Aleksy's and her father's deaths, and she would have it.

An entire portion of the wall dislodged, knocking into pipes and hurling toward the assassin. The assassin didn't have time to dodge before the rock slammed into her side, knocking her to the ground. The dirt opened for her to fall in, and then cocooned her body, trapping her inside the dirt wall and burying her alive.

But Magda wasn't fast enough. Pain flooded her body, and she looked down to see the axe on the ground in front of her, coated with blood, and a slash across her stomach.

The roots let go of Magda's wrists, and she fell to her knees, splashing into water that was already pooling around her from the open pipes. She clutched her stomach, feeling warm blood seeping across her palm. Water sprayed her across the face, but she didn't have the energy to shield herself. There was too much pain.

But she didn't have much time. The water was rising, and Ishani was unconscious.

Magda forced herself to move, trying to ignore the pain coursing through her body. She reached Ishani and looped her arms underneath her shoulders. She yelled in pain as she dragged Ishani through the water and back towards the rocks blocking the stairs. The water was rising rapidly, and Magda left a trickle of dark blood behind.

When they reached the rock wall blocking their escape, she let Ishani rest. The water was already a foot high and lapping at their shins.

"Magda!" Ravi yelled, peering through an opening in the rocks.

A wave of pain raced through Magda's body, and she caught herself before completely falling. The blood was seeping too fast from the wound in her stomach, and her energy was draining as quickly as the water was filling the cavern.

Ravi was scraping away at the rocks, creating a small opening. Odie was digging at another hole, trying to find a way through. "Can you squeeze through here?" Ravi asked, although they both knew the opening was impossibly small.

"I won't leave Ishani behind," Magda replied. Ishani was still alive, her chest rising and falling slightly as she leaned in a sitting position against the wall.

Odie barked, the scratching of his claws signaling that he hadn't stopped digging at the immovable rocks.

"And your...magic," Ravi said, as though he still didn't believe she had magic. "You can move earth, can't you?"

Magda extended her hand toward the boulders, trying to find the power. As she tried to channel the earth, another shooting pain rattled through her body. She let out a scream and her arm fell back to her side.

"Magda," Ravi's voice was pained. "I can go get help, but I don't want to leave you in case..."

The water was lapping at her knees now, and was starting to spill over to the other side of the rock wall. Magda knew that they were all running out of time.

"It's alright, Ravi," Magda said. "Whatever happens, just know that you—"

"Don't talk like that." Ravi reached through the crack in the rock, but he couldn't reach her. "I love you, Magda, and I told you that your battles are my battles, no matter the cost. Don't worry, I'll save you."

Ravi raced away to find help, but Magda knew they were out of time. She bit back tears.

Then Magda heard a whimper. Odie had slithered his way through an opening high in the rocks, jumping down on her side.

"No, Odie!" Magda yelled. She clutched her side as the pain intensified.

Odie nuzzled her, attempting to yank her clothing so she would stand up, but she could barely move, let alone climb over the top of the rocks.

"Bad dog!" Magda choked back a sob. "Go with Ravi!"

She leaned back against the dirt wall, the water almost reaching her shoulders. Odie's head tilted, his ears swiveling back as his tail drooped. After another moment, the dog padded forward and nuzzled his head against Magda's face.

Tears poured down Magda's cheeks as she laced her hand around Odie's neck and buried her face in his fur. "I love you too, Odie," she whispered.

The dog whimpered again.

"I'm so sorry I got us into this mess."

Odie let out a soft yap, nuzzling deeper against her.

The water had reached her neck, and she could feel the blood from her wound seeping out faster. She glanced across at Ishani, still unconscious, the water up to her chin from how she was angled.

If only Magda hadn't convinced them to come after the assassin, they would all be safe. She had just wanted revenge for her brother and father. She wanted the First Prince to pay.

Whoever the First Prince was, she hoped he died.

But there's so much I have to share with you.

Startled, Magda was more alert. The voice was like a whisper through the tunnel, but she wasn't the only one who sensed it. Odie was growling, his ears alert. Somehow, he sensed it too.

You're so much more than a Soul Guardian, Princess. You and I are so similar.

"Get out of my head!" she yelled. It was the voice from her dreams. But she wasn't dreaming.

Seems you need a little guidance. I have so much to teach you.

Then Magda felt a tingling warmth at her stomach as the water lapped over her wound. Startled, she glanced down and saw an icy blue sparkle bubbling to the surface.

This is your power. Own it.

Feeling a surge of magic rush through her fingertips, Magda focused in on her wound. She pressed her palm to the blood, seeing the icy-blue magic at her fingertips. The water swirled around her stomach, and seemed to race through her body, healing her entirely. For a brief moment she felt no fear or pain. She felt powerful.

She rose to her feet and peeled back the ripped fabric on her stomach to see that her wound was healed. Somehow, she had healed herself with the water. She snapped her head to her dog, who was sitting upright and alert.

"Did you see that?"

Odie tilted his head.

She waded in the water and faced the boulders blocking her from the exit. Staring at the obstacle before her, she channeled her magic. Earth and water coursed through her body, filling her with power she didn't know existed. Thrusting her hands toward the boulder, her magic ignited.

The water surrounding her crested over her body. It soared against the ceiling of the tunnel before barreling into the rocks like a tsunami. The boulders flew back as water and earth collided, her magic intertwining inside her.

The sound reverberated through the space. After the impact, mist and dirt fell around her, dusting her in water and earth. With Odie's help, she pulled Ishani up the stairs back into the assassin's hideout. The exit door was wide open, and there was no doubt Ravi would be racing back soon with every intention to rescue her.

But she had rescued herself, with magic she didn't even know she possessed. She had thought she wasn't a Life Guardian, she had Soul magic. But what was she now?

Odie barked at her side, and she knelt down beside him, scratching him behind the ear.

"We're safe," she laughed and he pummeled into her, his paws colliding with her chest and knocking her off balance. He licked her cheek until she couldn't take anymore, pushing him aside and sitting upright once more.

The voice returned to her head once more:

Are you ready for the answers now, Dear Princess?

A shiver ran up Magda's spine.

Her dog sniffed the blood still on her clothes, leftover from the wound in her stomach. It was completely healed, signaling she not only controlled the earth, but the water too.

Odie looked up at her and whimpered.

She petted his head before whispering, "Odie...can you keep a secret?"

Acknowledgments

Thank you so much to everyone who had a part in creating this world and the characters we have come to love over the past year writing this book. First, thank you to our friends and family, including Mom, Emily, Kirill, and Dan. You are all our first readers and biggest supporters.

Thank you to our incredible cover designer, Stefanie Saw, for bringing our vision to life so beautifully. We couldn't have done it without you.

Thank you to the colleagues who were all willing to support and read.

Thank you to our fabulous beta readers, arc readers, and friends who helped shape the final story. We loved and appreciated your ideas and input. And a huge thanks to our readers who continue to be with us on our journey as authors!

As indie authors, the most support you could give us is leaving a review! *The Mad King and the False Queen* is on Goodreads and Amazon to rate/review now.

We can't wait for you to continue Dagmara and Magdalena's story in *The First Prince and the Last Heir*. Available to pre-order!

About the Author

Amanda Abrom and Hope Abrom are sisters and co-authors originally from Lancaster, Pennsylvania. Currently, they live on two opposite sides of the US. Amanda lives in NYC with her husband and works in education while Hope works in LA at a post-production house as an editor. They first started pursuing creative projects together when they wrote the book and lyrics for an original musical, Royal Shadows, also a fantasy romance. *The Mad King and the False Queen* is the fifth book that they have co-authored, and they have plans for many more! In their spare time, they both enjoy seeing musicals, reading, traveling, and writing the next book!

Also by the Abrom Sisters

Designated Protector Series:
Book 1 Designated Protector
Book 2 Parallel Voyagers
Book 3 Forbidden Sorcerer

Made in the USA
Las Vegas, NV
22 April 2025